Troubled Blood

A *Strike* Novel

Part One

Robert Galbraith

W F HOWES LTD

This large print edition published in 2021 by
W F Howes Ltd
Unit 5, St George's House, Rearsby Business Park,
Gaddesby Lane, Rearsby, Leicester LE7 4YH

1 3 5 7 9 10 8 6 4 2

First published in the United Kingdom in 2020
by Sphere

A CIP catalogue record for this book is available
from the British Library

ISBN 978 1 00402 517 6

Typeset by Palimpsest Book Production Limited,
Falkirk, Stirlingshire

Printed and bound by
T J Books in the UK

Troubled Blood

To Barbara Murray,
social worker, WEA worker, teacher,
wife, mother, grandmother,
demon bridge player
and
world's best mother-in-law

There they her sought, and euery where inquired,
Where they might tydings get of her estate;
Yet found they none. But by what haplesse fate,
Or hard misfortune she was thence conuayd,
And stolne away from her beloued mate,
Were long to tell . . .

Edmund Spenser
The Faerie Queene

For, if it were not so, there would be something
disappearing into nothing, which is math-
ematically absurd.

Aleister Crowley
The Book of Thoth

PART I

Then came the iolly Sommer . . .

Edmund Spenser
The Faerie Queene

CHAPTER 1

And such was he, of whom I haue to tell,
The champion of true Iustice, Artegall . . .

Edmund Spenser
The Faerie Queene

'You're a Cornishman, born and bred,' said Dave Polworth irritably. '"Strike" isn't even your proper name. By rights, you're a Nancarrow. You're not going to sit here and say you'd call yourself English?'

The Victory Inn was so crowded on this warm August evening that drinkers had spilled outside onto the broad stone steps which led down to the bay. Polworth and Strike were sitting at a table in the corner, having a few pints to celebrate Polworth's thirty-ninth birthday. Cornish nationalism had been under discussion for twenty minutes, and to Strike it felt much longer.

'Would I call myself English?' he mused aloud. 'No, I'd probably say British.'

'Fuck off,' said Polworth, his quick temper

3

rising. 'You wouldn't. You're just trying to wind me up.'

The two friends were physical opposites. Polworth was short and spare as a jockey, weathered and prematurely lined, his sunburned scalp visible through his thinning hair. His T-shirt was crumpled, as though he had pulled it off the floor or out of a washing basket, and his jeans were ripped. On his left forearm was tattooed the black and white cross of St Piran; on his right hand was a deep scar, souvenir of a close encounter with a shark.

His friend Strike resembled an out-of-condition boxer, which in fact he was; a large man, well over six feet tall, with a slightly crooked nose, his dense dark hair curly. He bore no tattoos and, in spite of the perpetual shadow of the heavy beard, carried about him that well-pressed and fundamentally clean-cut air that suggested ex-police or ex-military.

'You were born here,' Polworth persisted. 'So you're Cornish.'

'Trouble is, by that standard, you're a Brummie.'

'Fuck off!' yelped Polworth again, genuinely stung. 'I've been here since I was two months old and my mum's a Trevelyan. It's identity – what you feel here,' and Polworth thumped his chest over his heart. 'My mum's family goes back centuries in Cornwall—'

'Yeah, well, blood and soil's never been my—'

'Did you hear about the last survey they done?'

4

said Polworth, talking over Strike. '"What's your ethnic origin?" they asked, and half – *half* – ticked "Cornish" instead of "English". Massive increase.'

'Great,' said Strike. 'What next? Boxes for Dumnones and Romans?'

'Keep using that patronising fucking tone,' said Polworth, 'and see where it gets you. You've been in London too fucking long, boy . . . There's nothing wrong with being proud of where you came from. Nothing wrong with communities wanting some power back from Westminster. The Scots are gonna lead the way, next year. You watch. When they get independence, that'll be the trigger. Celtic peoples right across the country are going to make their move.

'Want another one?' he added, gesturing towards Strike's empty pint glass.

Strike had come out to the pub craving a respite from tension and worry, not to be harangued about Cornish politics. Polworth's allegiance to Mebyon Kernow, the nationalist party he'd joined at sixteen, appeared to have gained a greater hold over him in the year or so since they had last seen each other. Dave usually made Strike laugh like almost nobody else, but he brooked no jokes upon Cornish independence, a subject that for Strike had all the appeal of soft furnishings or train-spotting. For a second Strike considered saying that he needed to get back to his aunt's house, but the prospect of that was almost more depressing than his old friend's invective against supermarkets that resisted putting the cross of St Piran on goods of Cornish origin.

'Great, thanks,' he said, passing his empty glass to Dave, who headed up to the bar, nodding left and right to his many acquaintances.

Left alone at the table, Strike's eyes roamed absently over the pub he'd always considered his local. It had changed over the years, but was still recognisably the place in which he and his Cornish mates had met in their late teens. He had an odd double impression of being exactly where he belonged, and where he'd never belonged, of intense familiarity and of separateness.

As his gaze moved aimlessly from timber floor to nautical prints, Strike found himself looking directly into the large, anxious eyes of a woman standing at the bar with a friend. She had a long, pale face and her dark, shoulder-length hair was streaked with grey. He didn't recognise her, but he'd been aware for the past hour that certain locals were craning their necks to look at him, or else trying to catch his eye. Looking away, Strike took out his mobile and pretended to be texting.

Acquaintances had a ready excuse for conversation, if he showed the slightest sign of encouraging them, because everyone in St Mawes seemed to know that his aunt Joan had received a diagnosis of advanced ovarian cancer ten days previously, and that he, his half-sister, Lucy, and Lucy's three sons had hastened at once to Joan and Ted's house to offer what support they could. For a week now

6

he'd been fielding enquiries, accepting sympathy and politely declining offers of help every time he ventured out of the house. He was tired of finding fresh ways of saying 'Yes, it looks terminal and yes, it's shit for all of us.'

Polworth pushed his way back to the table, carrying two fresh pints.

'There you go, Diddy,' he said, resuming his bar stool.

The old nickname hadn't been bestowed, as most people assumed, in ironic reference to Strike's size, but derived from 'didicoy', the Cornish word for gypsy. The sound of it softened Strike, reminding him why his friendship with Polworth was the most enduring of his life.

Thirty-five years previously, Strike had entered St Mawes Primary School a term late, unusually large for his age and with an accent that was glaringly different from the local burr. Although he'd been born in Cornwall, his mother had spirited him away as soon as she'd recovered from the birth, fleeing into the night, baby in her arms, back to the London life she loved, flitting from flat to squat to party. Four years after Strike's birth, she'd returned to St Mawes with her son and with her newborn, Lucy, only to take off again in the early hours of the morning, leaving Strike and his half-sister behind.

Precisely what Leda had said in the note she left on the kitchen table, Strike had never known. Doubtless she'd been having a spell of difficulty with a landlord or a boyfriend, or perhaps there was a music festival she particularly wanted to attend: it became difficult to live exactly as she pleased with two children in tow. Whatever the reason for her lengthening absence, Leda's sister-in-law, Joan, who was as conventional and orderly as Leda was flighty and chaotic, had bought Strike a uniform and enrolled him in the local school.

The other four-and-a-half-year-olds had gawped when he was introduced to the class. A few of them giggled when the teacher said his first name, Cormoran. He was worried by this school business, because he was sure that his mum had said she was going to 'home school' him. He'd tried to tell Uncle Ted that he didn't think his mum would want him to go, but Ted, normally so understanding, had said firmly that he had to, so there he was, alone among strangers with funny accents. Strike, who'd never been a great crier, had sat down at the old roll-top desk with a lump like an apple in his throat.

Why Dave Polworth, pocket don of the class, had decided to befriend the new boy had never been satisfactorily explained, even to Strike. It couldn't have been out of fear of Strike's size, because Dave's two best friends were hefty fishermen's sons, and Dave was in any case notorious as a fighter whose viciousness was inversely proportional to his height. By the end of that first day Polworth had become both friend and champion, making it his business to impress upon their classmates all the reasons that Strike was worthy of their respect: he was a Cornishman born, a nephew to Ted Nancarrow of the local lifeguard, he didn't know where his mum was and it wasn't his fault if he spoke funny.

Ill as Strike's aunt was, much as she had enjoyed having her nephew to stay for a whole week and even though he'd be leaving the following morning, Joan had virtually pushed him out of the house to celebrate 'Little Dave's' birthday that evening. She placed immense value on old ties and delighted in the fact that Strike and Dave Polworth were still mates, all these years later. Joan counted the fact of their friendship as proof that she'd been right to send him to school over his feckless mother's wishes and proof that Cornwall was Strike's true home, no matter how widely he might have wandered since, and even though he was currently London-based.

Polworth took a long pull on his fourth pint and said, with a sharp glance over his shoulder at the dark woman and her blonde friend, who were still watching Strike,

'Effing emmets.'

'And where would your garden be,' asked Strike, 'without tourists?'

'Be ansom,' said Polworth promptly. 'We get a ton of local visitors, plenty of repeat business.'

Polworth had recently resigned from a managerial position in an engineering firm in Bristol to work as head gardener in a large public garden a short distance along the coast. A qualified diver, an accomplished surfer, a competitor in Ironman competitions, Polworth had been relentlessly physical and restless since childhood, and time and office work hadn't tamed him.

'No regrets, then?' Strike asked.

'Fuck, no,' said Polworth fervently. 'Needed to get my hands dirty again. Need to get back outside. Forty next year. Now or never.'

Polworth had applied for the new job without telling his wife what he was doing. Having been offered the position, he'd quit his job and gone home to announce the fait accompli to his family.

'Penny come round, has she?' Strike asked.

'Still tells me once a week she wants a divorce,' Polworth answered indifferently. 'But it was better to present her with the fact, than argue the toss for five years. It's all worked out great. Kids love the new school, Penny's company let her transfer to the office in the Big City', by which Polworth meant Truro, not London. 'She's happy. Just doesn't want to admit it.'

Strike privately doubted the truth of this statement. A disregard for inconvenient facts tended to march hand in hand with Polworth's love of risk and romantic causes. However, Strike had problems enough of his own without worrying about Polworth's, so he raised his fresh pint and said, hoping to keep Polworth's mind off politics:

'Well, many happy returns, mate.'

10

'Cheers,' said Polworth, toasting him back. 'What d'you reckon to Arsenal's chances, then? Gonna qualify?'

Strike shrugged, because he feared that discussing the likelihood of his London football club securing a place in the Champions League would lead back to a lack of Cornish loyalties.

'How's your love life?' Polworth asked, trying a different tack.

'Non-existent,' said Strike.

Polworth grinned.

'Joanie reckons you're gonna end up with your business partner. That Robin girl.'

'Is that right?' said Strike.

'Told me all about it when I was round there, weekend before last. While I was fixing their Sky Box.'

'They didn't tell me you'd done that,' said Strike, again tipping his pint towards Polworth. 'That was good of you, mate, cheers.'

If he'd hoped to deflect his friend, he was unsuccessful.

'Both of 'em. Her and Ted,' said Polworth, 'both of 'em reckon it's Robin.'

And when Strike said nothing, Polworth pressed him, 'Nothing going on, then?'

'No,' said Strike.

'How come?' asked Polworth, frowning again. As with Cornish independence, Strike was refusing to embrace an obvious and desirable objective. 'She's a looker. Seen her in the paper. Maybe not

11

on a par with Milady Berserko,' Polworth acknowledged. It was the nickname he had long ago bestowed on Strike's ex-fiancée. 'But on the other hand, she's not a fucking nutcase, is she, Diddy?'

Strike laughed.

'Lucy likes her,' said Polworth. 'Says you'd be perfect together.'

'When were you talking to Lucy about my love life?' asked Strike, with a touch less complaisance.

'Month or so ago,' said Polworth. 'She brought her boys down for the weekend and we had them all over for a barbecue.'

Strike drank and said nothing.

'You get on great, she says,' said Polworth, watching him.

'Yeah, we do,' said Strike.

Polworth waited, eyebrows raised and looking expectant.

'It'd fuck everything up,' said Strike. 'I'm not risking the agency.'

'Right,' said Polworth. 'Tempted, though?'

There was a short pause. Strike carefully kept his gaze averted from the dark woman and her companion, who he was sure were discussing him.

'There might've been moments,' he admitted, 'when it crossed my mind. But she's going through a nasty divorce, we spend half our lives together as it is and I like having her as a business partner.'

Given their longstanding friendship, the fact that they'd already clashed over politics and that it was Polworth's birthday, he was trying not to let any hint of resentment at this line of questioning show. Every married person he knew seemed desperate to chivvy others into matrimony, no matter how poor an advertisement they themselves were for the institution. The Polworths, for instance, seemed to exist in a permanent state of mutual animosity. Strike had more often heard Penny refer to her husband as 'that twat' than by his name, and many was the night when Polworth had regaled his friends in happy detail of the ways in which he'd managed to pursue his own ambitions and interests at the expense of, or over the protests of, his wife. Both seemed happiest and most relaxed in the company of their own sex, and on those rare occasions when Strike had enjoyed hospitality at their home, the gatherings always seemed to follow a pattern of natural segregation, the women congregating in one area of the home, the men in another.

'And what happens when Robin wants kids?' asked Polworth.

'Don't think she's does,' said Strike. 'She likes the job.'

'They all say that,' said Polworth dismissively. 'What age is she now?'

'Ten years younger than us.'

'She'll want kids,' said Polworth confidently. 'They all do. And it happens quicker for women. They're up against the clock.'

'Well, she won't be getting kids with me. I don't

13

want them. Anyway, the older I get, the less I think I'm the marrying kind.'

'Thought that myself, mate,' said Polworth. 'But then I realised I'd got it all wrong. Told you how it happened, didn't I? How I ended up proposing to Penny?'

'Don't think so,' said Strike.

'I never told you about the whole Tolstoy thing?' asked Polworth, surprised at this omission.

Strike, who'd been about to drink, lowered his glass in amazement. Since primary school, Polworth, who had a razor-sharp intelligence but despised any form of learning he couldn't put to immediate, practical use, had shunned all printed material except technical manuals. Misinterpreting Strike's expression, Polworth said,

'Tolstoy. He's a writer.'

'Yeah,' said Strike. 'Thanks. How does Tolstoy—?'

'Telling you, aren't I? I'd split up with Penny the second time. She'd been banging on about getting engaged, and I wasn't feeling it. So I'm in this bar, telling my mate Chris about how I'm sick of her telling me she wants a ring – you remember Chris? Big guy with a lisp. You met him at Rozwyn's christening.

'Anyway, there's this pissed older guy at the bar on his own, bit of a ponce in his corduroy jacket, wavy hair, and he's pissing me off, to be honest, because I can tell he's listening, and I ask him what the fuck he's looking at and he looks me straight in the eye,' said Polworth, 'and he says:

14

"You can only carry a weight and use your hands, if you strap the weight to your back. Marry, and you get the use of your hands back. Don't marry, and you'll never have your hands free for anything else. Look at Mazankov, at Krupov. They've ruined their careers for the sake of women."

'I thought Mazankov and Krupov were mates of his. Asked him what the fuck he was telling me for. Then he says he's quoting this writer, Tolstoy.

'And we got talking and I tell you this, Diddy, it was a life-changing moment. The light bulb went on,' said Polworth, pointing at the air over his balding head. 'He made me see it clearly. The male predicament, mate. There I am, trying to get my hole on a Thursday night, heading home alone again, poorer, bored shitless; I thought of the money I've spent chasing gash, and the hassle, and whether I want to be watching porn alone at forty, and I thought, this is the whole point. What marriage is for. Am I going to do better than Penny? Am I enjoying talking shit to women in bars? Penny and me get on all right. I could do a hell of a lot worse. She's not bad-looking. I'd have my hole already at home, waiting for me, wouldn't I?'

'Pity she can't hear this,' said Strike. 'She'd fall in love with you all over again.'

'I shook that poncey bloke's hand,' said Polworth, ignoring Strike's sarcasm. 'Made him write me down the name of the book and all. Went straight out that bar, got a taxi to Penny's flat, banged on

15

the door, woke her up. She was fucking livid. Thought I'd come round because I was pissed, couldn't get anything better and wanted a shag. I said, "No, you dozy cow, I'm here because I wanna marry you."

'And I'll tell you the name of the book,' said Polworth. '*Anna Karenina.*' He drained his pint. 'It's shit.'

Strike laughed.

Polworth belched loudly, then checked his watch. He was a man who knew a good exit line and had no more time for prolonged leave-taking than for Russian literature.

'Gonna get going, Diddy,' he said, getting to his feet. 'If I'm back before half eleven, I'm on for a birthday blowie – which is the whole point I'm making, mate. Whole point.'

Grinning, Strike accepted Polworth's hand-shake. Polworth told Strike to convey his love to Joan and to call him next time he was down, then squeezed his way out of the pub, and disappeared from view.

CHAPTER 2

Heart, that is inly hurt, is greatly eas'd
With hope of thing, that may allay his
Smart . . .

Edmund Spenser
The Faerie Queene

Still grinning at Polworth's story, Strike now realised that the dark woman at the bar was showing signs of wanting to approach him. Her spectacled blonde companion appeared to be advising against it. Strike finished his pint, gathered up his wallet, checked his cigarettes were still in his pocket and, with the assistance of the wall beside him, stood up, making sure his balance was everything it should be before trying to walk. His prosthetic leg was occasionally uncooperative after four pints. Having assured himself that he could balance perfectly well, he set off towards the exit, giving unsmiling nods to those few locals whom he could not ignore without causing offence, and

17

reached the warm darkness outside without being importuned.

The wide, uneven stone steps that led down towards the bay were still crowded with drinkers and smokers. Strike wove his way between them, pulling out his cigarettes as he went.

It was a balmy August night and tourists were still strolling around the picturesque seafront. Strike was facing a fifteen-minute walk, part of it up a steep slope, back to his aunt and uncle's house. On a whim he turned right, crossed the street and headed for the high stone wall separating the car park and ferry point from the sea. Leaning against it, he lit a cigarette and stared out over the smoke grey and silver ocean, becoming just one more tourist in the darkness, free to smoke quietly without having to answer questions about cancer, deliberately postponing the moment when he'd have to return to the uncomfortable sofa that had been his bed for the past six nights.

On arrival, Strike had been told that he, the childless single man and ex-soldier, wouldn't mind sleeping in the sitting room 'because *you'll* sleep anywhere'. She'd been determined to shut down the possibility, mooted by Strike on the phone, that he might check into a bed and breakfast rather than stretch the house to capacity. Strike's visits were rare, especially in conjunction with his sister and nephews, and Joan wanted to enjoy his presence to the full, wanted to feel that she was, once again, the provider and nurturer, currently weakened by her first round of chemotherapy though she might be.

So the tall and heavy Strike, who'd have been far happier on a camp bed, had lain down uncomplainingly every night on the slippery, unyielding mass of satin-covered horsehair, to be woken each morning by his young nephews, who routinely forgot that they had been asked to wait until eight o'clock before barging into the sitting room. At least Jack had the decency to whisper apologies every time he realised that he'd woken his uncle. The eldest, Luke, clattered and shouted his way down the narrow stairs every morning and merely sniggered as he dashed past Strike on his way to the kitchen.

Luke had broken Strike's brand-new headphones, which the detective had felt obliged to pretend didn't matter in the slightest. His eldest nephew had also thought it amusing to run off into the garden with Strike's prosthetic leg one morning, and to stand waving it at his uncle through the window. When Luke finally brought it back, Strike, whose bladder had been very full and who was incapable of hopping up the steep stairs to the only toilet, had delivered Luke a quiet telling-off that had left the boy unusually subdued for most of the morning.

Meanwhile, Joan told Strike every morning, 'you slept well', without a hint of enquiry. Joan had a lifelong habit of subtly pressurising the family into telling her what she wanted to hear. In the days when Strike was sleeping in his office and facing imminent insolvency (facts that he had admittedly not shared with his aunt and uncle), Joan had told him happily 'you're doing awfully well' over the phone, and it had felt, as it always did, unnecessarily combative to challenge her optimistic declaration. After his lower leg had been blown off in Afghanistan, a tearful Joan had stood at his hospital bed as he tried to focus through a fog of morphine, and told him 'You feel comfortable, though. You aren't in pain.' He loved his aunt, who'd raised him for significant chunks of his childhood, but extended periods in her company made him feel stifled and suffocated. Her insistence on the smooth passing of counterfeit social coin from hand to hand, while uncomfortable truths were ignored and denied, wore him out.

Something gleamed in the water – sleek silver and a pair of soot-black eyes: a seal was turning lazily just below Strike. He watched its revolutions in the water, wondering whether it could see him and, for reasons he couldn't have explained, his thoughts slid towards his partner in the detective agency.

He was well aware that he hadn't told Polworth the whole truth about his relationship with Robin Ellacott, which, after all, was nobody else's business. The truth was that his feelings contained nuances and complications that he preferred not to examine. For instance, he had a tendency, when alone, bored or low-spirited, to want to hear her voice.

He checked his watch. She was having a day off, but there was an outside chance she'd still be awake and he had a decent pretext for texting: Saul Morris, their newest subcontractor, was owed his month's expenses, and Strike had left no instructions for sorting this out. If he texted about Morris, there was a good chance that Robin would call him back to find out how Joan was.

'Excuse me?' a woman said nervously, from behind him.

Strike knew without turning that it was the dark woman from the pub. She had a Home Counties accent and her tone contained that precise mixture of apology and excitement that he usually encountered in those who wanted to talk about his detective triumphs.

'Yes?' he said, turning to face the speaker.

Her blonde friend had come with her: or perhaps, thought Strike, they were more than friends. An indefinable sense of closeness seemed to bind the two women, whom he judged to be around forty. They wore jeans and shirts and the blonde in particular had the slightly weather-beaten leanness that suggests weekends spent hill walking or cycling. She was what some would call a 'handsome' woman, by which they meant that she was bare faced. High-cheekboned, bespectacled, her hair pulled back into a ponytail, she also looked stern.

The dark woman was slighter in build. Her large grey eyes shone palely in her long face. She had an air of intensity, even of fanaticism, about her in the half-light, like a medieval martyr.

'Are you . . . are you Cormoran Strike?' she asked.

'Yes,' he said, his tone uninviting.

'Oh,' she breathed, with an agitated little hand gesture. 'This is – this is so strange. I know you probably don't want to be – I'm sorry to bother you, I know you're off duty,' she gave a nervous laugh, 'but – my name's Anna, by the way – I wondered,' she took a deep breath, 'whether I could come – whether I could come and talk to you about my mother.'

Strike said nothing.

'She disappeared,' Anna went on. 'Margot Bamborough's her name. She was a GP. She finished work one evening, walked out of her practice and nobody's seen her since.'

'Have you contacted the police?' asked Strike.

Anna gave an odd little laugh.

'Oh yes – I mean, they knew – they investigated. But they never found anything. She disappeared,' said Anna, 'in 1974.'

The dark water lapped the stone and Strike thought he could hear the seal clearing its damp nostrils. Three drunk youths went weaving past, on their way to the ferry point. Strike wondered whether they knew the last ferry had been and gone at six.

'I just,' said the woman in a rush, 'you see – last week – I went to see a medium.'

Fuck, thought Strike.

He'd occasionally bumped up against the pur-veyors of paranormal insights during his detective career and felt nothing but contempt for them: leeches, or so he saw them, of money from the pockets of the deluded and the desperate.

A motorboat came chugging across the water, its engine grinding the night's stillness to pieces. Apparently this was the lift the three drunk boys were waiting for. They now began laughing and elbowing each other at the prospect of imminent seasickness.

'The medium told me I'd get a "leading",' Anna pressed on. 'She told me, "You're going to find out what happened to your mother. You'll get a leading and you must follow it. The way will become clear very soon." So when I saw you just now in the pub – *Cormoran Strike*, in the Victory – it just seemed such an incredible coincidence and I thought – I had to speak to you.'

A soft breeze ruffled Anna's dark, silver-streaked hair. The blonde said crisply,

'Come on, Anna, we should get going.'

She put an arm around the other's shoulders. Strike saw a wedding ring shining there.

'We're sorry to have bothered you,' she told Strike.

With gentle pressure, the blonde attempted to turn Anna away. The latter sniffed and muttered,

'Sorry. I . . . probably had too much wine.'

'Hang on.'

Strike often resented his own incurable urge to

23

know, his inability to leave an itch unscratched, especially when he was as tired and aggravated as he was tonight. But 1974 was the year of his own birth. Margot Bamborough had been missing as long as he'd been alive. He couldn't help it: he wanted to know more.

'Are you on holiday here?'

'Yes.' It was the blonde who had spoken. 'Well, we've got a second home in Falmouth. Our permanent base is in London.'

'I'm heading back there tomorrow,' said Strike (*What the fuck are you doing?* asked a voice in his head), 'but I could probably swing by and see you tomorrow morning in Falmouth, if you're free.'

'Really?' gasped Anna. He hadn't seen her eyes fill with tears, but he knew they must have done, because she now wiped them. 'Oh, that'd be *great*. Thank you. *Thank you!* I'll give you the address.'

The blonde showed no enthusiasm at the prospect of seeing Strike again. However, when Anna started fumbling through her handbag, she said, 'It's all right, I've got a card', pulled a wallet out of her back pocket, and handed Strike a business card bearing the name 'Dr Kim Sullivan, BPS Registered Psychologist', with an address in Falmouth printed below it.

'Great,' said Strike, inserting it into his own wallet. 'Well, I'll see you both tomorrow morning, then.'

'I've actually got a work conference call in the morning,' said Kim. 'I'll be free by twelve. Will that be too late for you?'

24

The implication was clear: you're not speaking to Anna without me present.

'No, that'll be fine,' said Strike. 'I'll see you at twelve, then.'

'Thank you so much!' said Anna.

Kim reached for Anna's hand and the two women walked away. Strike watched them pass under a street light before turning back towards the sea. The motorboat carrying the young drinkers had now chugged away again. It already looked tiny, dwarfed by the wide bay, the roar of its engine gradually deadened into a distant buzz.

Forgetting momentarily about texting Robin, Strike lit a second cigarette, took out his mobile and Googled Margot Bamborough.

Two different photographs appeared. The first was a grainy head-and-shoulders shot of an attractive, even-featured face with wide-set eyes, her wavy, dark blonde hair centre-parted. She was wearing a long-lapelled blouse over what appeared to be a knitted tank top.

The second picture showed the same woman looking younger and wearing the famous black corset of a Playboy Bunny, accessorised with black ears, black stockings and white tail. She was holding a tray of what looked like cigarettes, and smiling at the camera. Another young woman, identically dressed, stood beaming behind her, slightly bucktoothed and curvier than her willowy friend.

Strike scrolled down until he read a famous name in conjunction with Margot's.

. . . young doctor and mother, Margaret **'Margot' Bamborough**, whose disappearance on 11 October 1974 shared certain features with Creed's abductions of Vera Kenny and Gail Wrightman.

Bamborough, who worked at the St John's Medical Practice in Clerkenwell, had arranged to meet a female friend in the local Three Kings pub at six o'clock. She never arrived.

Several witnesses saw a small white van driving at speed in the area around the time that **Bamborough** would have been heading for her rendezvous.

DI Bill Talbot, who led the investigation into **Bamborough**'s disappearance, was convinced from an early stage that the young doctor had fallen victim to the serial killer known to be at large in the south east area. However, no trace of **Bamborough** was discovered in the basement flat where Dennis Creed imprisoned, tortured and killed seven other women.

Creed's trademark of beheading the corpses of his victims . . .

CHAPTER 3

But now of Britomart it here doth neede,
The hard aduentures and strange haps to tell

Edmund Spenser
The Faerie Queene

Had her day gone as planned, Robin Ellacott would have been tucked up in bed in her rented flat in Earl's Court at this moment, fresh from a long bath, her laundry done, reading a new novel. Instead, she was sitting in her ancient Land Rover, chilly from sheer exhaustion despite the mild night, still wearing the clothes she'd put on at four-thirty that morning, as she watched the lit window of a Pizza Express in Torquay. Her face in the wing mirror was pale, her blue eyes bloodshot, and the strawberry blonde hair currently hidden under a black beanie hat needed a wash.

From time to time, Robin dipped her hand into a bag of almonds sitting on the passenger seat beside her. It was only too easy to fall into a diet of fast food and chocolate when you were running surveillance, to snack more often than needed out of sheer boredom. Robin was trying to eat healthily in spite of her unsociable hours, but the almonds had long since ceased to be appetising, and she craved nothing more than a bit of the pizza she could see an overweight couple enjoying in the restaurant window. She could almost taste it, even though the air around her was tangy with sea salt and underlain by the perpetual fug of old Wellington boots and wet dog that imbued the Land Rover's ancient fabric seats.

The object of her surveillance, whom she and Strike had nicknamed 'Tufty' for his badly fitting toupee, was currently out of view. He'd disappeared into the pizzeria an hour and a half previously with three companions, one of whom, a teenager with his arm in a cast, was visible if Robin craned her head sideways into the space above the front passenger seat. This she did every five minutes or so, to check on the progress of the foursome's meal. The last time she had looked, ice cream was being delivered to the table. It couldn't, surely, be much longer.

Robin was fighting a feeling of depression which she knew was at least partly down to utter exhaustion, to the stiffness all over her body from many hours in the driving seat, and to the loss of her long-awaited day off. With Strike unavoidably absent from the agency for an entire week, she'd now worked a twenty-day stretch without breaks.

Their best subcontractor, Sam Barclay, had been supposed to take over the Tufty job today in Scotland, but Tufty hadn't flown to Glasgow as expected. Instead, he'd taken a surprise detour to Torquay, leaving Robin with no choice but to follow him.

There were other reasons for her low spirits, of course, one of which she acknowledged to herself; the other, she felt angry with herself for dwelling on.

The first, admissible, reason was her ongoing divorce, which was becoming more contentious by the week. Following Robin's discovery of her estranged husband's affair, they'd had one last cold and bitter meeting, coincidentally in a Pizza Express near Matthew's place of work, where they'd agreed to seek a no-fault divorce following a two-year separation. Robin was too honest not to admit that she, too, bore responsibility for the failure of their relationship. Matthew might have been unfaithful, but she knew that she'd never fully committed to the marriage, that she'd prioritised her job over Matthew on almost every occasion and that, by the end, she had been waiting for a reason to leave. The affair had been a shock, but a release, too.

However, during the twelve months that had elapsed since her pizza with Matthew, Robin had come to realise that far from seeking a 'no-fault' resolution, her ex-husband saw the end of the marriage as entirely Robin's responsibility and was determined to make her pay, both emotionally and financially, for her offence. The joint bank account, which held the proceeds of the sale of their old house, had been frozen while the lawyers wrangled over how much Robin could reasonably expect when she had been earning so much less than Matthew, and had – it had been strongly hinted in the last letter – married him purely with a view to obtaining a pecuniary advantage she could never have achieved alone.

Every letter from Matthew's lawyer caused Robin additional stress, rage and misery. She hadn't needed her own lawyer to point out that Matthew appeared to be trying to force her to spend money she didn't have on legal wrangling, to run down the clock and her resources until she walked away with as close to nothing as he could manage.

'I've never known a childless divorce be so contentious,' her lawyer had told her, words that brought no comfort.

Matthew continued to occupy almost as much space in Robin's head as when they'd been married. She thought she could read his thoughts across the miles and silence that separated them in their widely divergent new lives. He'd always been a bad loser. He had to emerge from this embarrassingly short marriage the winner, by walking away with all the money, and stigmatising Robin as the sole reason for its failure.

All of this was ample reason for her present mood, of course, but then there was the other reason, the one that was inadmissible, that Robin was annoyed with herself for fretting about.

It had happened the previous day, at the office. Saul Morris, the agency's newest subcontractor, was owed his month's expenses, so, after seeing Tufty safely back into the marital home in Windsor, Robin had driven back to Denmark Street to pay Saul.

Morris had been working for the agency for six weeks. He was an ex-police officer, an undeniably handsome man, with black hair and bright blue eyes, though something about him set Robin's teeth on edge. He had a habit of softening his voice when he spoke to her; arch asides and over-personal comments peppered their most mundane interactions, and no double entendre went unmarked if Morris was in the room. Robin rued the day when he'd found out that both of them were currently going through divorces, because he seemed to think this gave him fertile new ground for assumed intimacy.

She'd hoped to get back from Windsor before Pat Chauncey, the agency's new office manager, left, but it was ten past six by the time Robin climbed the stairs and found Morris waiting for her outside the locked door.

'Sorry,' Robin said, 'traffic was awful.'

She'd paid Morris back in cash from the new safe, then told him briskly she needed to get home, but he clung on like gum stuck in her hair, telling her all about his ex-wife's latest late-night texts.

31

Robin tried to unite politeness and coolness until the phone rang on her old desk. She'd ordinarily have let it go to voicemail, but so keen was she to curtail Morris's conversation that she said,

'I've got to get this, sorry. Have a nice evening,' and picked up the receiver.

'Strike Detective Agency, Robin speaking.'

'Hi, Robin,' said a slightly husky female voice. 'Is the boss there?'

Given that Robin had only spoken to Charlotte Campbell once, three years previously, it was perhaps surprising that she'd known instantly who was on the line. Robin had analysed these few words of Charlotte's to a perhaps ludicrous degree since. Robin had detected an undertone of laughter, as though Charlotte found Robin amusing. The easy use of Robin's first name and the description of Strike as 'the boss' had also come in for their share of rumination.

'No, I'm afraid not,' Robin had said, reaching for a pen while her heart beat a little faster. 'Can I take a message?'

'Could you ask him to call Charlotte Campbell? I've got something he wants. He knows my number.'

'Will do,' said Robin.

'Thanks very much,' Charlotte had said, still sounding amused. 'Bye, then.'

Robin had dutifully written down 'Charlotte Campbell called, has something for you' and placed the message on Strike's desk.

Charlotte was Strike's ex-fiancée. Their engagement had been terminated three years previously, on the very day that Robin had come to work at the agency as a temp. Though Strike was far from communicative on the subject, Robin knew that they'd been together for sixteen years ('on and off', as Strike tended to emphasise, because the relationship had faltered many times before its final termination), that Charlotte had become engaged to her present husband just two weeks after Strike had left her and that Charlotte was now the mother of twins.

But this wasn't all Robin knew, because after leaving her husband, Robin had spent five weeks living in the spare room of Nick and Ilsa Herbert, who were two of Strike's best friends. Robin and Ilsa had struck up their own friendship during that time, and still met regularly for drinks and coffees. Ilsa made very little secret of the fact that she hoped and believed that Strike and Robin would one day, and preferably soon, realise that they were 'made for each other'. Although Robin regularly asked Ilsa to desist from her broad hints, asserting that she and Strike were perfectly happy with a friendship and working relationship, Ilsa remained cheerfully unconvinced.

Robin was very fond of Ilsa, but her pleas for her new friend to forget any idea of matchmaking between herself and Strike were genuine. She was mortified by the thought that Strike might think she herself was complicit in Ilsa's regular attempts to engineer foursomes that increasingly had the appearance of double dates. Strike had declined the last two proposed outings of this type and, while the agency's current workload certainly made any kind of social life difficult, Robin had the uncomfortable feeling that he was well aware of Ilsa's ulterior motive. Looking back on her own brief married life, Robin was sure she'd never been guilty of treating single people as she now found herself treated by Ilsa: with a cheerful lack of concern for their sensibilities, and sometimes ham-fisted attempts to manage their love lives.

One of the ways in which Ilsa attempted to draw Robin out on the subject of Strike was to tell her all about Charlotte, and here, Robin felt guilty, because she rarely shut the Charlotte conversations down, even though she never left one of them without feeling as though she had just gorged on junk food: uncomfortable, and wishing she could resist the craving for more.

She knew, for instance, about the many me-or-the-army ultimatums, two of the suicide attempts ('The one on Arran wasn't a proper one,' said Ilsa scathingly. 'Pure manipulation') and about the ten days' enforced stay in the psychiatric clinic. She'd heard stories that Ilsa gave titles like cheap thrillers: the Night of the Bread Knife, the Incident of the Black Lace Dress and the Blood-Stained Note. She knew that in Ilsa's opinion, Charlotte was bad, not mad, and that the worst rows Ilsa and her husband Nick had ever had were on the subject of Charlotte, 'and she'd have bloody loved knowing that, too,' Ilsa had added.

And now Charlotte was phoning the office, asking Strike to call her back, and Robin, sitting outside the Pizza Express, hungry and exhausted, was pondering the phone call yet again, much as a tongue probes a mouth ulcer. If she was phoning the office, Charlotte clearly wasn't aware that Strike was in Cornwall with his terminally ill aunt, which didn't suggest regular contact between them. On the other hand, Charlotte's slightly amused tone had seemed to hint at an alliance between herself and Strike.

Robin's mobile, which was lying on the passenger seat beside the bag of almonds, buzzed. Glad of any distraction, she picked it up and saw a text message from Strike.

Are you awake?

Robin texted back:

No

As she'd expected, the mobile rang immediately.

'Well, you shouldn't be,' said Strike, without preamble. 'You must be knackered. What's it been, three weeks straight on Tufty?'

'I'm still on him.'

'What?' said Strike, sounding displeased. 'You're in Glasgow? Where's Barclay?'

'In Glasgow. He was ready in position, but Tufty didn't get on the plane. He drove down to Torquay instead. He's having pizza right now. I'm outside the restaurant.'

'The hell's he doing in Torquay, when the mistress is in Scotland?'

'Visiting his original family,' said Robin, wishing she could see Strike's face as she delivered the next bit of news. 'He's a bigamist.'

Her announcement was greeted with total silence.

'I was outside the house in Windsor at six,' said Robin, 'expecting to follow him to Stansted, see him safely onto the plane and let Barclay know he was on the way, but he didn't go to the airport. He rushed out of the house looking panicky, drove to a lock-up, took his case inside and came out with an entirely different set of luggage and minus his toupee. Then he drove all the way down here.

'Our client in Windsor's about to find out she's not legally married,' said Robin. 'Tufty's had this wife in Torquay for twenty years. I've been talking to the neighbours. I pretended I was doing a survey. One of the women along the street was at the original wedding. Tufty travels a lot for business, she said, but he's a lovely man. Devoted to his sons.

'There are two boys,' Robin continued, because Strike's stunned silence continued unabated, 'students, both in their late teens and both the absolute spit of him. One of them came off his motorbike yesterday – I got all this out of the

36

neighbour – he's got his arm in a cast and looks quite bruised and cut up. Tufty must've got news of the accident, so he came haring down here instead of going to Scotland.

'Tufty goes by the name of Edward Campion down here, not John – turns out John's his middle name, I've been searching the online records. He and the first wife and sons live in a really nice villa, view of the sea, massive garden.'

'Bloody hell,' said Strike. 'So our pregnant friend in Glasgow—'

'—is the least of Mrs-Campion-in-Windsor's worries,' said Robin. 'He's leading a triple life. Two wives and a mistress.'

'And he looks like a balding baboon. There's hope for all of us. Did you say he's having dinner right now?'

'Pizza with the wife and kids. I'm parked outside. I didn't manage to get pictures of him with the sons earlier, and I want to, because they're a total giveaway. Mini-Tuftys, just like the two in Windsor. Where d'you think he's been pretending to have been?'

'Oil rig?' suggested Strike. 'Abroad? Middle East? Maybe that's why he's so keen on keeping his tan topped up.'

Robin sighed.

'The client's going to be shattered.'

'So's the mistress in Scotland,' said Strike. 'That baby's due any minute.'

'His taste's amazingly consistent,' said Robin. 'If

you lined them up side by side, the Torquay wife, the Windsor wife and the mistress in Glasgow, they'd look like the same woman at twenty-year intervals.'

'Where are you planning to sleep?'

'Travelodge or a B&B,' said Robin, yawning again, 'if I can find anything vacant at the height of the holiday season. I'd drive straight back to London overnight, but I'm exhausted. I've been awake since four, and that's on top of a ten-hour day yesterday.'

'No driving and no sleeping in the car,' said Strike. 'Get a room.'

'How's Joan?' asked Robin. 'We can handle the workload if you want to stay in Cornwall a bit longer.'

'She won't sit still while we're all there. Ted agrees she needs some quiet. I'll come back down in a couple of weeks.'

'So, were you calling for an update on Tufty?'

'Actually, I was calling about something that just happened. I've just left the pub . . .'

In a few succinct sentences, Strike described the encounter with Margot Bamborough's daughter.

'I've just looked her up,' he said. 'Margot Bamborough, twenty-nine-year-old doctor, married, one-year-old daughter. Walked out of her GP practice in Clerkenwell at the end of a day's work, said she was going to have a quick drink with a female friend before heading home. The pub was only five minutes' walk away. The friend waited, but Margot never arrived and was never seen again.'

There was a pause. Robin, whose eyes were still fixed on the window of the pizza restaurant, said,

'And her daughter thinks you're going to find out what happened, nearly four decades later?'

'She seemed to be putting a lot of store on the coincidence of spotting me in the boozer right after the medium told her she'd get a "leading".'

'Hmm,' said Robin. 'And what do *you* think the chances are of finding out what happened after this length of time?'

'Slim to non-existent,' admitted Strike. 'On the other hand, the truth's out there. People don't just vaporise.'

Robin could hear a familiar note in his voice that indicated rumination on questions and possibilities.

'So you're meeting the daughter again tomorrow?'

'Can't hurt, can it?' said Strike.

Robin didn't answer.

'I know what you're thinking,' he said, with a trace of defensiveness. 'Emotionally overwrought client – medium – situation ripe for exploitation.'

'I'm not suggesting *you'd* exploit it—'

'Might as well hear her out, then, mightn't I? Unlike a lot of people, I wouldn't take her money for nothing. And once I'd exhausted all avenues—'

'I know you,' said Robin. 'The less you found out, the more interested you'd get.'

'Think I'd have her wife to deal with unless I

got results within a reasonable period. They're a gay couple,' he elaborated. 'The wife's a psychol—'

'Cormoran, I'll call you back,' said Robin, and without waiting for his answer, she cut the call and dropped the mobile back onto the passenger seat.

Tufty had just ambled out of the restaurant, followed by his wife and sons. Smiling and talking, they turned their steps towards their car, which lay five behind where Robin sat in the Land Rover. Raising her camera, she took a burst of pictures as the family drew nearer.

By the time they passed the Land Rover, the camera was lying in her lap and Robin's head was bowed over her phone, pretending to be texting. In the rear-view mirror she watched as the Tufty family got into their Range Rover and departed for the villa beside the sea.

Yawning yet again, Robin picked up her phone and called Strike back.

'Get everything you wanted?' he asked.

'Yeah,' said Robin, checking the photographs one-handedly with the phone to her ear, 'I've got a couple of clear ones of him and the boys. God, he's got strong genes. All four kids have got his exact features.'

She put the camera back into her bag.

'You realise I'm only a couple of hours away from St Mawes?'

'Nearer three,' said Strike.

'If you like—'

'You don't want to drive all the way down here, then back to London. You've just told me you're knackered.'

But Robin could tell that he liked the idea. He'd travelled down to Cornwall by train, taxi and ferry, because since he had lost a leg, long drives were neither easy nor particularly pleasurable.

'I'd like to meet this Anna. Then I could drive you back.'

'Well, if you're sure, that'd be great,' said Strike, now sounding cheerful. 'If we take her on, we should work the case together. There'd be a massive amount to sift through, cold case like this, and it sounds like you've wrapped up Tufty tonight.'

'Yep,' sighed Robin. 'It's all over except for the ruining of half a dozen lives.'

'*You* didn't ruin anyone's life,' said Strike bracingly. 'He did that. What's better: all three women find out now, or when he dies, with all the effing mess that'll cause?'

'I know,' said Robin, yawning again. 'So, do you want me to come to the house in St M—'

His 'no' was swift and firm.

'They – Anna and her partner – they're in Falmouth. I'll meet you there. It's a shorter drive for you.'

'OK,' said Robin. 'What time?'

'Could you manage half eleven?'

'Easily,' said Robin.

'I'll text you a place to meet. Now go and get some sleep.'

As she turned the key in the ignition, Robin became conscious that her spirits had lifted considerably. As though a censorious jury were watching, among them Ilsa, Matthew and Charlotte Campbell, she consciously repressed her smile as she reversed out of the parking space.

CHAPTER 4

Begotten by two fathers of one mother,
Though of contrarie natures each to other . . .

Edmund Spenser
The Faerie Queene

Strike woke shortly before five the following morning. Light was already streaming through Joan's thin curtains. Every night the horsehair sofa punished a different part of his body, and today he felt as though he had been punched in a kidney. He reached for his phone, noted the time, decided that he was too sore to fall back asleep, and raised himself to a sitting position.

After a minute spent stretching and scratching his armpits while his eyes acclimatised to the odd shapes rising on all sides in the gloom of Joan and Ted's sitting room, he Googled Margot Bamborough for a second time and, after a cursory examination of the picture of the smiling, wavy-haired doctor with widely spaced eyes, he scrolled through the results until he found a mention of

43

her on a website devoted to serial killers. Here he found a long article punctuated with pictures of Dennis Creed at various ages, from pretty, curly-haired blond toddler all the way through to the police mugshot of a slender man with a weak, sensual mouth and large, square glasses.

Strike then turned to an online bookstore, where he found an account of the serial killer's life, published in 1985 and titled *The Demon of Paradise Park*. It had been written by a well-respected investigative journalist, now dead. Creed's nondescript face appeared in colour on the cover, superimposed over ghostly black and white images of the seven women he was known to have tortured and killed. Margot Bamborough's face wasn't among them. Strike ordered the second-hand book, which cost £1, to be delivered to the office.

He returned his phone to its charging lead, put on his prosthetic leg, picked up his cigarettes and lighter, navigated around a rickety nest of tables with a vase of dried flowers on it and, being careful not to nudge any of the ornamental plates off the wall, passed through the doorway and down three steep steps into the kitchen. The lino, which had been there since his childhood, was icy cold on his remaining foot.

After making himself a mug of tea, he let himself out of the back door, still clad in nothing but boxers and a T-shirt, there to enjoy the cool of early morning, leaning up against the wall of the house, breathing in salt-laden air between puffs on his cigarette, and thinking about vanished mothers. Many times over the past ten days had his thoughts turned to Leda, a woman as different to Joan as the moon to the sun.

'Have you tried smoking yet, Cormy?' she'd once asked vaguely, out of a haze of blue smoke of her own creation. 'It isn't good for you, but God, I love it.'

People sometimes asked why social services never got involved with Leda Strike's family. The answer was that Leda had never stayed still long enough to present a stable target. Often her children remained in a school for mere weeks before a new enthusiasm seized her, and off they went, to a new city, a new squat, crashing on her friends' floors or, occasionally, renting. The only people who knew what was going on, and who might have contacted social services, were Ted and Joan, the one fixed point in the children's lives, but whether because Ted feared damaging the relationship between himself and his wayward sister, or because Joan worried that the children might not forgive her, they'd never done so.

One of the most vivid memories of Strike's childhood was also one of the rare occasions he could remember crying, when Leda had made an unannounced return, six weeks into Strike's first term at St Mawes Primary School. Amazed and angry that such definitive steps as enrolling him in school had been taken in her absence, she'd ushered him and his sister directly onto the ferry, promising them all manner of treats up in London. Strike had bawled, trying to explain to her that he and Dave Polworth had been going to explore smugglers' caves at the weekend, caves that might well have had no existence except in Dave's imagination, but which were no less real to Strike for that.

'You'll see the caves,' Leda had promised, plying him with sweets once they were on the train to London. 'You'll see what's-his-name soon, I promise.'

'Dave,' Strike had sobbed, 'he's called D-Dave.'

Don't think about it, Strike told himself, and he lit a second cigarette from the tip of his first.

'Stick, you'll catch your death, out there in boxers!'

He looked around. His sister was standing in the doorway, wrapped in a woollen dressing gown and wearing sheepskin slippers. They were physically so unalike that people struggled to believe that they were related, let alone half-siblings. Lucy was small, blonde and pink-faced, and greatly resembled her father, a musician not quite as famous as Strike's, but far more interested in maintaining contact with his offspring.

'Morning,' he said, but she'd already disappeared, returning with his trousers, sweatshirt, shoes and socks.

'Luce, it's not cold—'

'You'll get pneumonia. Put them on!'

Like Joan, Lucy had total confidence in her own judgement of her nearest and dearest's best

46

interests. With slightly better grace than he might have mustered had he not been about to return to London, Strike took his trousers and put them on, balancing awkwardly and risking a fall onto the gravel path. By the time he'd added a shoe and sock to his real foot, Lucy had made him a fresh mug of tea along with her own.

'I couldn't sleep, either,' she told him, handing over the mug as she sat down on the stone bench. It was the first time they'd been entirely alone all week. Lucy had been glued to Joan's side, insisting on doing all the cooking and cleaning while Joan, who found it inconceivable that she should sit down while the house was full of guests, hovered and fussed. On the rare moments that Joan wasn't present, one or more of Lucy's sons had generally been there, in Jack's case wanting to talk to Strike, the other two generally badgering Lucy for something.

'It's awful, isn't it?' said Lucy, staring out over the lawn and Ted's carefully tended flower-beds.

'Yeah,' sighed Strike. 'But fingers crossed. The chemo—'

'But

it won't cure her. It'll just prolong – pro—'

Lucy shook her head and dabbed at her eyes with a crumpled piece of toilet roll she pulled out of her dressing-gown pocket.

'I've rung her twice a week for nigh on twenty years, Stick. This place is a second home for our boys. She's the only mother I've ever known.'

Strike knew he oughtn't to rise to the bait. Nevertheless, he said,

'Other than our actual mother, you mean.'

'Leda wasn't my mother,' said Lucy coldly. Strike had never heard her say it in so many words, though it had often been implied. 'I haven't considered her my mother since I was fourteen years old. Younger, actually. *Joan's* my mother.'

And when Strike made no response, she said,

'You chose Leda. I know you love Joan, but we have entirely different relationships with her.'

'Didn't realise it was a competition,' Strike said, reaching for another cigarette.

'I'm only telling you how I feel!'

And telling me how I feel.

Several barbed comments about the infrequency of Strike's visits had already dropped from his sister's lips during their week of enforced proximity. He'd bitten back all irritable retorts. His primary aim was to leave the house without rowing with anyone.

'I always hated it when Leda came to take us away,' said Lucy now, 'but you were glad to go.'

He noted the Joan-esque statement of fact, the lack of enquiry.

'I wasn't always glad to go,' Strike contradicted her, thinking of the ferry, Dave Polworth and the smugglers' caves, but Lucy seemed to feel that he was trying to rob her of something.

'I'm just saying, you lost *your* mother years ago. Now I'm – I might be – losing mine.'

She mopped her eyes again with the damp toilet roll.

Lower back throbbing, eyes stinging with tiredness, Strike stood smoking in silence. He knew that Lucy would have liked to excise Leda for ever from her memory, and sometimes, remembering a few of the things Leda had put them through, he sympathised. This morning, though, the wraith of Leda seemed to drift on his cigarette smoke around him. He could hear her saying to Lucy, 'Go on and have a good cry, darling, it always helps', and 'Give your old mum a fag, Cormy'. He couldn't hate her.

'I can't *believe* you went out with Dave Polworth last night,' said Lucy suddenly. 'Your last night here!'

'Joan virtually shoved me out of the house,' said Strike, nettled. 'She loves Dave. Anyway, I'll be back in a couple of weeks.'

'Will you?' said Lucy, her eyelashes now beaded with tears. 'Or will you be in the middle of some case and just forget?'

Strike blew smoke out into the constantly lightening air, which had that flat blue tinge that precedes sunrise. Far to the right, hazily visible over the rooftops of the houses on the slope that was Hillhead, the division between sky and water was becoming clearer on the horizon.

'No,' he said, 'I won't forget.'

'Because you're good in a crisis,' said Lucy, 'I don't deny that, but it's keeping a commitment

49

going that you seem to have a problem with. Joan'll need support for months and months, not just when—'

'I know that, Luce,' said Strike, his temper rising in spite of himself. 'I understand illness and recuperation, believe it or—'

'Yeah, well,' said Lucy, 'you were great when Jack was in hospital, but when everything's fine you simply don't bother.'

'I took Jack out two weeks ago, what're you—?'

'You couldn't even make the effort to come to Luke's birthday party! He'd told all his friends you were going to be there—'

'Well, he shouldn't have done, because I told you *explicitly* over the phone—'

'You said you'd try—'

'No, *you* said I'd try,' Strike contradicted her, temper rising now, in spite of his best intentions. '*You* said "You'll make it if you can, though." Well, I couldn't make it, I told you so in advance and it's not my fault you told Luke differently—'

'I appreciate you taking Jack out every now and then,' said Lucy, talking over him, 'but has it never occurred to you that it would be nice if the other two could come, too? Adam *cried* when Jack came home from the War Rooms! And then you come down here,' said Lucy, who seemed determined to get everything off her chest now she'd started, 'and you only bring a present for Jack. What about Luke and Adam?'

'Ted called with the news about Joan and I set

straight off. I'd been saving those badges for Jack, so I brought them with me.'

'Well, how do you think that makes Luke and Adam feel? Obviously they think you don't like them as much as Jack!'

'I don't,' said Strike, finally losing his temper. 'Adam's a whiny little prick and Luke's a complete arsehole.'

He crushed out his cigarette on the wall, flicked the stub into the hedge and headed back inside, leaving Lucy gasping for air like a beached fish.

Back in the dark sitting room, Strike blundered straight into the table nest: the vase of dried flowers toppled heavily onto the patterned carpet and before he knew what he was doing he'd crushed the fragile stems and papery heads to dust beneath his false foot. He was still tidying up the fragments as best he could when Lucy strode silently past him towards the door to the stairs, emanating maternal outrage. Strike set the now empty vase back on the table and, waiting until he heard Lucy's bedroom door close, headed upstairs for the bathroom, fuming.

Afraid to use the shower in case he woke Ted and Joan, he peed, pulled the flush and only then remembered how noisy the old toilet was. Washing as best he could in tepid water while the cistern refilled with a noise like a cement mixer, Strike thought that if anyone slept through that, they'd have to be drugged.

Sure enough, on opening the bathroom door, he

came face to face with Joan. The top of his aunt's head barely came up to Strike's chest. He looked down on her thinning grey hair, into once forget-me-not blue eyes now bleached with age. Her frogged and quilted red dressing gown had the ceremonial dignity of a kabuki robe.

'Morning,' Strike said, trying to sound cheerful and achieving only a fake bonhomie. 'Didn't wake you, did I?'

'No, no, I've been awake for a while. How was Dave?' she asked.

'Great,' said Strike heartily. 'Loving his new job.'

'And Penny and the girls?'

'Yeah, they're really happy to be back in Cornwall.'

'Oh good,' said Joan. 'Dave's mum thought Penny might not want to leave Bristol.'

'No, it's all worked out great.'

The bedroom door behind Joan opened. Luke was standing there in his pyjamas, rubbing his eyes ostentatiously.

'You woke me up,' he told Strike and Joan.

'Oh, sorry, love,' said Joan.

'Can I have Coco Pops?'

'Of course you can,' said Joan fondly.

Luke bounded downstairs, stamping on the stairs to make as much noise as possible. He was gone barely a minute before he came bounding back towards them, glee etched over his freckled face.

'Granny, Uncle Cormoran's broken your flowers.'

You little shit.

'Yeah, sorry. The dried ones,' Strike told Joan. 'I knocked them over. The vase is fine—'

'Oh, they couldn't matter less,' said Joan, moving at once to the stairs. 'I'll fetch the carpet sweeper.'

'No,' said Strike at once, 'I've already—'

'There are still bits all over the carpet,' Luke said. 'I trod on them.'

I'll tread on you in a minute, arsehole.

Strike and Luke followed Joan back to the sitting room, where Strike insisted on taking the carpet sweeper from Joan, a flimsy, archaic device she'd had since the seventies. As he plied it, Luke stood in the kitchen doorway watching him, smirking while shovelling Coco Pops into his mouth. By the time Strike had cleaned the carpet to Joan's satisfaction, Jack and Adam had joined the early morning jamboree, along with a stony-faced Lucy, now fully dressed.

'Can we go to the beach today, Mum?'

'Can we swim?'

'Can I go out in the boat with Uncle Ted?'

'Sit down,' Strike told Joan. 'I'll bring you a cup of tea.'

But Lucy had already done it. She handed Joan the mug, threw Strike a filthy look, then turned back to the kitchen, answering her sons' questions as she went.

'What's going on?' asked Ted, shuffling into the room in pyjamas, confused by this break-of-dawn activity.

He'd once been nearly as tall as Strike, who

53

greatly resembled him. His dense, curly hair was now snow white, his deep brown face more cracked than lined, but Ted was still a strong man, though he stooped a little. However, Joan's diagnosis seemed to have dealt him a physical blow. He seemed literally shaken, a little disorientated and unsteady.

'Just getting my stuff together, Ted,' said Strike, who suddenly had an overpowering desire to leave. 'I'm going to have to get the first ferry to make the early train.'

'Ah,' said Ted. 'All the way back up to London, are you?'

'Yep,' said Strike, chucking his charging lead and deodorant back into the kit bag where the rest of his belongings were already neatly stowed. 'But I'll be back in a couple of weeks. You'll keep me posted, right?'

'You can't leave without breakfast!' said Joan anxiously. 'I'll make you a sandwich—'

'It's too early for me to eat,' lied Strike. 'I've had a cup of tea and I'll get something on the train. Tell her,' he said to Ted, because Joan wasn't listening, but scurrying for the kitchen.

'Joanie!' Ted called. 'He doesn't want anything!'

Strike grabbed his jacket off the back of a chair and hoisted the kit bag out to the hall.

'You should go back to bed,' he told Joan, as she hurried to bid him goodbye. 'I really didn't want to wake you. Rest, all right? Let someone else run the town for a few weeks.'

'I wish you'd stop smoking,' she said sadly.

Strike managed a humorous eye roll, then hugged her. She clung to him the way she had done whenever Leda was waiting impatiently to take him away, and Strike squeezed her back, feeling again the pain of divided loyalties, of being both battleground and prize, of having to give names to what was uncategorisable and unknowable.

'Bye, Ted,' he said, hugging his uncle. 'I'll ring you when I'm home and we'll fix up a time for the next visit.'

'I could've driven you,' said Uncle Ted feebly. 'Sure you don't want me to drive you?'

'I like the ferry,' lied Strike. In fact, the uneven steps leading down to the boat were almost impossible for him to navigate without assistance from the ferryman, but because he knew it would give them pleasure, he said, 'Reminds me of you two taking us shopping in Falmouth when we were kids.'

Lucy was watching him, apparently unconcerned, through the door from the sitting room. Luke and Adam hadn't wanted to leave their Coco Pops, but Jack came wriggling breathlessly into the tiny hall to say,

'Thanks for my badges, Uncle Corm.'

'It was a pleasure,' said Strike, and he ruffled the boy's hair. 'Bye, Luce,' he called. 'See you soon, Jack,' he added.

CHAPTER 5

He little answer'd, but in manly heart
His mightie indignation did forbeare,
Which was not yet so secret, but some part
Thereof did in his frouning face appeare . . .

Edmund Spenser
The Faerie Queene

The bedroom in the bed and breakfast where Robin spent the night barely had room for a single bed, a chest of drawers and a rickety sink plumbed into the corner. The walls were covered in a mauve floral wallpaper that Robin thought must surely have been considered tasteless even in the seventies, the sheets felt damp and the window was imperfectly covered by a tangled Venetian blind.

In the harsh glare of a single light bulb unsoftened by its shade of open wickerwork, Robin's reflection looked exhausted and ill-kempt, with purple shadows beneath her eyes. Her backpack contained only those items she always carried on surveillance jobs – a beanie hat, should she need to conceal her distinctive red-blonde hair, sunglasses, a change of top, a credit card and ID in a couple of different names. The fresh T-shirt she'd just pulled out of her backpack was heavily creased and her hair in urgent need of a wash; the sink was soapless and she'd omitted to pack toothbrush or toothpaste, unaware that she was going to be spending the night away from home.

Robin was back on the road by eight. In Newton Abbot she stopped at a chemist and a Sainsbury's, where she purchased, in addition to basic toiletries and dry shampoo, a small, cheap bottle of 4711 cologne. She cleaned her teeth and made herself as presentable as possible in the supermarket bathroom. While brushing her hair, she received a text from Strike:

I'll be in the Palacio Lounge café in The Moor, middle of Falmouth. Anyone will tell you where The Moor is.

The further west Robin drove, the lusher and greener the landscape became. Yorkshire-born, she'd found it extraordinary to see palm trees actually flourishing on English soil, back in Torquay. These twisting, verdant lanes, the luxuriance of the vegetation, the almost sub-tropical greenness was a surprise to a person raised among bare, rolling moors and hillside. Then there were the glints to her left of a quicksilver sea, as wide and gleaming as plate glass, and the tang of the salt now mixed with the citrus of her hastily purchased cologne. In spite of her tiredness she found her spirits buoyed by the glorious morning, and the idea of Strike waiting at journey's end.

She arrived in Falmouth at eleven o'clock, and drove in search of a parking space through streets packed with tourists and past shop doorways accreted in plastic toys and pubs covered in flags and multicoloured window boxes. Once she'd parked in The Moor itself – a wide open market square in the heart of the town – she saw that beneath the gaudy summertime trappings, Falmouth boasted some grand old nineteenth-century buildings, one of which housed the Palacio Lounge café and restaurant.

The high ceilings and classical proportions of what looked like an old courthouse had been decorated in a self-consciously whimsical style, which included garish orange floral wallpaper, hundreds of kitschy paintings in pastel frames, and a stuffed fox dressed as a magistrate. The clientele, which was dominated by students and families, sat on mismatched wooden chairs, their chatter echoing through the cavernous space. After a few seconds Robin spotted Strike, large and surly-looking at the back of the room, seeming far from happy beside a pair of families whose many young children, most of whom were wearing tie-dyed clothing, were racing around between tables.

Robin thought she saw the idea of standing to

greet her cross Strike's mind as she wound her way through the tables towards him, but if she was right, he decided against. She knew how he looked when his leg was hurting him, the lines around his mouth deeper than usual, as though he had been clenching his jaw. If Robin had looked tired in the dusty bed and breakfast mirror three hours previously, Strike looked utterly drained, his unshaven jaw appearing dirty, the shadows under his eyes dark blue.

'Morning,' he said, struggling to make himself heard over the merry shrieking of the hippy children. 'Get parked OK?'

'Just round the corner,' she said, sitting down.

'I chose this place because I thought it would be easy to find,' he said.

A small boy knocked into their table, causing Strike's coffee to slop over onto his plate, which was littered with croissant flakes, and ran off again. 'What d'you want?'

'Coffee would be great,' said Robin loudly, over the cries of the children beside them. 'How're things in St Mawes?'

'Same,' said Strike.

'I'm sorry,' said Robin.

'Why? It's not your fault,' grunted Strike.

This was hardly the greeting Robin had expected after a two-and-a-half drive to pick him up. Possibly her annoyance showed, because Strike added,

'Thanks for doing this. Appreciate it. *Oh, don't pretend you can't see me, dipshit,*' he added crossly,

59

as a young waiter walked away without spotting his raised hand.

'I'll go to the counter,' said Robin. 'I need the loo anyway.'

By the time she'd peed and managed to order a coffee from a harassed waiter, a tension headache had begun to pound on the left-hand side of her head. On her return to the table she found Strike looking like thunder, because the children at the next tables were now shrieking louder than ever as they raced around their oblivious parents, who simply shouted over the din. The idea of giving Strike Charlotte's telephone message right now passed through Robin's mind, only to be dismissed.

In fact, the main reason for Strike's foul mood was that the end of his amputated leg was agony. He'd fallen (*like a total tit*, as he told himself) while getting onto the Falmouth ferry. This feat required a precarious descent down worn stone steps without a handhold, then a step down into the boat with only the boatman's hand for assistance. At sixteen stone, Strike was hard to stabilise when he slipped, and slip he had, with the result that he was now in a lot of pain.

Robin took paracetamol out of her bag.

'Headache,' she said, catching Strike's eye.

'I'm not bloody surprised,' he said loudly, looking at the parents shouting at each other over the raucous yells of their offspring, but they didn't hear him. The idea of asking Robin for painkillers crossed Strike's mind, but this might engender enquiries and fussing, and he'd had quite enough of those in the past week, so he continued to suffer in silence.

'Where's the client?' she asked, after downing her pills with coffee.

'About five minutes' drive away. Place called Wodehouse Terrace.'

At this point, the smallest of the children racing around nearby tripped and smacked her face on the wooden floor. The child's shrieks and wails of pain pounded against Robin's eardrums.

'Oh, Daffy!' said one of the tie-dyed mothers shrilly, '*what* have you done?'

The child's mouth was bloody. Her mother crouched beside their table, loudly castigating and soothing, while the girl's siblings and friends watched avidly. The ferry-goers this morning had worn similar expressions when Strike had hit the deck.

'He's got a false leg,' the ferryman had shouted, partly, Strike suspected, in case anyone thought the fall was due to his negligence. The announcement had in no way lessened Strike's mortification or the interest of his fellow travellers.

'Shall we get going?' Robin asked, already on her feet.

'Definitely,' said Strike, wincing as he stood and picked up his holdall. 'Bloody kids,' he muttered, limping after Robin towards the sunlight.

61

CHAPTER 6

Faire Lady, hart of flint would rew
The vndeserued woes and sorrowes, which ye
  shew.

Edmund Spenser
The Faerie Queene

Wodehouse Terrace lay on a hill, with a wide view of the bay below. Many of the houses had had loft conversions, but Anna and Kim's, as they saw from the street, had been more extensively modified than any other, with what looked like a square glass box where once there had been roof.

'What does Anna do?' asked Robin, as they climbed the steps towards the deep blue front door.

'No idea,' said Strike, 'but her wife's a psychologist. I got the impression she isn't keen on the idea of an investigation.'

He pressed the doorbell. They heard footsteps on what sounded like bare wood, and the door was opened by Dr Sullivan, tall, blonde and bare-foot in jeans and a shirt, the sun glinting off her spectacles. She looked from Strike to Robin, apparently surprised.

'My partner, Robin Ellacott,' Strike explained.

'Oh,' said Kim, looking displeased. 'You do realise – this is only supposed to be an exploratory meeting.'

'Robin happened to be just up the coast on another case, so—'

'I'm more than happy to wait in the car,' said Robin politely, 'if Anna would rather speak to Cormoran alone.'

'Well – we'll see how Anna feels.'

Standing back to admit them, Kim added, 'Straight upstairs, in the sitting room.'

The house had clearly been remodelled through-out and to a high standard. Everywhere was bleached wood and glass. The bedroom, as Robin saw through an open door, had been relocated to the ground floor, along with what looked like a study. Upstairs, in the glass box they'd seen from the street, was an open-plan area combining kitchen, dining and sitting room, with a dazzling view of the sea.

Anna was standing beside a gleaming, expensive coffee machine, wearing a baggy blue cotton jumpsuit and white canvas shoes, which to Robin looked stylish and to Strike, frumpy. Her hair was tied back, revealing the delicacy of her bone structure.

'Oh, hello,' she said, starting at the sight of them. 'I didn't hear the door over the coffee machine.'

'Annie,' said Kim, following Strike and Robin into the room, 'this is Robin Ellacott, er – Cameron's partner. She's happy to go if you'd rather just talk to—'

'Cormoran,' Anna corrected Kim. 'Do people get that wrong a lot?' she asked Strike.

'More often than not,' he said, but with a smile. 'But it's a bloody stupid name.'

Anna laughed.

'I don't mind you staying,' she told Robin, advancing and offering a handshake. 'I think I read about you, too,' she added, and Robin pretended that she didn't notice Anna glancing down at the long scar on her forearm.

'Please, sit down,' said Kim, gesturing Strike and Robin to an inbuilt seating area around a low Perspex table.

'Coffee?' suggested Anna, and both of them accepted.

A ragdoll cat came prowling into the room, stepping delicately through the puddles of sunlight on the floor, its clear blue eyes like Joan's across the bay. After subjecting both Strike and Robin to dispassionate scrutiny, it leapt lightly onto the sofa and into Strike's lap.

'Ironically,' said Kim, as she carried a tray laden with cups and biscuits to the table, 'Cagney absolutely *loves* men.'

Strike and Robin laughed politely. Anna brought

over the coffee pot, and the two women sat down side by side, facing Strike and Robin, their faces in the full glare of the sun until Anna reached for a remote control, which automatically lowered cream-coloured sun blinds.

'Wonderful place,' said Robin, looking around.

'Thanks,' said Kim. '*Her* work,' she said, patting Anna's knee. 'She's an architect.'

Anna cleared her throat.

'I want to apologise,' she said, looking steadily at Strike with her unusual silver-grey eyes, 'for the way I behaved last night. I'd had a few glasses of wine. You probably thought I was a crank.'

'If I'd thought that,' said Strike, stroking the loudly purring cat, 'I wouldn't be here.'

'But mentioning the medium probably gave you entirely the wrong . . . because, believe me, Kim's already told me what a fool I was to go and see her.'

'I don't think you're a fool, Annie,' Kim said quietly. 'I think you're vulnerable. There's a difference.'

'May I ask what the medium said?' asked Strike.

'Does it matter?' asked Kim, looking at Strike with what Robin thought was mistrust.

'Not in an investigative sense,' said Strike, 'but as he – she? – is the reason Anna approached me—'

'It was a woman,' said Anna, 'and she didn't really tell me anything useful . . . not that I . . .'

With a nervous laugh, she shook her head and started again.

'I know it was a stupid thing to do. I – I've been through a difficult time recently – I left my firm and I'm about to turn forty and . . . well, Kim was away on a course and I – well, I suppose I wanted—'

She waved her hands dismissively, took a deep breath and said,

'She's quite an ordinary-looking woman who lives in Chiswick. Her house was full of angels – made of pottery and glass, I mean, and there was a big one painted on velvet over the fireplace.

'Kim,' Anna pressed on, and Robin glanced at the psychologist, whose expression was impassive, 'Kim thinks she – the medium – knew who my mother was – that she Googled me before I arrived. I'd given her my real name. When I got there, I simply said that my mother died a long time ago – although of course,' said Anna, with another nervous wave of her thin hands, 'there's no proof that my mother's dead – that's half the – but anyway, I told the medium she'd died, and that nobody had ever been clear with me about how it happened.

'So the woman went into a – well, I suppose you'd call it a trance,' Anna said, looking embarrassed, 'and she told me that people thought they were protecting me for my own good, but that it was time I knew the truth and that I would soon have a "leading" that would take me to it. And she said "your mother's very proud of you" and "she's always watching over you", and things like that, I suppose they're boilerplate – and then, at the end, "she lies in a holy place".

'"Lies in a holy place"?' repeated Strike.

'Yes. I suppose she thought that would be comforting, but I'm not a churchgoer. The sanctity or otherwise of my mother's final resting place – if she's buried – I mean, it's hardly my primary concern.'

'D'you mind if I take notes?' Strike asked.

He pulled out a notebook and pen, which Cagney the cat appeared to think were for her personal amusement. She attempted to bat the pen around as Strike wrote the date.

'Come here, you silly animal,' said Kim, getting up to lift the cat clear and put her back on the warm wooden floor.

'To begin at the beginning,' said Strike. 'You must've been very young when your mother went missing?'

'Just over a year old,' said Anna, 'so I can't remember her at all. There were no photographs of her in the house while I was growing up. I didn't know what had happened for a long time. Of course, there was no internet back then – anyway, my mother kept her own surname after marriage. I grew up as Anna Phipps, which is my father's name. If anybody had said "Margot Bamborough" to me before I was eleven, I wouldn't have known she had any connection to me.

'I thought Cynthia was my mum. She was my childminder when I was little,' she explained.

67

'She's a third cousin of my father's and quite a bit younger than him, but she's a Phipps, too, so I assumed we were a standard nuclear family. I mean – why wouldn't I?

'I do remember, once I'd started school, questioning why I was calling Cyn "Cyn" instead of "Mum". But then Dad and Cyn decided to get married, and they told me I could call her "Mum" now if I wanted to, and I thought, oh, I see, I had to use her name before, because they weren't married. You fill in the gaps when you're a child, don't you? With your own weird logic.

'I was seven or eight when a girl at school said to me, "That's not your real mum. Your real mum disappeared." It sounded mad. I didn't ask Dad or Cyn about it. I just locked it away, but I think, on some deep level, I sensed I'd just been handed the answer to some of the strange things I'd noticed and never been given answers to.

'I was eleven when I found out properly. By then, I'd heard other things from other kids at school. "Your real mum ran away" was one of them. Then one day, this really *poisonous* boy said to me, "Your mum was killed by a man who cut off her head."'

'I went home and I told my father what that boy had said. I wanted him to laugh, to say it was ridiculous, what a horrible little boy . . . but he turned white.

'That same evening he and Cynthia called me downstairs out of my bedroom, sat me down in the sitting room and told me the truth.

'And everything I thought I knew crumbled away,' said Anna quietly. 'Who thinks something like this has happened in their own family? I adored Cyn. I got on better with her than with my father, to tell you the truth. And then I found out that she wasn't my mum at all, and they'd both lied – lied in fact, lied by omission.

'They told me my mother walked out of her GP's practice one night and vanished. The last person to see her alive was the receptionist. She said she was off to the pub, which was five minutes up the road. Her best friend was waiting there. When my mother didn't turn up, the friend, Oonagh Kennedy, who'd waited an hour, thought she must have forgotten. She called my parents' house. My mother wasn't there. My father called the practice, but it was closed. It got dark. My mother didn't come home. My father called the police.

'They investigated for months and months. Nothing. No clues, no sightings – at least, that's what my father and Cyn said, but I've since read things that contradict that.

'I asked Dad and Cyn where my mother's parents were. They said they were dead. That turned out to be true. My grandfather died of a heart attack a couple of years after my mother disappeared and my grandmother died of a stroke a year later. My mother was an only child, so there were no other relatives I could meet or talk to about her.

'I asked for photographs. My father said he'd

got rid of them all, but Cyn dug some out for me, a couple of weeks after I found out. She asked me not to tell my father she'd done it; to hide them. I did: I had a pyjama case shaped like a rabbit and I kept my mother's photographs in there for years.'

'Did your father and stepmother explain to you what *might* have happened to your mother?' Strike asked.

'Dennis Creed, you mean?' said Anna. 'Yes, but they didn't tell me details. They said there was a chance she'd been killed by a – by a bad man. They had to tell me that much, because of what the boy at school had said.

'It was an appalling idea, thinking she might have been killed by Creed – I found out his name soon enough, kids at school were happy to fill me in. I started having nightmares about her, headless. Sometimes she came into my bedroom at night. Sometimes I dreamed I found her head in my toy chest.

'I got really angry with my father and Cyn,' said Anna, twisting her fingers together. 'Angry that they'd never told me, obviously, but I also started wondering what else they were hiding, whether they were involved in my mother disappearing, whether they'd wanted her out of the way, so they could marry. I went a bit off the rails, started playing truant . . . one weekend I took off and was brought home by the police. My father was livid. Of course, I look back, and after what had happened to my mother . . . obviously, me going missing, even for a few hours . . .

'I gave them hell, to tell you the truth,' said Anna shamefacedly. 'But all credit to Cyn, she stuck by me. She never gave up. She and Dad had had kids together by then – I've got a younger brother and sister – and there was family therapy and holidays with bonding activities, all led by Cyn, because my father certainly didn't want to do it. The subject of my mother just makes him angry and aggrieved. I remember him yelling at me, didn't I realise how terrible it was for *him* to have it all dragged up again, how did I think *he* felt . . .

'When I was fifteen I tried to find my mother's friend, Oonagh, the one she was supposed to be meeting the night she disappeared. They were Bunny Girls together,' said Anna, with a little smile, 'but I didn't know that at the time. I tracked Oonagh down in Wolverhampton, and she was quite emotional to hear from me. We had a couple of lovely phone calls. She told me things I really wanted to know, about my mother's sense of humour, the perfume she wore – Rive Gauche, I went out and blew my birthday money on a bottle next day – how she was addicted to chocolate and was an obsessive Joni Mitchell fan. My mother came more alive to me when I was talking to Oonagh than through the photographs, or anything Dad or Cyn had told me.

'But my father found out I'd spoken to Oonagh and he was furious. He made me give him Oonagh's number and called her and accused her of encouraging me to defy him, told her I was troubled, in therapy and what I didn't need was people "stirring". He told me not to wear the Rive Gauche, either. He said he couldn't stand the smell of it.

'So I never did meet Oonagh, and when I tried to reconnect with her in my twenties, I couldn't find her. She might have passed away, for all I know.'

'I got into university, left home and started reading everything I could about Dennis Creed. The nightmares came back, but it didn't get me any closer to finding out what really happened.

'Apparently the man in charge of the investigation into my mother's disappearance, a detective inspector called Bill Talbot, always thought Creed took her. Talbot will be dead by now; he was coming up for retirement anyway.

'Then, a few years out of uni, I had the bright idea of starting a website,' said Anna. 'My girlfriend at the time was tech-savvy. She helped me set it up. I was very naive,' she sighed. 'I said who I was and begged for information about my mother.

'You can probably imagine what happened. All kinds of theories: psychics telling me where to dig, people telling me my father had obviously done it, others telling me I wasn't really Margot's daughter, that I was after money and publicity, and some really malicious messages as well, saying my mother had probably run off with a lover and worse. A couple of journalists got in touch, too.

One of them ran an awful piece in the *Daily Express* about our family: they contacted my father and that was just about the final nail in the coffin for our relationship.

'It's never really recovered,' said Anna bleakly. 'When I told him I'm gay, he seemed to think I was only doing it to spite him. And Cyn's gone over to his side a bit, these last few years. She always says, "I've got a loyalty to your dad, too, Anna." So,' said Anna, 'that's where we are.'

There was a brief silence.

'Dreadful for you,' said Robin.

'It is,' agreed Kim, placing her hand on Anna's knee again, 'and I'm wholly sympathetic to Anna's desire for resolution, of course I am. But is it realistic,' she said, looking from Robin to Strike, 'and I mean this with no offence to you two, to think that you'll achieve what the police haven't, after all this time?'

'Realistic?' said Strike. 'No.'

Robin noticed Anna's downward look and the sudden rush of tears into her large eyes. She felt desperately sorry for the older woman, but at the same time she respected Strike's honesty, and it seemed to have impressed the sceptical Kim, too.

'Here's the truth,' Strike said, tactfully looking at his notes until Anna had finished drying her eyes with the back of her hand. 'I think we'd have a reasonable chance of getting hold of the old police file, because we've got decent contacts at the Met.

We can sift right through the evidence again, revisit witnesses as far as that's possible, basically make sure every stone's been turned over twice.

'But it's odds on that after all this time, we wouldn't find any more than the police did, and we'd be facing two major obstacles.

'Firstly, zero forensic evidence. From what I understand, literally no trace of your mother was ever found, is that right? No items of clothing, bus pass – nothing.'

'True,' mumbled Anna.

'Secondly, as you've just pointed out, a lot of the people connected with her or who witnessed anything that night are likely to have died.'

'I know,' said Anna, and a tear trickled, sparkling, down her nose onto the Perspex table. Kim reached out and put an arm around her shoulders. 'Maybe it's turning forty,' said Anna, with a sob, 'but I can't stand the idea that I'll go to my grave never knowing what happened.'

'I understand that,' said Strike, 'but I don't want to promise what I'm unlikely to be able to deliver.'

'Have there,' asked Robin, 'been any new leads or developments over the years?'

Kim answered. She seemed a little shaken by Anna's naked distress, and kept her arm around her shoulders.

'Not as far as we know, do we, Annie? But any information of that kind would probably have gone to Roy – Anna's father. And he might not have told us.'

'He acts as though none of it ever happened; it's how he copes,' said Anna, wiping her tears away. 'He pretends my mother never existed – except for the inconvenient fact that if she hadn't, I wouldn't be here.

'Believe it or not,' she said, 'it's the possibility that she just went away of her own accord and never came back, never wanted to see how I was doing, or let us know where she was, that really haunts me. That's the thing I can't bear to contemplate. My grandmother on my father's side, who I never loved – she was one of the meanest women I've ever met – took it upon herself to tell me that it had always been her private belief that my mother had simply run away. That she didn't like being a wife and a mother. That hurt me more than I can tell you, the thought that my mother would let everyone go through the horror of wondering what had happened to her, and never check that her daughter was all right . . .

'Even if Dennis Creed killed her,' said Anna, 'it would be terrible – awful – but it would be over. I could mourn rather than live with the possibility that she's out there somewhere, living under a different name, not caring what happened to us all.'

There was a brief silence, in which both Strike and Robin drank coffee, Anna sniffed, and Kim left the sofa area to tear off kitchen roll, which she handed to her wife.

A second ragdoll cat entered the room. She

75

subjected the four humans to a supercilious glare before lying down and stretching in a patch of sunlight.

'That's Lacey,' said Kim, while Anna mopped her face. 'She doesn't really like anyone, even us.'

Strike and Robin laughed politely again.

'How would this work?' asked Kim abruptly. 'How d'you charge?'

'By the hour,' said Strike. 'You'd get an itemised monthly bill. I can email you our rates,' he offered, 'but I'd imagine you two will want to talk this over properly before coming to a decision.'

'Yes, definitely,' said Kim, but as she gave Strike her email address she looked with concern again at Anna, who was sitting with head bowed, still pressing kitchen roll to her eyes at regular intervals.

Strike's stump protested at being asked to support his weight again so soon after sitting down, but there seemed little more to discuss, especially as Anna had regressed into a tearful silence. Slightly regretting the untouched plate of biscuits, the detective shook Anna's cool hand.

'Thanks, anyway,' she said, and he had the feeling that he had disappointed her, that she'd hoped he would make her a promise of the truth, that he would swear upon his honour to do what everyone else had failed to do.

Kim showed them out of the house.

'We'll call you later,' she said. 'This afternoon. Will that be all right?'

'Great, we'll wait to hear from you,' said Strike.

Robin glanced back as she and Strike headed down the sunlit garden steps towards the street, and caught Kim giving them a strange look, as though she'd found something in the pair of visitors that she hadn't expected. Catching Robin's eye, she smiled reflexively, and closed the blue door behind them.

CHAPTER 7

Long they thus traueiled in friendly wise,
Through countreyes waste, and eke well
edifyde . . .

Edmund Spenser
The Faerie Queene

As they headed out of Falmouth, Strike's mood turned to cheerfulness, which Robin attributed mainly to the interest of a possible new case. She'd never yet known an intriguing problem to fail to engage his attention, no matter what might be happening in his private life.

She was partially right: Strike's interest had certainly been piqued by Anna's story, but he was mainly cheered by the prospect of keeping weight off his prosthesis for a few hours, and by the knowledge that every passing minute put further distance between himself and his sister. Opening the car window, allowing the familiar sea air to rush bracingly inside the old car, he lit a cigarette and, blowing smoke away from Robin, asked,

78

'Seen much of Morris while I've been away?'

'Saw him yesterday,' said Robin. 'Paid him for his month's expenses.'

'Ah, great, cheers,' said Strike, 'I meant to remind you that needed doing. What d'you think of him? Barclay says he's good at the job, except he talks too much in the car.'

'Yeah,' said Robin noncommittally, 'he does like to talk.'

'Hutchins thinks he's a bit smarmy,' said Strike, subtly probing.

He'd noticed the special tone Morris reserved for Robin. Hutchins had also reported that Morris had asked him what Robin's relationship status was.

'Mm,' said Robin, 'well, I haven't really had enough contact with him to form an opinion.'

Given Strike's current stress levels and the amount of work the agency was struggling to cover, she'd decided not to criticise his most recent hire. They needed an extra man. At least Morris was good at the job.

'Pat likes him,' she added, partly out of mischief, and was amused to see, out of the corner of her eye, Strike turn to look at her, scowling.

'That's no bloody recommendation.'

'Unkind,' said Robin.

'You realise in a week's time it's going to be harder to sack her? Her probation period's nearly up.'

'I don't want to sack her,' said Robin. 'I think she's great.'

'Well, then, on your head be it if she causes trouble down the line.'

'It won't be on my head,' said Robin. 'You're not pinning Pat on me. Hiring her was a joint decision. You were the one who was sick of temps— '

'And you were the one who said "it might not be a bad idea to get a more traditional manager in" and "we shouldn't discount her because of her age"—'

'—I know what I said, and I stand by the age thing. We *do* need someone who understands a spreadsheet, who's organised, but you were the one who—'

'—I didn't want you accusing me of ageism.'

'—*you were the one who offered her the job,*' Robin finished firmly.

'Dunno what I was bloody thinking,' muttered Strike, flicking ash out of the window.

Patricia Chauncey was fifty-six and looked sixty-five. A thin woman with a deeply lined, monkeyish face and implausibly jet-black hair, she vaped continually in the office, but was to be seen drawing deeply on a Superking the moment her feet touched the pavement at the end of the day's work. Pat's voice was so deep and rasping that she was often mistaken for Strike on the phone. She sat at what once had been Robin's desk in the outer office and had taken over the bulk of the agency's phone-answering and administrative duties now that Robin had moved to full-time detection.

80

Strike and Pat's relationship had been combative from the start, which puzzled Robin, who liked them both. Robin was used to Strike's intermittent bouts of moodiness, and prone to give him the benefit of the doubt, especially when she suspected he was in pain, but Pat had no compunction about snapping 'Would a "thanks" kill you?' if Strike showed insufficient gratitude when she passed him his phone messages. She evidently felt none of the reverence some of their temps had displayed towards the now famous detective, one of whom had been sacked on the spot when Strike realised she was surreptitiously filming him on her mobile from the outer office. Indeed, the office manager's demeanour suggested that she lived in daily expectation of finding out things to Strike's discredit, and she'd displayed a certain satisfaction on hearing that the dent in one of the filing cabinets was due to the fact that he'd once punched it.

On the other hand, the filing was up to date, the accounts were in order, all receipts were neatly docketed, the phone was answered promptly, messages were passed on accurately, they never ran out of teabags or milk, and Pat had never once arrived late, no matter the weather and irrespective of Tube delays.

It was true, too, that Pat liked Morris, who was the recipient of most of her rare smiles. Morris was always careful to pay Pat his full tribute of blue-eyed charm before turning his attention to

Robin. Pat was already alert to the possibility of romance between her younger colleagues.

'He's lovely-looking,' she'd told Robin just the previous week, after Morris had phoned in his location so that the temporarily unreachable Barclay could be told where to take over surveillance on their biggest case. 'You've got to give him that.'

'I haven't got to give him anything,' Robin had said, a little crossly.

It was bad enough having Ilsa badger her about Strike in her leisure time without Pat starting on Morris during her working hours.

'Quite right,' Pat had responded, unfazed. 'Make him earn it.'

'Anyway,' said Strike, finishing his cigarette and crushing the stub out in the tin Robin kept for that purpose in the glove compartment, 'you've wrapped up Tufty. Bloody good going.'

'Thanks,' Robin said. 'But there's going to be press. Bigamy's always news.'

'Yeah,' said Strike. 'Well, it's going to be worse for him than us, but it's worth trying to keep our name out of it if we can. I'll have a word with Mrs-Campion-in-Windsor. So that leaves us,' he counted the names on his thick fingers, 'with Two-Times, Twinkletoes, Postcard and Shifty.'

It had become the agency's habit to assign nicknames to their targets and clients, mainly to avoid letting real names slip in public or in emails. Two-Times was a previous client of the agency, who'd recently resurfaced after trying other private detectives and finding them unsatisfactory. Strike and Robin had previously investigated two of his girlfriends. At a superficial glance, he seemed most unlucky in love, a man whose partners, initially attracted by his fat bank balance, seemed incapable of fidelity. Over time, Strike and Robin had come to believe that he derived obscure emotional or sexual satisfaction from being cheated on, and that they were being paid to provide evidence that, far from upsetting him, gave him pleasure. Once confronted with photographic evidence of her perfidy, the girlfriend of the moment would be confronted, dismissed and another found, and the whole pattern repeated. This time round, he was dating a glamour model who thus far, to Two-Times' poorly concealed disappointment, seemed to be faithful.

Twinkletoes, whose unimaginative nickname had been chosen by Morris, was a twenty-four-year-old dancer who was currently having an affair with a thirty-nine-year-old double-divorcee, notable mainly for her history of drug abuse and her enormous trust fund. The socialite's father was employing the agency to discover anything they could about Twinkletoes' background or behaviour, which could be used to prise his daughter away from him.

Postcard was, so far, an entirely unknown quantity. A middle-aged and, in Robin's opinion, fairly unattractive television weather forecaster had come to the agency after the police had said there was nothing they could do about the postcards that had begun to arrive at his place of work and, most worryingly, hand delivered to his house in the small hours. The cards made no threats; indeed, they were often no more than banal comments on the weatherman's choice of tie, yet they gave evidence of knowing far more about the man's movements and private life than a stranger should have. The use of postcards was also a peculiar choice, when persecution was so much easier, these days, online. The agency's subcontractor, Andy Hutchins, had now spent two solid weeks' worth of nights parked outside the weatherman's house, but Postcard hadn't yet shown themselves.

Last, and most lucrative, was the interesting case of Shifty, a young investment banker whose rapid rise through his company had generated a predictable amount of resentment among overlooked colleagues, which had exploded into full-blown suspicion when he'd been promoted to the second-in-command job ahead of three undeniably better qualified candidates. Exactly what leverage Shifty had on the CEO (known to the agency as Shifty's Boss or SB) was now a matter of interest not only to Shifty's subordinates, but to a couple of suspicious board members, who'd met Strike in a dark bar in the City to lay out their concerns. Strike's current strategy was to try to find out more about Shifty through his personal assistant, and to this end Morris had been given the job of chatting her up after hours, revealing neither his real name nor his occupation, but trying to gauge how deep her loyalty to Shifty ran.

'D'you need to be back in London by any particular time?' Strike asked, after a brief silence.

'No,' said Robin, 'why?'

'Would you mind,' said Strike, 'if we stop for food? I didn't have breakfast.'

Despite remembering that he had, in fact, had a plate full of croissant crumbs in front of him when she arrived at the Palacio Lounge, Robin agreed. Strike seemed to read her mind.

'You can't count a croissant. Mostly air.'

Robin laughed.

By the time they reached Subway at Cornwall Services, the atmosphere between the two of them had become almost light-hearted, notwithstanding their tiredness. Once Robin, mindful of her resolution to eat more healthily, had started on her salad and Strike had taken a few satisfying mouthfuls of his steak and cheese sandwich, he emailed Kim Sullivan their form letter about billing clients, then said,

'I had a row with Lucy this morning.'

Robin surmised that it must have been a bad one, for Strike to mention it.

'Five o'clock, in the garden, while I was having a quiet smoke.'

'Bit early for conflict,' said Robin, picking unenthusiastically through lettuce leaves.

'Well, it turns out we're competing in the Who

Loves Joan Best Handicap Stakes. Didn't even know I'd been entered.'

He ate in silence for a minute, then went on,

'It ended with me telling her I thought Adam's a whiny prick and Luke's an arsehole.'

Robin, who'd been sipping her water, inhaled, and was seized by a paroxysm of coughs. Diners at nearby tables glanced round as Robin spluttered and gasped. Grabbing a paper napkin from the table to mop her chin and her streaming eyes, she wheezed,

'What – on *earth* – did you say that for?'

'Because Adam's a whiny prick and Luke's an arsehole.'

Still trying to cough water out of her windpipe, Robin laughed, eyes streaming, but shook her head.

'Bloody hell, Cormoran,' she said, when at last she could talk properly.

'You haven't just had a solid week of them. Luke broke my new headphones, then ran off with my leg, the little shit. Then Lucy accuses me of favouring Jack. Of course I favour him – he's the only decent one.'

'Yes, but telling their *mother*—'

'Yeah, I know,' said Strike heavily. 'I'll ring and apologise.' There was a brief pause. 'But for fuck's sake,' he growled, 'why do I have to take all three of them out together? Neither of the others give a toss about the military. "Adam cried when you came back from the War Rooms", my arse. The little bastard didn't like that I'd bought Jack stuff, that's all. If Lucy had her way, I'd be taking them on group outings every weekend, and they'd *take turns* to choose; it'll be the zoo and effing go-karting, and everything that was good about me seeing Jack'll be ruined. I *like* Jack,' said Strike, with what appeared to be surprise. 'We're interested in the same stuff. What's with this mania for treating them all the same? Useful life lesson, I'd have thought, realising you aren't owed. You don't get stuff automatically because of who you're related to.

'But fine, she wants me to buy the other two presents,' and he framed a square in mid-air with his hands. '"Try Not Being a Little Shit". I'll get that made up as a plaque for Luke's bedroom wall.'

They bought a bag of snacks, then resumed their drive. As they turned out onto the road again, Strike expressed his guilt that he couldn't share the driving, because the old Land Rover was too much of a challenge with his false leg.

'It doesn't matter,' said Robin. 'I don't mind. What's funny?' she added, seeing Strike smirking at something he had found in their bag of food.

'English strawberries,' he said.

'And that's comical, why?'

He explained about Dave Polworth's fury that goods of Cornish origin weren't labelled as such, and his commensurate glee that more and more locals were putting their Cornish identity above English on forms.

'Social identity theory's very interesting,' said Robin. 'That and self-categorisation theory. I studied them at uni. There are implications for businesses as well as society, you know . . .'

She talked happily for a couple of minutes before realising, on glancing sideways, that Strike had fallen fast asleep. Choosing not to take offence, because he looked grey with tiredness, Robin fell silent, and other than the occasional grunting snore, there was no more communication to be had from Strike until, on the outskirts of Swindon, he suddenly jerked awake again.

'Shit,' he said, wiping his mouth with the back of his hand, 'sorry. How long was I asleep?'

'About three hours,' said Robin.

'Shit,' he said again, 'sorry,' and immediately reached for a cigarette. 'I've been kipping on the world's most uncomfortable sofa and the kids have woken me up at the crack of fucking dawn every day. Want anything from the food bag?'

'Yes,' said Robin, throwing the diet to the winds. She was in urgent need of a pick-me-up. 'Chocolate. English or Cornish, I don't mind.'

'Sorry,' Strike said for a third time. 'You were telling me about a social theory or something.'

Robin grinned.

'You fell asleep around the time I was telling you my fascinating application of social identity theory to detective practice.'

'Which is?' he said, trying to make up in politeness now what he had lost earlier.

Robin, who knew perfectly well that this was why he had asked the question, said,

'In essence, we tend to sort each other and ourselves into groupings, and that usually leads to an overestimation of similarities between members of a group, and an underestimation of the similarities between insiders and outsiders.'

'So you're saying all Cornishmen aren't rugged salt-of-the-earthers and all Englishmen aren't pompous arseholes?'

Strike unwrapped a Yorkie and put it into her hand.

'Sounds unlikely, but I'll run it past Polworth next time we meet.'

Ignoring the strawberries, which had been Robin's purchase, Strike opened a can of Coke and drank it while smoking and watching the sky turn bloody as they drew nearer to London.

'Dennis Creed's still alive, you know,' said Strike, watching trees blur out of the window. 'I was reading about him online this morning.'

'Where is he?' asked Robin.

'Broadmoor,' said Strike. 'He went to Wakefield initially, then Belmarsh, and was transferred to Broadmoor in '95.'

'What was the psychiatric diagnosis?'

'Controversial. Psychiatrists disagreed about whether or not he was sane at his trial. Very high

IQ. In the end the jury decided he was capable of knowing what he was doing was wrong, hence prison, not hospital. But he must've developed symptoms since that to justify medical treatment.

'On a very small amount of reading,' Strike went on, 'I can see why the lead investigator thought Margot Bamborough might have been one of Creed's victims. Allegedly, there was a small van seen speeding dangerously in the area, around the time she should have been walking towards the Three Kings. Creed used a van,' Strike elucidated, in response to Robin's questioning look, 'in some of the other known abductions.'

The lamps along the motorway had been lit before Robin, having finished her Yorkie, quoted:

'"She lies in a holy place".'

Still smoking, Strike snorted.

'Typical medium bollocks.'

'You think?'

'Yes, I bloody think,' said Strike. 'Very convenient, the way people can only speak in crossword clues from the afterlife. Come off it.'

'All right, calm down. I was only thinking out loud.'

'You could spin almost anywhere as "a holy place" if you wanted. Clerkenwell, where she disappeared – that whole area's got some kind of religious connection. Monks or something. Know where Dennis Creed was living in 1974?'

'Go on.'

'Paradise Park, Islington,' said Strike.

'Oh,' said Robin. 'So you think the medium *did* know who Anna's mother was?'

'If I was in the medium game, I'd sure as hell Google clients' names before they showed up. But it could've been a fancy touch designed to sound comforting, like Anna said. Hints at a decent burial. However bad her end was, it's purified by where her remains are. Creed admitted to scattering bone fragments in Paradise Park, by the way. Stamped them into the flower-beds.'

Although the car was still stuffy, Robin felt a small, involuntary shudder run through her.

'Fucking ghouls,' said Strike.

'Who?'

'Mediums, psychics, all those shysters . . . preying on people.'

'You don't think some of them believe in what they're doing? Think they really are getting messages from the beyond?'

'I think there are a lot of nutters in the world, and the less we reward them for their nuttery, the better for all of us.'

The mobile rang in Strike's pocket. He pulled it out.

'Cormoran Strike.'

'Yes, hello – it's Anna Phipps. I've got Kim here, too.'

Strike turned the mobile to speakerphone.

'Hope you can hear us all right,' he said, over the rumble and rattle of the Land Rover. 'We're still in the car.'

'Yes, it is noisy,' said Anna.

'I'll pull over,' said Robin, and she did so, turning smoothly onto the hard shoulder.

'Oh, that's better,' said Anna, as Robin turned off the engine. 'Well, Kim and I have talked it over, and we've decided: we *would* like to hire you.'

Robin felt a jolt of excitement.

'Great,' said Strike. 'We're very keen to help, if we can.'

'But,' said Kim, 'we feel that, for psychological and – well, candidly, financial – reasons we'd like to set a term on the investigation, because if the police haven't solved this case in nigh on forty years – I mean, you could be looking for the next forty and find nothing.'

'That's true,' said Strike. 'So—'

'We think a year,' said Anna, sounding nervous. 'What do you – does that seem reasonable?'

'It's what I would have suggested,' said Strike. 'To be honest, I don't think we've got much chance in anything under twelve months.'

'Is there anything more you need from me to get started?' Anna asked, sounding both nervous and excited.

'I'm sure something will occur to me,' said Strike, taking out his notebook to check a name, 'but it would be good to speak to your father and Cynthia.'

The other end of the line became completely silent. Strike and Robin looked at each other.

'I don't think there's any chance of that,' said Anna. 'I'm sorry, but if my father knew I was doing this, I doubt he'd ever forgive me.'

'And what about Cynthia?'

'The thing is,' came Kim's voice, 'Anna's father's been unwell recently. Cynthia is the more reasonable of the two on this subject, but she won't want anything to upset Roy just now.'

'Well, no problem,' said Strike, raising his eyebrows at Robin. 'Our first priority's got to be getting hold of the police file. In the meantime, I'll email you one of our standard contracts. Print it out, sign it and send it back, we'll get going.'

'Thank you,' said Anna and, with a slight delay, Kim said, 'OK, then.'

They hung up.

'Well, well,' said Strike. 'Our first cold case. This is going to be interesting.'

'And we've got a year,' said Robin, pulling back out onto the motorway.

'They'll extend that if we look as though we're onto something,' said Strike.

'Good luck with that,' said Robin sardonically. 'Kim's prepared to give us a year so she can tell Anna they've tried everything. I'll bet you a fiver right now we don't get any extensions.'

'I'll take that bet,' said Strike. 'If there's a hint of a lead, Anna's going to want to see it through to the end.'

The remainder of the journey was spent discussing

the agency's four current investigations, a conversation that took them all the way to the top of Denmark Street, where Strike got out.

'Cormoran,' said Robin, as he lifted the holdall out of the back of the Land Rover, 'there's a message on your desk from Charlotte Campbell. She called the day before yesterday and asked you to ring her back. She said she's got something you want.'

There was a brief moment where Strike simply looked at Robin, his expression unreadable.

'Right. Thanks. Well, I'll see you tomorrow. No, I won't,' he instantly contradicted himself, 'you've got time off. Enjoy.'

And with a slam of the rear door he limped off towards the office, head down, carrying his holdall over his shoulder, leaving an exhausted Robin no wiser as to whether he did or didn't want whatever it was that Charlotte Campbell had.

PART II

Then came the Autumne all in yellow clad . . .

Edmund Spenser
The Faerie Queene

CHAPTER 8

Full dreadfull thinges out of that balefull booke
He red . . .

Edmund Spenser
The Faerie Queene

When Strike and Robin broke the news of her husband's bigamy, the white-faced woman they now called the Second Mrs Tufty had sat in silence for a couple of minutes. Her small but charming house in central Windsor was quiet that Tuesday morning, her son and daughter at primary school, and she'd cleaned before they arrived: there was a smell of Pledge in the air and Hoover marks on the carpet. Upon the highly polished coffee table lay ten photographs of Tufty in Torquay, minus his toupee, laughing as he walked out of the pizza restaurant with the teenage boys who so strongly resembled the young children he'd fathered in Windsor, his arm around a smiling woman who might have been their client's older sister.

Robin, who could remember exactly how she'd felt when Sarah Shadlock's diamond earring had fallen out of her own marital bed, could only guess at the scale of pain, humiliation and shame behind the taut face. Strike was speaking conventional words of sympathy, but Robin would have bet her entire bank account that Mrs Tufty hadn't heard a word – and knew she'd been right when Mrs Tufty suddenly stood up, shaking so badly that Strike also struggled to his feet, mid-sentence, in case she needed catching. However, she walked jerkily past him out of the room. Shortly afterwards, they heard the front door open and spotted their client through the net curtain, approaching a red Audi Q3 parked in front of the house with a golf club in her hand.

'Oh shit,' said Robin.

By the time they reached her, the Second Mrs Tufty had smashed the windscreen and put several deep dents in the roof of the car. Gawping neighbours had appeared at windows and a pair of Pomeranians were yapping frenziedly behind glass in the house opposite. When Strike grabbed the four iron out of her hand, Mrs Tufty swore at him, tried to wrestle it back, then burst into a storm of tears.

Robin put her arm around their client and steered her firmly back into the house, Strike bringing up the rear, holding the golf club. In the kitchen, Robin instructed Strike to make strong coffee and find brandy. On Robin's advice, Mrs

Tufty called her brother and begged him to come, quickly, but when she'd hung up and begun scrolling to find Tufty's number, Robin jerked the mobile out of her well-manicured hand.

'Give it back!' said Mrs Tufty, wild-eyed and ready to fight. 'The bastard . . . the bastard . . . I want to talk to him . . . give it back!'

'Bad idea,' said Strike, putting coffee and brandy in front of her. 'He's already proven he's adept at hiding money and assets from you. You need a shit-hot lawyer.'

They remained with the client until her brother, a suited HR executive, arrived. He was annoyed that he'd been asked to leave work early, and so slow at grasping what he was being told that Strike became almost irate and Robin felt it necessary to intervene to stop a row.

'Fuck's sake,' muttered Strike, as they drove back towards London. '*He was already married to someone else when he married your sister.* How hard is that to grasp?'

'Very hard,' said Robin, an edge to her voice. 'People don't expect to find themselves in these kinds of situations.'

'D'you think they heard me when I asked them not to tell the press we were involved?'

'No,' said Robin.

She was right. A fortnight after they'd visited Windsor, they woke to find several tabloids carrying front-page exposés of Tufty and his three women, a picture of Strike in all the inside pages and his name in one of the headlines. He was news in his own right now, and the juxtaposition of famous detective and squat, balding, wealthy man who'd managed to run two families and a mistress was irresistible.

Strike had only ever given evidence at noteworthy court cases while sporting the full beard that grew conveniently fast when he needed it, and the picture the press used most often was an old one that showed him in uniform. Nevertheless, it was an ongoing battle to remain as inconspicuous as his chosen profession demanded, and being badgered for comment at his offices was an inconvenience he could do without. The storm of publicity was prolonged when both Mrs Tuftys formed an offensive alliance against their estranged husband. Showing an unforeseen taste for publicity, they not only granted a women's magazine a joint interview, but appeared on several daytime television programmes together to discuss their long deception, their shock, their newfound friendship, their intention to make Tufty rue the day he'd met either of them and to issue a thinly veiled warning to the pregnant mistress in Glasgow (who, astonishingly, seemed disposed to stand by Tufty) that she had another think coming if she imagined he'd have two farthings to rub together once his wives had finished with him.

September proceeded, cool and unsettled. Strike called Lucy to say sorry for being rude about her sons, but she remained cold even after the apology, doubtless because he'd merely expressed regret for voicing his opinion out loud, and hadn't retracted it. Strike was relieved to discover that her boys had weekend sporting fixtures now that school had started again, which meant he didn't have to sleep on the sofa on the next visit to St Mawes, and could devote himself to Ted and Joan without the distraction of Lucy's tense, accusatory presence.

Though as desperate to cook for him as ever, his aunt was already enfeebled by the chemotherapy. It was painful to watch her dragging herself around the kitchen, but she wouldn't sit down, even when Ted implored her to do so. On Saturday night, his uncle broke down after Joan had gone to bed, and sobbed into Strike's shoulder. Ted had once seemed an unperturbable, invulnerable bastion of strength to his nephew, and Strike, who could normally sleep under almost any conditions, lay awake past two in the morning, staring into the darkness that was deeper by far than a London night, wondering whether he should stay longer, and despising himself for deciding that it was right that he should return to London.

In truth, the agency was so busy that he felt guilty about the burden it was placing on Robin and his subcontractors by taking a long weekend in Cornwall. In addition to the five open cases still on the agency's books, he and Robin were juggling increased management demands made by the expanded workforce, and negotiating a year's extension on the office lease with the developer who'd bought their building. They were also trying, though so far without luck, to persuade one of the agency's police contacts to find and hand over the forty-year-old file on Margot Bamborough's disappearance. Morris was ex-Met, as was Andy Hutchins, their most longstanding subcontractor, a quiet, saturnine man whose MS was thankfully in remission, and both had tried to call in favours from former colleagues as well, but so far, responses to the agency's requests had ranged from 'mice have probably had it' to 'fuck off, Strike, I'm busy'.

One rainy afternoon, while tailing Shifty through the City, trying not to limp too obviously and in-wardly cursing the second pavement seller of cheap umbrellas who'd got in his way, Strike's mobile rang. Expecting to be given another problem to sort out, he was caught off guard when the caller said,

'Hi, Strike. George Layborn here. Heard you're looking at the Bamborough case again?'

Strike had only met DI Layborn once before, and while it had been in the context of a case where Strike and Robin had given material assistance to the Met, he hadn't considered their association close enough to ask Layborn for help on getting the Bamborough file.

'Hi, George. Yeah, you heard right,' said Strike, watching Shifty turn into a wine bar.

'Well, I could meet you tomorrow evening, if you fancy it. Feathers, six o'clock?' said Layborn.

So Strike asked Barclay to swap jobs, and headed

to the pub near Scotland Yard the following evening, where he found Layborn already at the bar, waiting for him. A paunchy, grey-haired, middle-aged man, Layborn bought both of them pints of London Pride, and they removed themselves to a corner table.

'My old man worked the Bamborough case, under Bill Talbot,' Layborn told Strike. 'He told me all about it. What've you got so far?'

'Nothing. I've been looking back at old press reports, and I'm trying to trace people who worked at the practice she disappeared from. Not much else I can do until I see the police file, but nobody's been able to help with that so far.'

Layborn, who had demonstrated a fondness for colourfully obscene turns of phrase on their only previous encounter, seemed oddly subdued tonight.

'It was a fucking mess, the Bamborough investigation,' he said quietly. 'Anyone told you about Talbot yet?'

'Go on.'

'He went off his rocker,' said Layborn. 'Proper mental breakdown. He'd been going funny before he took on the case, but you know, it was the seventies – looking after the workforce's mental health was for poofs. He'd been a good officer in his day, mind you. A couple of junior officers noticed he was acting odd, but when they raised it, they were told to eff off.

'He'd been heading up the Bamborough case six

103

months before his wife called an ambulance in the middle of the night and got him sectioned. He got his pension, but it was too late for the case. He died a good ten years ago, but I heard he never got over fucking up the investigation. Once he recovered he was mortified about how he'd behaved.'

'How was that?'

'Putting too much stock in his own intuitions, didn't take evidence properly, had no interest in talking to witnesses if they didn't fit his theory—'

'Which was that Creed abducted her, right?'

'Exactly,' said Layborn. 'Although Creed was still called the Essex Butcher back then, because he dumped the first couple of bodies in Epping Forest and Chigwell.' Layborn took a long pull on his pint. 'They found most of Jackie Aylett in an industrial bin. He's an animal, that one. Animal.'

'Who took over the case after Talbot?'

'Bloke called Lawson, Ken Lawson,' said Layborn, 'but he'd lost six months, the trail had gone cold and he'd inherited a right balls-up. Added to which, she was unlucky in her timing, Margot Bamborough,' Layborn continued. 'You know what happened a month after she vanished?'

'What?'

'Lord Lucan disappeared,' said Layborn. 'You try and keep a missing GP on the front pages after a peer of the realm's nanny gets bludgeoned to death and he goes on the run. They'd already used the Bunny Girl pictures – did you know Bamborough was a Bunny Girl?'

'Yeah,' said Strike.

'Helped fund her medical degree,' said Layborn, 'but according to my old man, the family didn't like that being dragged up. Put their backs right up, even though those pictures definitely got the case a bit more coverage. Way of the world,' he said, 'isn't it?'

'What did your dad think happened to her?' asked Strike.

'Well, to be honest,' sighed Layborn, 'he thought Talbot was probably right: Creed had taken her. There were no signs she meant to disappear – passport was still in the house, no case packed, no clothes missing, stable job, no money worries, young child.'

'Hard to drag a fit, healthy twenty-nine-year-old woman off a busy street without someone noticing,' said Strike.

'True,' said Layborn. 'Creed usually picked them off when they were drunk. Having said that, it was a dark evening and rainy. He'd pulled that trick before. And he was good at lulling women's suspicions and getting their sympathy. A couple of them walked into his flat of their own accord.'

'There was a van like Creed's seen speeding in the area, wasn't there?'

'Yeah,' said Layborn, 'and from what Dad told me it was never checked out properly. Talbot didn't want to hear that it might have been someone trying to get home for their tea, see. Routine work just wasn't done. For instance, I heard there was an old boyfriend of Bamborough's hanging around. I'm not saying the boyfriend killed her, but Dad told me Talbot spent half the interview trying to find out where this boyfriend had been on the night Helen Wardrop got attacked.'

'Who?'

'Prostitute. Creed tried to abduct her in '73. He had his failures, you know. Peggy Hiskett, she got away from him and gave the police a description in '71, but that didn't help them much. She said he was dark and stocky, because he was wearing a wig at the time and all padded out in a woman's coat. They caught him in the end because of Melody Bower. Nightclub singer, looked like Diana Ross. Creed got chatting to her at a bus stop, offered her a lift, then tried to drag her into the van when she said no. She escaped, gave the police a proper description and told them he'd said his house was off Paradise Park. He got careless towards the end. Arrogance did for him.'

'You know a lot about this, George.'

'Yeah, well, Dad was one of the first into Creed's basement after they arrested him. He wouldn't ever talk about what he saw in there, and he'd seen gangland killings, you name it . . . Creed's never admitted to Bamborough, but that doesn't mean he didn't do it. That cunt will keep people guessing till he's dead. Evil fucking bastard. He's played with the families of his known victims for years. Likes hinting he did more women, without giving any details. Some journalist interviewed him in the early eighties, but that was the last time they let anyone talk to him. The Ministry of Justice clamped down. Creed uses publicity as a chance to torment the families. It's the only power he's got left.'

Layborn drained the last of his pint and checked his watch.

'I'll do what I can for you with the file. My old man would've wanted me to help. It never sat right with him, what happened with that case.'

The wind was picking up by the time Strike returned to his attic flat. His rain-speckled windows rattled in their loose frames as he sorted carefully through the receipts in his wallet for those he needed to submit to the accountant.

At nine o'clock, after eating dinner cooked on his single-ringed hob, he lay down on his bed and picked up the second-hand biography of Dennis Creed, *The Demon of Paradise Park,* which he'd ordered a month ago and which had so far lain unopened on his bedside table. Having undone the button on his trousers to better accommodate the large amount of spaghetti he'd just consumed, he emitted a loud and satisfying belch, lit a cigarette, laid back against his pillows and opened the book to the beginning, where a timeline laid out the bare bones of Creed's long career of rape and murder.

1937 Born in Greenwell Terrace, Mile End.

1954	April: began National Service.
	November: raped schoolgirl **Vicky Hornchurch**, 15.
	Sentenced to 2 years, Feltham Borstal.
1955–61	Worked in a variety of short-lived manual and office jobs. Frequented prostitutes.
1961	July: raped and tortured shop assistant **Sheila Gaskins**, 22.
	Sentenced to 5 years HMP Pentonville.
1968	April: abducted, raped, tortured and murdered schoolgirl **Geraldine Christie**, 16.
1969	September: abducted, raped, tortured and murdered secretary and mother of one **Jackie Aylett**, 29.
	Killer dubbed 'The Essex Butcher' by press.
1970	January: moved to Vi Hooper's basement in Liverpool Road, near Paradise Park.
	Gained job as dry-cleaning delivery man.
	February: abducted dinner lady and mother of three **Vera Kenny**, 31. Kept in basement for three weeks. Raped, tortured and murdered.
	November: abducted estate agent **Noreen Sturrock**, 28. Kept in

basement for four weeks. Raped, tortured and murdered.

1971 August: failed to abduct pharmacist **Peggy Hiskett**, 34.

1972 September: abducted unemployed **Gail Wrightman**, 30. Kept imprisoned in basement. Raped and tortured.

1973 January: murdered Wrightman. December: failed to abduct prostitute and mother of one **Helen Wardrop**, 32.

1974 September: abducted hairdresser **Susan Meyer**, 27. Kept imprisoned in basement. Raped and tortured.

1975 February: abducted PhD student **Andrea Hooton**, 23. Hooton and Meyer were held concurrently in basement for 4 weeks. March: murdered Susan. April: murdered Andrea.

1976 January 25th: attempted to abduct nightclub singer **Melody Bower**, 26. January 31st: landlady Vi Hooper recognises Creed from description and photofit. February 2nd: Creed arrested.

Strike turned over the page and skim-read the introduction, which featured the only interview ever granted by Creed's mother, Agnes Waite.

. . . She began by telling me that the date given on Creed's birth certificate was false.

'It says he was born December 20th, doesn't it?' she asked me. 'That's not right. It was the night of November 19th. He lied about it when he registered the birth, because we were outside the time you were supposed to do it.'

'"He" was Agnes's stepfather, William Awdry, a man notorious in the local area for his violent temper . . .

'He took the baby out of my arms as soon as I'd had it and said he was going to kill it. Drown it in the outside toilet. I begged him not to. I pleaded with him to let the baby live. I hadn't known till then whether I wanted it to live or die, but once you've seen them, held them . . . and he was strong, Dennis, he wanted to live, you could tell.

'It went on for weeks, the threats, Awdry threatening to kill him. But by then the neighbours had heard the baby crying and probably heard what [Awdry] was threatening, as well. He knew there was no hiding it; he'd waited too long. So he registered the birth, but lied about the date, so nobody would ask why he'd done it so late. There wasn't nobody to say it had happened earlier, not anybody who'd count. They never got me a midwife or a nurse or anything . . .'

Creed often wrote me fuller answers than we'd had time for during face-to-face interviews. Months later he sent me the following, concerning his own suspicions about his paternity:

'I saw my supposed step-grandfather looking at me out of the mirror. The resemblance grew stronger as I got older. I had his eyes, the same shaped ears, his sallow complexion, his long neck. He was a bigger man than I was, a more masculine-looking man, and I think part of his great dislike of me came from the fact that he hated to see his own features in a weak and girlish form. He despised vulnerability . . .'

'Yeah, of course Dennis was his,' Agnes told me. 'He [Awdry] started on me when I was thirteen. I was never allowed out, never had a boyfriend. When my mother realised I was expecting, Awdry told her I'd been sneaking out to meet someone. What else was he going to say? And Mum believed him. Or she pretended to.'

Agnes fled her stepfather's overcrowded house shortly before Dennis's second birthday, when she was sixteen-and-a-half.

'I wanted to take Dennis with me, but I left in the middle of the night and I couldn't afford to make noise. I had nowhere to go, no job, no money. Just a boyfriend who said he'd look after me. So I went.'

She was to see her firstborn only twice more. When she found out William Awdry was serving nine months in jail for assault, she returned to her mother's house in hopes of snatching Dennis away.

'I was going to tell Bert [her first husband] he was my nephew, because Bert didn't know anything about that whole mess. But Dennis didn't remember me, I don't think. He wouldn't let go of my mum, wouldn't talk to me, and my mum told me it was too late now and I shouldn't have left him if I wanted him so bad. So I went away without him.'

The last time Agnes saw her son in the flesh was when she made a trip to his primary school and called him over to the fence to speak to her. Though he was barely five, Creed claimed in our second interview to remember this final meeting.

'She was a thin, plain little woman, dressed like a tart,' he told me. 'She didn't look like the other boys' mothers. You could tell she wasn't a respectable person. I didn't want the other children to see me talking to her. She said she was my mother and I told her it wasn't true, but I knew it was, really. I ran away from her.'

'He didn't want nothing to do with me,' said Agnes. 'I gave up after that. I wasn't going to go to the house if Awdry was there.

Dennis was in school, at least. He looked clean . . .

'I used to wonder about him, how he was and that,' Agnes said. 'Obviously, you do. Kids come out of you. Men don't understand what that is. Yeah, I used to wonder, but I moved north with Bert when he got the job with the GPO and I never went back to London, not even when my mum died, because Awdry had put it about that if I turned up he'd kick off.'

When I told Agnes I'd met Dennis a mere week before visiting her in Romford, she had only one point of curiosity.

'They say he's very clever, is he?'

I told her that he was, undoubtedly, very clever. It was the one point on which all his psychiatrists agreed. Warders told me he read extensively, especially books of psychology.

'I don't know where he got that from. Not me . . .

'I read it all in the papers. I saw him on the news, heard everything he did. Terrible, just terrible. What would make a person do that?

'After the trial was over, I thought back to him, all naked and bloody on the lino where I'd had him, with my stepfather standing over us, threatening to drown him, and I swear to you now,' said Agnes Waite, 'I wish I'd let it happen.'

113

Strike stubbed out his cigarette and reached for the can of Tennent's sitting beside the ashtray. A light rain pattered against his windows as he flicked a little further on in the book, pausing midway through chapter two.

. . . grandmother, Ena, was unwilling or unable to protect the youngest member of the household from her husband's increasingly sadistic punishments.

Awdry took a particular satisfaction in humiliating Dennis for his persistent bedwetting. His step-grandfather would pour a bucket of water over his bed, then force the boy to sleep in it. Creed recalled several occasions on which he was forced to walk to the corner shop without trousers, but still wearing sodden pyjama bottoms, to buy Awdry cigarettes.

'One took refuge in fantasy,' Creed wrote to me later. 'Inside my head I was entirely free and happy. But there were, even then, props in the material world that I enjoyed incorporating into my secret life. Items that attained a totemic power in my fantasies.'

By the age of twelve, Dennis had discovered the pleasures of voyeurism.

'It excited me,' he wrote, after our third interview, 'to watch a woman who didn't know she was being observed. I'd do it to my sisters, but I'd creep up to lit windows as well. If I got lucky, I'd see women or girls undressing, adjusting themselves or even a glimpse of nudity. I was aroused not only by the obviously sensual aspects, but by the sense of power. I felt I stole something of their essence from them, taking that which they thought private and hidden.'

He soon progressed to stealing women's underwear from neighbours' washing lines and even from his grandmother, Ena. These he enjoying wearing in secret, and masturbating in . . .

Yawning, Strike flicked on, coming to rest on a passage in chapter four.

. . . a quiet member of the mailroom staff at Fleetwood Electric, who astonished his colleagues when, on a works night out, he donned the coat of a female co-worker to imitate singer Kay Starr.

'There was little Dennis, belting out "Wheel of Fortune" in Jenny's coat,' an anonymous workmate told the press after Creed's arrest. 'It made some of the older men uncomfortable. A couple of them thought he was, you know, queer, after. But the younger ones, we all cheered him like anything. He came out of his shell a bit after that.'

But Creed's secret fantasy life didn't centre on a life of amateur theatrics or pub singing. Unbeknownst to anyone watching the tipsy sixteen-year-old onstage, his elaborate fantasies were becoming ever more sadistic . . .

Colleagues at Fleetwood Electric were appalled when 'little Dennis' was arrested for the rape and torture of Sheila Gaskins, 22, a shop assistant whom he'd followed off a late night bus. Gaskins, who survived the attack only because Creed was scared away by a nightwatchman who heard sounds down an alleyway, was able to provide evidence against him.

Convicted, he served five years in HMP Pentonville. This was the last time Creed would give way to sudden impulse.

Strike paused to light himself a fresh cigarette, then flicked ten chapters on through the book, until a familiar name caught his eye.

. . . Dr Margot Bamborough, a Clerkenwell GP, on October 11th 1974.

DI Bill Talbot, who headed the investigation, immediately noted suspicious similarities between the disappearance of the young GP and those of Vera Kenny and Gail Wrightman.

Both Kenny and Wrightman had been abducted on rainy nights, when the presence

116

of umbrellas and rainwashed windscreens provided handy impediments to would-be witnesses. There was a heavy downpour on the evening Margot Bamborough disappeared.

A small van with what were suspected to be fake number plates had been seen in both Kenny's and Wrightman's vicinities shortly before they vanished. Three separate witnesses came forward to say that a small white van of similar appearance had been seen speeding away from the vicinity of Margot Bamborough's practice that night.

Still more suggestive was the eyewitness account of a driver who saw two women in the street, one of whom seemed to be infirm or faint, the other supporting her. Talbot at once made the connection both with the drunk Vera Kenny, who'd been seen getting into a van with what appeared to be another woman, and the testimony of Peggy Hiskett, who'd reported the man dressed as a woman at a lonely bus stop, who'd tried to persuade her to drink a bottle of beer with him, becoming aggressive before, fortunately, she managed to attract the attention of a passing car.

Convinced that Bamborough had fallen victim to the serial killer now dubbed the Essex Butcher, Talbot—

Strike's mobile rang. Trying not to lose his page, Strike groped for it and answered it without looking at the caller's identity.

'Strike.'

'Hello, Bluey,' said a woman, softly.

Strike set the book on the bed, pages down. There was a pause, in which he could hear Charlotte breathing.

'What d'you want?'

'To talk to you,' she said.

'What about?'

'I don't know,' she half-laughed. 'You choose.'

Strike knew this mood. She was halfway into a bottle of wine or had perhaps enjoyed a couple of whiskies. There was a moment of drunkenness – not even of drunkenness, of alcohol-induced softening – where a Charlotte emerged who was endearing, even amusing, but not yet combative or maudlin. He'd asked himself once, towards the end of their engagement, when his own innate honesty was forcing him to face facts and ask hard questions, how realistic or healthy it was to wish for a wife forever very slightly drunk.

'You didn't call me back,' said Charlotte. 'I left a message with your Robin. Didn't she give it to you?'

'Yeah, she gave it to me.'

'But you didn't call.'

'What d'you want, Charlotte?'

The sane part of his brain was telling him to end the call, but still he held the phone to his ear, listening, waiting. She'd been like a drug to him for a long time: a drug, or a disease.

'Interesting,' said Charlotte dreamily. 'I thought she might have decided not to pass on the message.'

He said nothing.

'Are the two of you together yet? She's quite good-looking. And always there. On tap. So conven—'

'Why are you calling?'

'I've told you, I wanted to talk to you . . . d'you know what day it is today? The twins' first birthday. The entire *famille Ross* has turned up to fawn over them. This is the first moment I've had to myself all day.'

He knew, of course, that she'd had twins. There'd been an announcement in *The Times*, because she'd married into an aristocratic family that routinely announced births, marriages and deaths in its columns, although Strike had not, in fact, read the news there. It was Ilsa who'd passed the information on, and Strike had immediately remembered the words Charlotte had said to him, over a restaurant table she had tricked him into sharing with her, more than a year previously.

All that's kept me going through this pregnancy is the thought that once I've had them, I can leave.

But the babies had been born prematurely and Charlotte had not left them.

Kids come out of you. Men don't understand what that is.

There'd been two previous tipsy phone calls to

119

Strike like this one in the past year, both made late at night. He'd ended the first one mere seconds in, because Robin was trying to reach him. Charlotte had hung up abruptly a few minutes into the second.

'Nobody thought they'd live, did you know that?' Charlotte said now. 'It's,' she whispered, '*a miracle.*'

'If it's your kids' birthday, I should let you go,' said Strike. 'Goodnight, Char—'

'Don't go,' she said, suddenly urgent. 'Don't go, please don't.'

Hang up, said the voice in his head. He didn't.

'They're asleep, fast asleep. They don't know it's their birthday, the whole thing's a joke. Commemorating the anniversary of that fucking nightmare. It was hideous, they cut me open—'

'I've got to go,' he said. 'I'm busy.'

'*Please*,' she almost wailed. 'Bluey, I'm so unhappy, you don't know, I'm so fucking miserable—'

'You're a married mother of two,' he said brutally, 'and I'm not an agony aunt. There are anonymous services you can call if you need them. Goodnight, Charlotte.'

He cut the call.

The rain was coming down harder. It drummed on his dark windows. Dennis Creed's face was now the wrong way up on the cast-aside book. His light-lashed eyes seemed reversed in the upside-down face. The effect was unsettling, as though the eyes were alive in the photograph.

Strike opened the book again and continued to read.

CHAPTER 9

Faire Sir, of friendship let me now you pray,
That as I late aduentured for your sake,
The hurts whereof me now from battell stay,
Ye will me now with like good turne repay.

Edmund Spenser
The Faerie Queene

George Layborn still hadn't managed to lay hands on the Bamborough file when Robin's birthday arrived.

For the first time in her life, she woke on the morning of October the ninth, remembered what day it was and experienced no twinge of excitement, but a lowering sensation. She was twenty-nine years old today, and twenty-nine had an odd ring to it. The number seemed to signify not a landmark, but a staging post: 'Next stop: THIRTY'. Lying alone for a few moments in her double bed in her rented bedroom, she remembered what her favourite cousin, Katie, had said during Robin's last trip home, while Robin had been helping

Katie's two-year-old son make Play-Doh monsters to ride in his Tonka truck.

'It's like you're travelling in a different direction to the rest of us.'

Then, seeing something in Robin's face that made her regret her words, Katie had hastily added,

'I don't mean it in a bad way! You seem really happy. Free, I mean! Honestly,' Katie had said, with hollow insincerity, 'I really envy you sometimes.'

Robin hadn't known a second's regret for the termination of a marriage that, in its final phase, had made her deeply unhappy. She could still conjure up the mood, mercifully not experienced since, in which all colour seemed drained from her surroundings – and they had been pretty surroundings, too: she knew that the sea captain's house in Deptford where she and Matthew had finally parted had been a most attractive place, yet it was strange how few details she could remember about it now. All she could recall with any clarity was the deadened mood she'd suffered within those walls, the perpetual feelings of guilt and dread, and the dawning horror which accompanied the realisation that she had shackled herself to somebody whom she didn't like, and with whom she had next to nothing in common.

Nevertheless, Katie's blithe description of Robin's current life as 'happy' and 'free' wasn't entirely accurate. For several years now, Robin had watched Strike prioritise his working life over everything else – in fact, Joan's diagnosis had been the first occasion she'd known him to reallocate his jobs, and make something other than detection his top concern – and these days Robin, too, felt herself becoming taken over by the job, which she found satisfying to the point that it became almost all-consuming. Finally living what she'd wanted ever since she first walked through the glass door of Strike's office, she now understood the potential for loneliness that came with a single, driving passion.

Having sole possession of her bed had been a great pleasure at first: nobody sulking with their back to her, nobody complaining that she wasn't pulling her weight financially, or droning on about his promotion prospects; nobody demanding sex that had become a chore rather than a pleasure. Nevertheless, while she missed Matthew not at all, she could envisage a time (if she was honest, was perhaps already living it) when the lack of physical contact, of affection and even of sex – which for Robin was a more complicated prospect than for many women – would become, not a boon, but a serious absence in her life.

And then what? Would she become like Strike, with a succession of lovers relegated firmly to second place, after the job? No sooner had she thought this than she found herself wondering, as she'd done almost daily since, whether her partner had called Charlotte Campbell back.

Impatient with herself, she threw back the covers and, ignoring the packages lying on top of her chest of drawers, went to take a shower.

Her new home in Finborough Road occupied the top two floors of a terraced house. The bedrooms and bathroom were on the third floor, the public rooms on the fourth. A small terraced area lay off the sitting room, where the owner's elderly rough-coated dachshund, Wolfgang, liked to lie outside on sunny days.

Robin, who was under no illusions about property available in London for single women on an average wage, especially one with legal bills to pay, considered herself immensely fortunate to be living in a clean, well-maintained and tastefully decorated flat, with a double room to herself and a flatmate she liked. Her live-in landlord was a forty-two-year-old actor called Max Priestwood, who couldn't afford to run the place without a tenant. Max, who was gay, was what Robin's mother would have called ruggedly handsome: tall and broad-shouldered, with a full head of thick, dark blond hair and a perpetually weary look about his grey eyes. He was also an old friend of Ilsa's, who'd been at university with his younger brother.

In spite of Ilsa's assurances that 'Max is absolutely lovely', Robin had spent the first few months of her tenancy wondering whether she'd made a huge mistake in moving in with him, because he seemed sunk in what seemed perpetual gloom.

Robin tried her very best to be a good flatmate: she was naturally tidy, she never played music loudly or cooked anything very smelly; she made a fuss of Wolfgang and remembered to feed him if Max was out; she was punctilious when it came to replacing washing-up liquid and toilet roll; and she made a point of being polite and cheery whenever they came into contact, yet Max rarely if ever smiled, and when she first arrived, he'd seemed to find it an immense effort to talk to her. Feeling paranoid, Robin had wondered at first whether Ilsa had strong-armed Max into accepting her as a tenant.

Conversation had become slightly easier between them over the months of her tenancy, yet Max was never loquacious. Sometimes Robin was grateful for this monosyllabic tendency, because when she came in after working a twelve-hour stretch of surveillance, stiff and tired, her mind fizzing with work concerns, the last thing she wanted was small talk. At other times, when she might have preferred to go upstairs to the open-plan living area, she kept to her room rather than feel she was intruding upon Max's private space.

She suspected the main reason for Max's perennially low mood was his state of persistent unemployment. Since the West End play in which he had had a small part had ended four months ago, he hadn't managed to get another job. She'd learned quickly not to ask him whether he had any auditions lined up. Sometimes, even saying

'How was your day?' sounded unnecessarily judgemental. She knew he'd previously shared his flat with a long-term boyfriend, who by coincidence was also called Matthew. Robin knew nothing about Max's break-up except that his Matthew had signed over his half of the flat to Max voluntarily, which to Robin seemed remarkably generous compared with the behaviour of her own ex-husband.

Having showered, Robin pulled on a dressing gown and returned to her bedroom to open the packages that had arrived in the post over the past few days, and which she'd saved for this morning. She suspected her mother had bought the aromatherapy bath oils that were ostensibly from her brother Martin, that her veterinarian sister-in-law (who was currently pregnant with Robin's first niece or nephew) had chosen the homespun sweater, which was very much Jenny's own style, and that her brother Jonathan had a new girlfriend, who'd probably chosen the dangly earrings. Feeling slightly more depressed than she had before she'd opened the presents, Robin dressed herself all in black, which could take her through a day of paperwork at the office, a catch-up meeting with the weatherman whom Postcard was persecuting, all the way to birthday drinks that evening with Ilsa and Vanessa, her policewoman friend. Ilsa had suggested inviting Strike, and Robin had said that she would prefer it to be girls only, because she was trying to avoid any further occasions on which Ilsa might try and matchmake.

On the point of leaving her room, Robin's eye fell on a copy of *The Demon of Paradise Park* which she, like Strike, had bought online. Her copy was slightly more battered than his and had taken longer to arrive. She hadn't yet read much of it, partly because she was generally too tired of an evening to do anything other than fall into bed, but partly because what she had read had already caused a slight recurrence of the psychological symptoms she had carried with her ever since her forearm had been sliced open one dark night. Today, however, she stuffed it into her bag to read on the Tube.

A text from her mother arrived while Robin was walking to the station, wishing her a happy birthday and telling her to check her email account. This she did, and saw that her parents had sent her a one-hundred-and-fifty-pound voucher for Selfridges. This was a most welcome gift, because Robin had virtually no disposable income left, once her legal bills, rent and other living expenses had been paid, to spend on anything that might be considered self-indulgent.

Feeling slightly more cheerful as she settled into a corner of the train, Robin took *The Demon of Paradise Park* from her bag and opened it to the page she had last reached.

The coincidence of the first line caused her an odd inward tremor.

Chapter 5

Little though he realised it, Dennis Creed was released from prison on his true 29th birthday, 19th November, 1966. His grandmother, Ena, had died while he was in Brixton and there was no question of him returning to live with his step-grandfather. He had no close friends to call on, and anyone who might have been well disposed to him prior to his second rape conviction was, unsurprisingly, in no rush to meet or help him. Creed spent his first night as a free man in a hostel near King's Cross.

After a week sleeping in hostels or on park benches, Creed managed to find himself a single room in a boarding house. For the next four years, Creed would move between a series of rundown rooms and short-term, cash-in-hand jobs, interspersed with periods of rough living. He admitted to me later that he frequented prostitutes a good deal at this time, but in 1968 he killed his first victim.

Schoolgirl Geraldine Christie was walking home—

Robin skipped the next page and a half. She had no particular desire to read the particulars of the harm Creed had visited upon Geraldine Christie.

. . . until finally, in 1970, Creed secured himself a permanent home in the basement rooms of the boarding house run by Violet Cooper, a fifty-year-old ex-theatre dresser who, like his grandmother, was an incipient alcoholic. This now demolished house would, in time, become infamous as Creed's 'torture chamber'. A tall, narrow building of grubby brick, it lay in Liverpool Road, close to Paradise Park.

Creed presented Cooper with forged references, which she didn't bother to follow up, and claimed he'd recently been dismissed from a bar job, but that a friend had promised him employment in a nearby restaurant. Asked by defending counsel at his trial why she'd been happy to rent a room to an unemployed man of no fixed abode, Cooper replied that she was 'tender-hearted' and that Creed seemed 'a sweet boy, bit lost and lonely'.

Her decision to rent, first a room, then the entire basement, to Dennis Creed, would cost Violet Cooper dearly. In spite of her insistence during the trial that she had no idea what was happening in the basement of her boarding house, suspicion and opprobrium have been attached to the name Violet Cooper ever since. She has now adopted a new identity, which I agreed not to disclose.

'I thought he was a pansy,' Cooper says today. 'I'd seen a bit of it in the theatre. I felt sorry for him, that's the truth.'

A plump woman whose face has been ravaged by both time and drink, she admits that she and Creed quickly struck up a close friendship. At times during our converation she seemed to forget that young 'Den' who spent many evenings with her upstairs in her private sitting room, both of them tipsy and singing along to her collection of records, was the serial killer who dwelled in her basement.

'I wrote to him, you know,' she says. 'After he was convicted. I said, "If you ever felt anything for me, if any of it was real, tell me whether you did any of them other women. You've got nothing to lose now, Den," I says, "and you could put people's minds at rest."'

But the letter Creed wrote back admitted nothing.

'Sick, he is. I realised it, then. He'd just copied out the lyrics from an old Rosemary Clooney song we used to sing together, "Come On-A My House". You know the one . . . "*Come on-a my house, my house, I'm-a gonna give you candy . . .*" I knew then he hated me as much as he hated all them other women. Taunting me, he was.'

However, back in 1970, when Creed first moved into her basement, he'd been keen to ingratiate himself with his landlady, who admits he swiftly became a combination of son and confidant. Violet persuaded her friend Beryl Gould, who owned a dry-cleaner's, to give young Den a job as a delivery man, and this gave him access to the small van that would soon become notorious in the press . . .

Twenty minutes after boarding the train, Robin got out at Leicester Square. As she emerged into daylight, her mobile phone vibrated in her pocket. She pulled it out and saw a text from Strike. Drawing aside from the crowd emerging from the station, she opened it.

News: I've found Dr Dinesh Gupta, GP who worked with Margot at the Clerkenwell Practice in 1974. He's 80-odd but sounds completely compos mentis and is happy to meet me this afternoon at his house in Amersham. Currently watching Twinkletoes having breakfast in Soho. I'll get Barclay to take over from me at lunchtime and go straight to Gupta's. Any chance you could put off your meeting with Weatherman and come along?

Robin's heart sank. She'd already had to change the time of the weatherman's catch-up meeting once and felt it unfair to do so a second time, especially at such short notice. However, she'd have liked to meet Dr Dinesh Gupta.

I can't mess him around again, she typed back. **Let me know how it goes.**

Right you are, replied Strike.

Robin watched her mobile screen for a few more seconds. Strike had forgotten her birthday last year, realising his omission a week late and buying her flowers. Given that he'd seemed to feel guilty about the oversight, she'd imagined that he might make a note of the date and perhaps set an alert on his mobile this year. However, no 'Happy birthday, by the way!' appeared, so she put her mobile back in her pocket and, unsmiling, walked on towards the office.

CHAPTER 10

And if by lookes one may the mind aread,
He seemd to be a sage and sober syre . . .

Edmund Spenser
The Faerie Queene

'You are thinking,' said the small, spectacled, elderly doctor, who was dwarfed by both his suit and his upright armchair, 'that I look like Gandhi.'

Strike, who'd been thinking exactly that, was surprised into a laugh.

The eighty-one-year-old doctor appeared to have shrunk inside his suit; the collar and cuffs of his shirt gaped and his ankles were skinny in their black silk socks. Tufts of white hair appeared both in and over his ears, and he wore horn-rimmed spectacles. The strongest features in his genial brown face were the aquiline nose and dark eyes, which alone appeared to have escaped the ageing process, and were as bright and knowing as a wren's.

No speck of dust marred the highly polished coffee table between them, in what bore the appearance of a seldom-used, special occasion room. The deep gold of wallpaper, sofa and chairs glowed, pristine, in the autumn sunshine diffused by the net curtains. Four gilt-framed photographs hung in pairs on the wall on either side of the fringed drapes. Each picture showed a different dark-haired young woman, all wearing mortarboards and gowns, and holding degree certificates.

Mrs Gupta, a tiny, slightly deaf, grey-haired woman, had already told Strike what degrees each of her daughters had taken – two medicine, one modern languages and one computing – and how well each was doing in her chosen career. She'd also shown him pictures of the six grandchildren she and her husband had been blessed with so far. Only the youngest girl remained childless, 'but she will have them,' said Mrs Gupta, with a Joan-ish certainty. 'She'll never be happy without.'

Having provided Strike and her husband with tea served in china cups, and a plate of fig rolls, Mrs Gupta retreated to the kitchen, where *Escape to the Country* was playing with the sound turned up high.

'As it happens, my father met Gandhi as a young man when Gandhi visited London in 1931,' said Dr Gupta, selecting a fig roll. 'He, too, had studied law in London, you see, but a while after Gandhi. But ours was a wealthier family. Unlike Gandhi, my father could afford to

134

bring his wife to England with him. My parents decided to remain in the UK after Daddy qualified as a barrister.

'So my immediate family missed partition. Very fortunate for us. My grandparents and two of my aunts were killed as they attempted to leave East Bengal. Massacred,' said Dr Gupta, 'and both my aunts were raped before being killed.'

'I'm sorry,' said Strike, who, not having anticipated the turn the conversation had taken, had frozen in the act of opening his notebook and now sat feeling slightly foolish, his pen poised.

'My father,' said Dr Gupta, nodding gently as he munched his fig roll, 'carried the guilt with him to his grave. He thought he should have been there to protect them all, or to have died alongside them.

'Now, *Margot* didn't like hearing the truth about partition,' said Dr Gupta. 'We all wanted independence, naturally, but the transition was handled very badly, very badly indeed. Nearly three million went missing. Rapes. Mutilation. Families torn asunder. Dreadful mistakes made. Appalling acts committed.

'Margot and I had an argument about it. A friendly argument, of course,' he added, smiling. 'But Margot romanticised uprisings of people in distant lands. She didn't judge brown rapists and torturers by the same standards she would have applied to white men who drowned children for being the wrong religion. She believed, I think, like Suhrawardy, that "bloodshed and disorder are not necessarily evil in themselves, if resorted to for a noble cause".'

Dr Gupta swallowed his biscuit and added,

'It was Suhrawardy, of course, who incited the Great Calcutta Killings. Four thousand dead in a single day.'

Strike allowed a respectful pause to fill the room, broken only by the distant sound of *Escape to the Country*. When no further mention of bloodshed and terror was forthcoming, he took the opening that had been offered to him.

'Did you like Margot?'

'Oh yes,' said Dinesh Gupta, still smiling. 'Although I found some of her beliefs and her attitudes shocking. I was born into a traditional, though Westernised, family. Before Margot and I went into practice together, I had never been in daily proximity to a self-proclaimed *liberated* lady. My friends at medical school, and the partners in my previous practice, had all been men.'

'A feminist, was she?'

'Oh, very much so,' said Gupta, smiling. 'She would tease me about what she thought were my regressive attitudes. She was a great improver of people, Margot – whether they wished to be improved or not,' said Gupta, with a little laugh. 'She volunteered at the WEA, too. The Workers' Educational Association, you know? She'd come from a poor family, and she was a great proponent of adult education, especially for women.

'She would certainly have approved of my girls,' said Dinesh Gupta, turning in his armchair to point at the four graduation photographs behind him. 'Jheel still laments that we had no son, but I have no complaints. No complaints,' he repeated, turning back to face Strike.

'I understand from the General Medical Council records,' said Strike, 'that there was a third GP at the St John's practice, a Dr Joseph Brenner. Is that right?'

'Dr Brenner, yes, quite right,' said Gupta. 'I doubt he's still alive, poor fellow. He'd be over a hundred now. He'd worked alone in the area for many years before he came in with us at the new practice. He brought with him Dorothy Oakden, who'd done his typing for twenty-odd years. She became our practice secretary. An older lady – or so she seemed to me at the time,' said Gupta, with another small chuckle. 'I don't suppose she was more than fifty. Married late and widowed not long afterwards. I have no idea what became of her.'

'Who else worked at the practice?'

'Well, let's see . . . there was Janice Beattie, the district nurse, who was the best nurse I ever worked with. An Eastender by birth. Like Margot, she understood the privations of poverty from personal experience. Clerkenwell at that time was by no means as smart as it's become since. I still receive Christmas cards from Janice.'

'I don't suppose you have her address?' asked Strike.

'It's possible,' said Dr Gupta. 'I'll ask Jheel.'

He made to get up.

'Later, after we've talked, will be fine,' said Strike, afraid to break the chain of reminiscence. 'Please, go on. Who else worked at St John's?'

'Let's see, let's see,' said Dr Gupta again, sinking slowly back into his chair. 'We had two receptionists, young women, but I'm afraid I've lost touch with both of them . . . now, what were their names . . .?'

'Would that be Gloria Conti and Irene Bull?' asked Strike, who'd found both names in old press reports. A blurry photograph of both young women had shown a slight, dark girl and what he thought was probably a peroxide blonde, both of them looking distressed to be photographed as they entered the practice. The accompanying article in the *Daily Express* quoted 'Irene Bull, receptionist, aged 25', as saying *'It's terrible. We don't know anything. We're still hoping she'll come back. Maybe she's lost her memory or something.'* Gloria was mentioned in every press report he'd read, because she'd been the last known person to see Margot alive. *'She just said "Night, Gloria, see you tomorrow." She seemed normal, well, a bit tired, it was the end of the day and we'd had an emergency patient who'd kept her longer than she expected. She was a bit late to meet her friend. She put up her umbrella in the doorway and left.'*

'Gloria and Irene,' said Dr Gupta, nodding. 'Yes, that's right. They were both young, so they should

138

still be with us, but I'm afraid I haven't the faintest idea where they are now.'

'Is that everyone?' asked Strike.

'Yes, I think so. No, wait,' said Gupta, holding up a hand. 'There was the cleaner. A West Indian lady. What was her name, now?'

He screwed up his face.

'I'm afraid I can't remember.'

The existence of a practice cleaner was new information to Strike. His own office had always been cleaned by him or by Robin, although lately, Pat had pitched in. He wrote down 'Cleaner, West Indian'.

'How old was she, can you remember?'

'I really couldn't tell you,' said Gupta. He added delicately, 'Black ladies – they are much harder to *age*, aren't they? They look younger for longer. But I think she had several children, so not *very* young. Mid-thirties?' he suggested hopefully.

'So, three doctors, a secretary, two receptionists, a practice nurse and a cleaner?' Strike summarised.

'That's right. We had,' said Dr Gupta, 'all the ingredients of a successful business – but it was an unhappy practice, I'm afraid. Unhappy from the start.'

'Really?' said Strike, interested. 'Why was that?'

'Personal chemistry,' said Gupta promptly. 'The older I've grown, the more I've realised that the team is everything. Qualifications and experience are important, but if the team doesn't *gel* . . .' He interlocked his bony fingers, '. . . forget it!

You'll never achieve what you should. And so it was at St John's.

'Which was a pity, a very great pity, because we had potential. The practice was popular with ladies, who usually prefer consulting members of their own sex. Margot and Janice were both well liked.

'But there were internal divisions from the beginning. Dr Brenner joined us for the conveniences of a newer practice building, but he never acted as though he was part of the team. In fact, over time he became openly hostile to some of us.'

'Specifically, who was he hostile to?' asked Strike, guessing the answer.

'I'm afraid,' said Dr Gupta, sadly, 'he didn't like Margot. To be quite frank, I don't think Joseph Brenner liked *ladies*. He was rude to the girls on reception, as well. Of course, they were easier to bully than Margot. I think he respected Janice – she was very efficient, you know, and less combative than Margot – and he was always polite to Dorothy, who was fiercely loyal to him. But he took against Margot from the start.'

'Why was that, do you think?'

'Oh,' said Dr Gupta, raising his hands and letting them fall in a gesture of hopelessness, 'the truth is that Margot – now, I liked her, you understand, our discussions were always good-humoured – but she was a *Marmite* sort of person. Dr Brenner was no feminist. He thought a woman's place was at home with her children, and Margot leaving a baby at home and coming back out to work full time, he disapproved of that. Team meetings were very uncomfortable. He'd wait for Margot to start talking and then talk over her, very loudly.

'He was something of a bully, Brenner. He thought our receptionists were no better than they should be. Complained about their skirt lengths, their hairstyles.

'But actually, although he was *especially* rude to ladies, it's my opinion that he didn't really like *people*.'

'Odd,' said Strike. 'For a doctor.'

'Oh,' said Gupta, with a chuckle, 'that's by no means as unusual as you might think, Mr Strike. We doctors are like everybody else. It is a popular myth that all of us must love humanity in the round. The *irony* is that our biggest liability as a practice was Brenner himself. He was an addict!'

'Really?'

'Barbiturates,' said Gupta. 'Barbiturates, yes. A doctor couldn't get away with it these days, but he over-ordered them in massive quantities. Kept them in a locked cupboard in his consulting room. He was a very difficult man. Emotionally shut down. Unmarried. And this secret addiction.'

'Did you talk to him about it?' asked Strike.

'No,' said Gupta sadly. 'I put off doing so. I wanted to be sure of my ground before I broached the subject. From quiet enquiries I made, I suspected that he was still using his old practice address in addition to ours, doubling his order

141

and using multiple pharmacies. It was going to be tricky to prove what he was up to.

'I might never have realised if Janice hadn't come to me and said she'd happened to walk in on him when his cupboard was open, and seen the quantities he'd amassed. She then admitted that she'd found him slumped at his desk in a groggy state one evening after the last patient had left. I don't think it ever affected his judgement, though. Not *really*. I'd noticed that at the end of the day he might have been a little glazed, and so on, but he was nearing retirement. I assumed he was tired.'

'Did Margot know about this addiction?' asked Strike.

'No,' said Gupta, 'I didn't tell her, although I should have done. She was my partner and the person I ought to have confided in, so we could decide what to do.

'But I was afraid she'd storm straight into Dr Brenner's consulting room and confront him. Margot wasn't a woman to back away from doing what she thought was right, and I did sometimes wish that she would exercise a little more *tact*. The fallout from a confrontation with Brenner was likely to be severe. Delicacy was required – after all, we had no absolute proof – but then Margot went missing, and Dr Brenner's barbiturate habit became the least of our worries.'

'Did you and Brenner continue working together after Margot disappeared?' asked Strike.

'For a few months, yes, but he retired not long

afterwards. I continued to work at St John's for a short while, then got a job at another practice. I was glad to go. The St John's practice was full of bad associations.'

'How would you describe Margot's relationships with the other people at work?' Strike asked.

'Well, let's see,' said Gupta, taking a second fig roll. 'Dorothy the secretary never liked her, but I think that was out of loyalty to Dr Brenner. As I say, Dorothy was a widow. She was one of those *fierce* women who attach themselves to an employer they can defend and champion. Whenever Margot or I displeased or challenged Joseph in any way, our letters and reports were sure to go straight to the bottom of the typing pile. It was a joke between us. No computers in those days, Mr Strike. Nothing like nowadays – Aisha,' he said, indicating the top right-hand picture on the wall behind him, 'she types everything herself, a computer in her consulting room, everything computerised, which is much more efficient, but we were at the mercy of the typist for all our letters and reports.

'No, Dorothy didn't like Margot. Civil, but cold. Although,' said Gupta, who had evidently just remembered something, 'Dorothy *did* come to the barbecue, which was a surprise. Margot held a barbecue at her house one Sunday, the summer before she disappeared,' he explained. 'She knew that we weren't pulling together as a team, so she invited us all around to her house. The barbecue was supposed to . . .' and, wordlessly this time, he again illustrated the point by interlacing his fingers. 'I remember being surprised that Dorothy attended, because Brenner had declined. Dorothy brought her son, who was thirteen or fourteen, I think. She must have given birth late, especially for the seventies. A boisterous boy. I remember Margot's husband telling him off for smashing a valuable bowl.'

A fleeting memory of his nephew Luke carelessly treading on Strike's new headphones in St Mawes crossed the detective's mind.

'Margot and her husband had a very nice house out in Ham. The husband was a doctor too, a haematologist. Big garden. Jheel and I took our girls, but as Brenner didn't go, and Dorothy was offended by Margot's husband telling off her son, Margot's objective wasn't achieved, I'm afraid. The divisions remained entrenched.'

'Did everyone else attend?'

'Yes, I think so. No – wait. I don't think the cleaning lady – *Wilma!*' said Dr Gupta, looking delighted. 'Her name was Wilma! I had no idea I still knew it . . . but her surname . . . I'm not even sure I knew it back then . . . No, Wilma didn't come. But everyone else, yes.

'Janice brought her own little boy – he was younger than Dorothy's and far better behaved, as I remember. My girls spent the afternoon playing badminton with the little Beattie boy.'

'Was Janice married?'

'Divorced. Her husband left her for another woman. She got on with it, raised her son alone. Women like Janice always do get on with it. Admirable. Her life wasn't easy when I knew her, but I believe she married again, later, and I was glad when I heard about it.'

'Did Janice and Margot get along?'

'Oh yes. They had the gift of being able to disagree without taking personal offence.'

'Did they disagree often?'

'No, no,' said Gupta, 'but decisions must be made in a working environment. We were – or tried to be – a democratic business . . .'

'No, Margot and Janice were able to have rational disagreements without taking offence. I think they liked and respected each other. Janice was hit hard by Margot's disappearance. She told me the day I left the practice that a week hadn't passed since it happened that she hadn't dreamed about Margot.

'But none of us were ever quite the same afterwards,' said Dr Gupta quietly. 'One does not expect a friend to vanish into thin air without leaving a single trace behind them. There is something – uncanny about it.'

'There is,' agreed Strike. 'How did Margot get along with the two receptionists?'

'Well, now, Irene, the older of the two,' sighed Gupta, 'could be a handful. I remember her being – not rude, but a little cheeky – to Margot, at times. At the practice Christmas party – Margot

145

organised that, as well, still trying to force us all to get along, you know – Irene had rather a lot to drink. I remember a slight *contretemps*, but I really couldn't tell you what it was all about. I doubt it was anything serious. They seemed as amicable as ever the next time I saw them. Irene was quite hysterical after Margot disappeared.'

There was a short pause.

'*Some* of that may have been theatrics,' Gupta admitted, 'but the underlying distress was genuine, I'm sure.

'Gloria – poor little Gloria – *she* was devastated. Margot was more than an employer to Gloria, you know. She was something of an older sister figure, a mentor. It was Margot who wanted to hire her, even though Gloria had almost no relevant experience. And I must admit,' said Gupta judiciously, 'she turned out to be a good appointment. Hard worker. Learned fast. You only had to correct her once. I believe she was from an impoverished background. I know Dorothy looked down on Gloria. She could be quite unkind.'

'And what about Wilma, the cleaner?' asked Strike, reaching the bottom of his list. 'How did she get on with Margot?'

'I'd be lying if I said I could remember,' said Gupta. 'She was a quiet woman, Wilma. I never heard that they had any kind of problem.'

After a slight pause, he added,

'I hope I'm not inventing things, but I *seem* to remember that Wilma's husband was something of a bad lot. I *think* Margot told me that Wilma ought to divorce him. I don't know whether she said that directly to Wilma's face – though she probably did, knowing Margot . . . as a matter of fact,' he continued, 'I heard, after I left the practice, that Wilma had been fired. There was an allegation of drinking at work. She always had a Thermos with her. But I may be misremembering that, so please don't set too much store by it. As I say, I'd already left.'

The door to the sitting room opened.

'More tea?' enquired Mrs Gupta, and she removed the tray and the now-cooling teapot, telling Strike, who had risen to help her, to sit back down and not to be silly. When she'd left, Strike said,

'Could I take you back to the day Margot disappeared, Dr Gupta?'

Appearing to brace himself slightly, the little doctor said,

'Of course. But I must warn you: what I mostly remember about that day now is the account of it I gave the police at the time. Do you see? My actual memories are hazy. Mostly, I remember what I told the investigating officer.'

Strike thought this an unusually self-aware comment for a witness. Experienced in taking statements, he knew how wedded people became to the first account they gave, and that valuable information, discarded during that first edit, was often lost for ever beneath the formalised version that now stood in for actual memory.

'That's all right,' he told Gupta. 'Whatever you can remember.'

'Well, it was an entirely ordinary day,' said Gupta. 'The *only* thing that was *slightly* different was that one of the girls on reception had a dental appointment and left at half past two – Irene, that was.'

'We doctors were working as usual in our respective consulting rooms. Until half past two, both girls were on reception, and after Irene left, Gloria was there alone. Dorothy was at her desk until five, which was her regular departure time. Janice was at the practice until lunchtime, but off making house calls in the afternoon, which was quite routine. I saw Margot a couple of times in the back, where we had, not exactly a kitchen, but a sort of nook where we had a kettle and a fridge. She was pleased about Wilson.'

'About who?'

'Harold Wilson,' said Gupta, smiling. 'There'd been a general election the day before. Labour got back in with a majority. He'd been leading a minority government since February, you see.'

'Ah,' said Strike. 'Right.'

'I left at half past five,' said Gupta. 'I said goodbye to Margot, whose door was open. Brenner's door was closed. I assumed he was with a patient.

'Obviously, I can't speak with authority about what happened after I left,' said Gupta, 'but I can tell you what the others told me.'

'If you wouldn't mind,' said Strike. 'I'm particularly interested in the emergency patient who kept Margot late.'

'Ah,' said Gupta, now placing his fingertips together and nodding, 'you know about the mysterious dark lady. Everything I know about *her* came from little Gloria.

'We operated on a first-come, first-served basis at St John's. Registered patients came along and waited their turn, unless it was an emergency, of course. But this lady walked in off the street. She wasn't registered with the practice, but she had severe abdominal pain. Gloria told her to wait, then went to see whether Joseph Brenner would see her, because he was free, whereas Margot was still with her last registered patient of the day.

'Brenner made heavy weather of the request. While Gloria and Brenner were talking, Margot came out of her consulting room, seeing off her last patients, a mother and child, and offered to see the emergency herself as she was going from the practice to the pub with a friend, which was just up the road. Brenner, according to Gloria, said "good of you" or something like that – which was friendly, for Brenner – and he put on his coat and hat and left.

'Gloria went back into the waiting room to tell the lady Margot would see her. The lady went into the consulting room and stayed there longer than Gloria expected. Fully twenty-five, thirty minutes, which took the time to a quarter past six, and Margot was supposed to be meeting her friend at six.

'At last the patient came out of the consulting room and left. Margot came out shortly afterwards in her coat. She told Gloria that she was late for the pub, and asked Gloria to lock up. She walked out into the rain . . . and was never seen again.'

The door of the sitting room opened and Mrs Gupta reappeared with fresh tea. Again, Strike stood to help her, and was again shooed back into his chair. When she'd left, Strike asked,

'Why did you call the last patient "mysterious"? Because she was unregistered, or—?'

'Oh, you didn't know about that business?' said Gupta. 'No, no. Because there was much discussion afterwards as to whether or not she was actually a lady.'

Smiling at Strike's look of surprise, he said,

'Brenner started it. He'd walked out past her and told the investigating officer that he'd thought, on the brief impression he had of her, that she was a man and was surprised afterwards to hear that she was female. Gloria said she was a thickset young lady, dark – gypsy-ish, was her word – not a very *politically correct* term, but that's what Gloria said. Nobody else saw her, of course, so we couldn't judge.

'An appeal was put out for her, but nobody came forward, and in the absence of any information to the contrary, the investigating officer put a great deal of pressure on Gloria to say that she

150

thought the patient was really a man in disguise, or at least, that she could have been mistaken in thinking she was a lady. But Gloria insisted that she knew a lady when she saw one.'

'This officer being Bill Talbot?' asked Strike.

'Precisely,' said Gupta, reaching for his tea.

'D'you think he wanted to believe the patient was a man dressed as a woman because—'

'Because Dennis Creed sometimes cross-dressed? Yes,' said Gupta. 'Although we called him the Essex Butcher back then. We didn't know his real name until 1976. And the only physical description of the Butcher at the time said he was dark and squat – I suppose I see why Talbot was suspicious but . . .'

'Strange for the Essex Butcher to walk into a doctor's surgery in drag and wait his turn?'

'Well . . . quite,' said Dr Gupta.

There was a brief silence while Gupta sipped tea and Strike flicked back through his notes, checking that he had asked everything he wanted to know. It was Gupta who spoke first.

'Have you met Roy? Margot's husband?'

'No,' said Strike. 'I've been hired by her daughter. How well did you know him?'

'Only very slightly,' said Gupta.

He put the teacup down on the saucer. If ever Strike had seen a man with more to say, that man was Dinesh Gupta.

'What was your impression of him?' asked Strike, surreptitiously clicking the nib back out of his pen.

'Spoiled,' said Gupta. 'Very spoiled. A handsome man, who'd been made a prince by his mother. We Indian boys know something about that, Mr Strike. I met Roy's mother at the barbecue I mentioned. She singled me out for conversation. A snob, I should say. She didn't consider receptionists or secretaries worth her time. I had the strong impression that she thought her son had married beneath him. Again, this opinion is not unknown among Indian mothers. He's a haemophiliac, isn't he?' asked Gupta.

'Not that I've heard,' said Strike, surprised.

'Yes, yes,' said Gupta 'I think so, I think he is. He was a haematologist by profession, and his mother told me that he had chosen the specialty because of his own condition. You see? The clever, fragile little boy and the proud, overprotective mother.

'But then the little prince chose for a wife somebody utterly unlike his mother. Margot wasn't the kind of woman to leave her patients, or her adult learners, to rush home and cook Roy's dinner for him. Let him get his own, would have been her attitude . . . or the little cousin could have cooked, of course,' Gupta went on, with something of the delicacy he had brought to the mention of 'black ladies'. 'The young woman they paid to look after the baby.'

'Was Cynthia at the barbecue?'

'That was her name, was it? Yes, she was. I didn't talk to her. She was carrying Margot's daughter around, while Margot mingled.'

'Roy was interviewed by the police, I believe,' said Strike, who in fact took this for granted rather than knowing it for certain.

'Oh yes,' said Gupta. 'Now, *that* was a curious thing. Inspector Talbot told me at the start of my own police interview that Roy had been completely ruled out of their enquiries – which I've always thought was an odd thing to tell me. Don't you find it so? This was barely a week after Margot's disappearance. I suppose it was only just dawning on us all that there really was no mistake, no innocent explanation. We'd all had our hopeful little theories in the first couple of days. She'd maybe felt stressed, unable to cope, and gone off alone somewhere. Or perhaps there'd been an accident, and she was lying unconscious and unidentified in a hospital. But as the days went by, and the hospitals had been checked, and her photograph had been in all the papers and still there was no news, everything started to look more sinister.

'I found it most peculiar that Inspector Talbot informed me, unasked, that Roy wasn't under suspicion, that he had a complete alibi. Talbot struck all of us as peculiar, actually. Intense. His questions jumped around a lot.

'I *think* he was trying to reassure me,' said Gupta, taking a third fig roll and examining it thoughtfully as he continued. 'He wanted me to know that my brother doctor was in the clear, that I had nothing to fear, that he knew no doctor could have done anything so terrible as to abduct a woman, or – by then, we were all starting to fear it – to kill her . . .

'But Talbot thought it was Creed, of course, from the very start – and he was probably right,' sighed Gupta, sadly.

'What makes you think so?' asked Strike. He thought Gupta might mention the speeding van or the rainy night, but the answer was, he thought, a shrewd one.

'It's very difficult to dispose of a body as completely and cleanly as Margot's seems to have been hidden. Doctors know how death smells and we understand the legalities and procedures surrounding a dead human. The ignorant might imagine it is nothing more than disposing of a table of equivalent weight, but it is a very different thing, and a very difficult one. And even in the seventies, before DNA testing, the police did pretty well with fingerprints, blood groups and so forth.

'How has she remained hidden for so long? Somebody did the job very cleverly and if we know anything about Creed, it's that he's very clever, isn't that so? It was living ladies who betrayed him in the end, not dead. He knew how to render his corpses mute.'

Gupta popped the end of the fig roll in his mouth, sighed, brushed his hands fastidiously clean of crumbs, then pointed at Strike's legs and said,

'Which one is it?'

Strike didn't resent the blunt question, from a doctor.

'This one,' he said, shifting his right leg.

'You walk very naturally,' said Gupta, 'for a big man. I might not have known, if I hadn't read about you in the press. The prosthetics were not nearly as good in the old days. Wonderful, what you can buy now. Hydraulics reproducing natural joint action! Marvellous.'

'The NHS can't afford those fancy prosthetics,' said Strike, slipping his notebook back into his pocket. 'Mine's pretty basic. If it's not too much trouble,' he continued, 'could I ask you for the practice nurse's current address?'

'Yes, yes, of course,' said Gupta. He succeeded in rising from his armchair on the third attempt.

It took the Guptas half an hour to find, in an old address book, the last address they had for Janice Beattie.

'I can't swear it's current,' said Gupta, handing the slip of paper to Strike in the hall.

'It'll give me a head start on finding her, especially if she's got a different married name now,' said Strike. 'You've been very helpful, Dr Gupta. I really appreciate you taking the time to talk to me.'

'Of course,' said Dr Gupta, considering Strike with his shrewd, bright brown eyes, 'it would be a miracle if you found her, after all this time. But I'm glad somebody's looking again. Yes, I'm very glad somebody's looking.'

CHAPTER 11

It fortuned forth faring on his way,
He saw from far, or seemed for to see
Some troublous vprore or contentious fray

Edmund Spenser
The Faerie Queene

Strike walked back towards Amersham station, past the box hedges and twin garages of the professional middle classes, thinking about Margot Bamborough. She'd emerged from the old doctor's reminiscences as a vivid and forceful personality and, irrationally, this had been a surprise. In vanishing, Margot Bamborough had assumed in Strike's mind the insubstantiality of a wraith, as though it had always been predestined that she would one day disperse into the rainy dusk, never to return.

He remembered the seven women depicted on the front cover of *The Demon of Paradise Park*. They lived on in ghostly black and white, sporting the hairstyles that had become gradually more unfashionable with every day they'd been absent from their families and their lives, but each of those negative images represented a human whose heart had once beaten, whose ambitions and opinions, triumphs and disappointments had been as real as Margot Bamborough's, before they ran into the man who was paid the compliment of full colour in the cover photograph of the dreadful story of their deaths. Strike still hadn't finished the book, but knew that Creed had been responsible for the deaths of a diverse array of victims, including a schoolgirl, an estate agent and a pharmacist. That had been part of the terror of the Essex Butcher, according to the contemporary press: he wasn't confining his attacks to prostitutes who, it was implied, were a killer's natural prey. In fact, the only working girl who was known to have been attacked by him had survived.

Helen Wardrop, the woman in question, had told her story in a television documentary about Creed, which Strike had watched on YouTube a few nights previously while eating a Chinese takeaway. The programme had been salacious and melodramatic, with many poorly acted reconstructions and music lifted from a seventies horror movie. At the time of filming, Helen Wardrop had been a slack-faced, slow-spoken woman with dyed red hair and badly applied fake eyelashes, whose glazed affect and monotone suggested either tranquillisers or neurological damage. Creed had struck the drunk and screaming Helen what might have been a fatal blow to the head with a hammer in the course of trying to force her into the back of his van. She turned her head obligingly for the interviewer, to show the viewers a still-depressed area of skull. The interviewer told her she must feel very lucky to have survived. There was a tiny hesitation before she agreed with him.

Strike had turned off the documentary at that point, frustrated by the banality of the questioning. He, too, had once been in the wrong place at the wrong time, and bore the lifelong consequences, so he perfectly understood Helen Wardrop's hesitation. In the immediate aftermath of the explosion that had taken Strike's foot and shin, not to mention the lower half of Sergeant Gary Topley's body and a chunk of Richard Anstis's face, Strike had felt a variety of emotions which included guilt, gratitude, confusion, fear, rage, resentment and loneliness, but he couldn't remember feeling lucky. 'Lucky' would have been the bomb not detonating. 'Lucky' would have meant still having both his legs. 'Lucky' was what people who couldn't bear to contemplate horrors needed to hear maimed and terrorised survivors call themselves. He recalled his aunt's tearful assertion that he wasn't in pain as he lay in his hospital bed, groggy with morphine, her words standing in stark contrast to the first Polworth had spoken to him, when he visited Strike in Selly Oak Hospital.

'Bit of a fucker, this, Diddy.'

'It is, a bit,' Strike had said, his amputated leg

158

stretched in front of him, nerve endings insisting that the calf and foot were still there.

Strike arrived at Amersham station to discover he'd just missed a train back to London. He therefore sat down on a bench outside in the feeble autumn sunshine of late afternoon, took out his cigarettes, lit one, then examined his phone. Two texts and a missed call had come in while he'd been interviewing Gupta, his mobile on mute.

The texts were from his half-brother Al and his friend Ilsa, and could therefore wait, whereas the missed call was from George Layborn, whom he immediately phoned back.

'That you, Strike?'

'Yeah. You just phoned me.'

'I did. I've got it for you. Copy of the Bamborough file.'

'You're kidding!' said Strike, exhaling on a rush of exhilaration. 'George, that's phenomenal, I owe you big time for this.'

'Buy me a pint and mention me to the press if you ever find out who did it. "Valuable assistance." "Couldn't have done it without him." We can decide the wording after. Might remind this lot I deserve promotion. Listen,' added Layborn, more seriously, 'it's a mess. The file. Real mess.'

'In what way?'

'Old. Bits missing, from what I've seen, though they might just be in the wrong order – I haven't had time to go systematically through the whole thing, there's four boxes' worth here – but Talbot's record-keeping was all over the place and Lawson coming in and trying to make sense of it hasn't really helped. Anyway, for what it's worth, it's yours. I'll be over your way tomorrow and drop it in at the office, shall I?'

'Can't tell you how much I appreciate this, George.'

'My old man would've been dead happy to know someone was going to take another look,' said Layborn. 'He'd've loved to see Creed nailed for another one.'

Layborn rang off and Strike immediately lit a cigarette and called Robin to give her the good news, but his call went straight to voicemail. Then he remembered that she was in a meeting with the persecuted weatherman, so he turned his attention to the text from Al.

Hey bruv, it began, chummily.

Al was the only sibling on his father's side with whom Strike maintained any kind of ongoing relationship, spasmodic and one-sided though it was, Al making all the running. Strike had a total of six Rokeby half-siblings, three of whom he'd never even met, a situation which he felt no need to remedy, finding the stresses of his known relatives quite sufficient to be going on with.

As you know, the Deadbeats are celebrating 50 years together next year—

Strike hadn't known this. He'd met his father, Jonny Rokeby, who was lead singer of the Deadbeats, exactly twice in his life and most of the information he had about his rock-star father had come either from his mother Leda, the woman with whom he had carelessly fathered a child in the semi-public corner of a party in New York, or from the press.

As you know, the Deadbeats are celebrating 50 years together next year and (super confidential) they're going to drop a surprise new album on 24th May. We (families) are throwing them a big London bash that night at Spencer House to celebrate the launch. Bruv, it would mean the world to all of us, especially Dad, if you came. Gaby's had the idea of getting a picture taken of all the kids together, to give him as a present on the night. First ever. Getting it framed, as a surprise. Everyone's in. We just need you. Think about it, bruv.

Strike read this text through twice, then closed it without replying and opened Ilsa's, which was far shorter.

It's Robin's birthday, you total dickhead.

CHAPTER 12

With flattering wordes he sweetly wooed her,
And offered faire guiftes, t'allure her sight,
But she both offers and the offerer
Despysde, and all the fawning of the flatterer.

Edmund Spenser
The Faerie Queene

The television weatherman brought his wife to the catch-up meeting with Robin. Once ensconced in the agency's inner office, the couple proved hard to shift. The wife had arrived with a new theory to present to Robin, triggered by the most recent anonymous postcard to arrive by post at the television studio. It was the fifth card to feature a painting, and the third to have been bought at the National Portrait Gallery shop, and this had caused the weatherman's thoughts to turn to an ex-girlfriend, who'd been to art school. He didn't know where the woman was now, but surely it was worth looking for her?

Robin thought it was highly unlikely that an

ex-girlfriend would choose anonymous postcards to reconnect with a lost love, given the existence of social media and, indeed, the publicly available contact details for the weatherman, but she agreed diplomatically that this was worth looking into, and took down as many details of this long-vanished love interest as the weatherman could remember. Robin then ran through all the measures the agency was so far taking to trace the sender of the cards, and reassured husband and wife that they were continuing to watch the house at night, in the hopes that Postcard would show themselves.

The weatherman was a small man with reddish-brown hair, dark eyes and a possibly deceptive air of apology. His wife, a thin woman several inches taller than her husband, seemed frightened by the late-night hand deliveries, and slightly annoyed by her husband's half-laughing assertions that you didn't expect this sort of thing when you were a weatherman, because, after all, he was hardly the *film star* type, and who knew what this woman was capable of?

'Or man,' his wife reminded him. 'We don't *know* it's a woman, do we?'

'No, that's true,' said her husband, the smile fading slowly from his face.

When at last the couple had left, walking out past Pat, who was stoically typing away at her desk, Robin returned to the inner office and re-examined the most recent postcard. The painting on the front featured the portrait of a nineteenth-century man in a high cravat. *James Duffield Harding*. Robin had never heard of him. She flipped the card over. The printed message read:

HE ALWAYS REMINDS ME OF YOU.

She turned the card over again. The mousy man in side-whiskers *did* resemble the weatherman.

A yawn caught her by surprise. She'd spent most of the day clearing paperwork, authorising payment of bills and tweaking the rota for the coming fortnight to accommodate Morris's request for Saturday afternoon off, so that he could go and watch his three-year-old daughter perform in a ballet show. Checking her watch, Robin saw that it was already five o'clock. Fighting the low mood that had been held at bay by hard work, she tidied away the Postcard file, and switched her mobile ringer back on. Within seconds, it had rung: Strike.

'Hello,' said Robin, trying not to sound peeved, because as the hours had rolled by it had become clear to her that Strike had indeed forgotten her birthday yet again.

'Happy birthday,' he said, over the sound of what Robin could tell was a train.

'Thanks.'

'I've got something for you, but I won't be back for an hour, I've only just got on the train back from Amersham.'

Have you hell got something, thought Robin. *You forgot. You're just going to grab flowers on the way back to the office.*

Robin was sure Ilsa must have tipped Strike off, because Ilsa had called her just before the client had arrived, to tell Robin that she might be unavoidably late for drinks. She'd also asked, with unconvincing casualness, what Strike had bought her, and Robin had answered truthfully, 'Nothing'.

'That's nice, thanks,' Robin said now, 'but I'm just leaving. Going out for a drink tonight.'

'Oh,' said Strike. 'Right. Sorry – couldn't be helped, you know, with coming out here to meet Gupta.'

'No,' said Robin, 'well, you can leave them here in the office—'

'Yeah,' said Strike, and Robin noted that he didn't dispute the word 'them'. It was definitely going to be flowers.

'Anyway,' said Strike, 'big news. George Layborn's got hold of a copy of the Bamborough file.'

'Oh, that's great!' said Robin, enthusiastic in spite of herself.

'Yeah, isn't it? He's going to bring it over tomorrow morning.'

'How was Gupta?' asked Robin, sitting down on her side of the partners' desk which had replaced Strike's old single one.

'Interesting, especially about Margot herself,' said Strike, who became muffled as, Robin guessed, the train went through a tunnel. Robin pressed the mobile closer to her ear and said,

'In what way?'

'Dunno,' said Strike distantly. 'From the old photo, I wouldn't have guessed an ardent feminist. She sounds much more of a personality than I'd imagined, which is stupid, really – why shouldn't she have a personality, and a strong one?'

But Robin knew, somehow, what he meant. The hazy picture of Margot Bamborough, frozen in blurry time with her seventies middle parting, her wide, rounded lapels, her knitted tank top, seemed to belong to a long-gone, two-dimensional world of faded colour.

'Tell you the rest tomorrow,' said Strike, because their connection was breaking up. 'Reception's not great here. I can hardly hear you.'

'OK, fine,' said Robin loudly. 'Speak tomorrow.'

She opened the door into the outer office again. Pat was just turning off Robin's old PC, electronic cigarette sticking out of her mouth.

'Was that Strike?' she asked, crow-like, with her jet-black hair and her croak, the fake cigarette waggling.

'Yep,' said Robin, reaching for her coat and bag. 'He's on his way back from Amersham. Lock up as usual though, Pat, he can let himself in if he needs to.'

'Has he remembered your birthday yet?' asked Pat, who seemed to have taken sadistic satisfaction in news of Strike's forgetfulness that morning.

'Yes,' said Robin, and out of loyalty to Strike she added, 'he's got a present for me. I'll get it tomorrow.'

Pat had bought Robin a new purse. 'That old one was coming apart at the seams,' she said, when Robin unwrapped it. Robin, touched in spite of the fact that she might not have chosen bright red, had expressed warm thanks and at once transferred her money and cards across into the new one.

'Good thing about having one in a nice bright colour, you can always find it in your bag,' Pat had said complacently. 'What's that Scottish nutter got you?'

Barclay had left a small wrapped package with Pat to give to Robin that morning.

'Cards,' said Robin, smiling as she unwrapped the package. 'Sam was telling me all about these, look, when we were out on surveillance the other night. Cards showing Al-Qaeda's most wanted. They gave packs out to the American troops during the Iraq War.'

'What's he given you those for?' said Pat. 'What are you supposed to do with them?'

'Well, because I was interested, when he told me,' said Robin, amused by Pat's disdain. 'I can play poker with them. They've got all the right numbers and everything, look.'

'Bridge,' Pat had said. 'That's a proper game. I like a nice game of bridge.'

As both women pulled on their coats, Pat asked,

167

'Going anywhere nice tonight?'

'For a drink with a couple of friends,' said Robin. 'But I've got a Selfridges voucher burning a hole in my pocket. Think I might treat myself first.'

'Lovely,' croaked Pat. 'What d'you fancy?'

Before Robin could answer, the glass door behind her opened and Saul Morris entered, handsome, smiling and a little breathless, his black hair sleek, his blue eyes bright. With some misgiving, she saw the wrapped present and card clutched in his hand.

'Happy birthday!' he said. 'Hoped I'd catch you.'

And before Robin could prevent it, he'd bent down and kissed her on the cheek; no air kiss, this, but proper contact of lips and skin. She took half a step backwards.

'Got you a little something,' he said, apparently sensing nothing amiss, but holding out to her the gift and card. 'It's nothing really. And how's Moneypenny?' he said, turning to Pat, who had already removed her electronic cigarette to smile at him, displaying teeth the colour of old ivory.

'*Moneypenny*,' repeated Pat, beaming. 'Get on with you.'

Robin tore the paper from her gift. Inside was a box of Fortnum & Mason salted caramel truffles.

'Oh, *very* nice,' said Pat approvingly.

Chocolates, it seemed, were a far more appropriate gift for a young woman than a pack of cards with Al-Qaeda members on them.

'Remembered you like a bit of salted caramel,' said Morris, looking proud of himself.

Robin knew exactly where he'd got this idea, and it didn't make her any more appreciative.

A month previously, at the first meeting of the entire expanded agency, Robin had opened a tin of fancy biscuits that had arrived in a hamper sent by a grateful client. Strike had enquired why everything these days was salted caramel flavour, and Robin had replied that it didn't seem to be stopping him eating them by the handful. She'd expressed no personal fondness for the flavour, but Morris had evidently paid both too little and too much attention, treasuring up his lazy assumption for use at some later date.

'Thanks very much,' she said, with a bare minimum of warmth. 'I'm afraid I've got to dash.'

And before Pat could point out that Selfridges would still be there in a half an hour, Robin had slid past Morris and started down the metal stairs, his card still unopened in her hand.

Exactly why Morris grated on her so much, Robin was still pondering as she moved slowly around Selfridges' great perfume hall half an hour later. She'd decided to buy herself some new perfume, because she'd been wearing the same scent for five years. Matthew had liked it, and never wanted her to change, but her last bottle was down to the dregs, and she had a sudden urge to douse herself in something that Matthew wouldn't recognise, and possibly wouldn't even like. The cheap little bottle of 4711 cologne she'd bought on the way to Falmouth was nowhere near distinctive enough for a new signature scent, and so she wandered through a vast maze of smoked mirrors and gilded lights, between islands of seductive bottles and illuminated pictures of celebrities, each little domain presided over by black-clad sirens offering squirts and testing strips.

Was it pompous of her, she wondered, to think that Morris the subcontractor ought not to assume the right to kiss an agency partner? Would she mind if the generally reserved Hutchins kissed her on the cheek? No, she decided, she wouldn't mind at all, because she'd now known Andy over a year, and in any case, Hutchins would do the polite thing and make the greeting a matter of brief proximity of two faces, not a pressing of lips into her face.

And what about Barclay? He'd never kissed her, though he had recently called her 'ya numpty' when, on surveillance, she had accidentally spilled hot coffee all over him in her excitement at seeing their target, a civil servant, leaving a known brothel at two o'clock in the morning. But she hadn't minded Barclay calling her a numpty in the slightest. She'd *been* a numpty.

Turning a corner, Robin found herself facing the Yves Saint Laurent counter, and with a sudden sharpening of interest, her eyes focused on a blue, black and silver cylinder bearing the name Rive Gauche. Robin had never knowingly smelled Margot Bamborough's favourite perfume before.

'It's a classic,' said the bored-looking salesgirl,

watching Robin spraying Rive Gauche onto a fresh testing strip and inhaling.

Robin tended to rate perfumes according to how well they reproduced a familiar flower or foodstuff, but this wasn't a smell from nature. There was a ghostly rose there, but also something strangely metallic. Robin, who was used to fragrances made friendly with fruit and candy, set down the strip with a smile and a shake of her head and walked on.

So that was how Margot Bamborough had smelled, she thought. It was a far more sophisticated scent than the one Matthew had loved on Robin, which was a natural-smelling concoction of figs, fresh, milky and green.

Robin turned a corner and saw, standing on a counter directly ahead of her, a faceted glass bottle full of pink liquid: Flowerbomb, Sarah Shadlock's signature scent. Robin had seen it in Sarah and Tom's bathroom whenever she and Matthew had gone over for dinner. Since leaving Matthew, Robin had had ample time to realise that the occasions on which he had changed the sheets mid-week, because he'd 'spilled tea' or 'thought I'd do it today, save you doing it tomorrow' must have been as much to wash away that loud, sweet scent, as any other, more obviously incriminating traces that might have leaked from careful condoms.

'It's a modern classic,' said the hopeful salesgirl, who'd noticed Robin looking at the glass hand grenade. With a perfunctory smile, Robin shook her head and turned away. Now her reflection in the smoked glass looked simply sad, as she picked up bottles and smelled strips in a joyless hunt for something to improve this lousy birthday. She suddenly wished that she were heading home, and not out for drinks.

'What are you looking for?' said a sharp-cheekboned black girl, whom Robin passed shortly afterwards.

Five minutes later, after a brief, professional interchange, Robin was heading back towards Oxford Street with a rectangular black bottle in her bag. The salesgirl had been highly persuasive.

'. . . and if you want something *totally* different,' she'd said, picking up a fifth bottle, spraying a little onto a strip and wafting it around, 'try Fracas.'

She'd handed the strip to Robin, whose nostrils were now burning from the rich and varied assault of the past half hour.

'Sexy but grown-up, you know? It's a real classic.'

And in that moment, Robin, breathing in heady, luscious, oily tuberose, had been seduced by the idea of becoming, in her thirtieth year, a sophisticated woman utterly different from the kind of fool who was too stupid to realise that what her husband told her he loved, and what he liked taking into his bed, bore about as much resemblance as a fig to a hand grenade.

CHAPTER 13

Thence forward by that painfull way they pas,
Forth to an hill, that was both steepe and hy;
On top whereof a sacred chappell was,
And eke a little hermitage thereby.

Edmund Spenser
The Faerie Queene

In retrospect, Strike regretted the first gift he'd
ever given Robin Ellacott. He'd bought the
expensive green dress in a fit of quixotic extrava-
gance, feeling safe in giving her something so
personal only because she was engaged to another
man and he was never going to see her again, or
so he'd thought. She'd modelled it for Strike in
the course of persuading a saleswoman into indis-
cretions, and that girl's evidence, which Robin had
so skilfully extracted, had helped solve the case
that had made Strike's name and saved his agency
from bankruptcy. Buoyed by a tide of euphoria
and gratitude, he'd returned to the shop and made
the purchase as a grand farewell gesture. Nothing

else had seemed to encapsulate what he wanted to tell her, which was 'look what we achieved together', 'I couldn't have done it without you' and (if he was being totally honest with himself) 'you look gorgeous in this, and I'd like you to know I thought so when I saw you in it'.

But things hadn't panned out quite as Strike had expected, because within an hour of giving her the green dress he'd hired her as a full-time assistant. Doubtless the dress accounted for at least some of the profound mistrust Matthew, her fiancé, had henceforth felt towards the detective. Worse still, from Strike's point of view, it had set the bar uncomfortably high for future gifts. Whether consciously or not, he'd lowered expectations considerably since, either by forgetting to buy Robin birthday and Christmas gifts, or by making them as generic as was possible.

He purchased stargazer lilies at the first florist he could find when he got off the train from Amersham, and bore them into the office for Robin to find next day. He'd chosen them for their size and powerful fragrance. He felt he ought to spend more money than he had on the previous year's belated bunch, and these looked impressive, as though he hadn't skimped. Roses carried an unwelcome connotation of Valentine's Day, and nearly everything else in the florist's stock – admittedly depleted at half past five in the afternoon – looked a little bedraggled or underwhelming. The lilies were large and yet reassuringly impersonal, sculptural in quality and heavy with fragrance, and there was safety in their very boldness. They came from a clinical hothouse; there was no romantic whisper of quiet woods or secret garden about them: they were flowers of which he could say robustly 'nice smell', with no further justification for his choice.

Strike wasn't to know that Robin's primary association with stargazer lilies, now and for evermore, would be with Sarah Shadlock, who'd once brought an almost identical bouquet to Robin and Matthew's housewarming party. When she walked into the office the day after her birthday and saw the flowers standing there on the partners' desk, stuck in a vase full of water but still in their cellophane, with a large magenta bow on them and a small card that read 'Happy birthday from Cormoran' (no kiss, he never put kisses), she was affected exactly the same way she'd been by the hand-grenade-shaped bottle in Selfridges. She didn't want these flowers; they were a double irritant in reminding her of Strike's forgetfulness and Matthew's infidelity, and if she had to look at or smell them, she resolved, it wouldn't be in her own home.

So she'd left the lilies at the office, where they stubbornly refused to die, Pat conscientiously refilling their water every morning and taking such good care of them that they lived for nearly two weeks. Even Strike was sick of them by the end: he kept getting wafts of something that reminded him of his ex-girlfriend Lorelei's perfume, an unpleasant association.

By the time the waxy pink and white petals began to shrivel and fall, the thirty-ninth anniversary of Margot Bamborough's disappearance had passed unmarked and probably unnoticed by anyone except, perhaps, her family, Strike and Robin, who both registered the fateful date. Copies of the police records had been brought to the office as promised by George Layborn, and now lay in four cardboard boxes under the partners' desk, which was the only place the agency had room for them. Strike, who was currently the least encumbered by the agency's other cases, because he was holding himself in readiness to go back down to Cornwall should the need arise, set himself to work systematically through these files. Once he'd digested their contents, he intended to visit Clerkenwell with Robin, and retrace the route between the old St John's practice where Margot had last been seen alive, and the pub where her friend had waited for her in vain.

So, on the last day of October, Robin left the office at one o'clock and hurried, beneath a threatening sky and with her umbrella ready in her hand, onto the Tube. She was quietly excited by the prospect of this afternoon, the first she and Strike would spend working the Bamborough case together.

It was already drizzling slightly when Robin caught sight of Strike, standing smoking as he surveyed the frontage of a building halfway down St John's Lane. He turned at the sound of her heels on the wet pavement.

'Am I late?' she called, as she approached.

'No,' said Strike, 'I was early.'

She joined him, still holding her umbrella, and looked up at the tall, multi-storey building of brown brick, with large, metal-framed windows. It appeared to house offices, but there was no indication of what kind of businesses were operating inside.

'It was right here,' said Strike, pointing at the door numbered 29. 'The old St John's Medical Practice. They've remodelled the front of the building, obviously. There used to be a back entrance,' he said. 'We'll go round and have a shufti in a minute.'

Robin turned to look up and down St John's Lane, which was a long, narrow one-way street, bordered on either side by tall, multi-windowed buildings.

'Very overlooked,' commented Robin.

'Yep,' said Strike. 'So, let's begin with what Margot was wearing when she disappeared.'

'I already know,' said Robin. 'Brown corduroy skirt, red shirt, knitted tank top, beige Burberry raincoat, silver necklace and earrings, gold wedding ring. Carrying a leather shoulder bag and a black umbrella.'

'You should take up detection,' said Strike, mildly impressed. 'Ready for the police records?'

'Go on.'

'At a quarter to six on the eleventh of October 1974 only three people are known to have been inside this building: Margot, who was dressed exactly as you describe, but hadn't yet put on her raincoat; Gloria Conti, who was the younger of the two receptionists; and an emergency patient with abdominal pain, who'd walked in off the street. The patient, according to the hasty note Gloria took, was called "Theo question mark". In spite of the male name, and Dr Joseph Brenner's assertion that he thought the patient looked like a man, and Talbot trying hard to persuade her that Theo was a man dressed as a woman, Gloria never wavered in her assertion that "Theo" was a woman.

'All the other employees had left before a quarter to six, except Wilma the cleaner, who hadn't been there at all that day, because she didn't work Fridays. More of Wilma later.

'Janice, the nurse, was here until midday, then making house visits the rest of the afternoon and didn't return. Irene, the receptionist, left at half past two for a dental appointment and didn't come back. According to their statements, each of which were corroborated by some other witness, the secretary, Dorothy, left at ten past five, Dr Gupta at half past and Dr Brenner at a quarter to six. Police were happy with the alibis all three gave for the rest of the evening: Dorothy went home to her son and spent the evening watching

TV with him. Dr Gupta attended a large family dinner to celebrate his mother's birthday and Dr Brenner was with the spinster sister he shared his house with. Both Brenners were seen through the sitting-room window later that evening, by a dog walker.

'The last registered patients, a mother and child, were Margot's, and they left the practice shortly before Brenner did. The patients testified that Margot was fine when they saw her.

'From that point on, Gloria is the only witness. According to Gloria, Theo went into Margot's consulting room and stayed there longer than expected. At a quarter past six, Theo left, never to be seen at the practice again. A police appeal was subsequently put out for her, but nobody came forward.

'Margot left no notes about Theo. The assumption is that she intended to write up the consultation the following day, because her friend had now been waiting for her in the pub for a quarter of an hour and she didn't want to make herself even later.

'Shortly after Theo left, Margot came hurrying out of her consulting room, put on her raincoat, told Gloria to lock up with the emergency key, walked out into the rain, put up her umbrella, turned right and disappeared from Gloria's sight.'

Strike turned and pointed up the road towards a yellow stone arch of ancient appearance, which lay directly ahead of them.

'Which means she was heading in that direction, towards the Three Kings.'

For a moment, both of them looked towards the old arch that spanned the road, as though some shadow of Margot might materialise. Then Strike ground out his cigarette underfoot and said,

'Follow me.'

He walked the length of number 28, then paused to point up a dark passageway the width of a door, called Passing Alley.

'Good hiding place,' said Robin, pausing to look up and down the dark, vaulted corridor through the buildings.

'Certainly is,' said Strike. 'If somebody wanted to lie in wait for her, this is tailor made. Catch her by surprise, drag her up here – but after that, it'd get problematic.'

They walked along the short passage and emerged into a sunken garden area of concrete and shrubs that lay between two parallel streets.

'The police searched this whole garden area with sniffer dogs. Nothing. And if an assailant dragged her onwards, through there,' Strike pointed to the road that ran parallel to St John's Lane, 'onto St John Street, it would've been well-nigh impossible to go undetected. The street's far busier than St John's Lane. And that's assuming a fit, tall twenty-nine-year-old wouldn't have shouted and fought back.'

He turned to look at the back entrance.

'The district nurse sometimes went in the back,

rather than going through the waiting room. She had a little room to the rear of the building where she kept her own stuff and sometimes saw patients. Wilma the cleaner sometimes went out the back door as well. Otherwise it was usually locked.'

'Are we interested in people being able to enter or leave the building through a second door?' asked Robin.

'Not especially, but I want to get a feel for the layout. It's been nearly forty years: we've got to go back over everything.'

They walked back through Passing Alley to the front of the building.

'We've got one advantage over Bill Talbot,' said Strike. 'We know the Essex Butcher turned out to be slim and blond, not a swarthy thickset person of gypsy-ish appearance. Theo, whoever she was, wasn't Creed. Which doesn't necessarily make her irrelevant, of course.

'One last thing, then we're done with the practice itself,' said Strike, looking up at number 29. 'Irene, the blonde receptionist, told the police that Margot received two threatening, anonymous notes shortly before she disappeared. They're not in the police file, so we've only got Irene's statement to go on. She claims she opened one, and that she saw another on Margot's desk when bringing her tea. She says the one she read mentioned hellfire.'

'You'd think it was the secretary's job to open mail,' commented Robin. 'Not a receptionist's.'

'Good point,' said Strike, pulling out his note-book and scribbling, 'we'll check that . . . It seems relevant to add here that Talbot thought Irene was an unreliable witness: inaccurate and prone to exaggeration. Incidentally, Gupta said Irene and Margot had what he called a "contretemps" at a Christmas party. He didn't think it was a particularly big deal, but he'd remembered it.'

'And is Talbot—?'

'Dead? Yes,' said Strike. 'So's Lawson, who took over from him. Talbot's got a son, though, and I'm thinking of getting in touch with him. Lawson never had kids.'

'Go on, about the anonymous notes.'

'Well, Gloria, the other receptionist, said Irene showed her one of the notes, but couldn't remember what was in it. Janice, the nurse, confirmed that Irene had told her about them at the time, but said she hadn't personally seen them. Margot didn't tell Gupta about them – I called him to check.

'Anyway,' said Strike, giving the street one last sweeping look through the drizzle, 'assuming nobody abducted Margot right outside the prac-tice, or that she didn't get in a car yards from the door, she headed towards the Three Kings, which takes us this way.'

'D'you want to come under this umbrella?' Robin asked.

'No,' said Strike. His densely curling hair looked the same wet or dry: he had very little vanity.

They continued up the street and passed through St John's Gate, the ancient stone arch decorated with many small heraldic shields, emerging onto Clerkenwell Road, a bustling two-way street, which they crossed, arriving beside an old-fashioned scarlet phone box which stood at the mouth of Albemarle Way.

'Is that the phone box where the two women were seen struggling?' asked Robin.

Strike did a double take.

'You've read the case notes,' he said, almost accusingly.

'I had a quick look,' Robin admitted, 'while I was printing out Two-Times' bill last night. I didn't read everything; didn't have time. Just looked at a few bits and pieces.'

'Well, that *isn't* the phone box,' said Strike. 'The important phone box – or boxes – come later. We'll get to them in due course. Now follow me.'

Instead of proceeding into a paved pedestrian area that Robin, from her own scant research, knew Margot must have crossed if she had been heading for the Three Kings, Strike turned left, up Clerkenwell Road.

'Why are we going this way?' asked Robin, jogging to keep up.

'Because,' said Strike, stopping again and pointing up at a top window on the building opposite, which looked like an old brick ware-house, 'some time after six o'clock on the evening in question, a fourteen-year-old schoolgirl called

Amanda White swore she saw Margot at the top window, second from the right, banging her fists against the glass.'

'I haven't seen *that* mentioned online!' said Robin.

'For the good reason that the police concluded there was nothing in it.

'Talbot, as is clear from his notes, disregarded White because her story couldn't be fitted into his theory that Creed had abducted Margot. But Lawson went back to Amanda when he took over, and actually walked with her along this stretch of road.

'Amanda's account had a few things going for it. For one thing, she told the police unprompted that this had happened the evening after the general election, which she remembered because she had an argument with a Tory schoolfriend. The pair of them had been kept back after school for a detention. They'd then gone for a coffee together, over which the schoolfriend went into a huff when Mandy said it was good that Wilson had won, and refused to walk home with her.

'Amanda said she was still angry about her friend getting stroppy when she looked up and saw a woman pounding on the glass with her fists. The description she gave was a good one, although by this time, a full description of Margot's appearance and clothing had been in the press.

'Lawson contacted the business owner who worked on the top floor. It was a paper design company run by a husband and wife. They produced small runs of pamphlets, posters and invitations, that kind of stuff. No connection to Margot. Neither of them were registered with the St John's practice, because they lived out of the area. The wife said she sometimes had to thump the window frame to make it close. However, the wife in no way resembled Margot, being short, tubby and ginger-haired.'

'And someone would've noticed Margot on her way up to the third floor, surely?' said Robin, looking from the top window to the front door. She moved back from the kerb: cars were splashing through the puddles in the gutter. 'She'd have climbed the stairs or used the lift, and maybe rung the doorbell to get in.'

'You'd think so,' agreed Strike. 'Lawson concluded that Amanda had made an innocent mistake and thought the printer's wife was Margot.'

They returned to the point where they had deviated from what Robin thought of as 'Margot's route'. Strike paused again, pointing up the gloomy side road called Albemarle Way.

'Now, disregard the phone box, but note that Albemarle Way is the first side street since Passing Alley I think she could plausibly have entered – voluntarily or not – without necessarily being seen by fifty-odd people. Quieter, as you can see – but not *that* quiet,' admitted Strike, looking towards the end of Albemarle Way, where traffic was passing at a steady rate. Albemarle Way was narrower than

St John's Lane, but similar in being bordered by tall buildings in unbroken lines, which kept it permanently in shadow. 'Still a risk for an abductor,' said Strike, 'but if Dennis Creed was lurking somewhere in his van, waiting for a lone woman – any woman – to walk past in the rain, this is the place I can see it happening.'

It was at this moment, as a cold breeze whistled up Albemarle Way, that Strike caught a whiff of what he had thought were the dying stargazer lilies, but now realised was coming from Robin herself. The perfume wasn't exactly the same as the one that Lorelei had worn; his ex's had been strangely boozy, with overtones of rum (and he'd liked it when the scent had been an accompaniment to easy affection and imaginative sex; only later had he come to associate it with passive-aggression, character assassination and pleas for a love he could not feel). Nevertheless, this scent strongly resembled Lorelei's; he found it cloying and sickly.

Of course, many would say it was rich for him to have opinions about how women smelled, given that his signature odour was that of an old ashtray, overlain with a splash of Pour Un Homme on special occasions. Nevertheless, having spent much of his childhood in conditions of squalor, Strike found cleanliness a necessary trait in anyone he could find attractive. He'd liked Robin's previous scent, which he'd missed when she wasn't in the office.

'This way,' he said, and they proceeded through the rain into an irregular pedestrianised square. A few seconds later, Strike suddenly became aware that he'd left Robin behind, and walked back several paces to join her in front of St John Priory Church, a pleasingly symmetrical building of red brick, with long windows and two white stone pillars flanking the entrance.

'Thinking about her lying in a holy place?' he asked, lighting up again while the rain beat down on him. Exhaling, he held the cigarette cupped in his hand, to prevent its extinguishment.

'No,' said Robin, a little defensively, but then, 'yes, all right, maybe a bit. Look at this . . .'

Strike followed her through the open gates into a small garden of remembrance, open to the public and full (as Robin read off a small sign on the inner wall) of medicinal herbs, including many used in medieval times, in the Order of St John's hospitals. A white figure of Christ hung on the back wall, surrounded with the emblems of the four evangelists: the bull, the lion, the eagle and the angel. Fronds and leaves undulated gently beneath the rain. As Robin's eyes swept the small, walled garden, Strike, who'd followed her, said,

'I think we can agree that if somebody buried her in here, a cleric would have noticed disturbed earth.'

'I know,' said Robin. 'I'm just looking.'

As they returned to the street, she added,

'There are Maltese crosses everywhere, look. They were on that archway we just passed through, too.'

'It's the cross of the Knights Hospitaller. Knights of St John. Hence the street names and the emblem of St John ambulance; they've got their headquarters back in St John's Lane. If that medium Googled the area Margot went missing, she can't have missed Clerkenwell's associations with the Order of St John. I'll bet you that's where she got the idea for that little bit of "holy place" padding. But bear it in mind, because the cross is going to come up again once we reach the pub.'

'You know,' said Robin, turning to look back at the Priory, 'Peter Tobin, that Scottish serial killer – he attached himself to churches. He joined a religious sect at one point, under an assumed name. Then he got a job as a handyman at a church in Glasgow, where he buried that poor girl beneath the floorboards.'

'Churches are good cover for killers,' said Strike. 'Sex offenders, too.'

'Priests and doctors,' said Robin thoughtfully. 'It's hardwired in most of us to trust them, don't you think?'

'After the Catholic Church's many scandals? After Harold Shipman?'

'Yes, I think so,' said Robin. 'Don't you think we tend to invest some categories of people with unearned goodness? I suppose we've all got a need to trust people who seem to have power over life and death.'

'Think you're onto something there,' said Strike, as they entered a short pedestrian lane called Jerusalem Passage. 'I told Gupta it was odd that Joseph Brenner didn't like people. I thought that might be a basic job requirement for a doctor. He soon put me right.

'Let's stop here a moment,' Strike said, doing so. 'If Margot got this far – I'm assuming she'd've taken this route, because it's the shortest and most logical way to the Three Kings – this is the first time she'd have passed residences rather than offices or public buildings.'

Robin looked at the buildings around them. Sure enough, there were a couple of doors whose multiple buzzers indicated flats above.

'Is there a chance,' said Strike, 'however remote, that someone living along this lane could have persuaded or forced her inside?'

Robin looked up and down the street, the rain pattering onto her umbrella.

'Well,' she said slowly, 'obviously it *could* have happened, but it seems unlikely. Did someone wake up that day and decide they wanted to abduct a woman, reach outside and grab one?'

'Have I taught you nothing?'

'OK, fine: *means before motive*. But there are problems with the means, too. This is really overlooked as well. Does nobody see or hear her being abducted? Doesn't she scream or fight? And I

189

assume the abductor lives alone, unless their housemates are also in on the kidnapping?'

'All valid points,' admitted Strike. 'Plus, the police went door to door here. Everyone was questioned, though the flats weren't searched.

'But let's think this through . . . She's a doctor. What if someone shoots out of a house and begs her to come inside to look at an injured person – a sick relative – and once inside, they don't let her go? That'd be a good ploy for getting her inside, pretending there was a medical emergency.'

'OK, but that presupposes they knew she was a doctor.'

'The abductor could've been a patient.'

'But how did they know she'd be passing their house at that particular time? Had she alerted the whole neighbourhood that she was about to go to the pub?'

'Maybe it was a random thing, they saw her passing, they knew she was a doctor, they ran out and grabbed her. Or – I dunno, let's say there really was a sick or dying person inside, or someone's had an accident – perhaps there's an argument – she disagrees with the treatment or refuses to help – the fight becomes physical – she's accidentally killed.'

There was a short silence, while they moved aside for a group of chattering French students. When these had passed, Strike said,

'It's a stretch, I grant you.'

'We can find out how many of these buildings

are occupied by the same people they were thirty-nine years ago,' said Robin, 'but we've still got the problem of how they've kept her body hidden for nearly four decades. You wouldn't dare move, would you?'

'That's a problem, all right,' admitted Strike. 'As Gupta said, it's not like disposing of a table of equivalent weight. Blood, decomposition, infestation . . . plenty have tried keeping bodies on the premises. Crippen. Christie. Fred and Rose West. It's generally considered a mistake.'

'Creed managed it for a while,' said Robin. 'Boiling down severed hands in the basement. Burying heads apart from bodies. It wasn't the corpses that got him caught.'

'Are you reading *The Demon of Paradise Park*?' asked Strike sharply.

'Yes,' said Robin.

'D'you want that stuff in your head?'

'If it helps us with the case,' said Robin.

'Hmm. Just thinking of my health and safety responsibilities.'

Robin said nothing. Strike gave the houses a last, sweeping look, then invited Robin to walk on, saying,

'You're right, I can't see it. Freezers get opened, gas men visit and notice a smell, neighbours notice blocked drains. But in the interests of thoroughness, we should check who was living here at the time.'

They now emerged onto the busiest road they

had yet seen. Aylesbury Street was a wide road, lined with more office blocks and flats.

'So,' said Strike, pausing again on the pavement, 'if Margot's still walking to the pub, she would've crossed here and turned left, into Clerkenwell Green. But we're pausing to note that it was *there*,' Strike pointed some fifty yards to the right, 'that a small white van nearly knocked down two women as it sped away from Clerkenwell Green that evening. The incident was witnessed by four or five onlookers. Nobody got the registration number— '

'But Creed was putting fake licence plates on the delivery van he was using,' said Robin, 'so that might not help anyway.'

'Correct. The van seen by witnesses on the eleventh of October 1974 had a design on the side. The onlookers didn't all agree what it was, but two of them thought a large flower.'

'And we also know,' said Robin, 'that Creed was using removable paint on the van to disguise its appearance.'

'Correct again. So, on the surface, this looks like our first proper hint that Creed might've been in the area. Talbot, of course, wanted to believe that, so he was uninterested in the opinion of one of the witnesses that the van actually belonged to a local florist. However, a junior officer, presumably one of those who'd realised that his lead investigator was going quietly off his onion, went and questioned the florist, a man called Albert

Shimmings, who absolutely denied driving a speeding van in this area that night. He claimed he'd been giving his young son a lift in it, miles away.'

'Which doesn't necessarily mean it *wasn't* Shimmings,' said Robin. 'He might have been worried about being done for dangerous driving. No CCTV cameras . . . nothing to prove it one way or the other.'

'My thoughts exactly. If Shimmings is still alive, I think we should check his story. He might've decided it's worth telling the truth now a speeding charge can't stick. In the meantime,' said Strike, 'the matter of the van remains unresolved and we have to admit that one possible explanation is that Creed was driving it.'

'But where did he abduct Margot, if it *was* Creed in the van?' asked Robin. 'It can't've been back in Albemarle Way, because this isn't how he'd have left the area.'

'True. If he'd grabbed her in Albemarle Way, he'd've joined Aylesbury Street much further down and he definitely wouldn't have come via Clerkenwell Green – which leads us neatly to the Two Struggling Women by the Phoneboxes.'

They proceeded through the drizzle into Clerkenwell Green, a wide rectangular square which boasted trees, a pub and a café. Two telephone boxes stood in the middle, near parked cars and a bike stand.

'Here,' said Strike, coming to a halt between the

phone boxes, 'is where Talbot's craziness really starts messing with the case. A woman called Ruby Elliot, who was unfamiliar with the area, but trying to find her daughter and son-in-law's new house in Hayward's Place, was driving around in circles in the rain, lost.

'She passed these phone boxes and noticed two women struggling together, one of whom seemed, in her word, "tottery". She has no particularly distinct memory of them – remember, it's pouring with rain and she's anxiously trying to spot street signs and house numbers, because she's lost. All she can tell the police is that one of them was wearing a headscarf and the other a raincoat.

'The day after this detail appeared in the paper, a middle-aged woman of sound character came forward to say that the pair of women Ruby Elliot had seen had almost certainly been her and her aged mother. She told Talbot she'd been walking the old dear across Clerkenwell Green that night, taking her home after a little walk. The mother, who was infirm and senile, was wearing a rainhat, and she herself was wearing a raincoat similar to Margot's. They didn't have umbrellas, so she was trying to hurry her mother along. The old lady didn't take kindly to being rushed and there was a slight altercation here, right by the phone boxes. I've got a picture of the two of them, incidentally: the press got hold of it – "sighting debunked".

'But Talbot wasn't having it. He flat-out refused to accept that the two women hadn't been Margot and a man dressed like a woman. The way he sees it: Margot and Creed meet here by the phone boxes, Creed wrestles her into his van, which presumably was parked *there*—' Strike pointed to the short line of parked cars nearby, 'then Creed takes off at speed, with her screaming and banging on the sides of the van, exiting down Aylesbury Street.'

'But,' said Robin, 'Talbot thought *Theo* was Creed. Why would Creed come to Margot's surgery dressed as a woman, then walk out, leaving her unharmed, walk to Clerkenwell Green and grab her here, in the middle of the most public, over-looked place we've seen?'

'There's no point trying to make sense of it, because there isn't any. When Lawson took over the case, he went back to Fiona Fleury, which was the respectable middle-aged woman's name, questioned her again and came away completely satisfied that she and her mother had been the women Ruby Elliot saw. Again, the general election was useful, because Fiona Fleury remembered being tired and not particularly patient with her difficult mother, because she'd sat up late the night before, watching election coverage. Lawson concluded – and I'm inclined to agree with him – that the matter of the two struggling women had been resolved.'

The drizzle had thickened: raindrops were pounding on Robin's umbrella and rendering the hems of her trousers sodden. They now turned up

Clerkenwell Close, a curving street that rose towards a large and impressive church with a high, pointed steeple, set on higher ground.

'Margot can't have got this far,' said Robin.

'You say that,' said Strike, and to her surprise he paused again, looking ahead at the church, 'but we now reach one last alleged sighting.

'A church handyman – yeah, I know,' he added, in response to Robin's startled look, 'called Willy Lomax claims he saw a woman in a Burberry raincoat walking up the steps to St James-on-the-Green that evening, around the time Margot should've been arriving at the pub. He saw her from behind. These were the days, of course, when churches weren't locked up all the time.

'Talbot, of course, disregarded Lomax's evidence, because if Margot was alive and walking into churches, she couldn't have been speeding away in the Essex Butcher's van. Lawson couldn't make much of Lomax's evidence. The bloke stuck fast to his story: he'd seen a woman matching Margot's description go inside but, being a man of limited curiosity, didn't follow her, didn't ask her what she was up to and didn't watch to see whether she ever came out of the church again.

'And now,' said Strike, 'we've earned a pint.'

CHAPTER 14

In which there written was with cyphres old . . .

Edmund Spenser
The Faerie Queene

On the opposite side of the road from the church hung the sign of the Three Kings. The pub's curved, tiled exterior wall mirrored the bend in the road.

As she followed Strike inside, Robin had the strange sensation of walking back in time. Most of the walls were papered in pages from old music papers dating back to the seventies: a jumble of reviews, adverts for old stereo systems and pictures of pop and rock stars. Hallowe'en decorations hung over the bar, Bowie and Bob Marley looking down from framed prints, and Bob Dylan and Jimi Hendrix looked back at them from the opposite wall. As Robin sat down at a free table for two and Strike headed to the bar, she spotted a newspaper picture of Jonny Rokeby in tight leather trousers in the collage around the mirror. The pub looked as though it hadn't changed in many years; it might even have had these same frosted windows, these mismatched wooden tables, bare floorboards, round glass wall lamps and candles in bottles back when Margot's friend sat waiting for her in 1974.

For the first time, looking around this quirky, characterful pub, Robin found herself wondering exactly what Margot Bamborough had been like. It was odd how professional people's jobs defined them in the imagination. 'Doctor' felt, in many ways, like a complete identity. Waiting for her companion to buy the drinks, her eyes drifting from the skulls hanging from the bar to the pictures of dead rock stars, Robin was struck by the odd idea of a reverse nativity. The three Magi had journeyed towards a birth; Margot had set out for the Three Kings and, Robin feared, met death along the way.

Strike set Robin's wine in front of her, took a satisfying mouthful of Sussex Best, sat down and then reached inside his overcoat and pulled out a roll of papers. Robin noticed photocopied newspaper reports among the typed and handwritten pages.

'You've been to the British Library.'

'I was there all day yesterday.'

He took the top photocopy and showed it to Robin. It showed a small clipping from the *Daily Mail*, featuring a picture of Fiona Fleury and her

198

aged mother beneath the caption: *Essex Butcher Sighting 'Was Really Us'*. Neither woman would have been easy to mistake for Margot Bamborough: Fiona was a tall, broad woman with a cheery face and no waist; her mother was shrivelled with age and stooped.

'This is the first inkling that the press were losing confidence in Bill Talbot,' said Strike. 'A few weeks after this appeared, they were baying for his blood, which probably didn't help his mental health . . . Anyway,' he said, his large, hairy-backed hand lying flat on the rest of the photocopied paper. 'Let's go back to the one, incontrovertible fact we've got, which is that Margot Bamborough was still alive and inside the practice at a quarter to six that night.'

'At a quarter *past* six, you mean,' said Robin.

'No, I don't,' said Strike. 'The sequence of departures goes: ten past five, Dorothy. Half past five, Dinesh Gupta, who catches sight of Margot inside her consulting room before he leaves, and walks out past Gloria and Theo.

'Gloria goes to ask Brenner if he'll see Theo. He refuses. Margot comes out of her consulting room and her last scheduled patients, a mother and child, come out at the same time and leave, also walking out past Theo in the waiting room. Margot tells Gloria she's happy to see Theo. Brenner says "good of you" and leaves, at a quarter to six.

'From then on, we've only got Gloria's uncorroborated word for anything that happened. She's the only person claiming Theo and Margot left the surgery alive.'

Robin paused in the act of taking a sip of wine.

'Come on. You aren't suggesting they never left? That Margot's still there, buried under the floorboards?'

'No, because sniffer dogs went all over the building, as well as the garden behind it,' said Strike. 'But how's this for a theory? The reason Gloria was so insistent that Theo was a woman, not a man, was because he was her accomplice in the murder or abduction of Margot.'

'Wouldn't it have been more sensible to write down a girl's name instead of "Theo" if she wanted to hide a man's identity? And why would she ask Dr Brenner if he could see Theo, if she and Theo were planning to kill Margot?'

'Both good points,' admitted Strike, 'but maybe she knew perfectly well Brenner would refuse, because he was a cantankerous old bastard, and was trying to make the thing look natural to Margot. Humour me for a moment.

'Inert bodies are heavy, hard to move and diffi-cult to hide. A living, fighting woman is even harder. I've seen press photographs of Gloria and she was what my aunt would call a "slip of a girl", whereas Margot was a tall woman. I doubt Gloria could have killed Margot without help, and she definitely couldn't have lifted her.'

'Didn't Dr Gupta say Margot and Gloria were close?'

'*Means before motive*. The closeness could've been a front,' said Strike. 'Maybe Gloria didn't like being "improved" after all, and only acted the grateful pupil to allay Margot's suspicions.

'Be that as it may, the last time there are multiple witnesses to Margot's whereabouts was half an hour before she supposedly left the building. After that, we've only got Gloria's word for what happened.'

'OK, objection sustained,' said Robin.

'So,' said Strike, as he took his hand off the pile of paper, 'having granted me that, forget for a moment any alleged sightings of her at windows or walking into churches. Forget the speeding van. It's entirely possible that *none* of that had anything to do with Margot.

'Go back to the one thing we know for certain: Margot Bamborough was still alive at a quarter to six.

'So now we turn to three men the police considered plausible suspects at the time and ask ourselves where they were at a quarter to six on the eleventh of October 1974.'

'There you go,' he said, passing Robin a photocopy of a tabloid news story dated 24 October 1974. 'That's Roy Phipps, otherwise known as Margot's husband and Anna's dad.'

The photograph showed a handsome man of around thirty, who strongly resembled his daughter. Robin thought that if she had been looking to cast a poet in a cheesy movie, she'd have put Roy Phipps's headshot to the top of the pile. This was where Anna had got her long, pale face, her high forehead and her large, beautiful eyes. Phipps had worn his dark hair down to his long-lapelled collar in 1974, and he stared up out of this old newsprint harrowed, facing the camera, looking up from the card in his hand. The caption read: *Dr Roy Phipps, appealing to the public for help.*

'Don't bother reading it,' said Strike, already placing a second news story over the first. 'There's nothing in there you don't already know, but *this* one will give you a few titbits you don't.'

Robin bent obediently over the second news story, of which Strike had photocopied only half.

her husband, Dr Roy Phipps, who suffers from von Willebrand Disease, was ill at home and confined to bed at the marital home in Ham on the 11th October.

'Following several inaccurate and irresponsible press reports, we would like to state clearly that we are satisfied that Dr Roy Phipps had nothing to do with his wife's disappearance,' DI Bill Talbot, the detective in charge of the investigation, told newsmen. 'His own doctors have confirmed that walking and driving would both have been beyond Dr Phipps on the day in question and both Dr Phipps' nanny and his cleaner have given sworn statements confirming that Dr Phipps did not leave the house on the day of his wife's disappearance.'

'What's von Willebrand Disease?' asked Robin.

'A bleeding disorder. I looked it up. You don't clot properly. Gupta remembered that wrong; he thought Roy was a haemophiliac.

'There are three kinds of von Willebrand Disease,' said Strike. 'Type One just means you'd take a bit longer than normal to clot, but it shouldn't leave you bedbound, or unable to drive. I'm assuming Roy Phipps is Type Three, which can be as serious as haemophilia, and could lay him up for a while. But we'll need to check that.

'Anyway,' said Strike, turning over the next page. 'This is Talbot's record of his interview with Roy Phipps.'

'Oh God,' said Robin quietly.

The page was covered in small, slanting writing, but the most distinctive feature of the record were the stars Talbot had drawn all over it.

'See there?' said Strike, running a forefinger down a list of dates that were just discernible amid the scrawls. 'Those are the dates of the Essex Butcher abductions and attempted abductions.

'Talbot loses interest halfway down the list, look. On the twenty-sixth of August 1971, which is when Creed tried to abduct Peggy Hiskett, Roy was able to prove that he and Margot were on holiday in France.

'So that was that, as far as Talbot was concerned. If Roy hadn't tried to abduct Peggy Hiskett, he wasn't the Essex Butcher, and if he wasn't the

203

Essex Butcher, he couldn't have had anything to do with Margot's disappearance.

'But there's a funny thing at the bottom of Talbot's list of dates. All refer to Creed's activities except that last one. He's circled December twenty-seventh, with no year. No idea why he was interested in December twenty-seventh.'

'Or, presumably, why he went Vincent van Gogh all over his report?'

'The stars? Yeah, they're a feature on all Talbot's notes. Very strange. Now,' said Strike, 'let's see how a statement *should* be taken.'

He turned the page and there was a neatly type-written, double-spaced statement, four pages long, which DI Lawson had taken from Roy Phipps, and which had been duly signed on the final page by the haematologist.

'You needn't read the whole thing now,' said Strike. 'Bottom line is, he stuck to it that he'd been laid up in bed all day, as the cleaner and his nanny would testify.

'But now we go to Wilma Bayliss, the Phippses' cleaner. She also happened to be the St John's practice's cleaner. The rest of the practice didn't know at the time that she'd been doing some private work for Margot and Roy. Gupta told me that he thought Margot might've been encouraging Wilma to leave her husband, and giving her a bit of extra work might've been part of that scheme.'

'Why did she want Wilma to leave her husband?'

'I'm glad you asked that,' said Strike, and he turned over another piece of paper to show a tiny photocopied news clipping, which was dated in Strike's spiky and hard-to-read handwriting: 6 November 1972.

Rapist Jailed

Jules Bayliss, 36, of Leather Lane, Clerkenwell was today sentenced at the Inner London Crown Court to 5 years' jail for 2 counts of rape. Bayliss, who previously served two years in Brixton for aggravated assault, pleaded Not Guilty.

'Ah,' said Robin. 'I see.'

She took another slug of wine.

'Funnily enough,' she added, though she didn't sound amused, 'Creed got five years for his second rape as well. After they let him out, he started killing women as well as raping them.'

'Yeah,' said Strike. 'I know.'

For the second time, he considered questioning the advisability of Robin reading *The Demon of Paradise Park*, but decided against.

'I haven't yet managed to find out what became of Jules Bayliss,' he said, 'and the police notes regarding him are incomplete, so I can't be sure whether he was still in the nick when Margot was abducted.

'What's relevant to us is that Wilma told a different story to Lawson to the one she told Talbot

205

– although Wilma claimed she had, in fact, told Talbot, and that he didn't record it, which is possible, because, as you can see, his note-taking left a lot to be desired.

'Anyway, one of the things she told Lawson was that she'd sponged blood off the spare-room carpet the day Margot disappeared. The other was that she'd seen Roy walking through the garden on the day he was supposedly laid up in bed. She also admitted to Lawson that she hadn't actually seen Roy in bed, but she'd heard him talking from the master bedroom that day.'

'Those are . . . pretty major changes of story.'

'Well, as I say, Wilma's position was that she wasn't changing her story, Talbot simply hadn't recorded it properly. But Lawson seems to have given Wilma a very hard time about it, and he re-interviewed Roy on the strength of what she'd said, too. However, Roy still had Cynthia the nanny as his alibi, who was prepared to swear to the fact that he'd been laid up all day, because she was bringing him regular cups of tea in the master bedroom.

'I know,' he said, in response to Robin's raised eyebrows. 'Lawson seems to have had the same kind of dirty mind as us. He questioned Phipps on the precise nature of his relationship with Cynthia, which led to an angry outburst from Phipps, who said she was twelve years younger than he was and a cousin to boot.'

It flitted across both Strike's and Robin's minds

at this point that there were ten years separating them in age. Both suppressed this unbidden and irrelevant thought.

'According to Roy, the age difference and the blood relationship ought to have constituted a total prohibition on the relationship in the minds of all decent people. But as we know, he managed to overcome those qualms seven years later.

'Lawson also interrogated Roy about the fact that Margot had met an old flame for a drink three weeks before she died. In his rush to exonerate Roy, Talbot hadn't paid too much attention to the account of Oonagh Kennedy—'

'The friend Margot was supposed to be meeting in here?' said Robin.

'Exactly. Oonagh told both Talbot and Lawson that when Roy found out Margot had been for a drink with this old boyfriend, he'd been furious, and that he and Margot weren't talking to each other when she disappeared.

'According to Lawson's notes, Roy didn't like any of this being brought up—'

'Hardly surprising—'

'—and got quite aggressive. However, after speaking to Roy's doctors, Lawson was satisfied that Roy had indeed had a serious episode of bleeding after a fall in a hospital car park, and would have found it well nigh impossible to drive to Clerkenwell that evening, let alone kill or kidnap his wife.'

'He could have hired someone,' suggested Robin.

'They checked his bank accounts and couldn't find any suspicious payments, but that obviously doesn't mean he didn't find a way. He's a haematologist; he won't be lacking in brains.'

Strike took a further swig of beer.

'So that's the husband,' he said, flipping over the four pages of Roy's statement. 'Now for the old flame.'

'God above,' said Robin, looking down at another press photograph.

The man's thick, wavy hair reached well past his shoulders. He stood, unsmiling, with his hands on his narrow hips beside a painting of what appeared to be two writhing lovers. His shirt was open almost to his navel and his jeans were skin tight at the crotch and extremely wide at the ankle.

'I thought you'd enjoy that,' said Strike, grinning at Robin's reaction. 'He's Paul Satchwell, an artist – though not a very highbrow one, by the sounds of it. When the press got onto him, he was designing a mural for a nightclub. He's Margot's ex.'

'She's just gone *right* down in my estimation,' muttered Robin.

'Don't judge her too harshly. She met him when she was a Bunny Girl, so she was only nineteen or twenty. He was six years older than her and probably seemed like the height of sophistication.'

'In *that* shirt?'

'That's a publicity photo for his art show,' said Strike. 'It says so below. Possibly he didn't show as much chest hair in day-to-day life. The press got quite excited at the thought an ex-lover might be involved, and let's face it, a bloke who looked like that was a gift to the tabloids.'

Strike turned to another example of Talbot's chaotic note-taking, which like the first was covered in five-pointed stars and had the same list of dates, with scribbled annotations beside them.

'As you can see, Talbot didn't start with anything as mundane as "Where were you at a quarter to six on the night Margot disappeared?" He goes straight into the Essex Butcher dates, and when Satchwell told him he was celebrating a friend's thirtieth birthday on September the eleventh, which was when Susan Meyer was abducted, Talbot basically stopped asking him questions. But once again, we've got a date unconnected with Creed heavily circled at the bottom, with a gigantic cross beside it. April the sixteenth this time.'

'Where was Satchwell living when Margot disappeared?'

'Camden,' said Strike, turning the page to reveal, again, a conventional typewritten statement. 'There you go, look, it's in his statement to Lawson. Not all that far from Clerkenwell.

'To Lawson, Satchwell explained that after a gap of eight years, he and Margot met by chance in the street and decided to go for a catch-up drink. He was quite open with Lawson about this, presumably because he knew Oonagh or Roy would already have told them about it. He even told Lawson he'd have been keen to resume an affair with Margot, which seems a bit *too* helpful, although it was probably meant to prove he had nothing to hide. He said he and Margot had a volatile relationship for a couple of years when she was much younger, and that Margot finally ended it for good when she met Roy.

'Satchwell's alibi checked out. He told Lawson he was alone in his studio, which was also in Camden, for most of the afternoon on the day Margot disappeared, but took a phone call there round about five. Landlines – far harder to monkey about with than mobiles when you're trying to set up an alibi. Satchwell ate in a local café, where he was known, at half past six, and witnesses agreed they'd seen him. He then went home to change before meeting some friends in a bar around eight. The people he claimed to have been with confirmed it all and Lawson was satisfied that Satchwell was in the clear.

'Which brings us to the third, and, I'd have to say, most promising suspect – always excepting Dennis Creed. This,' said Strike, moving Satchwell's statement from the top of a now greatly diminished pile of paper, 'is Steve Douthwaite.'

If Roy Phipps would have been a lazy casting director's idea of a sensitive poet, and Paul Satchwell the very image of a seventies rock star, Steve Douthwaite would have been hired without hesitation to play the cheeky chap, the wisecracking upstart, the working-class Jack the Lad. He had dark, beady eyes, an infectious grin and a spiky mullet that reminded Robin of the young men featured on an old Bay City Rollers LP which Robin's mother, to her children's hilarity, still cherished. Douthwaite was holding a pint in one hand, and his other arm was slung around the shoulder of a man whose face had been cropped from the picture, but whose suit, like Douthwaite's, looked cheap, creased and shiny. Douthwaite had loosened his kipper tie and undone his top shirt button to reveal a neck chain.

'Ladykiller' Salesman Sought Over Missing Doctor

Police are anxious to trace the whereabouts of double-glazing salesman Steve Douthwaite, who has vanished following routine questioning over the disappearance of Dr Margot Bamborough, 29.

Douthwaite, 28, left no forwarding address after quitting his job and his flat in Percival Street, Clerkenwell.

A former patient of the missing doctor's, Douthwaite raised suspicion at the medical practice because of his frequent visits to see the pretty blonde doctor. Friends of the salesman describe him as 'smooth talking' and do not believe Douthwaite suffered any serious health issues. Douthwaite is believed to have sent Dr Bamborough gifts.

Douthwaite, who was raised in foster care,

has had no contact with friends since February 7th. Police are believed to have searched Douthwaite's home since he vacated it.

Tragic Affair

'He caused a lot of trouble round here, a lot of bad feeling,' said a co-worker at Diamond Double Glazing, who asked not to be named. 'Real Jack the Lad. He had an affair with another guy's wife. She ended up taking an overdose, left her kids without a mum. Nobody was sorry when Douthwaite took off, to be honest. We were happy to see the back of him. Too interested in booze and girls and not much cop at the job.'

Doctor Would Be 'A Challenge'

Asked what he thought Douthwaite's relationship with the missing doctor had been, his co-worker said,

'Chasing girls is all Steve cares about. He'd think a doctor was a challenge, knowing him.'

Police are eager to speak to Douthwaite again and appeal to any members of the public who might know his whereabouts.

When Robin had finished reading, Strike, who'd just finished his first pint, said,

'Want another drink?'

'I'll get these,' said Robin.

She went to the bar, where she waited beneath the hanging skulls and fake cobwebs. The barman had painted his face like Frankenstein's monster. Robin ordered drinks absent-mindedly, thinking about the Douthwaite article.

When she'd returned to Strike with a fresh pint, a wine and two packets of crisps, she said,

'You know, that article isn't fair.'

'Go on.'

'People don't necessarily tell their co-workers about their medical problems. Maybe Douthwaite *did* seem fine to his mates when they were all down the pub. That doesn't mean he didn't have anything wrong with him. He might have been mentally ill.'

'Not for the first time,' said Strike, 'you're bang on the money.'

He searched the small number of photocopied papers remaining in his pile and extracted another handwritten document, far neater than Talbot's and devoid of doodles and random dates. Somehow Robin knew, before Strike had said a word, that this fluid, rounded handwriting belonged to Margot Bamborough.

'Copies of Douthwaite's medical records,' said Strike. 'The police got hold of them. "Headaches, upset stomach, weight loss, palpitations, nausea, nightmares, trouble sleeping",' Strike read out. 'Margot's conclusion, on visit four – see there? – is "personal and employment-related difficulties, under severe strain, exhibiting signs of anxiety".'

'Well, his married girlfriend had killed herself,' said Robin. 'That'd knock anyone except a psychopath for six, wouldn't it?'

Charlotte slid like a shadow across Strike's mind.

'Yeah, you'd think. Also, look there. He'd been the victim of an assault shortly before his first visit to Margot. "Contusions, cracked rib." I smell angry, bereaved and betrayed husband.'

'But the paper makes it sound as though he was stalking Margot.'

'Well,' said Strike, tapping the photocopy of Douthwaite's medical notes, 'there are a hell of a lot of visits here. He saw her three times in one week. He's anxious, guilty, feeling unpopular, probably didn't expect his bit of fun to end in the woman's death. And there's a good-looking doctor offering no judgement, but kindness and support. I don't think it's beyond the realms of possibility to think he might have developed feelings for her.

'And look at this,' Strike went on, turning over the medical records to show Robin more typed statements. 'These are from Dorothy and Gloria, who both said Douthwaite came out of her room the last time he saw Margot, looking – well, this is Dorothy,' he said, and he read aloud, '"*I observed Mr Douthwaite leaving Dr Bamborough's surgery and noticed that he looked as though he had had a shock. I thought he also looked angry and distressed. As he walked out, he tripped over the toy truck of a boy in the waiting room and swore loudly. He seemed distracted and unaware of his surroundings."* And Gloria,' said Strike, turning over the page, 'says: *"I remember Mr Douthwaite leaving because he swore at a little boy. He looked as though he had just been given bad news. I thought he seemed scared and angry."*

'Now, Margot's notes of her last consultation with Douthwaite don't mention anything but the same old stress-related symptoms,' Strike went on, turning back to the medical records, 'so she definitely hadn't just diagnosed him with anything life-threatening. Lawson speculated that she might've felt he was getting over-attached, and told him he had to stop taking up valuable time that could be given to other patients, which Douthwaite didn't like hearing. Maybe he'd convinced himself his feelings were reciprocated. All the evidence suggests he was in a fragile mental state at the time.

'Anyway, four days after Douthwaite's last appointment, Margot vanishes. Tipped off by the surgery that there was a patient who seemed a bit over-fond of her, Talbot called him in for questioning. Here we go.'

Once again, Strike extracted a star-strewn scrawl from amid the typewritten pages.

'As usual, Talbot starts the interrogation by running through the list of Creed dates. Trouble is, Douthwaite doesn't seem to remember what he was doing on any of them.'

'If he was already ill with stress—' began Robin.

'Well, exactly,' said Strike. 'Being interrogated by

215

a police officer who thinks you might be the Essex Butcher wouldn't help your anxiety, would it?

'And look at this, Talbot adds a random date again: twenty-first February. But he also does something else. Can you make anything of that?'

Robin took the page from Strike and examined the last three lines of writing.

'Pitman shorthand,' said Robin.

'Can you read it?'

'No. I know a bit of Teeline; I never learned Pitman. Pat can do it, though.'

'You're saying she might be useful for once?'

'Oh sod off, Strike,' said Robin, crossly. 'You want to go back to temps, fine, but I like getting accurate messages and knowing the filing's up to date.'

She took a photograph on her phone and texted it to Pat, along with a request to translate it. Strike, meanwhile, was reflecting that Robin had never before called him 'Strike' when annoyed. Perversely, it had sounded more intimate than the use of his first name. He'd quite enjoyed it.

'Sorry for impugning Pat,' he said.

'I just told you to sod off,' said Robin, failing to suppress a smile. 'What did Lawson make of Douthwaite?'

'Well, unsurprisingly, when he tried to interview him and found out he'd left his flat and job, leaving no forwarding address, he got quite interested in him. Hence the tip-off to the papers. They were trying to flush him out.'

'And did it work?' asked Robin, now eating crisps.

'It did. Douthwaite turned up at a police station in Waltham Forest the day after the "Ladykiller" article appeared, probably terrified he'd soon have Fleet Street and Scotland Yard on his doorstep. He told them he was unemployed and living in a bedsit. Local police called Lawson, who went straight over there to interview him.

'There's a full account here,' said Strike, pushing some of the last pages of the roll he had brought with him towards Robin. 'All written by Lawson: "appears scared" – "evasive" – "nervous" – "sweating" – and the alibi's not good. Douthwaite says that on the afternoon of Margot's disappearance he was out looking for a new flat.'

'He claims he was already looking for a new place when she disappeared?'

'Coincidence, eh? Except that upon closer questioning he couldn't say which flats he'd seen and couldn't come up with the name of anyone who'd remember seeing him. In the end he said his flat-hunting had involved sitting in a local café and circling ads in the paper. Trouble was, nobody in the café remembered him being there.

'He said he'd moved to Waltham Forest because

he had bad associations with Clerkenwell after being interviewed by Talbot and made to feel as though he was under suspicion, and that, in any case, things hadn't been good for him at work since his affair with the co-worker's suicidal wife.'

'Well, that's credible enough,' said Robin.

'Lawson interviewed him twice more, but got nothing else out of him. Douthwaite came lawyered up to interview three. At that point, Lawson backed off. After all, they had nothing on Douthwaite, even if he was the fishiest person they interviewed. And it was – just – credible that the reason nobody had noticed him in the café was because it was a busy place.'

A group of drinkers in Hallowe'en costumes now entered the pub, giggling and clearly already full of alcohol. Robin noticed Strike casting an automatic eye over a young blonde in a rubber nurse's uniform.

'So,' she said, 'is that everything?'

'Almost,' said Strike, 'but I'm tempted not to show you this.'

'Why not?'

'Because I think it's going to feed your obsession with holy places.'

'I'm not—'

'OK, but before you look at it, just remember that nutters are always attracted by murders and missing person cases, all right?'

'Fine,' said Robin. 'Show me.'

Strike flipped over the piece of paper. It was a

photocopy of the crudest kind of anonymous note, featuring letters cut out of magazines.

If YOU WaNt TO kNOw WhEre MargOt BamBorOu gh IS

bURied DiG hERe

'Another St John's Cross,' said Robin.

'Yep. That arrived at Scotland Yard in 1985, addressed to Lawson, who'd already retired. Nothing else in the envelope.'

Robin sighed and leaned back in her chair.

'Nutter, obviously,' said Strike, now tapping his photocopied articles and statements back into a pile and rolling them up again. 'If you really knew where a body was buried, you'd include a bloody map.'

It was nearly six o'clock now, close to the hour at which a doctor had once left her practice and had never been seen again. The frosted pub windows were inky blue. Up at the bar, the blonde in the rubber uniform was giggling at something a man dressed as the Joker had told her.

'You know,' said Robin, glancing down at the papers sitting beside Strike's pint, 'she was late . . . it was pouring with rain . . .'

'Go on,' said Strike, wondering whether she was about to say exactly what he'd been thinking.

'Her friend was waiting in here, alone. Margot's late. She would've wanted to get here as quickly as possible. The simplest, most plausible explanation I can think of is that somebody offered her a lift. A car pulled up—'

'Or a van,' said Strike. Robin had, indeed, reached the same conclusion he had. 'Someone she knew—'

'Or someone who seemed safe. An elderly man—'

'Or what she thinks is a woman.'

'Exactly,' said Robin.

She turned a sad face to Strike.

'That's it. She either knew the driver, or the stranger seemed safe.'

'And who'd remember that?' said Strike. 'She was wearing a nondescript raincoat, carrying an umbrella. A vehicle pulls up. She bends down to the window, then gets in. No fight. No conflict. The car drives away.'

'And only the driver would know what happened next,' said Robin.

Her mobile rang: it was Pat Chauncey.

'She always does that,' said Strike. 'Text her, and she doesn't text back, she calls—'

'Does it matter?' said Robin, exasperated, and answered.

'Hi, Pat. Sorry to bother you out of hours. Did you get my text?'

'Yeah,' croaked Pat. 'Where did you find that?'

'It's in some old police notes. Can you translate it?'

'Yeah,' said Pat, 'but it doesn't make much sense.'

'Hang on, Pat, I want Cormoran to hear this,' said Robin, and she changed to speakerphone.

'Ready?' came Pat's rasping voice.

'Yes,' said Robin. Strike pulled out a pen and flipped over his roll of paper so that he could write on the blank side.

'It says: *"And that is the last of them, comma, the twelfth, comma, and the circle will be closed upon finding the tenth, comma"* – and then there's a word I can't read, I don't think it's proper Pitman – and after that another word, which phonetically says Ba – fom – et, full stop. Then a new sentence, *"Transcribe in the true book."*'

'Baphomet,' repeated Strike.

'Yeah,' said Pat.

'That's a name,' said Strike. 'Baphomet is an occult deity.'

'OK, well, that's what it says,' said Pat, matter-of-factly.

Robin thanked her and rang off.

'*"And that is the last of them, the twelfth, and the circle will be closed upon finding the tenth – unknown word – Baphomet. Transcribe in the true book,"*' Strike read back.

'How d'you know about Baphomet?' asked Robin.

'Whittaker was interested in all that shit.'

'Oh,' said Robin.

Whittaker was the last of Strike's mother's lovers, the man Strike believed had administered the overdose that had killed her.

'He had a copy of *The Satanic Bible*,' said Strike. 'It had a picture of Baphomet's head in a penta – shit,' he said, rifling back through the loose pages to find one of those on which Talbot had doodled many five-pointed stars. He frowned at it for a moment, then looked up at Robin.

'I don't think these are stars. They're pentagrams.'

PART III

. . . Winter, clothëd all in frieze . . .

Edmund Spenser
The Faerie Queene

CHAPTER 15

Wherein old dints of deepe woundes did remaine . . .

Edmund Spenser
The Faerie Queene

In the second week of November, Joan's chemo-therapy caused her white blood cell count to plummet dangerously, and she was admitted to hospital. Strike left Robin in charge of the agency, Lucy left her three sons in the care of her husband, and both hurried back to Cornwall.

Strike's fresh absence coincided with the monthly team meeting, which for the first time Robin led alone, the youngest and arguably least experienced investigator at the agency, and the only woman.

Robin wasn't sure whether she had imagined it, but she thought Hutchins and Morris, the two ex-policemen, put up slightly more disagreement about the next month's rota, and about the line they ought to take on Shifty, than they would have done had Strike been there. It was Robin's opinion that Shifty's PA, who'd now been extensively wined and dined at the agency's expense without revealing anything about the hold her boss might have over his CEO, ought to be abandoned as a possible source. She'd decided that Morris ought to see her one last time to wrap things up, allaying any suspicion about what he'd been after, after which Robin thought it time to try and infiltrate Shifty's social circle with a view to getting information direct from the man they were investigating. Barclay was the only subcontractor who agreed with Robin, and backed her up when she insisted that Morris was to leave Shifty's PA well alone. Of course, as Robin was well aware, she and Barclay had once gone digging for a body together, and such things create a bond.

The memory of the team meeting was still bothering her as she sat with her legs up on the sofa in the flat in Finborough Road later, now in pyjamas and a dressing gown, working on her laptop. Wolfgang the dachshund was curled at her bare feet, keeping them warm.

Max was out. He'd suddenly announced the previous weekend that he feared he was in danger of passing from 'introvert' to 'recluse', and had accepted an invitation to go to dinner with some actor friends, even though, in his bitter words on parting, 'They'll all be pitying me, but I suppose they'll enjoy that'. Robin had taken Wolfgang for a quick walk around the block at eleven, but otherwise had spent her evening on the Bamborough case, for which she'd had no time while Strike had been in St Mawes, because the other four cases on the agency's books were absorbing all working hours.

Robin hadn't been out since her birthday drinks with Ilsa and Vanessa, which hadn't been as enjoyable as she'd hoped. The conversation had revolved entirely around relationships, because Vanessa had arrived with a brand-new engagement ring on her finger. Since then, Robin had used pressure of work during Strike's absence to avoid nights out with either of her friends. Her cousin Katie's words, *it's like you're travelling in a different direction to the rest of us*, were hard to forget, but the truth was that Robin didn't want to stand in a bar while Ilsa and Vanessa encouraged her to respond to the advances of some overfamiliar, Morris-like man with a line in easy patter and bad jokes.

She and Strike had now divided between them the people they wished to trace and re-interview in the Bamborough case. Unfortunately, Robin now knew that at least four of her allocated people had passed beyond the reach of questioning.

After careful cross-referencing of old records, Robin had managed to identify the Willy Lomax who'd been the long-serving handyman of St James's Church, Clerkenwell. He'd died in 1989 and Robin had so far been unable to find a single confirmed relative.

Albert Shimmings, the florist and possible driver

of the speeding van seen on the night of Margot's disappearance, had also passed away, but Robin had emailed two men she believed to be his sons. She sincerely hoped she'd correctly identified them, otherwise an insurance agent and a driving instructor were both about to get truly mystifying messages. Neither had yet responded to her request to talk to them.

Wilma Bayliss, the ex-practice cleaner, had died in 2003. A mother of two sons and three daughters, she'd divorced Jules Bayliss in 1975. By the time she died, Wilma hadn't been a cleaner, but a social worker, and she'd raised a high-achieving family, including an architect, a paramedic, a teacher, another social worker and a Labour councillor. One of the sons now lived in Germany, but Robin nevertheless included him in the emails and Facebook messages she sent out to all five siblings. There'd been no response so far.

Dorothy Oakden, the practice secretary, had been ninety-one when she died in a North London nursing home. Robin hadn't yet managed to trace Carl, her only child.

Meanwhile, Margot's ex-boyfriend, Paul Satchwell, and the receptionist, Gloria Conti, were proving strangely and similarly elusive. At first Robin had been relieved when she'd failed to find a death certificate for either of them, but after combing telephone directories, census records, county court judgments, marriage and divorce certificates, press archives, social media and lists of company staff, she'd come up with nothing. The only possible explanations Robin could think of were changes of name (in Gloria's case, possibly by marriage) and emigration.

As for Mandy White, the schoolgirl who'd claimed to have seen Margot at a rainy window, there were so many Amanda Whites of approximately the right age to be found online that Robin was starting to despair of ever finding the right one. Robin found this line of inquiry particularly frustrating, firstly because there was a good chance that White was no longer Mandy's surname, and secondly because, like the police before her, Robin thought it highly unlikely that Mandy had actually seen Margot at the window that night.

Having examined and discounted the Facebook accounts of another six Amanda Whites, Robin yawned, stretched and decided she was owed a break. Setting her laptop down on a side table, she swung her legs carefully off the sofa so as not to disturb Wolfgang, and crossed the open-plan area that combined kitchen, dining and living rooms, to make herself one of the low-calorie hot chocolates she was trying to convince herself was a treat, because she was still, in the middle of this long, sedentary stretch of surveillance, trying to keep an eye on her waistline.

As she stirred the unappetising powder into boiling water, a whiff of tuberose mingled with the scent of synthetic caramel. In spite of her bath, Fracas still lingered in her hair and on her pyjamas.

This perfume, she'd finally decided, had been a costly mistake. Living in a dense cloud of tuberose made her feel not only perpetually on the verge of a headache, but also as though she were wearing fur and pearls in broad daylight.

Robin's mobile, which was lying on the sofa beside Wolfgang, rang as she picked up her laptop again. Startled from his sleep, the disgruntled dog rose on arthritic legs. Robin lifted him to safety before picking up her phone and seeing, to her disappointment, that it wasn't Strike, but Morris.

'Hi, Saul.'

Ever since the birthday kiss, Robin had tried to keep her manner on the colder side of professional when dealing with Morris.

'Hey, Robs. You said to call if I had anything, even if it was late.'

'Yes, of course.' *I never said you could call me 'Robs', though.* 'What's happened?' asked Robin, looking around for a pen.

'I got Gemma drunk tonight. Shifty's PA, you know. Under the influence, she told me she thinks Shifty's got something on his boss.'

Well, that's hardly news, thought Robin, abandoning the fruitless search for a writing implement.

'What makes her think so?'

'Apparently he's said stuff to her like, "Oh, he'll always take *my* calls, don't worry", and "I know where all the bodies are buried".'

An image of a cross of St John slid across Robin's mind and was dismissed.

'As a joke,' Morris added. 'He passed it off like he was joking, but it made Gemma think.'

'But she doesn't know any details?'

'No, but listen, seriously, give me a bit more time and I reckon I'll be able to persuade her to wear a wire for us. Not to blow my own horn here – can't reach, for one thing – no, seriously,' he said, although Robin hadn't laughed, 'I've got her properly softened up. Just give me a bit more time—'

'Look, I'm sorry, Saul, but we went over this at the meeting,' Robin reminded Morris, suppressing a yawn, which made her eyes water. 'The client doesn't want us to tell any of the employees we're investigating this, so we can't tell her who you are. Pressuring her to investigate her own boss is asking her to risk her job. It also risks blowing the whole case if she decides to tell him what's going on.'

'But again, not to toot—'

'Saul, it's one thing her confiding in you when she's drunk,' said Robin (why wasn't he listening? They'd been through this endlessly at the team meeting). 'It's another asking a girl with no investigative training to work for us.'

'She's all over me, Robin,' said Morris earnestly. 'It'd be crazy not to use her.'

Robin suddenly wondered whether Morris had slept with the girl. Strike had been quite clear that that wasn't to happen. She sank back down on the sofa. Her copy of *The Demon of Paradise Park* was warm, she noticed, from the dachshund lying on it. The displaced Wolfgang was now gazing at Robin from under the dining table, with the sad, reproachful eyes of an old man.

'Saul, I really think it's time for Hutchins to take over, to see what he can do with Shifty himself,' said Robin.

'OK, but before we make that decision, let me ring Strike and—'

'You're not ringing Strike,' said Robin, her temper rising. 'His aunt's – he's got enough on his plate in Cornwall.'

'You're so sweet,' said Morris, with a little laugh, 'but I promise you, Strike would want a say in this—'

'He left me in charge,' said Robin, anger rising now, 'and I'm telling you, you've taken it as far as you can with that girl. She doesn't know anything useful and trying to push her further could backfire badly on this agency. I'm asking you to give it up now, please. You can take over on Postcard tomorrow night, and I'll tell Andy to get to work on Shifty.'

There was a pause.

'I've upset you, haven't I?' said Morris.

'No, you haven't upset me,' said Robin. After all, 'upset' wasn't quite the same as 'enrage'.

'I didn't want to—'

'You haven't, Saul, I'm only reminding you what we agreed at the meeting.'

'OK,' he said. 'All right. Hey – listen. Did you

hear about the boss who told his secretary the company was in trouble?'

'No,' said Robin, through clenched teeth.

'He said, "I'm going to have to lay you or Jack off." She said, "Well, you'll have to jack off, because I've got a headache."'

'Ha ha,' said Robin. 'Night, Saul.'

Why did I say 'ha ha'?' she asked herself furiously, as she set down her mobile. Why didn't I just say, 'Stop telling me crap jokes?' Or say nothing! And why did I say sorry when I was asking him to do what we all agreed at the meeting? Why am I cosseting him?

She thought of all those times she'd pretended with Matthew. Faking orgasms had been nothing compared to pretending to find him funny and interesting through all those twice-told tales of rugby club jokes, through every anecdote designed to show him as the cleverest or the funniest man in the room. *Why do we do it?* she asked herself, picking up *The Demon of Paradise Park* without considering what she was doing. *Why do we work so hard to keep the peace, to keep them happy?*

Because, suggested the seven ghostly black and white faces behind Dennis Creed's, *they can turn nasty, Robin. You know just how nasty they can turn, with your scar up your arm and your memory of that gorilla mask.*

But she knew that wasn't why she'd humoured Morris, not really. She didn't expect him to become abusive or violent if she refused to laugh at his stupid jokes. No, this was something else.

The only girl in a family of boys, Robin had been raised, she knew, to keep everyone happy, in spite of the fact that her own mother had been quite the women's libber. Nobody had meant to do it, but she'd realised during the therapy she'd undertaken after the attack that had left her forearm forever scarred, that her family role had been that of 'easy child', the non-complainer, the conciliator. She'd been born just a year before Martin, who had been the Ellacotts' 'problem child': the most scattered and impetuous, the least academic and conscientious, the son who still lived at home at twenty-eight and the brother with whom she had least in common. (Though Martin had punched Matthew on the nose on her wedding day, and the last time she'd been home she'd found herself hugging him when he offered, on hearing how difficult Matthew was being about the divorce, to do it again.)

Wintry specks of rain were dotting the window behind the dining table. Wolfgang was fast asleep again. Robin couldn't face perusing the social media accounts of another fifty Amanda Whites tonight. As she picked up *The Demon of Paradise Park*, she hesitated. She'd made a rule for herself (because it had been a long, hard journey to reach the place where she was now, and she didn't want to lose her current good state of mental health) not to read this book after dark, or right before bed. After all, the information it contained could be found summarised online: there was no need to hear in his own words what Creed had done to each of the women he'd tortured and killed.

Nevertheless, she picked up her hot chocolate, opened the book to the page she had marked with a Tesco receipt, and began to read at the point she'd left off three days previously.

Convinced that Bamborough had fallen victim to the serial killer now dubbed the Essex Butcher, Talbot made enemies among his colleagues with what they felt was his obsessive focus on one theory.

'They called it early retirement,' said a colleague, 'but it was basically dismissal. They said he wasn't interested in anything other than the Butcher, but here we are, 9 years on, and no-one's ever found a better explanation, have they?'

Margot Bamborough's family failed to positively identify any of the unclaimed jewellery and underwear found in Creed's basement flat when he was arrested in 1976, although Bamborough's husband, Dr Roy Phipps, thought a tarnished silver locket which had been crushed, possibly by blunt force, might have resembled one that the doctor was believed to have been wearing when she disappeared.

However, a recently published account of Bamborough's life, *Whatever Happened to Margot Bamborough?* [4] written by the son of a close friend of the doctor, contains revelations about the doctor's private life which suggest a new line of enquiry – and a possible connection with Creed. Shortly before her disappearance, Margot Bamborough booked herself into the Bride Street Nursing Home in Islington, a private facility which in 1974 provided discreet abortions.

CHAPTER 16

Behold the man, and tell me Britomart,
If ay more goodly creature thou didst see;
How like a Gyaunt in each manly part
Beares he himselfe with portly maiestee . . .

Edmund Spenser
The Faerie Queene

Four days later, at a quarter past five in the morning, the 'Night Riviera' sleeper train pulled into Paddington station. Strike, who'd slept poorly, had spent long stretches of the night watching the ghostly grey blur of the so-called English Riviera slide past his compartment window. Having slept on top of the covers with his prosthesis still attached, he turned down the proffered breakfast on its plastic tray, and was among the first passengers to disembark into the station, kit bag over his shoulder.

There was a nip of frost in the early morning air and Strike's breath rose in a cloud before him as he walked down the platform, Brunel's steel

237

arches curving above him like the ribs of a blue whale's skeleton, cold dark sky visible through the glass ceiling. Unshaven and slightly uncomfortable on the stump that had missed its usual nightly application of soothing cream, Strike headed for a bench, sat down, lit a much-needed cigarette, pulled out his mobile and phoned Robin.

He knew she'd be awake, because she'd just spent the night parked in Strike's BMW outside the house of the weatherman, watching for Postcard. They'd communicated mostly by text while he'd been in Cornwall, while he divided his time between the hospital in Truro and the house in St Mawes, taking it in turns with Lucy to sit with Joan, whose hair had now fallen out and whose immune system appeared to have collapsed under the weight of the chemotherapy, and to minister to Ted, who was barely eating. Before returning to London, Strike had cooked a large batch of curry, which he left in the freezer, alongside shepherd's pies made by Lucy. When he raised his cigarette to his mouth he could still smell a trace of cumin on his fingers, and if he concentrated, he could conjure up the deadly smell of hospital disinfectant underlain with a trace of urine, instead of cold iron, diesel and the distant waftings of coffee from a nearby Starbucks.

'Hi,' said Robin, and at the sound of her voice Strike felt, as he had known he would, a slight easing of the knot of tension in his stomach. 'What's happened?'

'Nothing,' he said, slightly surprised, before he recollected that it was half past five in the morning. 'Oh – yeah, sorry, this isn't an emergency call, I've just got off the sleeper. Wondered whether you fancied getting breakfast before you head home to bed.'

'Oh, that'd be wonderful,' said Robin, with such genuine pleasure that Strike felt a little less tired, 'because I've got Bamborough news.'

'Great,' said Strike, 'so've I. Be good to have a catch-up.'

'How's Joan?'

'Not great. They let her go home yesterday. They've assigned her a Macmillan nurse. Ted's really low. Lucy's still down there.'

'You could've stayed,' said Robin. 'We can cope.'

'It's fine,' he said, screwing his eyes up against his own smoke. A shaft of wintry sunlight burst through a break in the clouds and illuminated the fag butts on the tiled floor. 'I've told them I'll go back for Christmas. Where d'you want to meet?'

'Well, I was planning to go to the National Portrait Gallery before I went home, so—'

'You were what?' said Strike.

'Planning to go to the National Portrait Gallery. I'll explain when I see you. Would you mind if we meet somewhere near there?'

'I can get anywhere,' said Strike, 'I'm right by the Tube. I'll head that way and whoever finds a café first can text the other.'

Forty-five minutes later, Robin entered Notes

café, which lay on St Martin's Lane and was already crowded, though it was so early in the morning. Wooden tables, some of them as large as the one in her parents' kitchen in Yorkshire, were crammed with young people with laptops and businessmen grabbing breakfast before work. As she queued at the long counter, she tried to ignore the various pastries and cakes spread out beneath it: she'd taken sandwiches with her to her overnight surveillance of the weatherman's house, and those, she told herself sternly, ought to suffice.

Having ordered a cappuccino, she headed for the back of the café, where Strike sat reading *The Times* beneath an iron chandelier that resembled a large spider. She seemed to have forgotten over the previous six days how large he was. Hunched over the newspaper, he reminded her of a black bear, stubble thick on his face, tucking into a bacon and egg ciabatta roll, and Robin felt a wave of liking simply for the way he looked. Or perhaps, she thought, she was merely reacting against clean-jawed, slim and conventionally handsome men who, like tuberose perfumes, seemed attractive until prolonged exposure made you crave escape.

'Hi,' she said, sliding into the seat opposite him.

Strike looked up, and in that moment, her long shining hair and her aura of good health acted upon him like an antidote to the fug of clinical decay in which he had spent the past five days.

'You don't look knackered enough to have been up all night.'

'I'll take that as a compliment and not as an accusation,' said Robin, eyebrows raised. 'I *was* up all night and Postcard still hasn't shown herself – or himself – but another card came yesterday, addressed to the television studio. It said Postcard loved the way he smiled at the end of Tuesday's weather report.'

Strike grunted.

Robin said, 'D'you want to go first on Bamborough, or shall I?'

'You first,' said Strike, still chewing, 'I'm starving.'

'OK,' said Robin. 'Well, I've got good news and bad. The bad news is nearly everyone I've been trying to trace is dead, and the rest might as well be.'

She filled Strike in on the deceased status of Willy Lomax, Albert Shimmings, Wilma Bayliss and Dorothy Oakden, and on the steps she'd taken, so far, to contact their relatives.

'Nobody's got back in touch except one of Shimmings' sons, who seems worried that we're journalists trying to pin Margot's disappearance on his father. I've written a reassuring email back. Hope it works.'

Strike, who had paused in his steady demolition of the roll to drink half a mug of tea, said,

'I've been having similar problems. That "two women struggling by the phone boxes" sighting is going to be nigh on impossible to check. Ruby Elliot, who saw them, and the Fleury mother and daughter, who almost certainly *were* them, are all dead as well. But they've both got living descendants, so I've fired off a few messages. Only one response so far, from a Fleury grandson who doesn't know what the hell I'm talking about. And Dr Brenner doesn't seem to have a single living relative that I can see. Never married, no kids, and a dead sister who didn't marry, either.'

'D'you know how many women there are out there called Amanda White?' sighed Robin.

'I can imagine,' said Strike, taking another large bite of roll. 'That's why I gave her to you.'

'You—?'

'I'm kidding,' he said, smirking at her expression. 'What about Paul Satchwell and Gloria Conti?'

'Well, if they're dead, they didn't die in the UK. But here's something really weird: I can't find a single mention of either of them after '75.'

'Coincidence,' said Strike, raising his eyebrows. 'Douthwaite, he of the stress headaches and the dead mistress, has disappeared as well. He's either abroad, or he's changed his identity. Can't find any address for him after '76, and no death certificate, either. Mind you, if I were in his shoes, I might've changed my name, as well. His press reviews weren't good, were they? Crap at his job, sleeping with a colleague's wife, sending flowers to a woman who then disappears—'

'We don't know it was flowers,' said Robin, into her coffee cup.

Other kinds of presents are available, Strike.

'Chocolates, then. Same applies. Harder to see why Satchwell and Conti took themselves off the radar, though,' said Strike, running his hand over his unshaven chin. 'The press interest in them died away fairly fast. And you'd have found Conti online if it was a simple case of a married name. There can't be as many "Gloria Contis" as there are Amanda Whites.'

'I've been wondering whether she went to live in Italy,' said Robin. 'Her dad's first name was Ricardo. She could've had relatives there. I've sent off a few Facebook enquiries to some Contis, but the only people who've responded so far don't know a Gloria. I'm pretending I'm doing genealogical research, because I'm worried she might not respond if I mention Margot straight off.'

'Think you're probably right,' said Strike, adding more sugar to his tea. 'Yeah, Italy's a good idea. She was young, might've fancied a change of scene. Satchwell disappearing's odd, though. That photo didn't suggest a shy man. You'd think he'd have popped up somewhere by now, advertising his paintings.'

'I've checked art exhibitions, auctions, galleries. It really is as though he dematerialised.'

'Well, I've made *some* progress,' said Strike, swallowing the last mouthful of his roll and pulling out his notebook. 'You can get a surprising amount of work done, sitting around in a hospital. I've found four living witnesses, and one of them's already agreed to talk: Gregory Talbot, son of Bill who went off his rocker and drew pentagrams all over the case file. I explained who I am and who hired me, and Gregory's quite amenable to a chat. I'm going over there on Saturday, if you want to come.'

'I can't,' said Robin, disappointed. 'Morris and Andy have both got family stuff on. Barclay and I have got to cover the weekend.'

'Ah,' said Strike, 'shame. Well, I've also found two of the women who worked with Margot at the practice,' said Strike, turning a page in his notebook. 'The nurse, Janice, is still going by her first married name, which helped. The address Gupta gave me was an old one, but I traced her from there. She's now in Nightingale Grove—'

'Very appropriate,' said Robin.

'—in Hither Green. And Irene Bull's now Mrs Irene Hickson, widow of a man who ran a successful building contractor's. She's living in Circus Street, Greenwich.'

'Have you phoned them?'

'I decided to write first,' said Strike. 'Older women, both living alone – I've set out who we are and who's hired us, so they've got time to check us out, make sure we're kosher, maybe check with Anna.'

'Good thinking,' said Robin.

'And I'm going to do the same with Oonagh Kennedy, the woman waiting for Margot in the pub that night, once I'm sure I've got the right one. Anna said she was in Wolverhampton, but the woman I've found is in Alnwick. She's the right age, but she's a retired *vicar*.'

Robin grinned at Strike's expression, which was a mixture of suspicion and distaste.

'What's wrong with vicars?'

'Nothing,' he said, adding a moment later, 'much. Depends on the vicar. But Oonagh was a Bunny Girl back in the sixties. She was standing beside Margot in one of the pictures the press used, named in one of the captions. Don't you think the transition from Bunny Girl to vicar is fairly unlikely?'

'Interesting life trajectory,' Robin admitted, 'but you're speaking to a temporary secretary who became a full-time detective. And speaking of Oonagh,' she added, drawing her copy of *The Demon of Paradise Park* out of her handbag and opening it. 'I wanted to show you something. There,' she said, holding it out to him. 'Read the bit I've marked with pencil.'

'I've already read the whole book,' said Strike. 'Which bit—?'

'Please,' Robin insisted, 'just read where I've marked.'

Strike wiped his hand on a paper napkin, took the book from Robin and read the paragraphs next to which she had made a thick pencil line.

Shortly before her disappearance, Margot Bamborough booked herself into the Bride Street Nursing Home in Islington, a private facility which in 1974 provided discreet abortions.

The Bride Street Nursing Home closed its doors in 1978 and no records exist to show whether Bamborough had the procedure. However, the possibility that she allowed a friend to use her name is mooted by the author of *Whatever Happened to Margot Bamborough?*, who notes that the Irish woman and fellow Bunny Girl Bamborough was supposedly meeting in the pub that night might have had good reason for maintaining the pub story, even after Bamborough's death.

Bride Street Nursing Home lay a mere eight minutes' walk from Dennis Creed's basement flat on Liverpool Road. The possibility remains, therefore, that Margot Bamborough never intended to go to the pub that night, that she told the lie to protect herself, or another woman, and that she may have been abducted, not from a street in Clerkenwell, but a short distance from Creed's house near Paradise Park.

'What the—?' began Strike, looking thunderstruck. 'My copy hasn't got this bit. You've got an extra three paragraphs!'

'I *thought* you hadn't read it,' said Robin, sounding satisfied. 'Yours can't be a first edition. Mine is. Look here,' she said, flicking to a place at the back of the book, while Strike still held it. 'See there, the endnote? "*Whatever Happened to Margot Bamborough?* by C. B. Oakden, published 1985." Except it wasn't published,' said Robin. 'It was pulped. The author of this,' she said, tapping *The Demon of Paradise Park*, 'must've got hold of an advance copy. I've been digging,' Robin went on. 'All this happened pre-internet, obviously, but I found a couple of mentions of it online, in legal articles about suing for libel to stop publication.

'Basically, Roy Phipps and Oonagh Kennedy brought a joint action against C. B. Oakden and won. Oakden's book was pulped and there was a hasty reprint of *The Demon of Paradise Park*, without the offending passage.'

'C. B. Oakden?' repeated Strike. 'Is he—?'

'Dorothy-the-practice-secretary's son. Exactly. Full name: Carl Brice Oakden. The last address I've got for him was in Walthamstow, but he's moved and I haven't managed to track him down yet.'

Strike re-read the paragraphs relating to the abortion clinic, then said,

'Well, if Phipps and Kennedy succeeded in suing to stop publication, they must have convinced a judge that this was partly or completely false.'

'Horrible thing to lie about, isn't it?' said Robin. 'Bad enough if he was saying Margot had the abortion, but hinting that Oonagh had it, and was covering up where Margot was that night—'

'I'm surprised he got it past lawyers,' said Strike.

'Oakden's publisher was a small press,' said Robin. 'I looked them up, too. They went out of business not long after he had his book pulped. Maybe they didn't bother with lawyers.'

'More fool them,' said Strike, 'but unless they had some kind of death wish, this can't have been *entirely* invented. He must've had something to base it on. And *this* bloke,' he held up *The Demon of Paradise Park*, 'was a proper investigative journalist. He wouldn't have theorised without seeing some proof.'

'Can we check with him, or is he—?'

'Dead,' said Strike, who sat for a moment, thinking, then went on:

'The appointment must've been made in Margot's name. The question is whether she had the procedure, or whether somebody used her name without her knowing.' Strike re-read the first few lines of the passage. 'And the date of the appointment isn't given, either. "Shortly before her disappearance" . . . weasel words. If the appointment had been made for the day she disappeared, the author would say so. That'd be a major revelation and it'd have been investigated by the police. "Shortly before her disappearance" is open to wide interpretation.'

'Coincidence, though, isn't it?' said Robin. 'Her making an appointment so close to Creed's house?'

'Yeah,' said Strike, but after a moment's consideration he said, 'I don't know. Is it? How many abortion clinics were there in London in 1974?'

Handing the book back to Robin, he continued, 'This might explain why Roy Phipps was jumpy about his daughter talking to Oonagh Kennedy. He didn't want her telling his teenage daughter her mother might've aborted her sibling.'

'I thought of that, too,' said Robin. 'It'd be an awful thing to hear. Especially when she's lived most of her life wondering whether her mother ran out on her.'

'We should try and get hold of a copy of *Whatever Happened to Margot Bamborough?*' said Strike. 'There might still be copies in existence if they got as far as printing them. He could've given some away. Review copies and the like.'

'I'm already on it,' said Robin. 'I've emailed a few different second-hand book places.'

This wasn't the first time she had found herself doing something for the agency that made her feel grubby.

'Carl Oakden was only fourteen when Margot disappeared,' she continued. 'Writing a book about her, milking the connection, claiming Margot and his mother were close friends—'

'Yeah, he sounds a common-or-garden shit,' Strike agreed. 'When did he leave his address in Walthamstow?'

'Five years ago.'

'Had a look on social media?'

'Yes. Can't find him.'

Strike's mobile vibrated in his pocket. Robin thought she saw a flicker of panic in his face as he fumbled to find it, and knew that he was thinking of Joan.

'Everything all right?' she asked, watching his expression darken as he looked down at his mobile screen.

Strike had just seen:

Bruv, can we please talk this over face to face? The launch and the new album are a big deal for Dad. All we're asking—

'Yeah, fine,' he said, stuffing the phone back in his pocket, the rest of the message unread. 'So, you wanted to go to—?'

For a moment, he couldn't remember the unlikely place Robin had told him she wanted to visit, and which was the reason they were currently sitting in this particular café.

'The National Portrait Gallery,' she said. 'Three of Postcard's postcards were bought in their gift shop.'

'Three of – sorry, what?'

He was distracted by what he'd just read. He'd been quite clear with his half-brother that he had no wish either to attend the party celebrating his father's new album, or to feature in the photograph with his half-siblings which was to be their congratulatory gift to him.

'Postcard's postcards – the person who's persecuting our weatherman,' she reminded him, before mumbling, 'it doesn't matter, it was just an idea I had.'

'Which was?'

'Well, the last-but-one picture Postcard sent was of a portrait they said "always reminded" them of our weatherman. So I thought . . . maybe they see that painting a lot. Maybe they work at the gallery. Maybe they secretly want him to know that, to come looking for them?'

Even as she said it, she thought the theory sounded far-fetched, but the truth was that they had absolutely no leads on Postcard. He or she had failed to turn up at the weatherman's house since they'd been watching it. Three postcards bought in a single place might mean something, or perhaps nothing at all. What else did they have?

Strike grunted. Unsure whether this indicated a lack of enthusiasm for her theory about Postcard, Robin returned her copy of *The Demon of Paradise Park* to her handbag and said,

'Heading for the office after this?'

'Yeah. I told Barclay I'll take over watching Twinkletoes at two.' Strike yawned. 'Might try and get a couple of hours' kip first.'

He pushed himself into a standing position.

'I'll call you and let you know how I get on with Gregory Talbot. And thanks for holding the fort while I was away. Really appreciate it.'

'No problem,' said Robin.

Strike hoisted his kit bag onto his shoulder and

limped out of the café. With a slight feeling of anti-climax, Robin watched him pause outside the window to light a cigarette, then walk out of sight. Checking her watch, Robin saw that there was still an hour and a half before the National Portrait Gallery opened.

There were doubtless more pleasurable ways of whiling away that time than in wondering whether the text that Strike had just received had come from Charlotte Campbell, but that was the distraction that occurred to Robin, and it occupied her for a surprising proportion of the time she had left to kill.

CHAPTER 17

But thou . . . whom frowning froward fate
Hath made sad witnesse of thy fathers fall . . .

Edmund Spenser
The Faerie Queene

Jonny Rokeby, who'd been almost entirely absent from his eldest son's life, had nevertheless been a constant, intangible presence, especially during Strike's childhood. Parents' friends had owned his father's albums, had Rokeby's poster on their bedroom walls as teenagers and regaled Strike with their fond memories of Deadbeats' concerts. A mother at the school gate had once begged the seven-year-old Strike to take a letter from her to his father. His mother had burned it later, at the squat where they were then staying.

Until he joined the army, where, by his choice, nobody knew either his father's name or his profession, Strike regularly found himself contemplated like a specimen in a jar, bothered by questions that under normal conditions would be considered personal and intrusive, and dealing with unspoken assumptions that had their roots in envy and spite.

Rokeby had demanded Leda take a paternity test before he'd accept that Strike was his son. When the test came back positive, a financial settlement had been reached which ought to have ensured that his young son would never again have to sleep on a dirty mattress in a room shared with near-strangers. However, a combination of his mother's profligacy and her regular disputes with Rokeby's representatives had merely ensured that Strike's life became a series of confusing bouts of affluence that usually ended in abrupt descents back into chaos and squalor. Leda was prone to giving her children wildly extravagant treats, which they enjoyed while wearing too-small shoes, and to taking off on trips to the Continent or to America to see her favourite bands in concert, leaving her children with Ted and Joan while she rode around in chauffeured cars and stayed in the best hotels.

He could still remember lying in the spare room in Cornwall, Lucy asleep in the twin bed beside him, listening to his mother and Joan arguing downstairs, because the children had arrived back at their aunt and uncle's in the middle of winter, without coats. Strike had twice been enrolled in private schools, but Leda had both times pulled him out again before he'd completed more than a couple of terms, because she'd decided that her son was being taught the wrong values. Every month, Rokeby's money melted away on hand-outs to friends and boyfriends, and in reckless ventures – Strike remembered a jewellery business, an arts magazine and a vegetarian restaurant, all of which failed, not to mention the commune in Norfolk that had been the worst experience of his young life.

Finally, Rokeby's lawyers (to whom the rock star had delegated all matters concerning the well-being of his son) tied up the paternity payments in such a way that Leda could no longer fritter the money away. The only difference this made to the teenage Strike's day-to-day life had been that the treats had stopped, because Leda wasn't prepared to have her spending scrutinised in the manner demanded by the new arrangement. From that point onwards, the paternity payments had sat accumulating quietly in an account, and the family had survived on the smaller financial contributions made by Lucy's father.

Strike had only met his father twice and had unhappy memories of both encounters. For his part, Rokeby had never asked why Strike's money remained unspent. A tax exile of long standing, he had a band to front, several homes to maintain, two exes and a current wife to keep happy, five legitimate and two illegitimate children. Strike, whose conception had been an accident, whose positive paternity test had broken up Rokeby's second marriage and whose whereabouts were usually uncertain, came low on his list of priorities.

Strike's uncle had provided the model of manhood to which Strike had aspired through his mother's many changes of lover, and a childhood spent in the long shadow cast by his biological father. Leda had always blamed Ted, the ex-military policeman, for Strike's unnatural interest in the army and investigation. Speaking from the middle of a blue haze of cannabis smoke, she would earnestly attempt to dissuade her son from a career in the army, lecturing him on Britain's shameful military history, on the inextricable links between imperialism and capitalism, and trying, without success, to persuade him to learn the guitar or, at the very least, to let his hair grow.

Yet with all the disadvantages and pain they had brought, Strike knew that the peculiar circumstances of his birth and upbringing had given him a head start as an investigator. He'd learned early how to colour himself according to his environment. From the moment he learned that penalties attached to not sounding like everyone else, his accent had switched between London and Cornwall. Before the loss of a leg had hampered his full range of physical movement, he'd been able, in spite of his distinctive size, to move and talk in ways that made him appear smaller than he really was. He'd also learned the value of concealing personal information, and of editing the stories you told about yourself, to avoid becoming entangled in other people's notions of who you must be. Most importantly of all, Strike had developed a sensitive radar for the changes in behaviour that marked the sudden realisation that he was a famous man's son. He'd been wise to the ways of manipulators, flatterers, liars, chancers and hypocrites ever since he was a child.

These dubious gifts were the best his father had given him, for, apart from child support, there'd never been a birthday card or a Christmas present. It had taken his leg being blown off in Afghanistan for Rokeby to send Strike a handwritten note. Strike had asked Charlotte, who had been sitting next to his hospital bed when he received it, to put it in the bin.

Since Strike had become of interest to the newspapers in his own right, Rokeby had made further tentative attempts to reconnect with his estranged son, going so far as to suggest in recent interviews that they were on good terms. Several of Strike's friends had sent him links to a recent online interview with Rokeby in which he'd spoken of his pride in Strike. The detective had deleted the messages without a response.

Strike was grudgingly fond of Al, the half-brother whom Rokeby had recently used as an emissary. Al's dogged pursuit of a relationship with Strike had been maintained in spite of his older brother's initial resistance. Al appeared to admire in Strike those qualities of self-reliance and independence that the latter had had no choice but to develop.

Nevertheless, Al was showing an antagonising bull-headedness in continuing to push Strike into celebrating an anniversary which meant nothing to Strike, except in serving as yet another reminder of how much more important Rokeby's band had always been to him than his illegitimate son. The detective resented the time he spent on Saturday morning, crafting a response to Al's latest text message on the subject. He finally chose brevity over further argument:

Haven't changed my mind, but no hard feelings or bitterness this end. Hope all goes well & let's get a beer when you're next in town.

Having taken care of this irksome bit of personal business, Strike made himself a sandwich, put on a clean shirt over his T-shirt, extracted from the Bamborough case file the page on which Bill Talbot had written his cryptic message in Pitman shorthand, and set off by car for West Wickham, where he had an appointment with Gregory Talbot, son of the late Bill.

Driving through intermittent sun and rain, and smoking as he went, Strike refocused his mind on business, mulling not only the questions he planned to ask the policeman's son, but also the various concerns related to the agency that had arisen since his return. Certain issues that needed his personal attention had been raised by Barclay the previous day. The Scot, who Strike was inclined to rate as his best investigator after Robin, had firstly expressed himself with characteristic bluntness on the subject of the West End dancer on whom they were supposed to be finding dirt.

'We're not gonnae get anythin' on him, Strike. If he's shaggin' some other bird, she must be livin' in his fuckin' wardrobe. I ken e's wi' oor lassie for her credit card, but he's too smart tae fuck up a good thing.'

'Think you're probably right,' said Strike, 'but I said we'd give the client three months, so we keep going. How're you getting on with Pat?' he added. He was hoping that somebody else found the new secretary as much of a pain in the arse as he did, but was disappointed.

'Aye, she's great. I ken she sounds like a bronchial docker, but she's very efficient. But if we're havin' an honest talk aboot new hires, here . . .' Barclay said, his large blue eyes looking up at his boss from under thick brows.

'Go on,' said Strike. 'Morris not pulling his weight?'

'I wouldnae say that, exactly.'

The Glaswegian scratched the back of his prematurely grey head, then said,

'Robin not mentioned anything to ye?'

'Has there been trouble between them?' asked Strike, more sharply.

'Not tae say trouble, exactly,' said Barclay slowly, 'but he doesnae like takin' orders from her. Makes that plain behind her back.'

'Well, that'll have to change. I'll have a word.'

'An' he's got his own ideas aboot the Shifty case.'

'Is that right?' said Strike.

'He still thinks he's gonnae win over the PA. Robin told him it wus time tae let it go, time tae put Hutchins in. She's found oot—'

'That Shifty belongs to Hendon Rifle Club, yeah, she emailed me. And she wants to get Hutchins in there, to try and befriend him. Smart plan. Shifty fancies himself a bit of a macho man, from all we know about him.'

'But Morris wants tae do it his way. He said tae her face he was happy wi' the new plan, but—'

'You think he's still seeing the PA?'

'"Seein'" might be a polite way o' puttin' it,' said Barclay.

So Strike had called Morris into the office and laid it down in plain language that he was to leave Shifty's PA alone, and concentrate for the next week on Two-Times' girlfriend. Morris had raised no objections: indeed, his capitulation had been tinged with obsequiousness. The encounter had left a slightly unpleasant aftertaste. Morris was, in nearly all respects, a desirable hire, with many good contacts in the force, but there had been something in his manner as he hurried to agree that denoted a slipperiness Strike couldn't like. Later that night, while Strike was following the taxi containing Twinkletoes and his girlfriend through the West End, he remembered Dr Gupta's interlaced fingers, and the old doctor's verdict that what made a successful business was the smooth functioning of a team.

Entering West Wickham, he found rows of suburban houses with bay windows, broad drives and private garages. The Avenue, where Gregory Talbot lived, was lined with solid family residences that spoke of conscientious middle-class owners who mowed their lawns and remembered bin day. The houses weren't as palatial as the detached houses on Dr Gupta's street, but were many times more spacious than Strike's attic flat over the office.

Turning into Talbot's drive, Strike parked his BMW behind a skip that blocked the front of the garage. As he switched off his engine, a pale, entirely bald man with large ears and steel-rimmed glasses opened his door looking cautiously excited. Strike knew from his online research that Gregory Talbot was a hospital administrator.

'Mr Strike?' he called, while the detective was getting carefully out of the BMW (the drive was slick with rain and the memory of tripping on the Falmouth ferry, still fresh).

'That's me,' said Strike, closing his car door and holding out his hand as Talbot came walking towards him. Talbot was shorter than Strike by a good six inches.

'Sorry about the skip,' he said. 'We're doing a loft conversion.'

As they approached the front door, a pair of twin girls Strike guessed to be around ten years old came bursting outside, almost knocking Gregory aside.

'Stay in the garden, girls,' called Gregory, though Strike thought the more pressing problem was surely that they had bare feet, and that the ground was cold and wet.

'*Thtay in the garden, girlth,*' imitated one of the twins. Gregory looked mildly over the top of his glasses at the twins.

'Rudeness isn't funny.'

'It bloody is,' said the first twin, to the raucous laughter of the second.

'Swear at me again, and there'll be no chocolate pudding for you tonight, Jayda,' said Gregory. 'Nor will you borrow my iPad.'

Jayda pulled a grotesque face but did not, in fact, swear again.

'We foster,' Gregory told Strike as they stepped inside. 'Our own kids have left home. Through to the right and have a seat.'

To Strike, who lived in a slightly Spartan minimalism by choice, the cluttered and very untidy room was unappealing. He wanted to accept Gregory's invitation to sit down, but there was nowhere he could do so without having to first shift a large quantity of objects, which felt rude. Oblivious to Strike's plight, Gregory glanced through the window at the twins. They were already running back indoors, shivering.

'They learn,' he said, as the front door slammed and the twins ran upstairs. Turning back to face the room, he became aware that none of the seats were currently useable.

'Oh, yeah, sorry,' he said, though with none of the embarrassment that Strike's Aunt Joan would have displayed had a casual visitor found her house in this state of disorder. 'The girls were in here this morning.'

Gregory swiftly cleared a leaking bubble-gun, two naked Barbie dolls, a child's sock, a number of small bits of brightly coloured plastic and half a satsuma off the seat of an armchair to allow Strike to sit down. He dumped the homeless objects onto a wooden coffee table that was already piled high with magazines, a jumble of remote controls, several letters and empty envelopes and further small plastic toys, including a good deal of Lego.

'Tea?' he offered. 'Coffee? My wife's taken the boys swimming.'

'Oh, there are boys, too?'

'Hence the loft conversion,' said Gregory. 'Darren's been with us nearly five years.'

While Gregory fetched hot drinks, Strike picked up the official sticker album of this year's Champions League, which he'd spotted lying on the floor beneath the coffee table. He turned the pages with a feeling of nostalgia for the days when he, too, had collected football stickers. He was idly pondering Arsenal's chances of winning the cup when a series of crashes directly overhead, which made the pendant light sway very slightly, made him look up. It sounded as though the twins were jumping on and off their bed. Setting the sticker book down, he pondered, without finding an answer, the question of what could have motivated Talbot and his wife to bring into their home children with whom they had no biological relationship. By the time Gregory reappeared with a tray, Strike's thoughts had travelled to Charlotte, who had always declared herself entirely un-maternal, and whose premature twins she'd vowed, while pregnant, to abandon to the care of her mother-in-law.

'Would you mind shifting—?' Gregory asked, eyes on the coffee table.

Strike hastened to move handfuls of objects off it, onto the sofa.

'Cheers,' said Gregory, setting down the tray. He scooped yet another mound of objects off the second armchair, dumped them, too, onto the now considerable pile on the sofa, picked up his mug, sat down and said,

'Help yourself,' indicating a slightly sticky sugar bowl and an unopened packet of biscuits.

'Thanks very much,' said Strike, spooning sugar into his tea.

'So,' said Gregory, looking mildly excited. 'You're trying to prove Creed killed Margot Bamborough.'

'Well,' said Strike, 'I'm trying to find out what happened to her and one possibility, obviously, is Creed.'

'Did you see, in the paper last weekend? One of Creed's drawings, selling for over a grand?'

'Missed that,' said Strike.

'Yeah, it was in the *Observer*. Self-portrait in pencil, done when he was in Belmarsh. Sold on a website where you can buy serial-killer art. Crazy world.'

'It is,' agreed Strike. 'Well, as I said on the phone, what I'd really like to talk to you about is your father.'

'Yes,' said Gregory, and some of his jauntiness left him. 'I, er, I don't know how much you know.'

'That he took early retirement, following a breakdown.'

'Well, yes, that's it in a nutshell,' said Gregory. 'His thyroid was at the bottom of it. Overactive and undiagnosed, for ages. He was losing weight, not sleeping . . . There was a lot of pressure on him, you know. Not just from the force; the press, as well. People were very upset. Well, you know – a missing doctor – Mum put him acting a bit oddly down to stress.'

'In what way was he acting oddly?'

'Well, he took over the spare room and wouldn't let anyone in there,' said Gregory, and before Strike could ask for more details, he continued: 'After they found out about his thyroid and got him on the right drugs, he went back to normal, but it was too late for his career. He got his pension, but he felt guilty about the Bamborough case for years. He blamed himself, you know, thinking that if he hadn't been so ill, he might've got him.

'Because Margot Bamborough wasn't the last

265

woman Creed took – I suppose you'll know all about that? He abducted Andrea Hooton after he took Bamborough. When they arrested him and went into the house and saw what was in the basement – the torture equipment and the photos he'd taken of the women – he admitted he'd kept some of them alive for months before he killed them.

'Dad was really upset when he heard that. He kept going back over it in his head, thinking if he'd caught him earlier, Bamborough and Hooton might've still been alive. He beat himself up for getting fixated—'

Gregory cut himself off.

'—distracted, you know.'

'So, even once your father had recovered, he still thought Creed had taken Margot?'

'Oh yeah, definitely,' said Gregory, looking mildly surprised that this was in question. 'They ruled out all the other possibilities, didn't they? The ex-boyfriend, that dodgy patient who had a thing for her, they all came up clean.'

Rather than answering this with his honest view, which was that Talbot's unfortunate illness had allowed valuable months to pass in which all suspects, Creed included, had had time to hide a body, cover up evidence, refine their alibis, or all three, Strike took from an inside pocket the piece of paper on which Talbot had written his Pitman message, and held it out to Gregory.

'Wanted to ask you about something. I think that's your father's handwriting?'

'Where did you get this?' asked Gregory, taking the paper cautiously.

'From the police file. It says: "*And that is the last of them, the twelfth, and the circle will be closed upon finding the tenth*" – and then there's an unknown word – "*Baphomet. Transcribe in the true book*",' said Strike, 'and I was wondering whether that meant anything to you?'

At that moment, there came a particularly loud crash from overhead. With a hasty 'excuse me', Gregory laid the paper on top of the tea tray and hurried from the room. Strike heard him climbing the stairs, and then a telling-off. It appeared that one of the twins had overturned a chest of drawers. Soprano voices united in exculpation and counter-accusation.

Through the net curtains, Strike now saw an old Volvo pulling up outside the house. A plump middle-aged brunette in a navy raincoat got out, followed by two boys, whom he guessed to be around fourteen or fifteen. The woman went to the boot of the car and took out two sports bags and several bags of shopping from Aldi. The boys, who'd begun to slouch towards the house, had to be called back to assist her.

Gregory arrived back at the sitting-room door just as his wife entered the hall. One of the teenage boys shoved his way past Gregory to survey the stranger with the amazement appropriate to spotting an escaped zoo animal.

'Hi,' said Strike.

The boy turned in astonishment to Gregory.

'Who's he?' he asked, pointing.

The second boy appeared beside the first, eyeing Strike with precisely the same mixture of wonder and suspicion.

'This is Mr Strike,' said Gregory.

His wife now appeared between the boys, placed a hand on their shoulders and steered them bodily away, smiling at Strike as she did so.

Gregory closed the door behind him and returned to his armchair. He appeared to have momentarily forgotten what he and Strike had been talking about before he had gone upstairs, but then his eye fell upon the piece of paper scrawled all over with his father's handwriting, dotted with pentagrams and with the cryptic lines in Pitman shorthand.

'D'you know why Dad knew Pitman shorthand?' he said, with forced cheerfulness. 'My mother was learning it at secretarial college, so he learned it as well, so he could test her. He was a good husband – and a good dad, too,' he added, a little defiantly.

'Sounds it,' said Strike.

There was another pause.

'Look,' said Gregory, 'they kept the – the specifics of Dad's illness out of the press at the time. He was a good copper and it wasn't his fault he got ill. My mother's still alive. She'd be devastated if it all got out now.'

'I can appreciate—'

'Actually, I'm not sure you can,' said Gregory, flushing slightly. He seemed a polite and mild man, and it was clear that this assertive statement cost him some effort. 'The families of some of Creed's victims, afterwards – there was a lot of ill feeling towards Dad. They blamed him for not getting Creed, for screwing it all up. People wrote to the house, telling him he was a disgrace. Mum and Dad ended up moving . . . From what you said on the phone, I thought you were interested in Dad's theories, not in – not in stuff like that,' he said, gesturing at the pentagram-strewn paper.

'I'm very interested in your father's theories,' said Strike. Deciding that a little duplicity was called for, or at least a little reframing of the facts, the detective added, 'Most of what your father wrote in the case file is entirely sound. He was asking all the right questions and he'd noticed—'

'The speeding van,' said Gregory quickly.

'Exactly,' said Strike.

'Rainy night, exactly like when Vera Kenny and Gail Wrightman were abducted.'

'Right,' said Strike, nodding.

'The two women who were struggling together,' said Gregory. 'That last patient, the woman who looked like a man. I mean, you've got to admit, you add all that together—'

'This is what I'm talking about,' said Strike. 'He might've been ill, but he still knew a clue when he saw one. All I want to know is whether the shorthand means anything I should know about.'

Some of Gregory's excitement faded from his face.

'No,' he said, 'it doesn't. That's just his illness talking.'

'You know,' said Strike slowly, 'your father wasn't the only one who saw Creed as satanic. The title of the best biography of him—'

'*The Demon of Paradise Park.*'

'Exactly. Creed and Baphomet have a lot in common,' said Strike.

In the pause that followed, they heard the twins running downstairs and loudly asking their foster mother whether she'd bought chocolate mousse.

'Look – I'd love you to prove it was Creed,' said Gregory at last. 'Prove Dad was right all along. There'd be no shame in Creed being too clever for him. He was too clever for Lawson, as well; he's been too clever for everyone. I know there wasn't any sign of Margot Bamborough in Creed's basement, but he never revealed where he'd put Andrea Hooton's clothes and jewellery, either. He was varying the way he disposed of bodies at the end. He was unlucky with Hooton, chucking her off the cliffs; unlucky the body was found so quickly.'

'All true,' said Strike.

Strike drank his tea while Gregory absent-mindedly chewed off a hangnail. A full minute passed before Strike decided that further pressure was required.

'This business about transcribing in the true book—'

He knew by Gregory's slight start that he'd hit the bullseye.

'—I wondered whether your father kept separate records from the official file – and if so,' said Strike, when Gregory didn't answer, 'whether they're still in existence.'

Gregory's wandering gaze fixed itself once more on Strike.

'Yeah, all right,' he said, 'Dad thought he was looking for something supernatural. We didn't know that until near the end, until we realised how ill he was. He was sprinkling salt outside our bedroom doors every night, to keep out Baphomet. He'd made himself what Mum thought was a home office in the spare room, but he was keeping the door locked.

'The night he was sectioned,' said Gregory, looking miserable, 'he came running out of it, ah, shouting. He woke us all up. My brother and I came out onto the landing. Dad had left the door to the spare room open, and we saw pentagrams all over the walls and lit candles. He'd taken up the carpet and made a magic circle on the floor to perform some kind of ritual, and he claimed . . . well, he thought he'd conjured some kind of demonic creature . . .

'Mum called 999 and an ambulance came and . . . well, you know the rest.'

'Must've been very distressing for all of you,' said Strike.

'Well, yeah. It was. While Dad was in hospital,

Mum cleaned out the room, took away his tarot cards and all the occult books, and painted over the pentagrams and the magic circle. It was all the more upsetting for her, because both had been committed churchgoers before Dad had his breakdown . . .'

'He was clearly very ill,' said Strike, 'which wasn't his fault, but he was still a detective and he still had sound copper sense. I can see it in the official record. If there's another set of records anywhere, especially if it contains stuff that isn't in the official file, it's an important document.'

Gregory chewed his nail again, looking tense. Finally, he seemed to reach a decision:

'Ever since we spoke on the phone, I've been thinking that maybe I should give you this,' he said, standing up and heading over to an overflowing bookcase in the corner. From the top, he took a large leather-bound notebook of old-fashioned type, which had a cord wrapped around it.

'This was the only thing that didn't get thrown away,' said Gregory, looking down at the note-book, 'because Dad wouldn't let go of it when the ambulance arrived. He said he had to record what the, ah, spirit had looked like, the thing he'd conjured . . . so the notebook got taken to hospital with him. They let him draw the demon, which helped the doctors understand what had been going on in his head, because at first he didn't want to talk to them. I found all this out after-wards; they protected me and my brother from it

272

while it was going on. After Dad got well, he kept the notebook, because he said if anything was a reminder to take his medicine, this was it. But I wanted to meet you before I made a decision.'

Resisting the urge to hold out his hand, Strike sat trying to look as sympathetic as his naturally surly features would allow. Robin was far better at conveying warmth and empathy; he'd watched her persuading recalcitrant witnesses many times since they'd gone into business together.

'You understand,' said Gregory, still clutching the notebook, and evidently determined to hammer the point home, 'he'd had a complete mental breakdown.'

'Of course,' said Strike. 'Who else have you shown that to?'

'Nobody,' said Gregory. 'It's been up in our attic for the last ten years. We had a couple of boxes of stuff from Mum and Dad's old house up there. Funny, you turning up just as the loft was being mucked out . . . maybe this is all Dad's doing? Maybe he's trying to tell me it's OK to pass this over?'

Strike made an ambiguous noise designed to convey agreement that the Talbots' decision to clear out their loft had been somehow prompted by Gregory's dead father, rather than the need to accommodate two extra children.

'Take it,' said Gregory abruptly, holding out the old notebook. Strike thought he looked relieved to see it pass into someone else's possession.

'I appreciate your trust. If I find anything in here I think you can help with, would it be all right to contact you again?'

'Yeah, of course,' said Gregory. 'You've got my email address . . . I'll give you my mobile number . . .'

Five minutes later, Strike was standing in the hall, shaking hands with Mrs Talbot as he prepared to return to his office.

'Lovely to meet you,' she said. 'I'm glad he's given you that thing. You never know, do you?'

And with the notebook in his hand, Strike agreed that you never did.

CHAPTER 18

So the fayre Britomart hauing disclo'ste
Her clowdy care into a wrathfull stowre,
The mist of griefe dissolu'd . . .

Edmund Spenser
The Faerie Queene

Robin, who'd recently given up many week-ends to cover the agency's workload, took the following Tuesday and Wednesday off at Strike's insistence. Her suggestion that she come into the office to look at the notebook Gregory Talbot had given Strike, and to go system-atically through the last box of the police file, which neither of them had yet had time to examine, had been sternly vetoed by the senior partner. Strike knew there was no time left this year for Robin to take all the leave she was owed, but he was determined that she should take as much as she could.

However, if Strike imagined that Robin derived much pleasure from her days off, he was wrong.

She spent Tuesday dealing with mundanities such as laundry and food shopping, and on Wednesday morning, set off for a twice-postponed appointment with her solicitor.

When she'd broken the news to her parents that she and Matthew were to divorce a little over a year after they'd married, her mother and father had wanted her to use a solicitor in Harrogate, who was an old family friend.

'I live in London. Why would I use a law firm in Yorkshire?'

Robin had chosen a lawyer in her late forties called Judith, whose dry humour, spiky grey hair and thick black-rimmed glasses had endeared her to Robin when first they met. Robin's feeling of warmth had abated somewhat over the ensuing twelve months. It was hard to maintain fondness for the person whose job it was to pass on the latest intransigent and aggressive communications from Matthew's lawyer. As the months rolled past, Robin noticed that Judith occasionally forgot or misremembered information pertinent to the divorce. Robin, who always took care to give her own clients the impression that their concerns were uppermost in her mind at all times, couldn't help wondering whether Judith would have been more meticulous if Robin had been richer.

Like Robin's parents, Judith had initially assumed that this divorce would be quick and easy, a matter of two signatures and a handshake. The couple had been married a little over a year and there were no children, not even a pet to argue over. Robin's parents had gone so far as to imagine that Matthew, whom they'd known since he was a child, must feel such shame at his infidelity that he'd want to compensate Robin by being generous and reasonable over the divorce. Her mother's growing fury towards her ex-son-in-law was starting to make Robin dread her phone calls home.

The offices of Stirling and Cobbs were a twenty-minute walk away from Robin's flat, on North End Road. Zipping herself into a warm coat, umbrella in hand, Robin chose to walk that morning purely for the exercise, because she'd spent so many long hours in her car of late, sitting outside the weatherman's house, waiting for Postcard. Indeed, the last time she'd walked for a whole hour had been inside the National Portrait Gallery, a trip that had been fruitless, except for one tiny incident that Robin had discounted, because Strike had taught her to mistrust the hunches so romanticised by the non-investigative public, which, he said, were more often than not born of personal biases or wishful thinking.

Tired, dispirited and knowing full well that nothing she was about to hear from Judith was likely to cheer her up, Robin was passing a bookie's when her mobile rang. Extracting it from her pocket took a little longer than usual, because she was wearing gloves, and she consequently sounded a little panicky when she finally managed to answer the unknown number.

'Yes, hello? Robin Ellacott speaking.'

'Oh, hi. This is Eden Richards.'

For a moment, Robin couldn't for the life of her think who Eden Richards was. The woman on the end of the line seemed to divine her dilemma, because she continued,

'Wilma Bayliss's daughter. You sent me and my brothers and sisters messages. You wanted to talk to us about Margot Bamborough.'

'Oh, yes, of course, thank you for calling me back!' said Robin, backing into the bookie's doorway, her finger in the ear not pressed against the phone, to block out the sound of traffic. Eden, she now remembered, was the oldest of Wilma's offspring, a Labour councillor from Lewisham.

'Yeah,' said Eden Richards, 'well, I'm afraid we don't want to talk to you. And I'm speaking for all of us here, OK?'

'I'm sorry to hear that,' said Robin, watching abstractedly as a passing Doberman Pinscher squatted and defecated on the pavement while its scowling owner waited, a plastic bag hanging from his hand. 'Can I ask why—?'

'We just don't want to,' said Eden. 'OK?'

'OK,' said Robin, 'but to be clear, all we're doing is checking statements that were made around the time Margot—'

'We can't speak for our mother,' said Eden. 'She's dead. We feel sorry for Margot's daughter, but we don't want to drag up stuff that – it's something we don't particularly want to relive, any of our

278

family. We were young when she disappeared. It was a bad time for us. So the answer's no, OK?'

'I understand,' said Robin, 'but I wish you'd reconsider. We aren't asking you to talk about anything pers—'

'You are, though,' said Eden. 'Yeah, you are. And we don't want to, OK? You aren't police. And by the way: my youngest sister's going through chemotherapy, so leave her alone, please. She doesn't need the grief. I'm going to go now. The answer's no, OK? Don't contact any of us again, please.'

And the line went dead.

'Shit,' said Robin out loud.

The owner of the Doberman Pinscher, who was now scooping a sizeable pile of that very substance off the pavement, said,

'You and me both, love.'

Robin forced a smile, stuffed her mobile back into her pocket and walked on. Shortly afterwards, still wondering whether she could have handled the call with Eden better, Robin pushed open the glass door of Stirling and Cobbs, Solicitors.

'*Well*,' said Judith five minutes later, once Robin was sitting opposite her in the tiny office full of filing cabinets. The monosyllable was followed by silence as Judith glanced over the documents in the file in front of her, clearly reminding herself of the facts of the case while Robin sat watching. Robin would much rather have sat for another five minutes in the waiting room than witness this casual and hasty revision of what was causing her so much stress and pain.

'Umm,' said Judith, 'yes . . . just checking that . . . yes, we had a response to ours on the fourteenth, as I said in my email, so you'll be aware that Mr Cunliffe isn't prepared to shift his position on the joint account.'

'Yes,' said Robin.

'So, I really think it's time to go to mediation,' said Judith Cobbs.

'And as I said in my reply to your email,' said Robin, wondering whether Judith had read it, 'I can't see mediation working.'

'Which is why I wanted to speak to you face to face,' said Judith, smiling. 'We often find that when the two parties have to sit down in the same room, and answer for themselves, especially with impartial witnesses present – I'd be with you, obviously – they become far less intransigent than they are by letter.'

'You said yourself,' Robin replied (blood was thumping in her ears: the sensation of not being heard was becoming increasingly common during these interactions), 'the last time we met – you agreed that Matthew seems to be trying to force this into court. He isn't really interested in the joint account. He can outspend me ten times over. He just wants to beat me. He wants a judge to agree that I married him for his bank account. He'll think it money well spent if he can point to some ruling that says the divorce was all my fault.'

'It's easy,' said Judith, still smiling, 'to attribute the worst possible motives to ex-partners, but he's clearly an intelligent—'

'Intelligent people can be as spiteful as anyone else.'

'True,' said Judith, still with an air of humouring Robin, 'but refusing to even *try* mediation is a bad move for both of you. No judge will look kindly on anyone who refuses to at least *try* and settle matters without recourse to the courts.'

The truth, as perhaps Judith and Robin both equally knew, was that Robin dreaded having to sit face to face with Matthew and the lawyer who had authored all those cold, threatening letters.

'I've *told* him I don't want the inheritance he got from his mother,' said Robin. 'All I want back out of that joint account is the money *my* parents put into our first property.'

'Yes,' said Judith, with a hint of boredom: Robin knew that she'd said exactly this, every time they'd met each other. 'But as you're aware, *his* position—'

'Is that I contributed virtually nothing to our finances, so he ought to keep the whole lot, because he went into the marriage out of love and I'm some kind of gold-digger.'

'This is obviously upsetting you,' said Judith, no longer smiling.

'We were together ten years,' said Robin, trying, with little success, to remain calm. 'When he was a student and I was working, I paid for everything. Should I have kept the receipts?'

'We can certainly make that point in mediation—'

'That'll just infuriate him,' said Robin.

She raised a hand to her face purely for the purpose of hiding it. She felt suddenly and perilously close to tears.

'OK, fine. We can try mediation.'

'I think that's the sensible thing to do,' said Judith Cobbs, smiling again. 'So, I'll contact Brophy, Shenston and—'

'I suppose I'll get a chance to tell Matthew he's a total shit, at least,' said Robin, on a sudden wave of fury.

Judith gave a small laugh.

'Oh, I wouldn't advise *that*,' she said.

Oh, wouldn't you really? thought Robin, as she hitched on another fake smile, and got up to leave.

A blustery, damp wind was blowing when she left the solicitor's. Robin trudged back towards Finborough Road, until finally, her face numb, her hair whipping into her eyes, she turned into a small café where, in defiance of her own healthy eating rules, she bought a large latte and a chocolate brownie. She sat and stared out at the rainswept street, enjoying the comfort of cake and coffee, until her mobile rang again.

It was Strike.

'Hi,' she said, through a mouthful of brownie. 'Sorry. Eating.'

'Wish I was,' he said. 'I'm outside the bloody theatre again. I think Barclay's right: we're not going to get anything on Twinkletoes. I've got Bamborough news.'

'So've I,' said Robin, who had managed to swallow the mouthful of brownie, 'but it isn't good news. Wilma Bayliss's children don't want to talk to us.'

'The cleaner's kids? Why not?'

'Wilma wasn't a cleaner by the time she died,' Robin reminded him. 'She was a social worker.'

Even as she said it, Robin wondered why she felt the need to correct him. Perhaps it was simply that if Wilma Bayliss was to be forever referred to as a cleaner, she, Robin, might as well be forever called 'the temp'.

'All right, why don't the *social worker's* kids want to talk to us?' asked Strike.

'The one who called me – Eden, she's the eldest – said they didn't want to drag up what had been a difficult time for the family. She said it had nothing to do with Margot – but then she contradicted herself, because when I said we only wanted to talk about Margot – I can't remember her exact words, but the sense was that talking about Margot's disappearance would involve them talking about the family's personal stuff.'

'Well, their father was in jail in the early seventies and Margot was urging Wilma to leave him,' said Strike. 'It's probably that. Think it's worth calling her back? Trying a bit more persuasion?'

'I don't think she's going to change her mind.'

'And she said she was speaking for her brothers and sisters, as well?'

'Yes. One of them's having chemotherapy. She warned me specifically away from her.'

'OK, avoid her, but one of the others might be worth a shot.'

'That'll annoy Eden.'

'Probably, but we've got nothing to lose now, have we?'

'S'pose not,' said Robin. 'So what's *your* news?'

'The practice nurse and the receptionist, the one who isn't Gloria Conti—'

'Irene Bull,' said Robin.

'Irene Bull, now Hickson, exactly – they're both happy to talk to us. Turns out they've been friends since the St John's practice days. Irene will be delighted to host Janice and us at her house on Saturday afternoon. I think we should both go.'

Robin turned her mobile to speakerphone so that she could check the rota she kept on her phone. The entry for Saturday read: *Strike's birthday/TT girlfriend.*

'I'm supposed to be following Two-Times' girl-friend,' said Robin, switching back from speakerphone.

'Sod that, Morris can do it,' said Strike. 'You can drive us – if you don't mind,' he added, and Robin smiled.

'No, I don't mind,' she said.

'Well, great,' said Strike. 'Enjoy the rest of your day off.'

He rang off. Robin picked up the rest of the brownie and finished it slowly, savouring every bite. In spite of the prospect of mediation with Matthew, and doubtless because of a much-needed infusion of chocolate, she felt a good deal happier than she had ten minutes previously.

CHAPTER 19

There did I finde mine onely faithfull frend
In heauy plight and sad perplexitie;
Whereof I sorie, yet my selfe did bend,
Him to recomfort with my companie.

Edmund Spenser
The Faerie Queene

Strike never told anyone that his birthday was imminent and avoided announcing it on the day itself. It wasn't that he didn't appreciate people remembering: indeed, he tended to be far more touched when they did than he ever let show, but he had an innate dislike of scheduled celebration and forced jollity, and of all inane practices, having 'Happy Birthday' sung to him was one of his least favourites.

As far back as he could remember, the day of his birth had brought up unhappy memories on which he chose, usually successfully, not to dwell. His mother had sometimes forgotten to buy him anything when he was a child. His biological father had never acknowledged the date. Birthdays were inextricably linked with the knowledge, which had long since become part of him, that his existence was accidental, that his genetic inheritance had been contested in court, and that the birth itself had been 'fucking hideous, darling, if men had to do it the human race would be extinct in a year'.

To his sister, Lucy, it would have been almost cruel to let a loved one's birthday pass without a card, a gift, a phone call or, if she could manage it, a party or at the very least a meal. This was why he usually lied to Lucy, pretending to have plans so as to avoid having to go all the way out to her house in Bromley and participate in a family dinner that she'd enjoy far more than he would. Not long ago, he'd happily have celebrated with a takeaway at his friends Nick and Ilsa's, but Ilsa had suggested Robin accompany Strike, and as Strike had decided many weeks ago that Ilsa's increasingly open attempts at matchmaking could only be successfully countered by a blanket refusal to cooperate, he'd pretended that he was going to Lucy's instead. The one joyless hope Strike had for his thirty-ninth birthday was that Robin would have forgotten it, because, if she did, his own omission would be cancelled out: they'd be quits.

He descended the metal stairs to the office on Friday morning and saw, to his surprise, two packages and four envelopes sitting beside the usual pile of mail on Pat's desk. The envelopes were all of different colours. Apparently, friends and family had decided to make sure birthday greetings reached him in time for the weekend.

'Is it your birthday?' Pat asked in her deep, gravelly voice, still staring at her monitor and typing, electronic cigarette jammed between her teeth as usual.

'Tomorrow,' said Strike, picking up the cards. He recognised the handwriting on three of them, but not the fourth.

'Many happy returns,' grunted Pat, over the clacking of her keyboard. 'You should've said.'

Some spirit of mischief prompted Strike to ask, 'Why? Would you've baked me a cake?'

'No,' said Pat indifferently. 'Might've got you a card, though.'

'Lucky I didn't say, then. One fewer tree's died.'

'It wouldn't have been a *big* card,' said Pat, unsmiling, her fingers still flying over the keyboard.

Grinning slightly, Strike removed himself, his cards and packages into the inner office, and later that evening took them upstairs with him, still unopened.

He woke on the twenty-third with his mind full of his trip to Greenwich with Robin later, and only remembered the significance of the day when he saw the presents and cards on the table. The packages contained a sweater from Ted and Joan, and a sweatshirt from Lucy. Ilsa, Dave Polworth and his half-brother Al had all sent joke cards which, while not actually making him laugh, were vaguely cheering.

He slipped the fourth card out of its envelope. It had a photograph of a bloodhound on the front, and Strike considered this for a second or two, wondering why it had been chosen. He'd never owned a dog, and while he had a mild preference for dogs over cats, having worked alongside a few in the military, he wouldn't have said dog-loving was one of his salient characteristics. Flicking the card open, he saw the words:

> Happy birthday Cormoran,
> Best,
> Jonny (Dad)

For a few moments, Strike merely looked at the words, his mind as blank as the rest of the card. The last time he'd seen his father's writing, he'd been full of morphine after his leg had been blown off. As a child, he'd occasionally caught a glimpse of his father's signature on legal documents sent to his mother. Then, he'd stared awestruck at the name, as though he were glimpsing an actual part of his father, as though the ink were blood, and solid proof that his father was a real human being, not a myth.

Quite suddenly, and with a force that shocked Strike, he found himself full of rage, rage on behalf of the small boy who would once have sold his soul to receive a birthday card from his father. He'd grown well beyond any desire to have contact with Jonny Rokeby, but he could still recall the acute pain his father's continual and implacable absence had so often caused him as a child: while the primary class was making Father's Day cards, for instance, or when strange adults questioned him about why he never saw Rokeby, or other children jeered at him, singing Deadbeats songs or telling him his mother had got pregnant with him purely to get Rokeby's money. He remembered the longing that was almost an ache, always most acute around birthdays and Christmas, for his father to send something, or phone: anything, to show that he knew Strike was alive. Strike hated the memory of these fantasies more than he hated remembering the pain caused by their eternal unfulfillment, but most of all he hated remembering the hopeful lies he'd told himself when, as a very young boy, he'd made excuses for his father, who probably didn't know that the family had moved yet again, who'd sent things to the wrong address, who wanted to know him but simply couldn't find him.

Where had Rokeby been when his son was a no-body? Where had Rokeby been every time Leda's life came off the rails, and Ted and Joan rode, again, to the rescue? Where had he been on any of the thousands of occasions when his presence might have meant something real, and genuine, rather than an attempt to look good to the papers?

Rokeby knew literally nothing about his son except that he was a detective, and *that* explained the fucking bloodhound. *Fuck you and fuck your fucking card.* Strike tore the card in half, then into quarters, and threw the pieces into the bin. But for a disinclination to trigger the fire alarm, he might have put a match to them.

Anger pulsed like a current through Strike all morning. He hated his own rage, as it showed that Rokeby still had some emotional hold on him, and by the time he set out for Earl's Court, where Robin was picking him up, he was not far off wishing that birthdays had never been invented.

Sitting in the Land Rover just outside the station entrance some forty-five minutes later, Robin watched Strike emerge onto the pavement, carrying a leather-bound notebook, and noted that he looked as grumpy as she'd ever seen him.

'Happy birthday,' she said, when he opened the passenger door. Strike immediately noticed the card and the small wrapped package lying on the dashboard.

Fuck.

'Cheers,' and climbed in beside her, looking even grumpier.

As Robin pulled out onto the road, she said,

'Is it turning thirty-nine that's upset you, or has something else happened?'

Having no desire to talk about Rokeby, Strike decided an effort was required.

'No, I'm just knackered. I was up late last night, going through the last box of the Bamborough file.'

'I wanted to do that on Tuesday, but you wouldn't let me!'

'You were owed time off,' said Strike shortly, tearing open the envelope of her card. 'You're *still* owed time off.'

'I know, but it would've been a lot more interesting than doing my ironing.'

Strike looked down at the front of Robin's card, which featured a watercolour picture of St Mawes. She must, he thought, have gone to some trouble to find it in London. 'Nice,' he said, 'thanks.'

Flipping it open, he read,

Many happy returns, love Robin x

She'd never put a kiss on any message to him before, and he liked it being there. Feeling slightly more cheerful, he unwrapped the small package that accompanied the card, and found inside a pair of replacement headphones of the kind Luke had broken while he'd been in St Mawes over the summer.

'Ah, Robin, that's – thanks. That's great. I hadn't replaced them, either.'

'I know,' said Robin, 'I noticed.'

As Strike put her card back in its envelope, he reminded himself that he really did need to get her a decent Christmas present.

'Is that Bill Talbot's secret notebook?' Robin asked, glancing sideways at the leather-bound book in Strike's lap.

'The very same. I'll show you after we've talked

to Irene and Janice. Batshit crazy. Full of bizarre drawings and symbols.'

'What about the last box of police records? Anything interesting?' Robin asked.

'Yes, as it goes. A chunk of police notes from 1975 had got mixed in with a bunch of later stuff. There were a few interesting bits.

'For instance, the practice cleaner, Wilma, was sacked a couple of months after Margot disappeared, but for petty theft, not drinking, which is what Gupta told me. Small amounts of money disappearing out of people's purses and pockets. I also found out a call was made to Margot's marital home on Anna's second birthday, from a woman claiming to be Margot.'

'Oh my God, that's horrible,' said Robin. 'A prank call?'

'Police thought so. They traced it to a phone box in Marylebone. Cynthia, the childminder-turned-second-wife, answered. The woman identified herself as Margot and told Cynthia to look after her daughter.'

'Did Cynthia think it was Margot?'

'She told police she was too shocked to really take in what the caller said. She thought it sounded a bit like her, but on balance it sounded more like someone imitating her.'

'What makes people do things like that?' Robin asked, in genuine perplexity.

'They're shits,' said Strike. 'There were also a bunch of alleged sightings of Margot after the day

293

she disappeared, in the last box. They were all disproven, but I've made a list and I'll email them to you. Mind if I smoke?'

'Carry on,' said Robin, and Strike wound down the window. 'I actually emailed *you* a tiny bit of information last night, too. *Very* tiny. Remember Albert Shimmings, the local florist—'

'—whose van people thought they saw speeding away from Clerkenwell Green? Yeah. Did he leave a note confessing to murder?'

'Unfortunately not, but I've spoken to his eldest son, who says that his dad's van *definitely* wasn't in Clerkenwell at half past six that evening. It was waiting outside his clarinet teacher's house in Camden, where his dad drove him every Friday. He says they told the police that at the time. His dad used to wait outside for him in the van and read spy novels.'

'Well, the clarinet lessons aren't in the records, but both Talbot and Lawson believed Shimmings when they spoke to him. Good to have it confirmed, though,' he added, lest Robin think he was being dismissive of her routine work. 'Well, that means there's still a possibility the van was Dennis Creed's, doesn't it?'

Strike lit up a Benson & Hedges, exhaled out of the window, and said,

'There was some interesting material on these two women we're about to meet, in that last box of notes. More stuff that came out when Lawson took over.'

'Really? I thought Irene had a dental appointment and Janice had house visits on the afternoon Margot disappeared?'

'Yeah, that's what their original statements said,' said Strike, 'and Talbot didn't check either woman's story. Took both at their word.'

'Presumably because he didn't think a woman could be the Essex Butcher?'

'Exactly.'

Strike pulled his own notebook out of his coat pocket and opened it to the pages he'd scribbled on Tuesday.

'Irene's first statement, which she gave to Talbot, said she'd had a grumbling toothache for a few days before Margot disappeared. Her friend Janice the nurse thought it might be an abscess, so Irene made an emergency appointment for three o'clock, leaving the practice at two-thirty. She and Janice were planning to go to the cinema that evening, but Irene's face was sore and swollen after having a tooth removed, so when Janice phoned her to see how the dentist's had gone, and to check whether she still wanted to go out that night, she said she'd rather stay at home.'

'No mobile phones,' mused Robin. 'Different world.'

'Exactly what I thought when I was going over this,' said Strike. 'These days Irene's mates would've expected a minute-by-minute commentary. Selfies from the dental chair.

'Talbot gave his officers to understand that he'd

personally contacted the dentist to check this story, but he hadn't. Wouldn't put it past him to have consulted a crystal ball.'

'Ha ha.'

'I'm not kidding. Wait till you see his notebook.'

Strike turned a page.

'Anyway, six months later, Lawson takes over the case and goes systematically back through every single witness and suspect in the file. Irene told the dentist story again, but half an hour after she left him, she panicked and asked to see him again. This time she admitted she'd lied.

'There'd never been any tooth pain. She hadn't visited the dentist. She said she'd been forced to do a lot of unpaid overtime at the surgery and resented it, and felt she was owed an afternoon off, so she faked toothache, pretended to have got an emergency appointment, then left the practice and went to the West End to do some shopping.

'She told Lawson that it was only when she got home – she was still living with her parents, incidentally – that it occurred to her that if she went out to meet Janice the nurse that evening, Janice might ask to see the place where the tooth had been extracted, or at least expect to see some swelling. So when Janice rang her to check they were still going to the cinema, she lied and said she didn't feel up to it.

'Lawson gave Irene quite a hard time, judging from his notes. Didn't she understand what a serious matter it was, lying to the police, people had been arrested for less, et cetera. He also put it to her that the new story showed she had no alibi for any point of the afternoon and evening, other than around half past six in the evening, when Janice rang her at home.'

'Where did Irene live?'

'Street called Corporation Row, which as it happens lies very close to the Three Kings, although not on the route Margot would have taken from the practice.

'Anyway, at the point alibis were mentioned, Irene became hysterical. She poured out a load of stuff about Margot having a lot of enemies, without being able to say who these enemies were, although she referred Lawson back to the anonymous letters Margot received.

'The next day, Irene went back to Lawson yet again, this time accompanied by her very angry father, who did her no favours by losing his temper at Lawson for daring to upset his daughter. In the course of this third interview, Irene presented Lawson with a receipt from Oxford Street, which was marked 3.10 p.m. on the day Margot disappeared. The receipt was for cash. Lawson probably took a lot of pleasure in telling Irene and her dad that all the receipt proved was that *somebody* had gone shopping on Oxford Street that day.'

'Still – a receipt for the right day, right time—'

'Could've been her mother's. A friend's.'

'Why would they have kept it for six months?'

'Why would she?'

Robin considered the matter. She regularly kept receipts, but these were matters of expenses while doing surveillance, to be presented to the accountant.

'Yeah, maybe it is odd she still had it,' she conceded.

'But Lawson never managed to get anything further out of her. I don't think he genuinely suspected her, mind you. I get the impression he just didn't like her. He pressed her very hard on the anonymous notes she claimed to have seen, the ones mentioning hellfire. I don't think he believed in them.'

'I thought the other receptionist confirmed she'd seen one?'

'She did. Nothing to say they weren't in cahoots, though. No trace of the notes was ever found.'

'But that'd be a serious lie,' said Robin. 'With the fake dental appointment, I can see why she fibbed and why she'd have been frightened to admit it afterwards. Lying about anonymous notes in the context of a missing person, though . . .'

'Ah, but don't forget, Irene was already telling the story of the anonymous notes before Margot went missing. It's more of the same, isn't it? The two receptionists could've invented these threatening notes for the pleasure of starting a malicious rumour, then found it impossible to back away from the lie after Margot disappeared.

'Anyway,' said Strike, flicking over a couple of pages, 'so much for Irene. Now for her best buddy, the practice nurse.

'Janice's original statement was that she drove around all afternoon, making house calls. The last visit, which was to an old lady with multiple health issues, kept her longer than she expected. She left there around six and hurried straight to a call box to ring Irene at home, to see whether they were still on for the cinema that evening. Irene said she didn't feel up to it, but Janice had already got herself a babysitter, and was desperate to see the movie – James Caan, *The Gambler* – so she went anyway. Watched the movie alone, then went back to the neighbour's, picked up her son and went home.

'Talbot didn't bother to check any of this, but a zealous junior officer did, on his own initiative, and it all checked out. All the patients confirmed that Janice had been at their houses at the right times. The babysitter confirmed that Janice returned to pick up her son when expected. Janice also produced a half-torn ticket for the movie out of the bottom of her handbag. Given that this was less than a week after Margot disappeared, it doesn't seem particularly fishy, her still having it. On the other hand, a torn ticket is no more proof that she sat through the movie than the receipt is proof Irene went shopping.'

He threw his cigarette end out of the window.

'Where did Janice's last patient of the day live?'

asked Robin, and Strike knew that her mind was running on distances and timings.

'Gopsall Street, which is about a ten-minute drive from the practice. It would've been *just* possible for a woman in a car to have intercepted Margot on the way to the Three Kings, assuming Margot was walking very slowly, or was delayed somewhere along the route, or left the practice later than Gloria said she did. But it would've required luck, because as we know, some of the path Margot would've taken was pedestrianised.'

'And I can't really see why you'd make arrangements with a friend to go to the cinema if you were planning to abduct someone,' said Robin.

'Nor can I,' said Strike. 'But I'm not finished. When Lawson takes over the case he finds out that Janice lied to Talbot as well.'

'You're kidding.'

'Nope. Turned out she didn't actually have a car. Six weeks before Margot disappeared, Janice's ancient Morris Minor gave up the ghost and she sold it for scrap. From that time onwards, she was making all her house calls by public transport and on foot. She hadn't wanted to tell anyone at the practice that she was carless, in case they told her she couldn't do her job. Her husband had walked out, leaving her with a kid. She was saving up to get a new car, but she knew it was going to take a while, so she pretended the Morris Minor was in the garage, or that it was easier to get the bus, if anyone asked.'

'But if that's true—'

'It is. Lawson checked it all out, questioned the scrap yard and everything.'

'—then that surely puts her completely out of the frame for an abduction.'

'I'm inclined to agree,' said Strike. 'She could've got a cab, of course, but the cabbie would've had to be in on the abduction, too. No, the interesting thing about Janice is that in spite of believing she was entirely innocent, Talbot interviewed her a total of seven times, more than any other witness or suspect.'

'*Seven times?*'

'Yep. He had a kind of excuse at first. She was a neighbour of Steve Douthwaite's, Margot's acutely stressed patient. Interviews two and three were all about Douthwaite, who Janice knew to say hello to. Douthwaite was Talbot's preferred candidate for the Essex Butcher, so you can follow his thought processes – you *would* question neighbours if you thought someone might be butchering women at home. But Janice wasn't able to tell Talbot anything about Douthwaite beyond what we already know, and Talbot still kept going back to her. After the third interview, he stopped asking her about Douthwaite and things got very strange indeed. Among other things, Talbot asked whether she'd ever been hypnotised, whether she'd be prepared to try it, asked her all about her dreams and urged her to keep a diary of them so he could read it, and also to make him a list of her most recent sexual partners.'

'He did *what*?'

'There's a copy of a letter from the Commissioner in the file,' said Strike drily, 'apologising to Janice for Talbot's behaviour. All in all, you can see why they wanted him off the force as fast as possible.'

'Did his son tell you any of that?'

Strike remembered Gregory's earnest, mild face, his assertion that Bill had been a good father and his embarrassment as the conversation turned to pentagrams.

'I doubt he knew about it. Janice doesn't seem to have made a fuss.'

'Well,' said Robin, slowly. 'She *was* a nurse. Maybe she could tell he was ill?'

She considered the matter for a few moments, then said,

'It'd be frightening, though, wouldn't it? Having the investigating officer coming back to your house every five minutes, asking you to keep a dream diary?'

'It'd put the wind up most people. I'm assuming the explanation is the obvious one – but we should ask her about it.'

Strike glanced into the back and saw, as he'd hoped, a bag of food.

'Well, it is your birthday,' said Robin, her eyes still on the road.

'Fancy a biscuit?'

'Bit early for me. You carry on.'

As he leaned back to fetch the bag, Strike noticed that Robin smelled again of her old perfume.

CHAPTER 20

And if that any ill she heard of any,
She would it eeke, and make much worse by
telling,
And take great ioy to publish it to many,
That euery matter worse was for her melling.

Edmund Spenser
The Faerie Queene

Irene Hickson's house lay in a short, curving Georgian terrace of yellow brick, with arched windows and fanlights over each black front door. It reminded Robin of the street where she'd spent the last few months of her married life, in a rented house that had been built for a sea merchant. Here, too, were traces of London's trading past. The lettering over an arched window read *Royal Circus Tea Warehouse*.

'Mr Hickson must've made good money,' said Strike, looking up at the beautifully proportioned frontage as he and Robin crossed the street. 'This is a long way from Corporation Row.'

Robin rang the doorbell. They heard a shout of 'Don't worry, I'll get it!' and a few seconds later, a short, silver-haired woman opened the door to them. Dressed in a navy sweater, and trousers of the kind that Robin's mother would have called 'slacks', she had a round pink and white face. Blue eyes peeked out from beneath a blunt fringe that Robin suspected she might have cut herself.

'Mrs Hickson?' asked Robin.

'Janice Beattie,' said the older woman. 'You're Robin, are you? An' you're—'

The retired nurse's eyes swept down over Strike's legs in what looked like professional appraisal.

'—Corm'ran, is that 'ow you say it?' she asked, looking back up into his face.

'That's right,' said Strike. 'Very good of you to see us, Mrs Beattie.'

'Oh, no trouble at all,' she said, backing away to let them in. 'Irene'll be wiv us in a mo.'

The naturally upturned corners of the nurse's mouth and the dimples in her full cheeks gave her a cheerful look even when she wasn't smiling. She led them through a hall that Strike found oppressively over-decorated. Everything was dusky pink: the flowered wallpaper, the thick carpet, the dish of pot-pourri that sat on the telephone table. The distant sound of a flush told them exactly where Irene was.

The sitting room was decorated in olive green, and everything that could be swagged, flounced, fringed or padded had been. Family photographs in silver frames were crowded on side tables, the largest of which showed a heavily tanned forty-something blonde who was cheek to cheek over fruit-and-umbrella-laden cocktails with a florid gentlemen who Robin assumed was the late Mr Hickson. He looked quite a lot older than his wife. A large collection of porcelain figurines stood upon purpose-built mahogany shelves against the shiny olive-green wallpaper. All represented young women. Some wore crinolines, others twirled parasols, still others sniffed flowers or cradled lambs in their arms.

'She collects 'em,' said Janice, smiling as she saw where Robin was looking. 'Lovely, aren't they?'

'Oh yes,' lied Robin.

Janice didn't seem to feel she had the right to invite them to sit down without Irene present, so the three of them remained standing beside the figurines.

'Have you come far?' she asked them politely, but before they could answer, a voice that commanded attention said,

'Hello! Welcome!'

Like her sitting room, Irene Hickson presented a first impression of over-embellished, over-padded opulence. Just as blonde as she'd been at twenty-five, she was now much heavier, with an enormous bosom. She'd outlined her hooded eyes in black, pencilled her sparse brows into a high, Pierrot-ish arch and painted her thin lips in scarlet. In a mustard-coloured twinset, black trousers, patent heels and a large quantity of gold jewellery, which included clip-on earrings so heavy that they were stretching her already long lobes, she advanced on them in a potent cloud of amber perfume and hairspray.

'How d'you do?' she said, beaming at Strike as she offered her hand, bracelets jangling. 'Has Jan told you? What happened this morning? *So* strange, with you coming today; *so* strange, but I've lost *count* of the number of times things like that happen to me.' She paused, then said dramatically, '*My Margot shattered.* My Margot Fonteyn, on the top shelf,' she said, pointing to a gap in the china figurines. 'Fell apart into a million pieces when I ran the feather duster over her!'

She paused, waiting for astonishment.

'That *is* odd,' said Robin, because it was clear Strike wasn't going to say anything.

'*Isn't it?*' said Irene. 'Tea? Coffee? Whatever you want.'

'I'll do it, dear,' said Janice.

'Thank you, my love. Maybe make both?' said Irene. She waved Strike and Robin graciously towards armchairs. 'Please, sit down.'

The armchairs placed Strike and Robin within view of a window framed in tasselled curtains, through which they could see a garden with intricate paving and raised beds. It had an Elizabethan air, with low box hedges and a wrought iron sundial.

'Oh, the garden was all my Eddie,' said Irene, following their gaze. 'He *loved* his garden, bless his heart. *Loved* this house. It's why I'm still here, although it's too big for me now, really . . . Excuse me. I haven't been well,' she added in a loud whisper, making quite a business of lowering herself onto the sofa and placing cushions carefully around herself. 'Jan's been a *saint.*'

'I'm sorry to hear that,' said Strike. 'That you've been unwell, I mean, not that your friend's a saint.'

Irene gave a delighted peal of laughter and Robin suspected that if Strike had been sitting slightly nearer, Irene might have playfully cuffed him. With an air of giving Strike privileged information, she half-mouthed:

'Irritable bowel syndrome. It flares up. The pain is sometimes – *well.* The funny thing is, I was *fine* all the time I was away – I've been staying with my eldest daughter, they're in Hampshire, that's why I didn't get your letter straight away – but the moment I got home, I called Jan, I said, you'll have to come, I'm in *that much pain* – and my GP's no use,' she added, with a little moue of disgust. '*Woman.* All my own fault, according to her! I should be cutting out everything that makes life worth living – I was telling them, Jan,' she said, as her friend backed into the room with a laden tea tray, 'that you're a *saint.*'

'Oh, carry on. Everyone likes a good review,' said Janice cheerfully. Strike was halfway out of his chair to help her with the tray, on which stood

307

both teapot and cafetière, but like Mrs Gupta she refused help, depositing it on a padded ottoman. An assortment of chocolate biscuits, some foil-wrapped, lay on a doily; the sugar bowl had tongs and the flowered fine bone china suggested 'for best'. Janice joined her friend on the sofa and poured out the hot drinks, serving Irene first.

'Help yourself to biscuits,' Irene told her visitors, and then, eyeing Strike hungrily, 'So – the famous Cameron Strike! I nearly had a *heart attack* when I saw your name at the bottom of the letter. And you're going to try and crack Creed, are you? Will he talk to you, do you think? Will they let you go and see him?'

'We're not that far along yet,' said Strike with a smile, as he took out his notebook and uncapped his pen. 'We've got a few questions, mainly background, that you two might be able—'

'Oh, *anything* we can do to help,' said Irene eagerly. '*Anything.*'

'We've read both your police statements,' said Strike, 'so unless—'

'Oh dear,' interrupted Irene, pulling a mock-fearful expression. 'You know all about me being a naughty girl, then? About the dentist and that, do you? There'll be young girls out there doing it, right now, fibbing to get a few hours off, but just my luck I picked the day Margot – sorry, I don't mean that,' Irene said, catching herself. 'I don't. This is how I get myself in trouble,' she said, with a little laugh. '*Steady, girl*, Eddie would've said, wouldn't he Jan?' she said, tapping her friend on the arm. 'Wouldn't he have said, *steady, girl?*'

'He would,' said Janice, smiling and nodding.

'I was going to say,' Strike continued, 'that unless either of you have got anything to add—'

'Oh, don't think we haven't thought about it,' interrupted Irene again. 'If we'd remembered anything else we'd have been *straight* down the police station, wouldn't we, Jan?'

'—I'd like to clarify a few points.

'Mrs Beattie,' said Strike, looking at Janice, who was absentmindedly stroking the underside of her wedding ring, which was the only piece of jewellery she wore, 'one thing that struck me when I read the police notes was how many times Inspector Talbot—'

'Oh, you and me both, Cameron,' Irene interrupted eagerly, before Janice could open her mouth. 'You and me both! I know *exactly* what you're going to ask – *why did he keep pestering Jan?* I told her at the time – didn't I, Jan? – I said, this isn't right, you should report it, but you didn't, did you? I mean, I know he was having a breakdown, blah blah blah – *you'll* know all about that,' she said, with a nod towards Strike, that simultaneously conveyed a compliment and an eagerness to fill him in should he require it, 'but ill men are still *men*, aren't they?'

'Mrs Beattie,' repeated Strike, slightly louder, 'why do *you* think Talbot kept interviewing you?'

Irene took the broad hint and allowed Janice to answer, but her self-restraint lasted only until Janice hit her stride, at which point she set up a murmured counterpoint, echoing Janice's words, adding agreement and emphasis, and giving the general impression that she feared that if she did not make a noise every few seconds, Strike might forget she was there.

'I dunno, in all honesty,' said Janice, still fiddling with her wedding ring. 'The first few times 'e saw me it was straightforward questions—'

'At first it was, yeah,' murmured Irene, nodding along.

'—about what I done that day, you know, what I could tell 'im about people coming to see Margot, because I knew a lot of the patients—'

'We got to know them all, working at the practice,' said Irene, nodding.

'—but then, it was like 'e thought I 'ad . . . well, *special powers*. I know that sounds bonkers, but I don't fink—'

'Oho, well, *I* do,' said Irene, her eyes on Strike.

'—no, I honestly *don't* fink 'e was – you know—' Janice seemed embarrassed even to say it, '*keen* on me.'E *did* ask inappropriate things, but I could tell 'e wasn't right, you know – in the 'ead. It was an 'orrible position to be in, honestly,' Janice said, switching her gaze to Robin. 'I didn't feel like I could *tell* anyone.'E was police! I just 'ad to keep sitting there while 'e asked me about me *dreams*. And after the first few interviews that's all he wanted to talk about, me past boyfriends and stuff, nothing about Margot or the patients—'

'He was interested in *one* patient, though, wasn't—?' began Robin.

'Duckworth!' piped up Irene excitedly.

'Douthwaite,' said Strike.

'Douthwaite, yes, that's who I meant,' muttered Irene, and to cover a slight embarrassment she helped herself to a biscuit, which meant that for a few moments, at least, Janice was able to talk uninterrupted.

'Yeah, 'e did ask me about Steve,' said Janice, nodding, ''cause 'e lived in my block of flats, down Percival Street.'

'Did you know Douthwaite well?' asked Robin.

'Not really. Ackshly, I never knew 'im at all until 'e got beaten up. I come 'ome late and found a load of people on the landing with 'im. People knew I was a nurse so – there's me wiv my son Kevin under one arm and shopping in the other hand – but Steve was in a right state, so I 'ad to 'elp. 'E didn't want the police called, but 'e'd 'ad the sort of beating that can leave you wiv internal injuries. The ovver geezer 'ad used a bat. Jealous 'usband—'

'Who had *completely* the wrong end of the stick, didn't he?' interrupted Irene. 'Because Douthwaite was queer!' she said, with a shout of laughter. 'He was only *friends* with the wife, but this jealous idiot thinks—'

311

'Well, I don't *know* if Steve was queer—' began Janice, but there was no stopping Irene.

'—man – woman – two and two makes five! My Eddie was *exactly the same* – Jan, bear me out, what was Eddie like?' she said, tapping Janice's arm again. '*Exactly* the same, wasn't he? I remember once, I said, "Eddie, you think if I so much *look* at a man – he can be queer, he can be Welsh—" But after you told me, Jan, I thought, yeah, that Duckworth – Douth-thing – *is* a bit camp. When he came in the surgery afterwards, I could see it. Good-looking, but a bit soft.'

'But I don't know wevver 'e *was* queer, Irene, I didn't know 'im well enough to—'

'He kept coming back to see you,' Irene chided her. 'You told me he did. Kept coming back to your place for tea and sympathy and telling you all his problems.'

'It were only a couple of times,' said Janice. 'We'd chat, passing on the stairs, and one time 'e 'elped me with my shopping and come in for a cup of tea.'

'But he asked you—' prompted Irene.

'I'm getting to that, dear,' said Janice, with what Strike thought was remarkable patience. ''E was getting 'eadaches,' she told Strike and Robin, 'an' I told 'im 'e needed to go and see a doctor for 'eadaches, I couldn't diagnose 'im. I mean, I felt a bit sorry for 'im, but I didn't want to get in the 'abit of 'olding out-of-hours clinics in me flat. I 'ad Kevin to look after.'

'So you think Douthwaite's visits to Margot were

because of his health?' asked Robin. 'Not because he had a romantic interest in—?'

'He *did* send her chocolates one time,' said Irene, 'but if you ask me, it was more like she was an agony aunt.'

'Well, 'e 'ad these 'ead pains and 'e was def'nitely nervous. Depressed, maybe,' said Janice. 'Everyone 'ad blamed him for what happened to that poor girl 'oo killed 'erself, but I don't know . . . and some of me ovver neighbours told me there were young men coming in and out of his flat—'

'There you are,' said Irene triumphantly. 'Queer!'

'Might not've been that,' said Janice. 'Coulda just been 'is mates, or drugs, or stuff falling off the back of a lorry . . . One fing I do know, 'cause people talked, locally: the 'usband of that girl who killed 'erself was knockin' twelve bells out of 'er. Tragedy, really. But the papers pinned it all on Steve an' 'e ran. Well, sex sells better'n domestic violence, doesn't it? If you find Steve,' she added, 'tell 'im I said 'ello. It wasn't fair, what the papers did.'

Robin had been trained by Strike to organise her interviews and notes into the categories of people, places and things. She now asked both women,

'Were there any other patients you can ever remember giving cause for alarm at the practice, or perhaps having an unusual relationship with Marg—?'

'*Well*,' said Irene, '*remember*, Jan, there was that one with the beard down to here . . .' She placed her hand at waist level, '. . . remember? *What* was he called? Apton? Applethorpe? Jan, you remember. You *do* remember, Jan, he stank like a tramp and you had to go round his house once. He used to wander around near St John's. I think he lived on Clerkenwell Road. Sometimes he had his kid with him. Really *funny*-looking kid. Massive ears.'

'Oh, *them*,' said Janice, her frown disappearing. 'But they weren't Margot's—'

'Well, *he* was stopping people on the street, afterwards, telling them he'd killed Margot!' Irene told Strike excitedly. 'Yeah! He was! He stopped Dorothy! Of course, *Dorothy* wasn't going to tell the police, not Dorothy, she was all "load of stuff and nonsense", "he's a lunatic", but I said to her, "What if he actually *did* do it, Dorothy, and you haven't told anyone?" Now, Applethorpe was a proper nutcase. He had a girl locked up—'

'She weren't *locked up*, Irene,' said Janice, for the first time showing a trace of impatience. 'Social work said she were agoraphobic, but she weren't being kept there against 'er *will*—'

'She was peculiar,' said Irene stubbornly. 'You told me she was. I think someone should've taken the kid away, personally. You said the flat was filthy—'

'You can't take people's children off them because they 'aven't cleaned the 'ouse!' said Janice firmly. She turned back to Strike and Robin. 'Yeah, I visited the Applethorpes, just the once, but I don't fink they ever met Margot. See, it was diff'rent then: doctors 'ad their own lists, and the

Applethorpes were registered with Brenner.'E asked me to go round for 'im, check on the kid.'

'Do you remember the address? Street name?'

'Oh gawd,' said Janice, frowning. 'Yeah, I think it was Clerkenwell Road. I think so. See, I only visited the once. The kid 'adn't been well and Dr Brenner wanted 'im checked and 'e'd never make an 'ouse call if 'e could avoid it. Anyway, the kid was on the mend, but I spotted right off the dad was—'

'Nutcase—' said Irene, nodding along.

'—jittery, bit out of it,' said Janice. 'I went in the kitchen to wash my 'ands and there was a load of benzedrine lying in full view on the worktop. I warned both the parents, now the kid was walking, to put it away somewhere safe—'

'*Really* funny-looking kid,' interposed Irene.

'—and I went to Brenner after, an' I said, "Dr Brenner, that man's abusing benzedrine." It was proper addictive, we all knew it by then, even in '74.'Course, Brenner thought I was being *presumptuous*, queryin' 'is prescriptions. But I was worried, so I called social work wivout telling Brenner, and they were very good. They were already keeping a close eye on the family.'

'But the mother—' said Irene.

'You can't decide for other people what makes 'em 'appy, Irene!' said Janice. 'The mum loved that kid, even if the dad was – well, 'e *was* odd, poor sod,' Janice conceded. ''E thought 'e was a kind of – I don't know what you'd call it – a guru,

315

or a magic man. Thought 'e could put the evil eye on people.'E told me that durin' the 'ouse call. You do meet people wiv weird ideas, nursin'. I just used to say, "Really? 'Ow interesting." There's no point challenging 'em. But Applethorpe thought he could ill-wish people – that's what we used to call it, in the old days.'E was worried 'is little boy 'ad got German measles because he'd got cross with 'im.'E said 'e could do that to people . . . He died 'imself, poor sod. Year after Margot vanished.'

'Did he?' said Irene, with a trace of disappointment.

'Yeah. It would've been after you left, after you married Eddie. I remember, street cleaners found him early in the morning, curled up and dead under the Walter Street bridge.'Eart attack. Keeled over and there was nobody there to 'elp him. Wasn't that old, neither. I remember Dr Brenner being a bit twitchy about it.'

'Why was that?' asked Strike.

'Well, 'e'd prescribed the Bennies the man was abusin', 'adn't 'e?'

To Robin's surprise, a fleeting smile passed over Strike's face.

'But it weren't just Applethorpe,' Janice went on, who didn't seem to have noticed anything odd in Strike's response. 'There was—'

'Oh, *tons* of people swore blind they'd heard something, or had a hunch, blah blah blah,' said Irene, rolling her eyes, 'and there was us, you know, who were actually *involved*, it was terrible, just –

excuse me,' she said, putting her hand on her stomach, 'I must just nip to the – sorry.'

Irene left the room in something of a hurry. Janice looked after her, and it was hard, given her naturally smiley face, to tell whether she was more concerned or amused.

'She'll be fine,' she told Strike and Robin quietly. 'I 'ave *told* 'er the doc's probably right tellin' 'er to lay off the spicy food, but she wanted a curry last night . . . she gets lonely. Rings me up to come over. I stayed overnight. Eddie only died last year. Nearly ninety, bless 'im.'E *adored* Irene and the girls. She misses 'im something rotten.'

'Were you about to tell us somebody else had claimed to know what happened to Margot?' Strike prompted her gently.

'What? Oh, yeah . . . Charlie Ramage.'E 'ad an 'ot tub and sauna business. Wealfy man, so you'd think 'e 'ad better things to do with 'is time than make up stories, but there you go, people are funny.'

'What did he say?' asked Robin.

'Well, see, motorbikes were Charlie's 'obby.'E 'ad loads of 'em, and 'e used to go on these long rides all over the country.'E 'ad a bad smash and 'e was at 'ome wiv two broken legs, so I was droppin' in sev'ral times a week . . . this would've been a good two years after Margot disappeared. Well, Charlie was a man 'oo liked to talk, and one day, out of a clear blue sky, 'e swears blind 'e met Margot, about a week after she went missing, in

Leamington Spa. But, you know,' Janice said, shaking her head. 'I didn't take it very serious. Lovely man, but like I say, 'e liked to talk.'

'What exactly did he tell you?' asked Robin.

'Said 'e'd been on one of 'is bike trips up north, and 'e stopped outside this big church in Leamington Spa, and 'e was leaning against the wall 'avin' a cup of tea an' a sandwich, an' there was this woman walking in the graveyard on the other side of the railings, lookin' at the graves. Not like she was in mourning or anyfing, just interested. Black 'air, accordin' to Charlie. An' 'e called out to 'er, "Nice place, innit?" and she turned to look at 'im and – well, 'e swore blind it was Margot Bamborough, wiv 'er 'air dyed.'E said 'e told 'er she looked familiar and she looked upset and hurried off.'

'And he claimed this happened a week after she disappeared?' asked Robin.

'Yeah, 'e said 'e recognised 'er because 'er picture was still all over the papers at the time. So I says, "Did you go to the police about this, Charlie?" And 'e says, "Yeah, I did," an' 'e told me 'e was friends with a policeman, quite an 'igh up bloke, an' 'e told 'is friend. But I never saw or 'eard anyfing about it after, so, you know . . .'

'Ramage told you this story in 1976?' Strike asked, making a note.

'Yeah, musta been,' said Janice, frowning in an effort to remember, as Irene walked back into the room. 'Because they'd got Creed by then. That's 'ow it came up.''E'd been reading about the trial in the papers and then 'e says, cool as you like, "Well, I don't fink 'e done anyfing to Margot Bamborough, because I reckon I seen 'er after she disappeared."'

'Did Margot have any connection with Leamington Spa, as far as you know?' asked Robin.

'What's this?' said Irene sharply.

'Nuffing,' said Janice. 'Just a stupid story some patient told me. Margot in a graveyard wiv dyed hair. *You* know.'

'In Leamington Spa?' said Irene, looking displeased. Robin had the impression that she greatly resented having left Janice in the spotlight while she was forced back to the bathroom. 'You never told me that. Why didn't you tell me?'

'Oh . . . well, it was in '76,' said Janice, looking slightly cowed. 'You must've just 'ad Sharon. You 'ad better fings to fink about than Charlie Ramage telling porkies.'

Irene helped herself to another biscuit, frowning slightly.

'I'd like to move on to the practice itself,' said Strike. 'How did you find Margot to—'

'To work with?' said Irene, loudly, who seemed to feel it was her turn, having missed out on several minutes of Strike's attention. 'Well, speaking *personally*—'

Her pause was that of an epicure, savouring the prospect of coming pleasure.

'—to be *totally* honest, she was one of those

people who think they know best about *everything*. She'd tell you how to live your life, how to do the filing, how to make a cup of tea, blah blah blah—'

'Oh, Irene, she weren't *that* bad,' muttered Janice. 'I liked—'

'Jan, *come on*,' said Irene loftily. 'She'd never got over being the clever clogs in her family and thought all the rest of us were thick as mince! Well, maybe she didn't think *you* were,' said Irene, with an eye roll, as her friend shook her head, 'but she did me. Treated me like a moron. *Patronising* isn't it. Now, I didn't dislike her!' Irene added quickly. 'Not *dislike*. But she was *picky*. Veee-ry pleased with herself. We'd *completely* forgotten we came from a two-up, two-down in Stepney, put it that way.'

'How did *you* find her?' Robin asked Janice.

'Well—' began Janice, but Irene talked over her.

'*Snobby*. Jan, *come on*. She marries herself a rich consultant – *that* was no two-up, two-down, that place out in Ham! Proper eye-opener it was, seeing what she'd married into, and then she has the gall to come into work preaching the liberated life to the rest of us: marriage isn't the be all and end all, don't stop your career, blah blah blah. And *always* finding fault.'

'What did she—?'

'How you answered the phone, how you spoke to patients, how you dressed, even – *"Irene, I don't think that top's appropriate for work."* She was a bloody Bunny Girl! The hypocrisy of her! I didn't dislike her,' Irene insisted. 'I didn't, truly, I'm just trying to give you the full – oh, and she wouldn't let us make her hot drinks, would she, Jan? Neither of the *other* two doctors ever complained we didn't know what to do with a teabag.'

'That's not why—' began Janice.

'Jan, *come on*, you *remember* how fussy—'

'Why would *you* say she didn't like people making her drinks?' Strike asked Janice. Robin could tell that his patience was wearing thin with Irene.

'Oh, that was 'cause of when I was washing up mugs one day,' said Janice. 'I tipped the dregs out of Dr Brenner's and I found an—'

'*Atomal* pill, wasn't it?' asked Irene.

'—Amytal capsule, stuck to the bottom. I knew what it was from the col—'

'Blue,' interjected Irene, nodding, 'weren't they?'

'Blue 'Eavens, they used to call them on the street, yeah,' said Janice. 'Downers. I always made sure everyone knew I didn't 'ave nuffing like that in me nurse's bag, when I was out makin' 'ouse calls. You 'ad to be careful, in case you got mugged.'

'How did you know it was Dr Brenner's cup?' asked Strike.

''E always used the same one, wiv his old university's coat of arms on,' said Janice. 'There'd 'ave been 'ell to pay if anyone else touched it.' She hesitated, 'I don't know wevver – if you've talked to Dr Gupta—'

'We know Dr Brenner was addicted to barbiturates,' Strike said. Janice looked relieved.

'Right – well, I knew 'e must've dropped it in there, accidental, when he was taking some. Probably didn't realise, thought it 'ad rolled away on the floor. There'd have been a lot of questions asked, usually, at a doctor's surgery, finding drugs in a drink. If something gets into someone's tea by accident, that's serious.'

'How much harm would a single capsule—?' Robin began.

'Oh, no *real* harm,' said Irene knowledgeably, 'would it, Jan?'

'No, a single capsule, that's not even a full dose,' said Janice. 'You'd've felt a bit sleepy, that's all. Anyway, Margot come out the back to make the tea when I was tryin' to get the pill off the bottom of the mug with a teaspoon. We 'ad a sink and a kettle and a fridge just outside the nurse's room. She saw me trying to scrape the pill out. So it weren't *fussiness*, 'er making 'er own drinks after that. It were precautionary. I took extra care to make sure I was drinking out of me own mug, as well.'

'Did you tell Margot how you thought the pill had got in the tea?' asked Robin.

'No,' said Janice, 'because Dr Gupta 'ad asked me not to mention Brenner's problem, so I just said "must've been an accident", which was *technically* true. I expected her to call a staff meeting and hold an enquiry—'

'Ah, well, you know my theory about why she didn't do that,' said Irene.

'Irene,' said Janice, shaking her head. 'Honestly—'

'*My* theory,' said Irene, ignoring Janice, 'is Margot thought someone *else* had put the pill in Brenner's drink, and if you're asking me *who*—'

'*Irene*,' said Janice again, clearly urging restraint, but Irene was unstoppable.

'—I'll tell you – *Gloria*. That girl was as rough as hell and she came from a criminal background – no, I'm saying it, Jan, I'm sure Cameron wants to know *everything* what was going on at that practice—'

''Ow can Gloria putting something in Brenner's tea – and by the way,' Janice said to Strike and Robin, '*I* don't fink she did—'

'Well, as I was on the desk with Gloria every day, Jan,' said Irene loftily, '*I* knew what she was really like—'

'—but even if she *did* put the pill in 'is tea, Irene, 'ow could that 'ave anything to do with Margot disappearin'?'

'*I* don't know,' said Irene, who seemed to be getting cross, 'but they're interested in who was working there and what went on – aren't you?' she demanded of Strike, who nodded. With a '*See?*' to Janice, Irene plunged on, 'So: Gloria came from a really rough family, a Little Italy family—'

Janice tried to protest, but Irene overrode her again.

'She *did*, Jan! One of her brothers was drug dealing, that sort of thing, she told me so! That Atomal capsule might not've come from Brenner's store at all! She could've got it off one of her brothers. Gloria *hated* Brenner. He was a miserable old sod, all right, always having a go at us. She said to me once, "Imagine living with him. If I was his sister I'd poison the old bastard's food," and Margot heard her, and told her off, because there were patients in the waiting room, and it wasn't professional, saying something like that about one of the doctors.

'Anyway, when Margot never did anything about the pill in Brenner's mug, I thought, *that's because she knows who did it.* She didn't want her little pet in trouble. Gloria was her *project*, see. Gloria spent half her time in Margot's consulting room being lectured on feminism while I was left to hold the fort on reception . . . she'd've let Gloria away with murder, Margot would. Total blind spot.'

'Do either of you know where Gloria is now?' asked Strike.

'No idea. She left not long after Margot disappeared,' said Irene.

'I never saw her again after she left the practice,' said Janice, who looked uncomfortable, 'but Irene, I don't fink we should be flinging accusations—'

'Do me a favour,' said Irene abruptly to her friend, a hand on her stomach, 'and fetch that medicine off the top of the fridge for me, will you? I'm still not right. And would anyone like more tea or coffee while Jan's there?'

Janice got up uncomplainingly, collected empty cups, loaded the tray and set off for the kitchen.

Robin got up to open the door for her, and Janice smiled at her as she passed. While Janice's footsteps padded away down the thickly carpeted hall, Irene said, unsmiling,

'*Poor* Jan. She's had an awful life, really. Like something out of Dickens, her childhood. Eddie and I helped her out financially a few times, after Beattie left her. She calls herself "Beattie", but he never married her, you know,' said Irene. 'Awful, isn't it? And they had a kid, too. I don't think he ever really wanted to be there, and then he walked out. Larry, though – I mean, he wasn't the brightest tool in the box,' Irene laughed a little, 'but he thought the world of her. I think she thought she could do better at first – Larry worked for Eddie, you know – not on the management side, he was just a builder, but in the end, I think she realised – well, you know, not everyone's prepared to take on a kid . . .'

'Could I ask you about the threatening notes to Margot you saw, Mrs Hickson?'

'Oh, yes, of course,' said Irene, pleased. 'So *you* believe me, do you? Because the police didn't.'

'There were two, you said in your statement?'

'That's right. I wouldn't've opened the first one, only Dorothy was off, and Dr Brenner told me to sort out the post. Dorothy was *never* off usually. It was because her son was having his tonsils out. Spoiled little so-and-so, he was. That was the *only* time I ever saw her upset, when she told me she was taking him into hospital the next day. Hard

325

as nails, usually – but she was a widow, and he was all she had.'

Janice reappeared with refilled teapot and cafetière. Robin got up and took the heavy teapot and cafetière off the tray for her. Janice accepted her help with a smile and a whispered 'thanks', so that she didn't interrupt Irene.

'What did the note say?' Strike asked.

'Well, it's *ages* ago, now,' said Irene. Janice handed her a packet of indigestion tablets, which Irene took with a brief smile, but no thanks. 'But from what I remember . . .' she popped pills out of the blister pack, 'let me see, I want to get this right . . . it was *very* rude. It called Margot the c-word, I remember *that*. And said hellfire waited for women like her.'

'Was it typed? Printed?'

'Written,' said Irene. She took a couple of tablets with a sip of tea.

'What about the second one?' said Strike.

'I don't know what that said. I had to go into her consulting room to give her a message, see, and I saw it lying on her desk. Same writing, I recognised it at once. She didn't like me seeing it, I could tell. Screwed it up and threw it in the bin.'

Janice passed round fresh cups of tea and coffee. Irene helped herself to another chocolate biscuit.

'I doubt you'll know,' said Strike, 'but I wondered if you ever had any reason to suspect that Margot was pregnant before she—'

'How d'you know about that?' gasped Irene, looking thunderstruck.

'She *was*?' said Robin.

'Yes!' said Irene. 'See – Jan, don't look like that, honestly – I took a call from a nursing home, while she was out on a house call! They called the practice to confirm she'd be in next day . . .' and she mouthed the next few words, '*for an abortion!*'

'They told you what procedure she was going in for, over the phone?' asked Robin.

For a moment, Irene looked rather confused.

'They – well, no – actually, I – well, I'm not proud of it, but I called the clinic back. Just nosy. You do that kind of thing when you're young, don't you?'

Robin hoped her reciprocal smile looked sincerer than Irene's.

'When was this, Mrs Hickson, can you remember?' Strike asked.

'Not long before she disappeared. Four weeks? Something like that?'

'Before or after the anonymous notes?'

'I don't – after, I think,' said Irene. 'Or was it? I can't remember . . .'

'Did you talk to anyone else about the appointment?'

'Only Jan, and she told me off. Didn't you, Jan?'

'I know you didn't mean any 'arm,' muttered Janice, 'but patient confidentiality—'

'Margot wasn't *our* patient. It's a different thing.'

'And you didn't tell the police about this?' Strike asked her.

'No,' said Irene, 'because I – well, I shouldn't've known, should I? Anyway, how could it have anything to do with her disappearing?'

'Apart from Mrs Beattie, did you tell anyone else about it?'

'No,' said Irene defensively, 'because – I mean, I wouldn't have told anyone *else* – you kept your mouth shut, working at a doctor's surgery. I could've told all kinds of people's secrets, couldn't I? Being a receptionist, I saw files, but of course you didn't say anything, I knew how to keep secrets, it was part of the job . . .'

Expressionless, Strike wrote 'protesting too much' in his notebook.

'I've got another question, Mrs Hickson, and it might be a sensitive one,' Strike said, looking up again. 'I heard you and Margot had a disagreement at the Christmas party.'

'*Oh*,' said Irene, her face falling. '*That*. Yes, well—'

There was a slight pause.

'I was cross about what she'd done to Kevin. Jan's son. Remember, Jan?'

Janice looked confused.

'Come on, Jan, you *do*,' said Irene, tapping Janice's arm again. 'When she took him into her consulting room and blah blah blah.'

'*Oh*,' said Janice. For a moment, Robin had the distinct impression that Janice was truly cross with her friend this time. 'But—'

'You remember,' said Irene, glaring at her.

328

'I . . . yeah,' said Janice. 'Yeah, I *was* angry about that, all right.'

'Jan had kept him off school,' Irene told Strike. 'Hadn't you, Jan? How old was he, six? And then—'

'What exactly happened?' Strike asked Janice.

'Kev had a tummy ache,' said Janice. 'Well, schoolitis, really. My neighbour 'oo sometimes looked after 'im wasn't well—'

'Basically,' interrupted Irene, 'Jan brought Kevin to work and—'

'Could Mrs Beattie tell the story?' Strike asked.

'Oh – yes, of course!' said Irene. She put her hand back on her abdomen again and stroked it, with a long-suffering air.

'Your usual childminder was ill?' Strike prompted Janice.

'Yeah, but I was s'posed to be at work, so I took Kev wiv me to the practice and give 'im a colouring book. Then I 'ad to change a lady's dressing in the back room, so I put Kev in the waiting room. Irene and Gloria were keeping an eye on him for me. But then Margot – well, she took 'im into her consulting room and examined 'im, stripped 'im off to the waist and everything. She *knew* 'e was my son an' she *knew* why 'e was there, but she took it upon herself . . . I was angry, I can't lie,' said Janice quietly. 'We 'ad words. I said, "All you 'ad to do was wait until I'd seen the patient and I'd've come in wiv 'im while you looked at him."

329

'And I've got to say, when I put it to her straight, she backed down right away and apologised. No,' Janice said, because Irene had puffed herself up, 'she *did*, Irene, she apologised, said I was quite right, she shouldn't have seen him without me, but 'e'd been holding his tummy and she acted on instinct. It wasn't badly intentioned. She just, sometimes—'

'—put people's backs up, that's what I'm saying,' said Irene. 'Thought she was above everyone else, she knew best—'

'—rushed in, I was going to say. But she were a good doctor,' said Janice, with quiet firmness. 'You 'ear it all, when you're in people's 'ouses, you 'ear what the patients think of them, and Margot was well liked. She took time. She was kind – she *was*, Irene, I know she got on your wick, but that's what the patients—'

'Oh, well, maybe,' said Irene, with an if-you-say-so inflection. 'But she didn't have much competition at St John's, did she?'

'Were Dr Gupta and Dr Brenner unpopular?' Strike asked.

'Dr Gupta was lovely,' said Janice. 'A very good doctor, although some patients didn't want to see a brown man, and that's the truth. But Brenner was an 'ard man to like. It was only after he died that I understood why he might've—'

Irene gave a huge gasp and then began, unexpectedly, to laugh.

'*Tell them what you collect, Janice.* Go on!' She

330

turned to Strike and Robin. 'If this isn't the *creepiest*, most *morbid*—'

'I don't *collect* 'em,' said Janice, who had turned pink. 'They're just something I like to *save*—'

'*Obituaries!* What d'you think of that? The rest of us collect china or snow globes, blah blah blah, but Janice collects—'

'*It isn't a collection*,' repeated Janice, still pink-faced. 'All it is—' She addressed Robin with a trace of appeal. 'My mum couldn't read—'

'*Imagine*,' said Irene complacently, stroking her stomach. Janice faltered for a moment, then said,

'—yeah, so . . . Dad wasn't bothered about books, but 'e used to bring the paper 'ome, and that's 'ow I learned to read. I used to cut out the best stories.'Uman interest, I s'pose you'd call them. I've never been that interested in fiction. I can't see the point, things somebody's made up.'

'Oh, I *love* a good novel,' breathed Irene, still rubbing her stomach.

'Anyway . . . I dunno . . . when you read an obituary, you find out 'oo people've *really* been, don't you? If it's someone I know, or I nursed, I keep 'em because, I dunno, I felt like *somebody* should. You get your life written up in the paper – it's an achievement, isn't it?'

'Not if you're Dennis Creed, it isn't,' said Irene. Looking as though she'd said something very clever she reached forwards to take another biscuit, and a deafening fart ripped through the room.

Irene turned scarlet. Robin thought for one

331

horrible moment that Strike was going to laugh, so she said loudly to Janice,

'Did you keep Dr Brenner's obituary?'

'Oh, yeah,' said Janice, who seemed completely unperturbed by the loud noise that had just emanated from Irene. Perhaps she was used to far worse, as a nurse. 'An' it explained *a lot.*'

'In what way?' asked Robin, determinedly not looking at either Strike or Irene.

''E'd been into Bergen-Belsen, one of the first medical men in there.'

'God,' said Robin, shocked.

'I know,' said Janice. ''E never talked about it. I'd never 'ave known, if I 'adn't read it in the paper. What 'e must have seen . . . mounds of bodies, dead kids . . . I read a library book about it. Dreadful. Maybe that's why 'e was the way 'e was, I dunno. I felt sorry, when I read it. I 'adn't seen 'im in years by the time 'e died. Someone showed me the obituary, knowing I'd been at St John's, and I kept it as a record of him. You could forgive Brenner a lot, once you saw what 'e'd witnessed, what 'e'd been through . . . but that's true of everyone, really, innit? Once you know, ev'rything's explained. It's a shame you often *don't* know until it's too late to – you all right, love?' she said to Irene.

In the wake of the fart, Robin suspected that Irene had decided the only dignified cover-up was to emphasise that she was unwell.

'D'you know, I think it's stress,' she said, her

332

hand down the waistband of her trousers. 'It always flares up when I'm . . . sorry,' she said with dignity to Strike and Robin, 'but I'm afraid I don't think I . . .'

'Of course,' said Strike, closing his notebook. 'I think we've asked everything we came for, anyway. Unless there's anything else,' he asked the two women, 'that you've remembered that seems odd, in retrospect, or out of place?'

'We've fort, 'aven't we?' Janice asked Irene. 'All these years . . . we've talked about it, obviously.'

'It *must've* been Creed, mustn't it?' said Irene, with finality. 'What other explanation is there? Where else could she have gone? *Do* you think they'll let you in to see him?' she asked Strike again, with a last flicker of curiosity.

'No idea,' he said, getting to his feet. 'Thanks very much for your hospitality, anyway, and for answering our questions . . .'

Janice saw them out. Irene waved wordlessly as they left the room. Robin could tell that the interview had fallen short of her expectation of enjoyment. Awkward and uncomfortable admissions had been forced from her; the picture she'd painted of her young self had not been, perhaps, everything she would have wished – and nobody, Robin thought, shaking hands with Janice at the door, would particularly enjoy farting loudly in front of strangers.

CHAPTER 21

Well then, sayd Artegall, let it be tride.
First in one ballance set the true aside.
He did so first; and then the false he layd
In th'other scale . . .

Edmund Spenser
The Faerie Queene

'Well, I'm no doctor,' said Strike, as they crossed the road back to the Land Rover, 'but I blame the curry.'

'Don't,' said Robin, laughing against her will. She couldn't help but feel a certain vicarious embarrassment.

'You weren't sitting as near her as I was,' said Strike, as he got back into the car. 'I'm guessing lamb bhuna—'

'Seriously,' said Robin, half-laughing, half-disgusted, 'stop.'

As he drew his seatbelt back over himself, Strike said,

'I need a proper drink.'

'There's a decent pub not far from here,' said Robin. 'I looked it up. The Trafalgar Tavern.'

Looking up the pub was doubtless yet another Nice Thing that Robin had chosen to do for his birthday, and Strike wondered whether it was her intention to make him feel guilty. Probably not, he thought, but that, nevertheless, was the effect, so he passed no comment other than to ask,

'What did you think of all that?'

'Well, there were a few cross-currents, weren't there?' said Robin, steering out of the parking space. 'And I think we were told a couple of lies.'

'Me too,' said Strike. 'Which ones did you spot?'

'Irene and Janice's row at the Christmas party, for starters,' said Robin, turning out of Circus Street. 'I don't think it was really about Margot examining Janice's son – although I *do* think Margot examined Kevin without permission.'

'So do I,' said Strike. 'But I agree: I don't think that's what the row was about. Irene forced Janice to tell that story, because she didn't want to admit the truth. Which makes me wonder . . . Irene getting Janice to come to her house, so we can interview them both together: was that so Irene could make sure Janice didn't tell us anything she wouldn't want told? That's the trouble with friends you've had for decades, isn't it? They know too much.'

Robin, who was busy trying to remember the route to the Trafalgar she'd memorised that morning, thought at once about all those stories

Ilsa had told her about Strike and Charlotte's relationship. Ilsa had told her Strike had refused an invitation to go over to their house that evening for dinner, claiming that he had a prior arrangement with his sister. Robin found it hard to believe this, given Strike's and Lucy's recent row. Perhaps she was being paranoid, but she'd also wondered whether Strike wasn't avoiding being in her company outside work hours.

'You don't suspect Irene, do you?'

'Only of being a liar, a gossip and a compulsive attention-seeker,' said Strike. 'I don't think she's bright enough to have abducted Margot Bamborough and not given herself away in forty years. On the other hand, lies are always interesting. Anything else catch your interest?'

'Yes. There was something funny about that Leamington Spa story, or rather, Irene's reaction when she heard Janice talking about it . . . I think Leamington Spa meant something to her. And it was odd that Janice *hadn't* told her what that patient said. You'd think she definitely would have done, given that they're best friends, and they both knew Margot, and they've stayed in touch all these years. Even if Janice thought that man Ramage was making it all up, why wouldn't she tell Irene?'

'Another good point,' said Strike, looking thoughtfully at the neo-classical façade of the National Maritime Museum as they drove past wide stretches of beautifully manicured emerald lawn. 'What did you think of Janice?'

'Well, when we were allowed to hear her speak, she seemed quite decent,' said Robin cautiously. 'She seemed fair-minded about Margot and Douthwaite. Why she puts up with being treated as Irene's skivvy, though . . .'

'Some people need to be needed . . . and there might be a sense of obligation, if Irene was telling the truth about her and her husband helping Janice out financially when she needed it.'

Strike spotted the pub Robin had chosen from a distance. Large and opulent-looking, with many balconies and awnings, not to mention window-baskets and coats of arms, it stood on the bank of the Thames. Robin parked and they proceeded past black iron bollards to the paved area where many wooden tables afforded a view over the river, in the midst of which a life-size black statue of the diminutive Lord Nelson faced the water.

'See?' said Robin, 'you can sit outside and smoke.'

'Isn't it a bit cold?' said Strike.

'This coat's padded. I'll get the—'

'No, I will,' said Strike firmly. 'What d'you want?

'Just a lime and soda, please, as I'm driving.'

As Strike walked into the pub, there was a sudden chorus of 'Happy Birthday to You'. For a split-second, seeing helium balloons in the corner, he was horror-struck, thinking that Robin had brought him here for a surprise party; but a bare heartbeat later, it registered that he didn't recognise a single face, and that the balloons formed the figure 80. A tiny woman with lavender hair was beaming at the top of a table full of family: flashes went off as she blew out the candles on a large chocolate cake. Applause and cheers followed, and a toddler blew a feathered whistle.

Strike headed towards the bar, still slightly shaken, taking himself to task for having imagined, for a moment, that Robin would have arranged a surprise party for him. Even Charlotte, with whom he'd had the longest and closest relationship of his life, had never done that. Indeed, Charlotte had never allowed anything as mundane as his birthday to interfere with her own whims and moods. On Strike's twenty-seventh, when she'd been going through one of her intermittent phases of either rampant jealousy, or rage at his refusal to give up the army (the precise causes of their many scenes and rows tended to blur in his mind), she'd thrown his wrapped gift out of a third-floor window in front of him.

But, of course, there were other memories. His thirty-third birthday, for instance. He'd just been discharged from Selly Oak hospital, and was walking for the first time on a prosthesis, and Charlotte had taken him back to her flat in Notting Hill, cooked for him, and returned from the kitchen at the end of the meal holding two cups of coffee, stark naked and more beautiful than any woman he had ever seen. He'd laughed and gasped at the same time. He hadn't had sex for nearly two years. The night that had followed would probably never be forgotten by him, nor the way she had sobbed in his arms afterwards, telling him that he was the only man for her, that she was afraid of what she felt, afraid that she was evil for not regretting his missing lower leg if it brought her back to him, if it meant that, at last, she could look after him as he had always looked after her. And close to midnight, Strike had proposed to her, and they'd made love again, and then talked through to dawn about how he was going to start his detective agency, and she'd told him she didn't want a ring, that he was to save his money for his new career, at which he would be magnificent.

Drinks and crisps purchased, Strike returned to Robin, who was sitting on an outside bench, hands in her pockets, looking glum.

'Cheer up,' said Strike, speaking to himself as much as to her.

'Sorry,' said Robin, though she didn't really know why she was apologising.

He sat down beside her, rather than opposite, so both of them faced the river. There was a small shingle beach below them, and waves lapped the cold pebbles. On the opposite bank rose the steel-coloured office blocks of Canary Wharf; to their left, the Shard. The river was the colour of lead on this cold November day. Strike tore one of the crisp packets down the middle so that both could help themselves. Wishing she'd asked for coffee instead of a cold drink, Robin took a sip of her lime and soda, ate a couple of crisps, returned her hands to her pockets, then said,

'I know this isn't the attitude, but honestly . . . I don't think we're going to find out what happened to Margot Bamborough.'

'What's brought this on?'

'I suppose Irene misremembering names . . . Janice going along with her, covering up the reason for the Christmas party row . . . it's such a long time ago. People are under no obligation to tell the truth to us now, even if they can remember it. Factor in people getting wedded to old theories, like that whole thing about Gloria and the pill in Brenner's mug, and people wanting to make themselves important, pretending to know things and . . . well, I'm starting to think we're attempting the impossible here.'

A wave of tiredness had swept over Robin while sitting in the cold, waiting for Strike, and in its wake had come hopelessness.

'Pull yourself together,' said Strike bracingly. 'We've already found out two big things the police never knew.' He pulled out his cigarettes, lit one, then said, 'Firstly: there was a big stock of barbiturates on the premises where Margot worked. Secondly: Margot Bamborough might well have had an abortion.

'Taking the barbiturates first,' he said, 'are we overlooking something very obvious, which is that there were means on the premises to put someone to sleep?'

'Margot wasn't put to sleep,' said Robin, gloomily munching crisps. 'She walked out of there.'

'Only if we assume—'

'—Gloria wasn't lying. I know,' said Robin. 'But how do she and Theo – because Theo's still got to be in on it, hasn't she? How did Gloria and Theo administer enough barbiturates to render Margot unconscious? Don't forget, if Irene's telling the truth, Margot wasn't letting anyone else make her drinks at that point. And from what Janice said about dosage, you'd need a lot of pills to make someone actually unconscious.'

'Well reasoned. So, going back to that little story about the pill in the tea—'

'Didn't you believe it?'

'I did,' said Strike, 'because it seems a totally pointless lie. It's not interesting enough to make an exciting anecdote, is it, a single pill? It does reopen the question of whether Margot knew about or suspected Brenner's addiction, though. She might've noticed him being odd in his manner. Downers would make him drowsy. Perhaps she'd seen he was slow on the uptake. Everything we've found out about Margot suggests that if she thought Brenner was behaving unprofessionally, or might be dangerous to patients, she'd have waded straight in and confronted him. And we've just heard a lot of interesting background on Brenner, who sounds like a traumatised, unhappy and lonely man. What if Margot threatened him with being struck off? Loss of status and prestige,

341

to a man who has virtually nothing else in his life? People have killed for less.'

'He left the surgery before she did, that night.'

'What if he waited for her? Offered her a lift?'

'If he did, I think she'd have been suspicious,' said Robin. 'Not that he wanted to hurt her, but that he was going to shout at her, which would've been in character, from what we know of *him*. I'd rather have walked in the rain, personally. And she was a lot younger than him, and tall and fit. I can't remember now where he lived . . .'

'With his unmarried sister, about twenty minutes' drive from the practice. The sister said he'd arrived home at the usual time. A dog-walking neighbour confirmed they'd seen him through the window round about eleven . . .

'But I can think of one other possibility regarding those barbiturates,' Strike went on. 'As Janice pointed out, they had street value, and by the sounds of it, Brenner had amassed a big stock of them. We've got to consider the possibility that some outsider knew there were valuable drugs on the premises, set out to nick them, and Margot got in the way.'

'Which takes us back to Margot dying on the premises, which means—'

'Gloria and Theo come back into the frame. Gloria and Theo might have planned to take the drugs themselves. And we've just heard—'

'—about the drug-dealing brother,' said Robin. 'Why the sceptical tone?'

'Irene was determined to have a go at Gloria, wasn't she?'

'She was, yeah, but the fact that Gloria had a drug-dealing brother is information worth knowing, as is the fact that there were a stack of drugs on the premises that were ripe for nicking. Brenner wouldn't have wanted to admit he had them in the first place, so probably wouldn't have reported the theft, which makes for a situation open to exploitation.'

'A criminal brother doesn't make a person criminal in themselves.'

'Agreed, but it makes me even keener to find Gloria. The term "person of interest" fits her pretty accurately . . .

'And then there's the abortion,' said Strike. 'If Irene's telling the truth about the nursing home calling to confirm the appointment—'

'*If*,' said Robin.

'I don't think that was a lie,' said Strike. 'For the opposite reason to the pill in Brenner's cup. That lie's too big. People don't make things like that up. Anyway, she told Janice about it at the time, and their little row about patient confidentiality rings true. And C. B. Oakden must've based the story on something. I wouldn't be at all surprised if that tip-off came from Irene. She doesn't strike me as a woman who'd turn down a chance to speculate or gossip.'

Robin said nothing. She'd only once in her life had to face the possibility that she might be pregnant, and could still remember the relief that had flooded her when it became clear that she wasn't, and wouldn't have to face still more contact with strangers, and another intimate procedure, more blood, more pain.

Imagine aborting your husband's child, she thought. Could Margot really have done that, when she already had that child's sister at home? What had been going through her mind, a month before she disappeared? Perhaps she'd been quietly breaking down, like Talbot? The past few years had taught Robin how very mysterious human beings were, even to those who thought they knew them best. Infidelity and bigamy, kinks and fetishes, theft and fraud, stalking and harassment: she'd now delved into so many secret lives she'd lost count. Nor did she hold herself superior to any of the deceived and duped who came to the agency, craving truth. Hadn't she thought she knew her own husband back to front? How many hundreds of nights had they lain entwined like Siamese twins, whispering confidences and sharing laughter in the dark? She'd spent nearly half her life with Matthew, and not until a hard, bright diamond ear stud had appeared in their bed had she realised that he was living a life apart, and was not, and perhaps never had been, the man she thought she knew.

'You don't want to think she had an abortion,' said Strike, correctly deducing at least part of the reason for Robin's silence. She didn't answer, instead asking,

'You haven't heard back from her friend Oonagh, have you?'

'Didn't I tell you?' said Strike. 'Yeah, I got an email yesterday. She *is* a retired vicar, and she'd be delighted to meet us when she comes down to London to do some Christmas shopping. Date to be confirmed.'

'That's good,' said Robin. 'You know, I'd like to talk to someone who actually *liked* Margot.'

'Gupta liked her,' said Strike. 'And Janice, she's just said so.'

Robin ripped open the second bag of crisps.

'Which is what you'd expect, isn't it?' she said. 'That people would at least *pretend* they liked Margot, after what happened. But Irene didn't. Don't you find it a bit . . . *excessive* . . . to be holding on to that much resentment, forty years later? She really put the boot in. Wouldn't you think it was . . . I don't know, more *politic* . . .'

'To claim to be friends?'

'Yes . . . but maybe Irene knew there were far too many witnesses to the fact that they *weren't* friends. What did you think of the anonymous notes? True or false?'

'Good question,' said Strike, scratching his chin. 'Irene really enjoyed telling us Margot had been called "the c-word", but "hellfire" doesn't sound like the kind of thing she'd invent. I'd have expected something more in the "uppity bitch" line.'

He drew out his notebook again, and scanned the notes he'd made of the interview.

'Well, we still need to check these leads out, for what they're worth. Why don't you follow up Charlie Ramage and Leamington Spa, and I'll look into the Bennie-abusing Applethorpe?'

'You just did it again,' said Robin.

'Did what?'

'Smirked when you said "Bennies". What's so funny about benzedrine?'

'Oh—' Strike chuckled. 'I was just reminded of something my Uncle Ted told me. Did you ever watch *Crossroads*?'

'What's *Crossroads*?'

'I always forget how much younger you are,' Strike said. 'It was a daytime soap opera and it had a character in it called Benny. He was – well, these days you'd call him special needs. Simple. He wore a woolly hat. Iconic character, in his way.'

'You were thinking of him?' said Robin. It didn't seem particularly amusing.

'No, but you need to know about him to understand the next bit. I assume you know about the Falklands War.'

'I'm younger than you, Strike. I'm not pig-ignorant.'

'OK, right. So, the British troops who went over there – Ted was there, 1982 – nicknamed the locals "Bennies", after the character on *Crossroads*. Command gets wind of this, and the order comes down the line, "Stop calling these people we've just liberated Bennies". So,' said Strike, grinning, 'They started calling them "Stills".'

'"Stills"? What does "Stills" mean?'

'"Still Bennies,"' said Strike, and he let out a great roar of laughter. Robin laughed, too, but mostly at Strike's amusement. When his guffaws had subsided, both watched the river for a few seconds, drinking and, in Strike's case, smoking, until he said,

'I'm going to write to the Ministry of Justice. Apply for permission to visit Creed.'

'Seriously?'

'We've got to try. The authorities always thought Creed assaulted or killed more women than he was done for. There was jewellery in his house and bits of clothing nobody ever identified. Just because everyone thinks it's Creed—'

'—doesn't mean it isn't,' agreed Robin, who followed the tortured logic perfectly.

Strike sighed, rubbed his face, cigarette still poking out of his mouth, then said,

'Want to see exactly how crazy Talbot was?'

'Go on.'

Strike pulled the leather-bound notebook out of the inside pocket of his coat and handed it to her. Robin opened it and turned the pages in silence.

They were covered in strange drawings and diagrams. The writing was small, meticulously neat but cramped. There was much underlining and circling of phrases and symbols. The pentagram recurred. The pages were littered with names, but none connected with the case: Crowley, Lévi, Adams and Schmidt.

'Huh,' she said quietly, stopping on a particularly heavily embellished page on which a goat's head with a third eye looked balefully up at her. 'Look at this . . .'

She bent closer.

'He's using astrological symbols.'

'He's what?' said Strike, frowning down at the page she was perusing.

'That's Libra,' said Robin, pointing at a symbol towards the bottom of the page. 'It's my sign, I used to have a keyring with that on it.'

'He's using bloody *star signs*?' said Strike, pulling the book back towards him, looking so disgusted that Robin started to laugh again.

Strike scanned the page. Robin was right. The circles drawn around the goat's head told him something else, too.

'He's calculated the full horoscope for the moment he thought she was abducted,' he said. 'Look at the date there. The eleventh of October 1974. Half past six in the evening . . . fuck's sake. *Astrology* . . . he was out of his tree.'

'What's your sign?' asked Robin, trying to work it out.

'No idea.'

'Oh sod off,' said Robin.

He looked at her, taken aback.

'You're being affected!' she said. 'Everyone knows their star sign. Don't pretend to be above it.'

Strike grinned reluctantly, took a large drag on his cigarette, exhaled, then said,

'Sagittarius, Scorpio rising, with the sun in the first house.'

11/10/74 6.30pm

ΚΕΦΑΛΗ Α
THE SABBATH OF THE GOAT
To beget is to die; to die is to beget.
Cast the Seed into the Field of Night.
CROWLEY

SCHMIDT ADVISES
REASSESSMENT
BAPHOMET
BAPHOMET

♀ = goddess of intelligence & justice in ♑
SHE IS WITH BAPHOMET

WHO?

Medium Coeli ♑ Baphomet makes his mark, fulfils an AMBITION

= careless mistakes by ♑? MAYBE NARROW ESCAPE? Van?

SCHMIDT SAYS ♅ IS ♑ !

WHO?

AC ♈

♄ in House of Death
CROWLEY: 'manner of death will be singular'
WHO?

♀ in 7th house, House of Marriage. ♀ in ♏ - temper, hidden depths.

Stellium in 6th house, House of Health, clear danger for all medical people. Baphomet fakes illness? Medical emergency?

6th House also SERVANTS

☽ in 4th DEVOTED MOTHER

Indication of overbearing/conceited/bullying individual ♌?

Significant? But 'the sign of ♑ is rough, harsh, dark, even blind; It is divinely unscrupulous, sublimely careless of result' CROWLEY

♈ 'the hair is often light brown or reddish; the eyes are somewhat blue and cold - body well-formed, very rarely accumulates fat' ADAMS so ♈ true subject and clearly not ♑ BUT CLOSE TO SCENE OF ABDUCTION?

WHO?

Southern node in ♊
Cauda Draconis: CROWLEY says SUDDEN LOSSES
2nd House, House of Possessions: TROPHIES TAKEN FROM HER
ADAMS: ♊ in speech is logical and clear - ♊??

SCHMIDT CORRECTS TO ♓ ✓

Baphomet's ruler in ♋
'Holy, holy, holy, unto One Hundred and Fifty Six times holy be OUR LADY that rideth upon THE BEAST!' CROWLEY

♋ knows something, possibly subconscious, has had prior contact with ♑?

She disappeared during ♎ SIGNIFICANT?
♎ = JUSTICE/ADJUSTMENT Was she pursuing justice?

Dr ♎ perfect example of type. ADAMS says head is long-skulled, features small, regular and pleasing, hair very dark brown or black, tendency to grow low on forehead – gentleness – amiability – 'things may be very wrong without people perceiving it. ♎ is the one who discovers the trouble and proceeds to adjust it.' 'A disruption gives him the most terrible agony of spirit.' '♎ IS THE MOST TRUSTWORTHY OF THE SIGNS' ... but also Crowley?

♑
It is the sign of antagonism and fatality.
It is the goat of lust attacking the heavens with its horns.
- Eliphas Levi

'You're—' Robin began to laugh. 'Did you just pull that out of your backside, or is it real?'

'Of course, it's not fucking *real*,' said Strike. '*None* of it's real, is it? But yeah. That's what my *natal horoscope* says. Stop bloody laughing. Remember who my mother was. She loved all that shit. One of her best mates did my full horoscope for her when I was born. I should have recognised that straight off,' he said, pointing at the goat drawing. 'But I haven't been through this properly yet, haven't had time.'

'So what does having the sun in the first house mean?'

'It means nothing, it's all bollocks.'

Robin could tell that he didn't want to admit that he'd remembered, which made her laugh some more. Half-annoyed, half-amused, he muttered,

'Independent. Leadership.'

'Well—'

'It's all bollocks, and we've got enough mystic crap swimming round this case without adding star signs. The medium and the holy place, Talbot and Baphomet—'

'—Irene and her broken Margot Fonteyn,' said Robin.

'Irene and her broken fucking Margot Fonteyn,' Strike muttered, rolling his eyes.

A fine shower of icy rain began to fall, speckling the table top and over Talbot's notebook, which Strike closed before the ink could run. In unspoken agreement, both got up and headed back towards the Land Rover.

The lavender-haired old lady who shared Strike's birthday was now being helped into a nearby Toyota by what looked like two daughters. All around her car stood family, smiling and talking under umbrellas. Just for a moment, as he pulled himself back inside the Land Rover, Strike wondered where he'd be if he lived to eighty, and who'd be there with him.

CHAPTER 22

And later times thinges more vnknowne shall
* show.*
Why then should witlesse man so much
* misweene*
That nothing is but that which he hath seene?
What if within the Moones fayre shining
* spheare,*
What if in euery other starre vnseene
Of other worldes he happily should heare?

Edmund Spenser
The Faerie Queene

Strike got himself a takeaway that night, to eat alone in his attic flat. As he upended the Singapore noodles onto his plate, he inwardly acknowledged the irony that, had Ilsa not been so keen to act as midwife to a romantic relationship between himself and Robin, he might now have been sitting in Nick and Ilsa's flat in Octavia Road, enjoying a laugh with two of his old friends and indeed with Robin herself, whose company had never yet palled on him, through the many long hours they had worked together.

Strike's thoughts lingered on his partner while he ate, on the kiss on the well-chosen card, on the headphones and the fact that she was now calling him Strike in moments of annoyance, or when the two of them were joking, all of them clear signs of increasing intimacy. However stressful the divorce proceedings, of which she'd shared few details, however little she might consciously be seeking romance, she was nevertheless a free agent.

Not for the first time, Strike wondered exactly how egotistical it was to suspect that Robin's feelings towards him might be warmer than those of pure friendship. He got on with her better than he'd ever got on with any woman. Their mutual liking had survived all the stresses of running a business together, the personal trials each had endured since they had met, even the major disagreement that had once seen him sack her. She'd hurried to the hospital when he had found himself alone with a critically ill nephew, brooking, he had no doubt, the displeasure of the ex-husband Strike never forgot to call 'that arsehole' inside his own head.

Nor was Strike unconscious of Robin's good looks: indeed, he'd been fully aware of them ever since she'd taken off her coat in his office for the first time. But her physical appeal was less of a threat to his peace of mind than the deep, guilty liking for being, currently, the main man in her life. Now that the possibility of something more lay in front of him, now that her husband was gone, and she was single, he found himself seriously wondering what would happen, should they act upon what he was beginning to suspect was a mutual attraction. Could the agency, for which they'd both sacrificed so much, which for Strike represented the culmination of all his ambitions, survive the partners falling into bed together? However he reframed this question, the answer always came back 'no', because he was certain, for reasons that had to do with past trauma, not from any particularly puritanical streak, that what Robin sought, ultimately, was the security and permanence of marriage.

And he wasn't the marrying kind. No matter the inconveniences, what he craved at the end of a working day was his private space, clean and ordered, organised exactly as he liked it, free of emotional storms, from guilt and recriminations, from demands to service Hallmark's idea of romance, from a life where someone else's happiness was his responsibility. The truth was that he'd always been responsible for some woman: for Lucy, as they grew up together in squalor and chaos; for Leda, who lurched from lover to lover, and whom he had sometimes had to physically protect as a teenager; for Charlotte, whose volatility and self-destructive tendencies had been given many different names by therapists and psychiatrists, but whom he had loved in spite of it all. He was alone now, and at a kind of peace. None of the affairs or one-night stands he'd had since Charlotte had touched the essential part of him. He'd sometimes wondered since whether Charlotte had not stunted his ability to feel deeply.

Except that, almost against his will, he did care about Robin. He felt familiar stirrings of a desire to make her happy that irked him far more than the habit he'd developed of looking determinedly away when she bent over a desk. They were friends, and he hoped they'd always be friends, and he suspected the best way to guarantee that was never see each other naked.

When he'd washed up his plate, Strike opened the window to admit the cold night air, reminding himself that every woman he knew would have been complaining immediately about the draught. He then lit a cigarette, opened the laptop he'd brought upstairs and drafted a letter to the Ministry of Justice, explaining that he'd been hired by Anna Phipps, setting out his proven credentials as an investigator both within the army and outside it, and requesting permission to visit and question Dennis Creed in Broadmoor.

Once finished, he yawned, lit his umpteenth cigarette of the day and went to lie down on his bed, as usual undoing his trousers first. Picking up *The Demon of Paradise Park*, he turned to the final chapter.

The question that haunts the officers who entered Creed's basement in 1976 and saw for themselves the combination of jail and torture chamber that he'd constructed there, is whether the 12 women he is known to have assaulted, raped and/or killed represent the total tally of his victims.

In our final interview, Creed, who that morning had been deprived of privileges following an aggressive outburst against a prison officer, was at his least communicative and most cryptic.

Q: People suspect there may have been more victims.
A: Is that right?
Q: Louise Tucker. She was sixteen, she'd run away—
A: You journalists love putting ages on people, don't you? Why is that?
Q: Because it paints a picture. It's a detail we can all identify with. D'you know anything about Louise Tucker?
A: Yeah. She was sixteen.
Q: There was unclaimed jewellery in your basement. Unclaimed pieces of clothing.
A: . . .
Q: You don't want to talk about the unclaimed jewellery?
A: . . .

Q: Why don't you want to talk about those unclaimed items?

A: . . .

Q: Does any part of you think, "I've got nothing to lose, now. I could put people's minds at rest. Stop families wondering"?

A: . . .

Q: You don't think, it would be a kind of reparation? I could repair something of my reputation?

A: [laughs] "Reputation" . . . you think I spend my days worrying about my reputation? You people really don't [indistinguishable]

Q: What about Kara Wolfson? Disappeared in '73.

A: How old was she?

Q: Twenty-six. Club hostess in Soho.

A: I don't like whores.

Q: Why's that?

A: Filthy.

Q: You frequented prostitutes.

A: When there was nothing else on offer.

Q: You tried – Helen Wardrop was a prostitute. And she got away from you. Gave a description to the police.

A: . . .

Q: You tried to abduct Helen in the same area Kara was last seen.

A: . . .

Q: What about Margot Bamborough?

A: . . .

Q: A van resembling your van was seen speeding in the area she disappeared.

A: . . .

Q: If you abducted Bamborough, she'd have been in your basement at the same time as Susan Meyer, wouldn't she?

A: . . . Nice for her.

Q: Was it nice for her?

A: Someone to talk to.

Q: Are you saying you were holding both Bamborough and Meyer at the same time?

A: [smiles]

Q: What about Andrea Hooton? Was Bamborough dead when you abducted Andrea?

A: . . .

Q: You threw Andrea's body off cliffs. That was a change in your m.o. Was she the first body you threw off there?

A: . . .

Q: You don't want to confirm whether you abducted Margot Bamborough?

A: [smiles]

Strike put down the book and lay for a while, smoking and thinking. Then he reached for Bill Talbot's leather-bound notebook, which he'd earlier thrown onto his bed when taking off his coat.

Flicking through the densely packed pages, looking for something comprehensible, something he could connect with a solid fact or reference point, he suddenly placed a thick finger in the book to stop the pages turning, his attention caught by a sentence written mostly in English that seemed familiar.

12th (♓) found. Therefore AS EXPECTED killer is ♑

It was an effort to get up and fetch his own notebook, but this he did. Slumping back onto his bed, he found the sentence that Pat had translated for him from Pitman shorthand:

And that is the last of them, the twelfth, and the circle will be closed upon finding the tenth – unknown word – Baphomet. Transcribe in the true book.

The unknown word, Strike realised, was the same symbol that followed the word 'Killer' in Talbot's notebook.

With a feeling of both exasperation and curiosity, Strike picked up his phone and Googled 'astrological symbols'.

A few minutes later, having read a couple of astrological web pages with an expression of mild distaste, he'd successfully interpreted Talbot's sentence. It read: '*Twelfth (Pisces) found. Therefore AS EXPECTED killer is Capricorn.*'

Pisces was the twelfth sign of the zodiac, Capricorn the tenth. Capricorn was also the sign of the goat, which Talbot, in his manic state, appeared to have connected with Baphomet, the goat-headed deity.

'Fuck's sake,' muttered Strike, turning to a fresh page in his notebook and writing something.

An idea now occurred to him: those strange, unexplained dates with crosses beside them on all the male witnesses' statements. He wondered whether he could be bothered to get up and go downstairs to fetch the relevant pages from the boxes of police records. With a sigh, he decided that the answer was yes. He did up his flies, heaved himself to his feet, and fetched the office keys from their hook by the door.

Ten minutes later, Strike returned to his bedroom with both his laptop and a fresh notebook. As he settled down on top of the duvet again, he noticed that the screen of his mobile, which was lying on the duvet, was now lit up. Somebody had tried to call him while he'd been downstairs. Expecting it to be Lucy, he picked up the phone and looked at it.

He'd just missed a call from Charlotte. Strike lay the phone back down again and opened his laptop. Slowly and painstakingly, he set to work matching the unexplained dates on each male suspect's witness statements with the relevant sign of the zodiac. If his hunch that Talbot had been checking the men's star signs was correct, Steven Douthwaite was a Pisces, Paul Satchwell was an Aries and Roy Phipps, who'd been born on the twenty-seventh of December . . . was a Capricorn.

12th (♓) found. Therefore AS EXPECTED killer is ♑

'Capricornus is divinely unscrupulous, sublimely careless of result... thou hast no right but to do thy will. Do that, and no other shall say nay. For pure will, unassuaged of purpose, delivered from the lust of result, is every way perfect.' – Crowley

Husband can't be true ♑, Adams says ♑ materialistic, severe, hard-bitten, thin lipped, 'eyes small and piercing'

SCHMIDT EXPLAINS ⟶ NOT ♑ BUT ♋

resourceful, sensitive, musical
"I am the secret serpent coiled about to spring; in my coiling there is joy." - CROWLEY

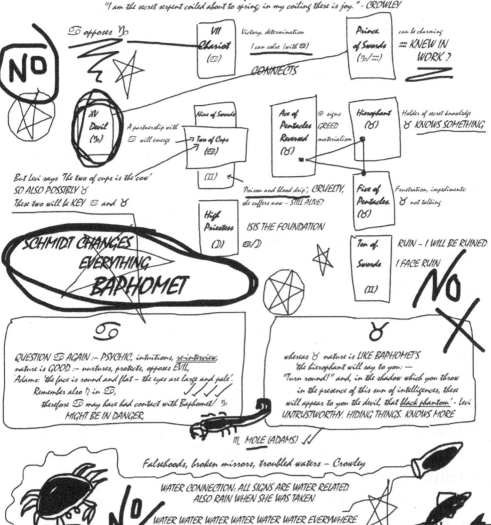

♋ opposes ♑

NO

VII
Chariot
(♋)

Victory, determination
I can solve (with ♋)

CONNECTS

Prince
of Swords
(♑/♒)

can be charming
♒ KNEW IN WORK ?

XV
Devil
(♑)

A partnership with
♋ will emerge

Nine of Swords

Two of Cups
(♋)

(II)

Ace of
Pentacles
Reversed
(♉)

⊕ signs
GREED
materialism

Hierophant
(♉)

Holder of secret knowledge
♉ KNOWS SOMETHING

But Levi says 'The two of cups is the cow'
SO ALSO POSSIBLY ♉
These two will be KEY ♋ and ♉

High
Priestess
(☽)

'Poison and blood drip', CRUELTY,
she suffers now – STILL ALIVE?

ISIS THE FOUNDATION
♋/☽

Five of
Pentacles
(♉)

Frustration, impediments:
♉ not talking

Ten of
Swords
(II)

RUIN – I WILL BE RUINED
I FACE RUIN

NO ✕

SCHMIDT CHANGES
EVERYTHING
BAPHOMET

♋

QUESTION ♋ AGAIN :– PSYCHIC, intuitions, <u>re-interview</u>,
nature is GOOD :– nurtures, protects, opposes EVIL,
Adams: 'the face is round and flat – the eyes are large and pale'.
Remember also ☽ in ♋,
therefore ♋ may have had contact with Baphomet/ ♑
MIGHT BE IN DANGER.

♉

whereas ♉ nature is LIKE BAPHOMET'S
'the hierophant will say to you: —
"Turn round!" and, in the shadow which you throw
in the presence of this sun of intelligences, these
will appear to you the devil, that black phantom' - Levi
UNTRUSTWORTHY. HIDING THINGS. KNOWS MORE

♏ MOLE (ADAMS)

Falsehoods, broken mirrors, troubled waters – Crowley

WATER CONNECTION: ALL SIGNS ARE WATER RELATED.
ALSO RAIN WHEN SHE WAS TAKEN

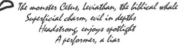 NO

WATER WATER WATER WATER WATER WATER EVERYWHERE

♒ worried about how ♏ died? SCHMIDT AGREES W ADAMS

Did ♒ challenge ♓ about ♏? Was ♋ there, did ♋ witness? ♋ is kind, instinct is to protect, INTERVIEW AGAIN.
♏ and ♒ are connected WATER WATER also ♋ and ♑ HAS A FISH'S TAIL.

The monster Cetus, Leviathan, the biblical whale
Superficial charm, evil in depths
Headstrong, enjoys spotlight
A performer, a liar

Yet Talbot had cleared Roy Phipps of involvement early in the case.

'So that makes no fucking sense,' muttered Strike to the empty room.

He put down his laptop and picked up Talbot's notebook again, reading on from the assertion that Margot's killer must be Capricorn.

'Christ almighty,' Strike muttered, trying, but not entirely succeeding, to find sense among the mass of esoteric ramblings with the aid of his astrological websites. As far as he could tell, Talbot appeared to have absolved Roy Phipps from suspicion on the grounds that he wasn't really a Capricorn, but some sign that Strike couldn't make head nor tail of, and which he suspected Talbot might have invented.

Returning to the notebook, Strike recognised the Celtic cross layout of tarot cards from his youth. Leda fancied herself a reader of tarot; many times had he seen her lay out the cards in the very formation Talbot had sketched in the middle of the page. He had never, however, seen the cards given astrological meanings before, and wondered whether this, too, had been Talbot's own invention.

His mobile buzzed again. He picked it up.

Charlotte had sent him a photograph. A naked photograph, of herself holding two coffees. The accompanying message said **6 years ago tonight. I wish it was happening again. Happy Birthday, Bluey x**

Against his will, Strike stared at the body no sentient heterosexual man could fail to desire, and at the face Venus would envy. Then he noticed the blurring along her lower stomach, where she'd airbrushed out her Caesarean scar. This took care of his burgeoning erection. Like an alcoholic pushing away brandy, he deleted the picture and returned to Talbot's notebook.

CHAPTER 23

It is the mynd, that maketh good or ill,
That maketh wretch or happie, rich or poore:
For some, that hath abundance at his will,
Hath not enough, but wants in greatest store;
And other, that hath litle, askes no more,
But in that litle is both rich and wise.

Edmund Spenser
The Faerie Queene

Eleven days later, Robin was woken at 8 a.m.
by her mobile ringing, after barely an hour's
sleep. She'd spent the night on another
pointless vigil outside the house of the persecuted
weatherman, and had returned to her flat in Earl's
Court to grab a couple of hours' sleep before
hurrying out again to interview Oonagh Kennedy
with Strike, in the café at Fortnum & Mason.
Completely disorientated, she knocked a couple
of items off the bedside table as she groped in the
dark for her phone.

''Lo?''

'Robin?' said a happy shout in her ear. 'You're an aunt!'

'I'm what, sorry?' she muttered.

Wisps of her dreams still clung about her: Pat Chauncey had been asking her out to dinner, and had been deeply hurt that she didn't want to go.

'You're an aunt! Jenny's just had the baby!'

'Oh,' said Robin, and very slowly her brain computed that this was Stephen, her elder brother, on the line. 'Oh, that's wonderful . . . what—?'

'A girl!' said Stephen jubilantly. 'Annabel Marie. Eight pounds eight ounces!'

'Wow,' said Robin, 'that's – is that big? It seems—'

'I'm sending you a picture now!' said Stephen. 'Got it?'

'No – hang on,' said Robin, sitting up. Bleary-eyed, she switched to speakerphone to check her messages. The picture arrived as she was peering at the screen: a wrinkled, bald red baby swaddled in a hospital robe, fists balled up, looking furious to have been forced from a place of quiet, padded darkness into the brightness of a hospital ward.

'Just got it. Oh, Stephen, she's . . . she's beautiful.'

It was a lie, but nevertheless, tears prickled in the exhausted Robin's eyes.

'My God, Button,' she said quietly; it was Stephen's childhood nickname. 'You're a dad!'

'I know!' he said. 'Insane, isn't it? When are you coming home to see her?'

'Soon,' Robin promised. 'I'm back for Christmas. Give Jenny all my love, won't you?'

'I will, yeah. Gonna call Jon now. See you soon, Robs.'

The call was cut. Robin lay in darkness, staring at the brightly lit picture of the crumpled baby, whose puffy eyes were screwed up against a world she seemed to have decided already was not much of a place. It was quite extraordinary to think of her brother Stephen as a father, and that the family now had one more member.

Robin seemed to hear her cousin Katie's words again: *It's like you're travelling in a different direction to the rest of us.* In the old days with Matthew, before she'd started work at the agency, she'd expected to have children with him. Robin had no strong feelings *against* having children, it was simply that she knew, now, that the job she loved would be impossible if she were a mother, or at least, that it would stop being the job she loved. Motherhood, from her limited observation of those her age who were doing it, seemed to demand as much from a woman as she could possibly give. Katie had talked of the perennial tug on her heart when she wasn't with her son, and Robin had tried to imagine an emotional tether even stronger than the guilt and anger with which Matthew had tried to retain her. The problem wasn't that Robin didn't think she'd love her child. On the contrary, she thought it likely that she would love that child to the extent that this job, for which she had voluntarily sacrificed a marriage, her safety, her sleep and her financial security, would have to be sacrificed in return. And how would she feel, afterwards, about the person who'd made that sacrifice necessary?

Robin turned on the light and bent to pick up the things she had knocked off her bedside table: an empty glass, thankfully unbroken, and the thin, flimsy paperback entitled *Whatever Happened to Margot Bamborough?* by C. B. Oakden, which Robin had received in the post the previous morning, and which she'd already read.

Strike didn't yet know that she had managed to get hold of a copy of Oakden's book and Robin had been looking forward to showing him. She had a couple more fragments of Bamborough news, too, but now, perhaps because of her sheer exhaustion, the feeling of anticipation at sharing them had disappeared. Deciding that she wouldn't be able to get back to sleep, she got out of bed.

As she showered, Robin realised, to her surprise, that she was crying.

This is ridiculous. You don't even want a baby. Get a grip of yourself.

When Robin arrived upstairs, dressed, with her hair blow-dried and concealer applied to the shadows under her eyes, she found Max eating toast in the kitchen.

'Morning,' he said, looking up from a perusal of the day's news on his phone. 'You all right?'

'Fine,' said Robin, with forced brightness. 'Just found out I'm an aunt. My brother Stephen's wife gave birth this morning.'

'Oh. Congratulations,' said Max, politely interested. 'Um . . . boy or girl?'

'Girl,' said Robin, turning on the coffee machine.

'I've got about eight godchildren,' said Max gloomily. 'Parents love giving the job to childless people. They think we'll put more effort in, having no kids of our own.'

'True,' said Robin, trying to maintain her cheery tone. She'd been made godmother to Katie's son. The christening had been the first time she'd been in the church in Masham since her wedding to Matthew.

She took a mug of black coffee back to her bedroom, where she opened up her laptop and decided to set down her new information on the Bamborough case in an email to Strike before they met. They might not have much time together before Oonagh Kennedy's interview, so this would expedite discussion.

Hi,

Few bits and pieces on Bamborough before I see you:

• Charles Ramage, the hot tub millionaire, is dead. I've spoken to his son, who couldn't confirm the story about the

Margot sighting, but remembered Janice nursing his father after his crash and said Ramage Snr liked her and 'probably told her all his stories, he had loads of them'. Said his father never minded exaggerating if it made a story better, but was not a liar and 'had a good heart. Wouldn't have told a lie about a missing woman.' Also confirmed that his father was close friends with a 'senior police officer' (couldn't remember rank or first name) called Greene. Ramage Snr's widow is still alive and living in Spain, but she's his second wife and the son doesn't get on with her. I'm trying to get a contact number/email address for her.

- I'm 99% sure I've found the right Amanda White, who's now called Amanda Laws. Two years ago she posted a piece on Facebook about people disappearing, which included Margot. She said in the comment that she'd been personally involved in the Margot disappearance. I've sent her a message but nothing back yet.

- I've got hold of a copy of *Whatever Happened to Margot Bamborough?* and read it (it's not long). Judging by what we know about Margot so far, it looks full of inaccuracies. I'll bring it with me this morning.

See you in a bit x

Sleep-deprived, Robin had added the kiss automatically and had sent the email before she could retract it. It was one thing to put a kiss on a birthday card, quite another to start adding them to work emails.

Shit.

She could hardly write a PS saying 'Ignore that kiss, my fingers did it without me meaning to.' That would draw attention to the thing if Strike hadn't thought anything of it.

As she closed her laptop, her mobile screen lit up: she'd received a long, excited text from her mother about baby Annabel Marie's perfection, complete with a photograph of herself cradling her new granddaughter, Robin's father beaming over his wife's shoulder. Robin texted back:

She's gorgeous!

even though the baby was quite as unprepossessing in the new photograph as she'd been in the old. Yet she wasn't really lying: the fact of Annabel's birth *was* somehow gorgeous, an everyday miracle, and Robin's mysterious shower tears had been partly in acknowledgement of the fact.

As the Tube sped her towards Piccadilly Circus,

Robin took out her copy of C. B. Oakden's book, which she'd found at a second-hand bookshop in Chester, and flicked through it again. The dealer had said the book had been in his shop for several years, and had arrived in a job lot of books he'd taken off the hands of the family of an elderly local woman who'd died. Robin suspected that the dealer hadn't known of the book's murky legal status before Robin's email enquiry, but he appeared to have no particular moral qualms about selling it. As long as Robin guaranteed by phone that she wouldn't reveal where she'd got it, he was happy to part with it, for a hefty mark-up. Robin only hoped Strike would think the price justified, once he'd read it.

Robin's particular copy appeared to have escaped pulping because it had been one of the author's free copies, which must have been given to him before the court decision. An inscription on the fly-leaf read: *To Auntie May, with every good wish, CB Oakden (Carl)*. To Robin, 'with every good wish' seemed an affected, grandiose message to send an aunt.

Barely a hundred pages long, the flimsy paperback had a photograph of Margot as a Bunny Girl on the cover, a picture familiar to Robin because it had appeared in so many newspaper reports of her disappearance. Half cut off in this enlarged picture was a second Bunny Girl, who Robin knew to be Oonagh Kennedy. The photograph was reproduced in its entirety in the middle of the paperback, along with other pictures which Robin thought Strike would agree were the most valuable part of the book, though only, she feared, in terms of putting faces to names rather than helping the investigation.

Robin got off the Tube at Piccadilly Circus and walked in a strong wind up Piccadilly, beneath swaying Christmas lights, wondering where she might find a baby present for Stephen and Jenny. Having passed no appropriate shops, she arrived outside Fortnum & Mason with an hour to spare before the projected meeting with Oonagh Kennedy.

Robin had often passed the famous store since she had lived in London, but never gone inside. The ornate frontage was duck-egg blue and the windows, dressed for Christmas, some of the most beautiful in the city. Robin peered through clear circles of glass surrounded by artificial snow, at heaps of jewel-like crystallised fruits, silk scarves, gilded tea canisters, and wooden nutcrackers shaped like fairy-tale princes. A gust of particularly cold, rain-flecked wind whipped at her, and, without conscious thought, Robin allowed herself to be swept inside the sumptuous seasonal fantasy, through a door flanked by a doorman in an overcoat and top hat.

The store was carpeted in scarlet. Everywhere were mountains of duck-egg blue packaging. Close at hand she saw the very truffles that Morris had bought her for her birthday. Past marzipan fruits and biscuits she walked, until she glimpsed the café at the back of the ground floor where they'd agreed to meet Oonagh. Robin turned back. She didn't want to see the retired vicar before the allotted time, because she wanted to reason herself into a more business-like frame of mind before an interview.

'Excuse me,' she asked a harried-looking woman selecting marzipan fruits for a client, 'd'you sell anything for children in—?'

'Third floor,' said the woman, already moving away.

The small selection of children's goods available were, in Robin's view, exorbitantly priced, but as Annabel's only aunt, and only London-based relative, she felt a certain pressure to give a suitably metropolitan gift. Accordingly, she purchased a large, cuddly Paddington bear.

Robin was walking away from the till with her duck-egg carrier bag when her mobile rang. Expecting it to be Strike, she saw instead an unknown number.

'Hi, Robin here.'

'Hi, Robin. It's Tom,' said an angry voice.

Robin couldn't for the life of her think who Tom was. She mentally ran through the cases the agency was currently working on – Two-Times, Twinkletoes, Postcard, Shifty and Bamborough – trying in vain to remember a Tom, while saying with what she intended to be yes-of-course-I-know-who-you-are warmth,

'Oh, hi!'

'*Tom Turvey*,' said the man, who didn't appear fooled.

'Oh,' said Robin, her heart beginning to beat uncomfortably fast, and she drew back into an alcove where pricey scented candles stood on shelves.

Tom Turvey was Sarah Shadlock's fiancé. Robin had had no contact with him since finding out that their respective partners had been sleeping together. She'd never particularly liked him, nor had she ever found out whether he knew about the affair.

'Thanks,' said Tom. 'Thanks a *fucking bunch*, Robin!'

He was close to shouting. Robin distanced the mobile a little from her ear.

'Excuse me?' she said, but she suddenly seemed to have become all nerves and pulse.

'Didn't bother fucking telling me, eh? Just walked away and washed your hands, did you?'

'Tom—'

'She's told me *fucking* everything, and you knew a year ago and I find out today, *four weeks before my wedding*—'

'Tom, I—'

'Well, I hope you're fucking happy!' he bellowed. Robin removed the phone from her ear and held it at arm's length. He was still clearly audible as he yelled, 'I'm the only one of us who hasn't been fucking around, and I'm the one who's been *fucked over*—'

Robin cut him off. Her hands were shaking.

'*Excuse me*,' said a large woman, who was trying to see the candles on the shelves behind Robin, who mumbled an apology and walked away, until she reached a curving iron banister, beyond which was a large, circular expanse of thin air. Looking down, she saw the floors had been cut out, so that she was able to see right into the basement, where compressed people were criss-crossing the space with baskets laden with expensive hams and bottles of wine. Head spinning, hardly aware of what she was doing, Robin turned and headed blindly back towards the department exit, trying not to bump into tables piled with fragile china. Down the red carpeted stairs she walked, trying to breathe herself back to calm, trying to make sense of what she'd just heard.

'Robin.'

She walked on, and only when somebody said '*Robin*' again did she turn and realise Strike had just entered the store via a side door from Duke Street. The shoulders of his overcoat were studded with glimmering raindrops.

'Hi,' she said, dazed.

'You all right?'

For a split-second she wanted to tell him everything: after all, he knew about Matthew's affair, he knew how her marriage had ended and he'd met Tom and Sarah. However, Strike himself looked tense, his mobile gripped in his hand.

'Fine. You?'

'Not great,' he said.

The two of them moved aside to allow a group of tourists into the store. In the shadow of the wooden staircase Strike said,

'Joan's taken a turn for the worse. They've readmitted her to hospital.'

'Oh God, I'm so sorry,' said Robin. 'Listen – go to Cornwall. We'll cope. I'll interview Oonagh, I'll take care of everything—'

'No. She specifically told Ted she didn't want us all dashing down there again. But that's not like her . . .'

Strike seemed every bit as scattered and distracted as Robin felt, but now she pulled herself together. *Screw Tom, screw Matthew and Sarah.*

'Seriously, Cormoran, go. I can take care of work.'

'They're expecting me in a fortnight for Christmas. Ted says she's desperate to have us all at home. It's supposed to be just for a couple of days, the hospital thing.'

'Well, if you're sure . . .' said Robin. She checked her watch. 'We've got ten minutes until Oonagh's supposed to be here. Want to go to the café and wait for her?'

'Yeah,' said Strike. 'Good thinking, I could use a coffee.'

'God Rest Ye Merry, Gentlemen' trilled from the speakers as they entered the realm of crystallised fruits and expensive teas, both lost in painful thought.

CHAPTER 24

. . . my delight is all in ioyfulnesse,
In beds, in bowres, in banckets, and in feasts:
And ill becomes you with your lofty creasts,
To scorne the ioy, that Ioue is glad to seeke . . .

Edmund Spenser
The Faerie Queene

The café was reached by a flight of stairs that placed it on a higher level than the shop floor, which it overlooked. Once he and Robin had sat down at a table for four by the window, Strike sat silently looking down into Jermyn Street, where passers-by were reduced to moving mushrooms, eclipsed by their umbrellas. He was a stone's throw from the restaurant in which he'd last seen Charlotte.

He'd received several more calls from her since the nude photograph on his birthday, plus several texts, three of which had arrived the previous evening. He'd ignored all of them, but somewhere at the back of his anxiety about Joan scuttled a familiar worry about what Charlotte's next move was going to be, because the texts were becoming increasingly overwrought. She had a couple of suicide attempts in her past, one of which had almost succeeded. Three years after he'd left her, she was still trying to make him responsible for her safety and her happiness, and Strike found it equally infuriating and saddening. When Ted had called Strike that morning with the news about Joan, the detective had been in the process of looking up the telephone number of the merchant bank where Charlotte's husband worked. If Charlotte threatened suicide, or sent any kind of final message, Strike intended to call Jago.

'Cormoran,' Robin said.

He looked round. A waiter had arrived at the table. When both had ordered coffee, and Robin some toast, each relapsed into silence. Robin was looking away from the window towards the shoppers stocking up on fancy groceries for Christmas down on the shop floor and re-running Tom Turvey's outburst in her head. The aftershocks were still hitting her. *Four weeks before my fucking wedding.* It must have been called off. Sarah had left Tom for Matthew, the man she'd wanted all along, and Robin was sure she wouldn't have left Tom unless Matthew had shown himself ready to offer her what Tom had: diamonds and a change of name. *I'm the only one of us who hasn't been fucking around.* Everyone had been unfaithful, in Tom's opinion, except poor Tom . . . so Matthew must have told his old friend that she, Robin, had been sleeping with someone else (which meant Strike, of course, of whom Matthew had been perennially jealous and suspicious from the moment Robin had gone to work for him). And even now that Tom knew about Matthew and Sarah, after his old friend's duplicity and treachery had been revealed, Tom still believed the lie about Robin and Strike. Doubtless he thought his current misery was all Robin's fault, that if she hadn't succumbed to Strike, the domino effect of infidelity would never have been started.

'You sure you're all right?'

Robin started and looked around. Strike had come out of his own reverie and was looking at her over his coffee cup.

'Fine,' she said. 'Just knackered. Did you get my email?'

'Email?' said Strike, reaching for the phone in his pocket. 'Yeah, but I haven't read it, sorry. Dealing with other—'

'Don't bother now,' said Robin hastily, inwardly cringing at the thought of that accidental kiss, even in the midst of her new troubles. 'It isn't particularly important, it'll keep. I did find this, though.'

She took the copy of *Whatever Happened to Margot Bamborough?* out of her bag and passed it over the table, but before Strike could express his surprise, she muttered,

'Give it back, give it back now,' tugged it back out of his hand and stuffed it into her bag.

A stout woman was heading towards them across the café. Two bulging bags of Christmas fare were dangling from her hands. She had the full cheeks and large square front teeth of a cheerful-looking chipmunk, an aspect that in her youthful photos had added a certain cheeky charm to her prettiness. The hair that once had been long, dark and glossy was now chin-length and white, except at the front, where a dashing bright purple streak had been added. A large silver and amethyst cross bounced on her purple sweater.

'Oonagh?' said Robin.

'Dat's me,' she panted. She seemed nervous. 'The *queues*! Well, what do I expect, Fortnum's at Christmas? But fair play, dey *do* a lovely mustard.'

Robin smiled. Strike drew out the chair beside him.

'T'anks very much,' said Oonagh, sitting down.

Her Irish accent was attractive, and barely eroded by what Robin knew had been a longer residence in England than in the country of her birth.

Both detectives introduced themselves.

'Very nice to meet you,' Oonagh said, shaking hands before clearing her throat nervously. 'Excuse me. I was *made up* to get yer message,' she told Strike. 'Years and years I've spent, wondering why Roy never hired someone, because he's got the money to do it and the police never got anywhere. So little Anna called you in, did she? God bless that gorl, *what* she must've gone through . . . Oh, hello,' she said to the waiter, 'could I have a cappuccino and a bit of that carrot cake? T'ank you.'

When the waiter had gone, Oonagh took a deep breath and said,

'I know I'm rattlin' on. I'm nervous, that's the truth.'

'There's nothing to be—' began Strike.

'Oh, there is,' Oonagh contradicted him, looking sober. 'Whatever happened to Margot, it can't be anything good, can it? Nigh on forty years I've prayed for that girl, prayed for the truth and prayed God would look after her, alive or dead. She was the best friend I ever had and – sorry. I knew this would happen. Knew it.'

She picked up her unused cloth napkin and mopped her eyes.

'Ask me a question,' she said, half-laughing. 'Save me from meself.'

Robin glanced at Strike, who handed the interview to her with a look as he pulled out his notebook.

'Well, perhaps we can start with how you and Margot met?' Robin suggested.

'We can, o' course,' said Oonagh. 'That would've been '66. We were both auditioning to be Bunny Girls. You'll know all about that?'

Robin nodded.

'I had a decent figure then, believe it or not,' said Oonagh, smiling as she gestured down at her tubby torso, although she seemed to feel little regret for the loss of her waist.

Robin hoped Strike wasn't going to take her to task later for not organising her questions according to the usual categories of *people, places and things,* but she judged it better to make this feel more like a normal conversation, at least at first, because Oonagh was still visibly nervous.

'Did you come over from Ireland, to try and get the job?' asked Robin.

'Oh no,' said Oonagh. 'I was already in London. I kinda run away from home, truth be told. You're lookin' at a convent gorl with a mammy as strict as a prison warder. I had a week's wages from a clothes shop in Derry in my pocket, and my mammy gave me one row too many. I walked out, got on the ferry, came to London and sent a postcard home to tell 'em I was alive and not to worry. My mammy didn't speak to me for t'irty years.

'I was waitressing when I heard they were opening a Playboy Club in Mayfair. Well, the money was *crazy* good compared to what you could earn in a normal place. T'irty-five pounds a week, we started on. That's near enough six hundred a week, nowadays. There was nowhere else in London was going to pay a working-class gorl that. It was more than most of our daddies earned.'

'And you met Margot at the club?'

'I met her at the audition. Knew *she'd* get hired the moment I looked at her. She had the figure of a model: all legs, and the girl *lived* on sugar. She was t'ree years younger than me, and she lied about her age so they'd take – oh, t'ank you very much,' said Oonagh, as the waiter placed her cappuccino and carrot cake in front of her.

'Why was Margot auditioning?' Robin asked.

'Because her family had nothing – and I mean, *nothing*, now,' Oonagh said. 'Her daddy had an accident when she was four. Fell off a step-ladder, broke his back. Crippled. That's why she had no brothers and sisters. Her mammy used to clean people's houses. *My* family had more than the Bamboroughs and nobody ever got rich farming a place the size of ours. But the Bamboroughs were not-enough-to-eat poor.

'She was such a clever girl, but the family needed help. She got herself into medical school, told the university she'd have to defer for a year, then headed straight for the Playboy Club. We took to each other straight away, in the audition, because she was *so funny*.'

'Was she?' said Robin. Out of the corner of her eye, she saw Strike look up from his notebook in surprise.

'Oh, Margot Bamborough was the funniest person I ever knew in my life,' said Oonagh. 'In my *loife*, now. We used to laugh till we cried. I've never laughed like that since. Proper cockney accent and she could just make you laugh until you *dropped*.

'So we started work together, and they were *strict*, mind you,' said Oonagh, now forking cake into her mouth as she talked. 'Inspected before you walked out on the floor, uniform on properly, nails done, and then there were *rules* like you've no idea. They used to put plain-clothes detectives in the club to catch us out, make sure we weren't giving out our full names or our phone numbers.

'If you were any good at it, you could put a tidy bit of money away. Margot graduated to cigarette girl, selling them out of a little tray. She was popular with the men because she was so funny. She hardly spent a penny on herself. She split the lot between a savings account for medical school and the rest she gave her mammy. Worked every hour they'd let her. Bunny Peggy, she called herself, because she didn't want any of the punters to know her real name. I was Bunny *Una*, because nobody knew how to say "Oonagh". We got all kinds of offers – you had to say no, of course. But it was nice to be asked, right enough,' said Oonagh, and perhaps picking up on Robin's surprise, she smiled and said,

'Don't think Margot and I didn't know *exactly* what we were doin', corseted up with bunny ears on our heads. What you maybe don't realise is a woman couldn't get a mortgage in dose days without a man co-signing the forms. Same with credit cards. I squandered my money at first, but I learned better, learned from Margot. I got smart, I started saving. I ended up buying my own flat with cash. Middle-class gorls, with their mammies and daddies paying their way, they could afford to burn their bras and have hairy armpits. Margot and I, we did what we had to.

'Anyway, the Playboy Club was sophisticated. It wasn't a knocking shop. It had licences it would've lost if things got seedy. We had women guests, too. Men used to bring their wives, their dates. The worst we had was a bit of tail-pulling, but if a club member got really handsy, he lost his membership. You should've seen what I had to put up with in my job before that: hands up my skirt when I bent over a table, and worse. They looked after us at the Playboy Club. Members weren't allowed to date Bunny Girls – well, in t'eory. It happened. It happened to Margot. I was angry at her for that, I said, you're risking everything, you fool.'

'Was this Paul Satchwell?' asked Robin.

'It was indeed,' said Oonagh. 'He'd come to the club as someone's guest, he wasn't a member, so Margot t'ought it was a grey area. I was still worried she was going to lose the job.'

'You didn't like him?'

'No, I didn't like him,' said Oonagh. 'T'ought he was Robert Plant, so he did, but Margot fell for him hook, line and sinker. She didn't go out a lot, see, because she was saving. I'd been round the nightclubs in my first year in London; I'd met plenty of Satchwells. He was six years older than she was, an artist and he wore his jeans so tight you could see his cock and balls right through them.'

Strike let out an involuntary snort of laughter. Oonagh looked at him.

'Sorry,' he muttered. 'You're, ah, not like most vicars I've met.'

'I don't t'ink the Good Lord will mind me mentioning cocks and balls,' said Oonagh airily. 'He made 'em, didn't he?'

'So they started dating?' asked Robin.

'They did,' said Oonagh. '*Mad* passion, it was. You could *feel* the heat off the two of them. For Margot – see, before Satchwell, she'd always had *tunnel vision* about life, you know, eyes on the prize: become a doctor and save her family. She was cleverer than any of the boys she knew, and men don't like that much *nowadays*. She was taller than half of them, as well. She told me she'd never had a man interested in her brains before Satchwell. *Interested in her brains*, my aunt Nelly. The girl had a body like Jane Birkin. Oh, and it wasn't only *his* looks, either, she said. He'd read t'ings. He could talk about art. He could talk for the *hour* about art, right enough. I heard him. Well, *I* don't know a Monet from a poster of Margate, so I'm no judge, but it sounded a load of old bollocks to me.

'But he'd take Margot out to a gallery and educate her about art, then he'd take her home to bed. Sex makes fools of us all,' sighed Oonagh Kennedy. 'And he was her very first and it was obvious, you know,' she nodded at Robin, 'he knew what he was doing, so it was all that much more important to her. Mad in love, she was. *Mad*.

'Then, one night, just a couple o' weeks before she was supposed to be starting medical school, she turns up at my flat *howling*. She'd dropped in on Paul unexpected after work and there was another woman at the flat with him. Naked. *Modelling*, he told her. Modelling – at midnight. She turned round and ran. He went chasin' after her, but she jumped in a taxi and came to mine.

'*Heartbroken*, she was. All night, we sat up talking, me saying "You're better off without him", which was no more than the truth. I said to her, "Margot, you're about to start medical school. The place'll be *wall to wall* with handsome, clever boys training to be doctors. You won't remember Satchwell's *name* after a week or two."

'But then, near dawn, she told me a t'ing I've never told anyone before.'

Oonagh hesitated. Robin tried to look politely but warmly receptive.

'She'd let him take pictures of her. You know. *Pictures*. And she was scared, she wanted them back. I said to her, why in God's name would you let him do such a t'ing, Margot? Because it would've *killed* her mother. The pride they had in her, their only daughter, their brilliant gorl. If those photos turned up anywhere, a magazine or I don't know what, they'd have never lived it down, boastin' up and down their street about their Margot, the genius.

'So I said, I'll come with you and we'll get them back. So we went round there early and banged on his door. The bastard – excuse me, now,' she said. 'You'll rightly say, that's not a Christian attitude, but wait till you hear. Satchwell said to Margot, "I'll speak to you, but not your nanny." Your *nanny*.

'Well, now. I spent ten years working with domestic abuse survivors in Wolverhampton and it's one of the *hallmarks* of an abuser, if their victim isn't compliant, it's because she's under someone *else's* control. Her *nanny*.

'Before I know what's going on, she's inside and I'm stuck on the other side of a closed door. He'd pulled her in and slammed it in my face. I could hear them shouting at each other. Margot was giving as good as she got, God bless her.

'And then, and this is what I *really* wanted to tell you,' said Oonagh, 'and I want to get it right. I told that Inspector Talbot and he didn't listen to a word I was saying, and I told the one who took over, what was his name—?'

'Lawson?' asked Robin.

'Lawson,' said Oonagh, nodding. 'I told both of 'em: I could hear Margot and Paul screaming at each other through the door, Margot telling him to give her the pictures and the negatives – different world, you see. Negatives, you had to get, if you didn't want more copies made. But he refused. He said they were *his copyright*, the dirty bastard – so then I heard Margot say, and this is the important bit, "If you show those pictures to anyone, if they ever turn up in print, I'll go straight to the police and I'll tell them all about your little *pillow* dream—"'

'"Pillow dream"?' repeated Robin.

'That's what she said. And he hit her. A smack loud enough to hear through solid wood, and I heard her shriek. Well, I started hammering and kicking the door. I said, unless he opened it I was going for the police *right now. That* put the fear o' God into him. He opened the door and Margot comes out, hand to her face, it was bright red, you could see his finger marks, and I pulled her behind me and I said to Satchwell, "Don't you *ever* come near her again, and you heard what she said. There'll be trouble if those pictures turn up anywhere."

'And I swear to you, he looked murderous. He stepped right up to me, the way a man will when he wants to remind you what he could do, if he wanted. Almost standing on my toes, he was. I didn't shift,' said Oonagh Kennedy. 'I stood my ground, but I was scared, I won't deny it. And he said to Margot, "Have you told her?" And Margot says, "She doesn't know anything. Yet." And he says, "Well, you know what'll happen if I find out you've talked." And he mimed – well, never mind. It was an – an obscene pose, I suppose you'd say. One of the pictures he'd taken. And he walked back into his flat and slammed the door.'

'Did Margot ever tell you what she meant by the "pillow dream"?' asked Robin.

'She wouldn't. You might t'ink she was scared,

but . . . you know, I t'ink it's just women,' sighed Oonagh. 'We're socialised that way, but maybe Mother Nature's got a hand in it. How many kids would survive to their first birthday if their mammies couldn't forgive 'em?

'Even that day, with his handprint across her face, she didn't want to tell me, because there was a bit of her that didn't want to hurt him. I saw it all the bloody time with my domestic abuse survivors. Women still protecting them. Still worrying about them! Love dies hard in some women.'

'Did she see Satchwell after that?'

'I wish to *God* I could say she didn't,' said Oonagh, shaking her head, 'but yes, she did. They couldn't stay away from each other.

'She started her degree course, but she was that popular at the club, they let her go part time, so I was still seeing a lot of her. One day, her mammy called the club because her daddy had taken sick, but Margot hadn't come in. I was terrified: where was Margot, what had happened to her, why wasn't she there? I've often t'ought back to that moment, you know, because when it happened for real, I was so sure at first she'd turn up, like she had the first time.

'Anyway, when she saw how upset I'd been, t'inking she'd gone missing, she told me the truth. She and Satchwell had started things up again. She had all the old excuses down: he swore he'd never hit her again, he'd cried his eyes out about it, it was the worst mistake of his life, and anyway, she'd provoked him. I told her, "If you can't see him now for what he is, after what he did to you first time round . . ." Anyway, they split again and, surprise, surprise, he not only knocked her around again, he kept her locked in his flat all day, so she couldn't get to work. That was the first shift she'd ever missed. She nearly lost the job over it, and had to make up some cock-and-bull story.

'So then at last,' said Oonagh, 'she tells me she's learned her lesson, I was right all along, she's never going back to him, that's it, *finito*.'

'Did she get the photographs back?' asked Robin.

'First t'ing I asked, when I found out they were back together. She said he'd told her he'd destroyed them. She believed it, too.'

'You didn't?'

'O' course I didn't,' said Oonagh. 'I'd seen him, when she t'reatened him with his *pillow dream*. That was a frightened man. He'd never have destroyed anyt'ing that gave him bargaining power over her.

'Would it be all right if I get another cappuccino?' asked Oonagh apologetically. 'My t'roat's dry, all this talking.'

'Of course,' said Strike, hailing a waiter, and ordering fresh coffees all round.

Oonagh pointed at Robin's Fortnum's bag.

'Been stocking up for Christmas, too?'

'Oh, no, I've been buying a present for my new niece. She was born this morning,' said Robin, smiling.

'Congratulations,' said Strike, who was surprised Robin hadn't already told him.

'Oh, how lovely,' said Oonagh. 'My fifth grand-child arrived last month.'

The interval while waiting for the fresh coffees was filled by Oonagh showing Robin pictures of her grandchildren, and Robin showing Oonagh the two pictures she had of Annabel Marie.

'*Gorgeous*, isn't she?' said Oonagh, peering through her purple reading glasses at the picture on Robin's phone. She included Strike in the question, but, seeing only an angry-looking, bald monkey, his acquiescence was half-hearted.

When the coffees had arrived and the waiter moved away again, Robin said,

'While I remember . . . would you happen to know if Margot had family or friends in Leamington Spa?'

'Leamington Spa?' repeated Oonagh, frowning. 'Let's see . . . one of the gorls at the club was from . . . no, that was King's Lynn. They're similar sorts of names, aren't they? I can't remember anyone from there, no . . . Why?'

'We've heard a man claimed to have seen her there, a week after she disappeared.'

'There were a few sightings after, right enough. Nothing in any of them. None of them made sense. Leamington Spa, that's a new one.'

She took a sip of her cappuccino. Robin asked,

'Did you still see a lot of each other, once Margot went off to medical school?'

'Oh yeah, because she was still working at the club part time. How she did it all, studying, working, supporting her family . . . living on nerves and chocolate, skinny as ever. And then, at the start of her second year, she met Roy.'

Oonagh sighed.

'Even the cleverest people can be bloody *stupid* when it comes to their love lives,' she said. 'In fact, I sometimes t'ink, the cleverer they are with books, the stupider they are with sex. Margot t'ought she'd learned her lesson, that she'd grown up. She couldn't see that it was *classic* rebound. He might've *looked* as different from Satchwell as you could get, but really, it was more of the same.

'Roy had the kind of background Margot would've loved. Books, travel, culture, you know. See, there were gaps in what Margot knew. She was insecure about not knowing about the right fork, the right words. "Napkin" instead of "serviette". All that snobby English stuff.

'Roy was mad for her, mind you. It wasn't all one way. I could see what the appeal was: she was like nothing he'd ever known before. She shocked him, but she fascinated him: the Playboy Club and her work ethic, her feminist ideas, supporting her mammy and daddy. They had arguments, intellectual arguments, you know.

'But there was something *bloodless* about the man. Not *wet* exactly, but—' Oonagh gave a sudden laugh. '"Bloodless" – you'll know about his bleeding problem?'

'Yes,' said Robin. 'Von Something Disease?'

'Dat's the one,' said Oonagh. 'He'd been cossetted and wrapped up in cotton wool all his life by his mother, who was a *horror*. I met her a few times. That woman gave me the respect you'd give something you'd got stuck on your shoe.

'And Roy was . . . still waters run deep, I suppose sums it up. He didn't show a lot of emotion. *Their* flirtation wasn't all sex, it really *was* ideas with them. Not that he wasn't good-looking. He was handsome, in a kind of . . . *limp* way. As different from Satchwell as you could imagine. Pretty boy, all eyes and floppy hair.

'But he was a manipulator. A little bit of disapproval here, a cold look there. He loved how different Margot was, but it still made him uncomfortable. He wanted a woman the exact opposite to his mother, but he wanted Mammy to approve. So the fault lines were dere from the beginning.

'And he could *sulk*,' said Oonagh. 'I *hate* a sulker, now. My mother was the same. T'irty years she wouldn't talk to me, because I moved to London. She finally gave in so she could meet her grandchildren, but then my sister got tipsy at Christmas and let it slip I'd left the church and joined the Anglicans, we were finished for ever. Playboy, she could forgive. Proddy, never.

'Even when they were dating, Roy would stop talking to Margot for days at a time. She told me once he cut her off for a week. She lost patience, she said, "I'm off." That brought him round sharp enough. I said, what was he sulking about? And it was the club. He hated her working there. I said, "Is *he* offering to support your family, while you study?" "Oh, he doesn't like the idea of other men ogling me," she says. Girls like that idea, that little bit of possessiveness. They t'ink it means he only wants her, when o' course, it's the other way round. He only wants her available to *him*. *He's* still free to look at other girls, and Roy had other people interested in him, girls from his own background. He was a pretty boy with a lot of family money. Well,' said Oonagh, 'look at little cousin Cynthia, lurking in the wings.'

'Did you know Cynthia?' asked Robin.

'Met her once or twice, at their house. Mousy little thing. She never spoke more than two words to me,' said Oonagh. 'But she made Roy feel good about himself. Laughing loike a drain at all his jokes. Such as they were.'

'Margot and Roy must have married right after medical school, did they?'

'Dat's right. I was a bridesmaid. She went into general practice. Roy was a high-flier, he went into one of the big teaching hospitals, I can't remember which.

'Roy's parents had this very nice big house with huge lawns and all the rest of it. After his father died, which was just before they had Anna, the mother made it over to Roy. Margot's name wasn't on the deeds, I remember her telling me dat. But Roy loved the idea of bringing up his family in the same house he'd grown up in, and it was beautiful, right enough, out near Hampton Court. So the mother-in-law moved out and Roy and Margot moved in.

'Except, of course, the mother-in-law felt she had the right to walk back in any time she felt like it, because she'd given it to them and she still looked on it as more hers than Margot's.'

'Did you and Margot still see a lot of each other?' asked Robin.

'We did,' said Oonagh. 'We used to try and meet at least once every couple of weeks. Real best friends, we were. Even after she married Roy, she wanted to hold on to me. They had their middle-class friends, o' course, but I t'ink,' said Oonagh, her voice thickening, 'I t'ink she knew I'd always be on her side, you see. She was moving in circles where she felt alone.'

'At home, or at work, too?' asked Robin.

'At home, she was a fish out of water,' said Oonagh. 'Roy's house, Roy's family, Roy's friends, Roy's everyt'ing. She *saw* her own mammy and daddy plenty, but it was hard, the daddy being in his wheelchair, to get him out to the big house. I t'ink the Bamboroughs felt intimidated by Roy and his mother. So Margot used to go back to Stepney to see them. She was still supporting them financially. Ran herself ragged between all her different commitments.'

'And how were things at work?'

'Uphill, all the way,' said Oonagh. 'There weren't

that many women doctors back then, and she was young and working class and that practice she ended up at, the St John's one, she felt alone. It wasn't a happy place,' said Oonagh, echoing Dr Gupta. 'Being Margot, she wanted to try and make it better. That was Margot's whole ethos: make it better. Make it work. Look after everyone. Solve the problem. She tried to bring them together as a team, even though she was the one being bullied.'

'Who was bullying her?'

'The old fella,' said Oonagh. 'I can't remember the names, now. There were two other doctors, isn't that right? The old one and the Indian one. She said *he* was all right, the Indian fella, but she could feel the disapproval off him, too. They had an argument about the pill, she told me. GPs could give it to unmarried women if they wanted – when it was first brought out, it was married women only – but the Indian lad, he still wouldn't hand it out to unmarried women. The first family planning clinics started appearing the same year Margot disappeared. We talked about them. Margot said, t'ank God for it, because she was sure the women coming to their clinic weren't able to get it from either of the other doctors.

'But it wasn't only them. She had trouble with the other staff. I don't t'ink the nurse liked her, either.'

'Janice?' said Robin.

'Was it Janice?' said Oonagh, frowning.

'Irene?' suggested Strike.

'She was blonde,' said Oonagh. 'I remember, at the Christmas party—'

'You were there?' said Robin, surprised.

'Margot *begged* me to go,' said Oonagh. 'She'd set it up and she was afraid it was going to be awful. Roy was working, so *he* couldn't go. This was just a few months after Anna was born. Margot had been on maternity leave and they'd got another doctor in to cover for her, a man. She was convinced the place had worked better without her. She was hormonal and tired and dreading going back. Anna would only have been two or three months old. Margot brought her to the party, because she was breastfeeding. She'd organised the Christmas party to try and make a bit of a fresh start with them all, break the ice before she had to go back in.'

'Go on about Irene,' said Robin, conscious of Strike's pen hovering over his notebook.

'Well, she got drunk, if she's the blonde one. She'd brought some man with her to the party. Anyway, towards the end of the night, Irene accused Margot of *flirting* with the man. Did you ever in your loife hear anything more ridiculous? There's Margot standing there with her new baby in her arms, and the girl having a *proper* go at her. Was she not the nurse? It's so long ago . . .'

'No, Irene was the receptionist,' said Robin.

'I t'ought that was the little Italian girl?'

'Gloria was the other one.'

'Oh, Margot *loved* her,' said Oonagh. 'She said

the girl was very clever but in a bad situation. She never gave me details. I t'ink the girl had seen her for medical advice and o' course, Margot wouldn't have shared anything about her health. She took all of dat very seriously. No priest in his confessional treated other people's secrets with more respect.'

'I want to ask you about something sensitive,' said Robin tentatively. 'There was a book about Margot, written in 1985, and you—'

'Joined with Roy to stop it,' said Oonagh at once. 'I did. It was a pack o' lies from start to finish. You know what he wrote, obviously. About—'

Oonagh might have left the Catholic Church, but she baulked at the word.

'—the termination. It was a filthy lie. I never had an abortion and nor did Margot. She'd have told me, if she was thinking about it. We were best friends. Somebody used her name to make dat appointment. I don't know who. The clinic didn't recognise her picture. She'd never been there. The very best t'ing in her life was Anna and she'd *never* have got rid of another baby. *Never.* She wasn't religious, but she'd have t'ought that was a sin, all right.'

'She wasn't a churchgoer?' Robin asked.

'At'eist t'rough and t'rough,' said Oonagh. 'She t'ought it was all superstition. Her mammy was chapel, and Margot reacted against it. The church kept women down, was the way Margot looked at it, and she said to me, "If there's a God, why'd my daddy, who's a good man, have to fall off that step-ladder? Why's my family have to live the life we've had?" Well, Margot couldn't tell me anything about hypocrisy and religion I didn't already know. I'd left the Catholics by then. Doctrine of papal infallibility. No contraception, no matter if women died having their eleventh.

'My own mammy t'ought she was God's deputy on this earth, so she did, and some of the nuns at my school were pure bitches. Sister Mary Theresa – see there?' said Oonagh, pushing her fringe out of her eyes to reveal a scar the size of a five-pence piece. 'She hit me round the head wit' a metal set square. Blood everywhere. "I expect you deserved it," Mammy said.

'Now, I'll tell you who reminded me of Sister Mary Theresa,' said Oonagh. 'Would *she* have been the nurse, now? The older one at Margot's practice?'

'D'you mean Dorothy?'

'She was a widow, the one I'm t'inking of.'

'Yes, that was Dorothy, the secretary.'

'Spit image of Sister Mary Theresa, the eyes on her,' said Oonagh. 'I got cornered by her at the party. They're drawn to the church, women like dat. Nearly every congregation's got a couple. Outward observance, inward poison. They say the words, you know "Father forgive me, for I have sinned", but the Dorothys of this world, they don't believe they *can* sin, not really.

'One t'ing life's taught me: where there's no

capacity for joy, there's no capacity for goodness,' said Oonagh Kennedy. 'She had it in for Margot, that Dorothy. I told her I was Margot's best friend and she started asking nosy questions. How we'd met. Boyfriends. How Margot met Roy. None of her bloody business.

'Then she started talking about the old doctor, whatever his name was. There was a bit of Sister Mary Theresa in her, all right, but dat woman's god was sitting a desk away. I told Margot about the talk I'd had with her afterwards, and Margot said I was right. Dorothy was a mean one.'

'It was Dorothy's son who wrote the book about Margot,' said Robin.

'*Was it her son?*' gasped Oonagh. 'Was it? Well, *there you are*. Nasty pieces of work, the pair of them.'

'When was the last time you saw Margot?' Robin asked.

'Exactly two weeks before the night she disappeared. We met at The T'ree Kings then, too. Six o'clock, I had a night off from the club. There were a couple of bars nearer the practice, but she didn't want to run into anyone she worked with after hours.'

'Can you remember what you talked about that night?'

'I remember everyt'ing,' said Oonagh. 'You'll think that's an exaggeration, but it isn't. I started by giving her a row about going for a drink with Satchwell, which she'd told me about on the

401

phone. They'd bumped into each other in the street.

'She said he seemed different to how he used to be and that worried me, I'm not going to lie. She wasn't built for an affair, but she was unhappy. Once we got to the pub, she told me the whole story. He'd asked to see her again and she'd said no. I believed her, and I'll tell you why: because she looked so damn miserable that she'd said no.

'She seemed worn down, that night. Unhappy like I'd never seen her before. She said Roy hadn't been talking to her for ten days when she ran into Satchwell. They'd had a row about his mother walking in and out of the house like she owned it. Margot wanted to redecorate, but Roy said it'd break his mother's heart if they got rid of any of the things his father loved. So there was Margot, an outsider in her own home, not even allowed to change the ornaments.

'Margot said she'd had a line from *Court and Spark* running through her head, all day long. Joni Mitchell's album, *Court and Spark*,' she said, seeing Robin's puzzlement. '*That* was Margot's religion. Joni Mitchell. She *raved* about that album. It was a line from the song "The Same Situation". "*Caught in my struggle for higher achievements, And my search for love that don't seem to cease.*" I can't listen to that album to this day. It's too painful.

'She told me she went straight home after havin' the drink with Paul and told Roy what had just

402

happened. I think partly she felt guilty about going for the drink, but partly she wanted to jolt him awake. She was tired and miserable and she was saying *someone else wanted me, once.* Human nature, isn't it? "Wake up," she was saying. "You can't just ignore me and cut me off and refuse all compromises. I can't live like this."

'Well, being Roy, he wasn't the type to fire up and start throwing things. I t'ink she'd have found it easier if he had. He was furious, all right, but he showed it by gettin' colder and more silent.

'I don't t'ink he said another word to her until the day she disappeared. She told me on the phone when we arranged the drink for the eleventh, "I'm still living in a silent order." She sounded hopeless. I remember thinking then, "She's going to leave him."

'When we met in the pub that last time, I said to her, "Satchwell's not the answer to whatever's wrong with you and Roy."

'We talked about Anna, too. Margot would've given anything to take a year or two out and concentrate on Anna, and that's exactly what Roy and his mother had wanted her to do, stay home with Anna and forget working.

'But she couldn't. She was still supporting her parents. Her mammy was ill now, and Margot didn't want her out cleaning houses any more. While she was working, she could look Roy in the face and justify all the money she was giving them, but his mother wasn't going to let her precious, delicate son work for the benefit of a pair o' chain-smokin' Eastenders.'

'Can you remember anything else you talked about?'

'We talked about the Playboy Club, because I was leaving. I'd got my flat and I was thinking of going and studying. Margot was all for it. What I didn't tell her was, I was thinking of a t'eology degree, what with her attitude to religion.

'We talked about politics, a bit. We both wanted Wilson to win the election. And I told her I was worried I still hadn't found The One. Over t'irty, I was. That was old, then, for finding a husband.

'Before we said goodbye that night, I said, "Don't forget, there's always a spare room at my place. Room for a bassinet, as well."'

Tears welled again in Oonagh's eyes and trickled down her cheeks. She picked up her napkin and pressed it to her face.

'I'm sorry. Forty years ago, but it feels like yesterday. They don't disappear, the dead. It'd be easier if they did. I can see her so clearly. If she walked up those steps now, part of me wouldn't be surprised. She was such a *vivid* person. For her to disappear like that, just thin air where she was . . .'

Robin said nothing until Oonagh had wiped her face dry, then asked,

'What can you remember about arranging to meet on the eleventh?'

'She called me, asked to meet same place, same time. I said yes, o' course. There was something funny in the way she said it. I said, "Everything all right?" She said, "I need to ask your advice about something. I might be going mad. I shouldn't really talk about it, but I t'ink you're the only one I can trust."'

Strike and Robin looked at each other.

'Was that not written down anywhere?'

'No,' said Strike.

'No,' said Oonagh, and for the first time she looked angry. 'Well, I can't say I'm surprised.'

'Why not?' asked Robin.

'Talbot was away with the fairies,' said Oonagh. 'I could see it in the first five minutes of my interview. I called Roy, I said, "That man isn't right. Complain, tell them you want someone else on the case." He didn't, or if he did, nothing was done.

'And Lawson t'ought I was some silly little Bunny Girl,' said Oonagh. 'Probably t'ought I was tellin' fibs, trying to make myself interesting off the back of my best friend disappearing. Margot Bamborough was more like a sister than a friend to me,' said Oonagh fiercely, 'and the on'y person I've ever really talked to about her is my husband. I cried all over him, two days before we got married, because she should've been there. She should've been my matron of honour.'

'Have you got any idea what she was going to ask your advice about?' asked Robin.

'No,' said Oonagh. 'I've t'ought about it often since, whether it could have had anything to do with what happened. Something about Roy, perhaps, but then why would she say she shouldn't talk about it? We'd already talked about Roy. I'd told her as plain as I could, the last time we met, she could come and live with me if she left, Anna as well.

'Then I t'ought, maybe it's something a patient has told her, because like I said, she was scrupulous about confidentiality.

'Anyway, I walked up that hill in the rain to the pub on the eleventh. I was early, so I went to have a look at that church there, over the road, big—'

'Wait,' said Strike sharply. 'What kind of coat were you wearing?'

Oonagh didn't seem surprised by the question. On the contrary, she smiled.

'You're t'inking of the old gravedigger, or whoever he was? The one who t'ought he saw Margot going in there? I *told* them at the time it was me,' said Oonagh. 'I wasn't wearing a raincoat, but it was beige. My hair was darker than Margot's, but it was the same kind of length. I *told* them, when they asked me, did I think Margot might've gone into the church before meeting me – I said, no, she hated church. *I* went there! That was me!'

'Why?' asked Strike. 'Why did you go in there?'

'I was being called,' said Oonagh simply.

Robin repressed a smile, because Strike looked almost embarrassed at the answer.

'God was calling me back,' said Oonagh. 'I kept going into Anglican churches, t'inking, is this the answer? There was so much about the Catholics I couldn't take, but still, I could feel the pull back towards Him.'

'How long d'you think you were in the church?' asked Robin, to give Strike time to recover himself.

'Five minutes or so. I said a little prayer. I was asking for guidance. Then I walked out again, crossed the road and went into the pub.

'I waited nearly the full hour before I called Roy. At first I t'ought, she's been delayed by a patient. Then I t'ought, no, she must've forgotten. But when I called the house, Roy said she wasn't there. He was quite short with me. I wondered whether somethin' more had happened between them. Maybe Margot had snapped. Maybe I was going to get home and find her on the doorstep with Anna. So I went dashin' home, but she wasn't there.

'Roy called at nine to see whether I'd had any contact. That's when I started to get really worried. He said he was going to call the police.

'You'll know the rest,' said Oonagh quietly. 'It was like a nightmare. You put all your hopes on t'ings that are less and less likely. Amnesia. Knocked down by a car and unconscious somewhere. She's run away somewhere to t'ink.

'But I knew, really. She'd never've left her baby girl, and she'd *never* have left without telling me. I knew she was dead. I could tell the police t'ought it was the Essex Butcher, but me . . .'

'But you?' prompted Robin gently.

'Well, I kept t'inking, t'ree weeks after Paul Satchwell comes back into her life, she vanishes for ever. I know he had his little alibi, all his arty friends backing him up. I said to Talbot and Lawson: ask him about the pillow dream. Ask him what that means, the pillow dream he was so frightened Margot would tell people about.

'Is that in the police notes?' she asked Strike, turning to look at him. 'Did either of them ask Satchwell about the pillow dream?'

'No,' said Strike slowly. 'I don't think they did.'

CHAPTER 25

All those were idle thoughtes and fantasies,
Deuices, dreames, opinions vnsound,
Shewes, visions, sooth-sayes, and prophesies;
And all that fained is, as leasings, tales, and
lies.

Edmund Spenser
The Faerie Queene

Three evenings later, Strike was to be found sitting in his BMW outside a nondescript terraced house in Stoke Newington. The Shifty investigation, now in its fifth month, had so far yielded no results. The restive trustees who suspected that their CEO was being blackmailed by the ambitious Shifty were making ominous noises of discontent, and were clearly considering taking their business elsewhere.

Even after being plied with gin by Hutchins, who'd succeeded in befriending him at the rifle club, Shifty had remained as close lipped as ever about the hold he had over his boss, so it was time, Strike had decided, to start tailing SB himself. It was just possible that the CEO, a rotund, pinstriped man with a bald patch like a monk's tonsure, was still indulging in the blackmailable behaviour that Shifty had uncovered and that had leveraged him into a promotion that neither Shifty's CV, nor his personality, justified.

Strike was sure Shifty wasn't exploiting a simple case of infidelity. SB's current wife had the immaculate, plastic sheen of a doll newly removed from cellophane and Strike suspected it would take more than her husband having an affair to make her relinquish her taloned grip on a black American Express card, especially as she'd been married barely two years and had no children to guarantee a generous settlement.

Christmas tree lights twinkled in almost every window surrounding Strike. The roof of the house beside him had been hung with brilliant blue-white icicles that burned the retina if looked at too long. Wreaths on doors, glass panels decorated with fake snow and the sparkle of orange, red and green reflected in the dirty puddles all reminded Strike that he really did need to start buying Christmas gifts to take to Cornwall.

Joan had been released from hospital that morning, her drugs adjusted, and determined to get home and start preparing for the family festivities. Strike would need to buy presents not only for Joan and Ted but for his sister, brother-in-law and nephews. This was an irksome extra chore, given the amount of work the agency currently had on its books. Then he reminded himself that he had to buy something for Robin, too, something better than flowers. Strike, who disliked shopping in general, and buying gifts in particular, reached for his cigarettes to ward off a dim sense of persecution.

Having lit up, Strike took from his pocket the copy of *Whatever Happened to Margot Bamborough?* which Robin had given him, but which he hadn't yet had time to read. Small tags marked the places Robin thought might be of some interest to the investigation.

With a quick glance at the still-closed front door of the house he was watching, Strike opened the book and skim-read a couple of pages, looking up at regular intervals to check that SB hadn't yet emerged.

The first chapter, which Robin hadn't marked, but which Strike flicked through anyway, dealt summarily with Margot's childhood and adolescence. Unable to gain access to anybody with particularly clear memories of his subject, Oakden had to fall back on generalities, supposition and a good deal of padding. Thus Strike learned that Margot Bamborough 'would have dreamed of leaving poverty behind', 'would have been caught up in the giddy atmosphere of the 1960s' and 'would have been aware of the possibilities for consequence-free sex offered by the contraceptive pill'. Word count was boosted by the information

411

that the mini-skirt had been popularised by Mary Quant, that London was the heart of a thriving music scene and that the Beatles had appeared on America's *Ed Sullivan Show* around the time of Margot's nineteenth birthday. 'Margot would have been excited by the possibilities offered to the working classes in this new, egalitarian era,' C. B. Oakden informed his readers.

Chapter two ushered in Margot's arrival at the Playboy Club, and here, the sense of strain that had suffused the previous chapter vanished. C. B. Oakden evidently found Playboy Bunny Margot a far more inspiring subject than child Margot, and he devoted many paragraphs to the sense of freedom and liberation she would have felt on lacing herself tightly into her Bunny costume, putting on false ears and judiciously padding the cups of her costume to ensure that her breasts appeared of sufficient fullness to satisfy her employer's stringent demands. Writing eleven years after her disappearance, Oakden had managed to track down a couple of Bunny Girls who remembered Margot. Bunny Lisa, who was now married with two children, reminisced about having 'a good laugh' with her, and being 'devastated' by her disappearance. Bunny Rita, who ran her own marketing business, said that she was 'really bright, obviously going places', and thought 'it must've been dreadful for her poor family'.

Strike glanced up again at the front of the house into which SB had disappeared. Still no sign of him. Turning back to C. B. Oakden, the bored Strike skipped ahead to the first place Robin had marked as of interest.

After her successful stint at the Playboy Club, the playful and flirtatious Margot found it hard to adapt to the life of a general practitioner. At least one employee at the St John's practice says her manner was out of place in the setting of a consulting room.

"She didn't keep them at a proper distance, that was the trouble. She wasn't from a background that had a lot of professional people. A doctor's got to hold himself above the patients.

"She recommended that book *The Joy of Sex*, to a woman who went to see her. I heard people in the waiting room talking about it, after. Giggling, you know. A doctor shouldn't be telling people to read things like that. It reflects poorly on the whole practice. I was embarrassed for her.

"The one who was keen on her, the young fellow who kept coming back to see her, buying her chocolates and what have you – if she was telling people about different sex positions, you can see how men got the wrong idea, can't you?"

There followed several paragraphs that had clearly been cribbed from the press, covering the suicide of Steve Douthwaite's married ex-girlfriend, his sudden flight from his job and the fact that Lawson had re-interviewed him several times. Making the most of his scant material, Oakden managed to suggest that Douthwaite had been at best disreputable, at worst, dangerous: a feckless drifter and an unprincipled lady's man, in whose vicinity women had a habit of dying or disappearing. It was with a slight snort of sudden amusement, therefore, that Strike read the words,

> Now calling himself Stevie Jacks, Douthwaite currently works at Butlin's holiday camp in Clacton-on-Sea—

After glancing up again to check that SB hadn't yet emerged, Strike read on:

> where he runs events for the campers by day and performs in the cabaret by night. His "Longfellow Serenade" is a particular hit with the ladies. Dark-haired Douthwaite/ Jacks remains a handsome man, and clearly popular with female campers.
> "I've always liked singing," he tells me in the bar after the show. 'I was in a band when I was younger but it broke up. I came to Butlin's once when I was a kid, with my foster family. I always thought it looked a laugh, being a Redcoat. Plenty of big-time entertainers got their start here, you know."

When talk turns to Margot Bamborough, however, a very different side to this cheeky cabaret singer appears.

"The press wrote a load of balls. I never bought her chocolates or anything else, that was just made up to make me look like some kind of creep. I had a stomach ulcer and headaches. I'd been through a bad time."

After refusing to explain why he'd changed his name, Douthwaite left the bar.

His colleagues at the holiday camp expressed their shock that "Stevie" had been questioned by the police over the disappearance of the young doctor.

"He never told us anything about it," said Julie Wilkes, 22. "I'm quite shocked, actually. You'd think he'd have told us. He never said 'Jacks' wasn't his real name, either."

Oakden treated his readers to a brief history of Butlin's, and ended the chapter with a paragraph of speculation on the opportunities a predatory man might find at a holiday camp.

Strike lit another cigarette, then flicked ahead to the second of Robin's markers, where a short passage dealt with Jules Bayliss, husband of the office-cleaner-turned-social-worker, Wilma. The only piece of new information here was that convicted rapist Bayliss had been released on bail in January 1975, a full three months after Margot went missing. Nevertheless, Oakden asserted that

Bayliss 'would have got wind' of the fact that Margot was trying to persuade his wife to leave him, 'would have been angry that the doctor was pressurising his wife to break up the family' and 'would have had many criminal associations in his own community'. The police, Oakden informed his readers, 'would have looked carefully into the movements of any of Bayliss's friends or relatives on the eleventh of October, so we must conclude,' he finished, anticlimactically, 'that no suspicious activity was uncovered.'

Robin's third tab marked the pages dealing with the abortion at Bride Street Nursing Home. Oakden ushered in this part of his story with considerable fanfare, informing his readers that he was about to reveal facts that had never before been made public.

What followed was interesting to Strike only in as far as it proved that an abortion had definitely taken place on the fourteenth of September 1974, and that the name given by the patient had been Margot Bamborough. As proof, Oakden reprinted photographs of the Bride Street medical records that had been provided by an unidentified employee of the nursing home, which had closed down in 1978. Strike supposed the unnamed employee would no longer have been fearful for their job when Oakden had come offering money for information in the eighties. The unnamed employee also told Oakden that the woman who had had the procedure didn't resemble the picture of

Margot that had subsequently appeared in the papers.

Oakden then posed a series of rhetorical questions that he and his foolhardy publishers appeared to think circumvented libel laws. Was it possible that the woman who had the abortion had used Margot's name with her support and consent? In which case, who might Margot have been most eager to assist? Was it not most likely that a Roman Catholic would be particularly worried about anyone finding out she had had an abortion? Was it not also the case that complications could arise from such a procedure? Might Margot have returned to the vicinity of the Bride Street Nursing Home on the eleventh of October to visit somebody who had been readmitted to the clinic? Or to ask advice on behalf of that person? Could Margot possibly have been abducted, not from Clerkenwell, but from a street or two away from Dennis Creed's basement?

To which Strike answered mentally, *no, and you deserved to have your book pulped, pal.* The string of events suggested by Oakden had clearly been put together in a determined attempt to place Margot in the vicinity of Creed's basement on the night she disappeared. 'Complications' were necessary to explain Margot returning to the nursing home a month after the abortion, but they couldn't be Margot's own, given that she was fit, well and working at the St John's practice all the way up to her disappearance. Once attributed to a best friend, however, undefined 'complications' could serve two purposes: to give Margot a reason to head back to the clinic to visit Oonagh, and Oonagh a reason to lie about both women's whereabouts that night. All in all, Strike considered Oakden lucky not to have been sued, and surmised that fear of the resultant publicity was all that had held Roy and Oonagh back.

He flicked forward to Robin's fourth tab and, after checking again that the front door of the house he was watching remained closed, read the next marked passage.

"I saw her as clearly as I can see you now. She was standing at that window, *pounding* on it, as if she wanted to attract attention. I especially remember, because I was reading *The Other Side of Midnight* at the time and just thinking about women and what they go through, you know, and I looked up and I saw her.

"If I close my eyes, she's there, it's like a snapshot in my head and it's haunted me ever since, to be honest. People have said to me since, 'you're making it up' or 'you need to let it go', but I'm not changing my story just because other people don't believe it. What would that make me?"

The small printers who then occupied the top floor of the building was run by husband and wife team Arnold and Rachel Sawyer.

Police accepted their assurance that Margot Bamborough had never set foot on the premises, and that the woman seen by Mandy that night was probably Mrs Sawyer herself, who claimed one of the windows needed to be hit to close properly.

However, an odd connection between A&R Printing and Margot Bamborough went unnoticed by police. A&R's first major printing job was for the now-closed night-club Drudge – the very nightclub for which Paul Satchwell, Margot's lover, had designed a risqué mural. Satchwell's designs subsequently featured on flyers printed by A&R Printing, so it is likely that he and the Sawyers would have been in touch with each other.

Might this suggest . . .

'Fuck's sake,' muttered Strike, turning the page and dropping his eyes to a brief paragraph Robin had marked with a thick black line.

However, ex-neighbour Wayne Truelove thinks that Paul Satchwell subsequently went abroad.

"He talked to me about going travelling. I don't think he was making a lot of money from his art and after the police questioned him, he told me he was thinking of clearing out for a bit. Probably smart, going away."

Robin's fifth and final tab came towards the end of the book, and after again checking that SB's car was parked where he had left it, and that the front door of the house had not opened, Strike read:

A month after Margot's disappearance, her husband Roy visited the St John's practice. Roy, who had been unable to conceal his bad temper at the practice barbecue that summer, was unsurprisingly subdued on this visit.

Dorothy remembers: "He wanted to speak to us all, to thank us for cooperating with the police. He looked ill. Hardly surprising.

"We'd boxed up her personal effects because we had a locum working out of her room. The police had already searched it. We put her personal effects together. There was hand cream and her framed degree certificate and a photo of him, Roy, holding their daughter. He looked through the box and got a bit emotional, but then he picked up this thing that she'd had on her desk. It was one of those little wooden figures, like a Viking. He said 'Where did this come from? Where did she get this?' None of us knew, but I thought he seemed upset by it.

"He probably thought a man had given

it her. Of course, the police were looking into her love life by then. Awful thing, not to be able to trust your wife."

Strike glanced up yet again at the house, saw no change, and flicked to the end of the book, which concluded in a final burst of speculation, supposition and half-baked theory. On the one hand, Oakden implied that Margot had brought tragedy on herself, that fate had punished her for being too sexual and too bold, for cramming herself into a corset and bunny ears, for hoisting herself hubristically out of the class into which she had been born. On the other hand, she seemed to have lived her life surrounded by would-be killers. No man associated with Margot escaped Oakden's suspicion, whether it was 'charming but feckless Stevie Douthwaite-turned-Jacks', 'domineering blood specialist Roy Phipps', 'resentful rapist Jules Bayliss', 'hot-tempered womaniser Paul Satchwell' or 'notorious sex monster Dennis Creed'.

Strike was on the point of closing the book when he noticed a line of darker page edges in the middle, suggesting photographs, and opened it again.

Other than the familiar press headshot and the picture of Margot and Oonagh in their Bunny Girl costumes – Oonagh curvaceous and grinning broadly, Margot statuesque, with a cloud of fair hair – there were only three photos. All were of poor quality and featured Margot only incidentally.

The first was captioned: 'The author, his mother and Margot'. Square-jawed, iron-grey-haired, and wearing winged glasses, Dorothy Oakden stood facing the camera with her arm around a skinny freckle-faced boy with a pageboy haircut, who had screwed up his face into a grimace that distorted his features. Strike was reminded of Luke, his eldest nephew. Behind the Oakdens was a long expanse of striped lawn and, in the distance, a sprawling house with many pointed gables. Objects appeared to be protruding out of the lawn close to the house: upon closer examination, Strike concluded that they were the beginnings of walls or columns: it looked as though a summerhouse was under construction.

Walking across the lawn behind Dorothy and Carl, unaware that she was being photographed, was Margot Bamborough, barefooted, wearing denim shorts and a T-shirt, carrying a plate and smiling at somebody out of shot. Strike deduced that this picture had been taken at the staff barbecue Margot had organised. The Phipps house was certainly grander than he'd imagined.

After looking up once more to check that SB's car remained parked where he'd left it, Strike turned to the last two pictures, both of which featured the St John's practice Christmas party.

Tinsel had been draped over the reception desk and the waiting room cleared of chairs, which had been stacked in corners. Strike searched for Margot in both pictures and found her, baby Anna in her arms, talking to a tall black woman he assumed was Wilma Bayliss. In the corner of the picture was a slim, round-eyed woman with feathered brown hair, who Strike thought might be a young Janice.

In the second picture, all heads were turned away from the camera or partially obscured, except one. A gaunt, unsmiling older man in a suit, with his hair slicked back, was the only person who seemed to have been given notice that the picture was about to be taken. The flash had turned his eyes red. The picture was captioned 'Margot and Dr Joseph Brenner', though only the back of Margot's head was visible.

In the corner of this picture were three men who, judging from their coats and jackets, had just arrived at the party. The darkness of their clothing made a solid block of black on the right-hand side of the photo. All had their backs to the camera, but the largest, whose face was slightly turned to the left, displayed one long black sideburn, a large ear, the tip of a fleshy nose and a drooping eye. His left hand was raised in the act of scratching his face. He was wearing a large gold ring featuring a lion's head.

Strike examined this picture until noises out on the street made him look up. SB had just emerged from the house. A plump blonde in carpet slippers was standing on her doormat. She raised a hand and patted SB gently on the top of the head, as you would pet a child or a dog. Smiling, SB bade her farewell, then turned and walked back towards his Mercedes.

Strike threw the copy of *Whatever Happened to Margot Bamborough?* into the passenger seat. Waiting for SB to pull out into the road, he set off in pursuit.

After five minutes or so, it became clear that his quarry was driving back to his home in West Brompton. One hand on the steering wheel, Strike groped for his mobile, then pressed the number of an old friend. The call went straight to voicemail.

'Shanker, it's Bunsen. Need to talk to you about something. Let me know when I can buy you a pint.'

CHAPTER 26

All were faire knights, and goodly well beseene,
But to faire Britomart they all but shadowes
beene.

Edmund Spenser
The Faerie Queene

With five active cases on the agency's books, and only four days to go until Christmas, two of the agency's subcontractors succumbed to seasonal flu. Morris fell first: he blamed his daughter's nursery, where the virus had swept like wildfire through toddlers and parents alike. He continued to work until a high temperature and joint pain forced him to telephone in his apologies, by which time he'd managed to pass the bug to a furious Barclay, who in turn had transmitted it to his own wife and young daughter.

'Stupid arsehole shoulda stayed at home instead o' breathin' all over me in the car,' Barclay ranted hoarsely over the phone to Strike early on the morning of the twentieth, while Strike was opening up the office. The last full team meeting before Christmas was to have taken place at ten o'clock, but as two of the team were now unable to attend, Strike had decided to cancel. The only person he hadn't been able to reach was Robin, who he assumed was on the Tube. Strike had asked her to come in early so they could catch up with the Bamborough case before everyone else arrived.

'We're supposedtae be flying to Glasgow the morra,' Barclay rasped, while Strike put on the kettle. 'The wean's in that much pain wi' her ears—'

'Yeah,' said Strike, who was feeling sub-standard himself, doubtless due to tiredness, and too much smoking. 'Well, feel better and get back whenever you can.'

'Arsehole,' growled Barclay, and then, 'Morris, I mean. Not you. Merry fuckin' Christmas.'

Trying to convince himself that he was imagining the tickle in his throat, the slight clamminess of his back and the pain behind his eyes, Strike made himself a mug of tea, then moved through to the inner office and pulled up the blinds. Wind and heavy rain were causing the Christmas lights strung across Denmark Street to sway on their cables. Just as they'd done on the five previous mornings, the decorations reminded Strike that he still hadn't started his Christmas shopping. He took a seat on his accustomed side of the partners' desk, knowing that he'd now left the job so late that he would be forced to execute it within a couple of hours, which at least obviated the tedious preliminary of carefully considering what anyone might like. Rain lashed the window behind him. He'd have liked to go back to bed.

He heard the glass door open and close.

'Morning,' Robin called from the outer office. 'It's *vile* out there.'

'Morning,' Strike called back. 'Kettle's just boiled and team meeting's cancelled. That's Barclay down with flu as well.'

'Shit,' said Robin. 'How're *you* feeling?'

'Fine,' said Strike, now sorting out his various Bamborough notes.

But when Robin entered the inner office, carrying tea in one hand and her own notebook in the other, she didn't think Strike looked fine at all. He was paler than usual, his forehead looked shiny and there were grey shadows around his eyes. She closed the office door and sat down opposite him without passing comment.

'Not much point to a team meeting anyway,' muttered Strike. 'Fuck-all progress on any of the cases. Twinkletoes is clean. The worst you can say about him is he's with her for the money, but her dad knew that from the start. Two-Times' girl-friend isn't cheating and Christ only knows what Shifty's got on SB. You saw my email about the blonde in Stoke Newington?'

'Yes,' said Robin, whose face had been whipped

into high colour by the squally weather. She was trying to comb her hair back into some semblance of tidiness with her fingers. 'Nothing come up on the address?'

'No. If I had to guess, I'd say she's a relative. She patted him on the head as he left.'

'Dominatrix?' suggested Robin.

There wasn't much she hadn't learned about the kinks of powerful men since joining the agency.

'It occurred to me, but the way he said goodbye . . . they looked . . . cosy. But he hasn't got a sister and she looked younger than him. Would cousins pat each other on the head?'

'Well, Sunday night's all wrong for a normal counsellor or a therapist, but patting's quasi-parental . . . life coach? Psychic?'

'That's a thought,' said Strike, stroking his chin. 'Stockholders wouldn't be impressed if he's making business decisions based on what his fortune teller in Stoke Newington's telling him. I was going to put Morris on to the woman over Christmas, but he's out of action, Hutchins is on Two-Times' girl and I'm supposed to be leaving for Cornwall day after tomorrow. You're off to Masham when – Tuesday?'

'No,' said Robin, looking anxious. 'Tomorrow – Saturday. We did discuss this back in September, remember? I swapped with Morris so I could—'

'Yeah, yeah, I remember,' lied Strike. His head was starting to throb, and the tea wasn't making

428

his throat feel much more comfortable. 'No problem.'

But this, of course, meant that if he was going to give Robin a Christmas present, he'd have to buy it and get it to her by the end of the day.

'I'd try and get a later train,' said Robin, 'but obviously, with it being Christmas—'

'No, you're owed time off,' he said brusquely. 'You shouldn't be working just because those careless bastards got flu.'

Robin, who had a strong suspicion that Barclay and Morris weren't the only people at the agency with flu, said,

'D'you want more tea?'

'What? No,' said Strike, feeling unreasonably resentful at her for, as he saw it, forcing him to go shopping. 'And Postcard's a washout, we've got literally noth—'

'I might – *might* – have something on Postcard.'

'What?' said Strike, surprised.

'Our weatherman got another postcard yesterday, sent to the television studio. It's the fourth one bought in the National Portrait Gallery shop, and it's got an odd message on it.'

She pulled the postcard from her bag and handed it over the desk to Strike. The picture on the front reproduced a self-portrait of Joshua Reynolds, his hand shading his eyes in the stereotypical pose of one staring at something indistinct. On the back was written:

> I hope I'm wrong, but I think you sent someone to my work, holding some of my letters. Have you let someone else see them? I really hope you haven't. Were you trying to scare me? You act like you're so kind and down-to-earth, no airs and graces. I'd have thought you'd have the decency to come yourself if you've got something to say to me. If you don't understand this, ignore.

Strike looked up at Robin.

'Does this mean . . .?'

Robin explained that she'd bought the same three postcards that Postcard had previously sent from the gallery shop, then roamed the gallery's many rooms, holding the postcards so that they were visible to all the guides she passed, until an owlish woman in thick-lensed glasses had appeared to react at the sight of them, and disappeared through a door marked 'Staff Only'.

'I didn't tell you at the time,' Robin said, 'because I thought I might've imagined it, and she also looked exactly like the kind of person I'd imagined Postcard to be, so I was worried I was doing a Talbot, chasing my own mad hunches.'

'But you're not off your rocker, are you? That was a bloody good idea, going to the shop, and this,' he brandished the postcard of the Reynolds, 'suggests you hit the bullseye first throw.'

'I didn't manage to get a picture of her,' said Robin, trying not to show how much pleasure Strike's praise had given her, 'but she was in Room 8 and I can describe her. Big glasses, shorter than me, thick brown hair, bobbed, probably fortyish.'

Strike made a note of the description.

'Might nip along there myself before I head for Cornwall,' he said. 'Right, let's get on with Bamborough.'

But before either could say another word, the phone rang in the outer office. Glad to have something to complain about, Strike glanced at his watch, heaved himself to his feet and said,

'It's nine o'clock, Pat should—'

But even as he said it, they both heard the glass door open, Pat's unhurried tread and then, in her usual rasping baritone,

'Cormoran Strike Detective Agency.'

Robin tried not to smile as Strike dropped back into his chair. There was a knock on the door, and Pat stuck her head inside,

'Morning. Got a Gregory Talbot on hold for you.'

'Put him through,' said Strike. 'Please,' he added, detecting a martial look in Pat's eye, 'and close the door.'

She did so. A moment later, the phone rang on the partners' desk and Strike switched it to speakerphone.

'Hi, Gregory, Strike here.'

'Yes, hello,' said Gregory, who sounded anxious. 'What can I do for you?'

'Er, well, you know how we were clearing out the loft?'

'Yes,' said Strike.

'Well, yesterday I unpacked an old box,' said Gregory, sounding tense, 'and I found something hidden under Dad's commendations and his uniform—'

'Not *hidden*,' said a querulous female voice in the background.

'I didn't know it was there,' said Gregory. 'And now my mother—'

'Let me talk to him,' said the woman in the background.

'My mother would like to talk to you,' said Gregory, sounding exasperated.

A defiant, elderly female voice replaced Gregory's.

'Is this Mr Strike?'

'It is.'

'Gregory's told you all about how the police treated Bill at the end?'

'Yes,' said Strike.

'He could have kept working once he got treatment for his thyroid, but they didn't let him. He'd given them *everything*, the force was his *life*. Greg says he's given you Bill's notes?'

'That's right,' said Strike.

'Well, after Bill died I found this *can* in a box

432

in the shed and it had the Creed mark on it – you've read the notes, you know Bill used a special symbol for Creed?'

'Yes,' said Strike.

'I couldn't take everything with me into sheltered accommodation, they give you virtually *no* storage space, so I put it into the boxes to go in Greg and Alice's attic. I quite forgot it was there until Greg started looking through his dad's things yesterday. The police have made it *quite* clear they weren't interested in Bill's theories, but Greg says you are, so you should have it.'

Gregory came back on the line. They heard movement that seemed to indicate that Gregory was moving away from his mother. A door closed.

'It's a can containing a reel of old 16mm film,' he told Strike, his mouth close to the receiver. 'Mum doesn't know what's on there. I haven't got a camera to run it, but I've held a bit up to the light and . . . it looks like a dirty movie. I was worried about putting it out for the binmen—'

Given that the Talbots were fostering children, Strike understood his qualms.

'If we give it to you – I wonder—'

'You'd rather we didn't say where we got it?' Strike said, eyes on Robin's. 'I can't see why we'd need to.'

Robin noticed that he hadn't promised, but Gregory seemed happy.

'I'll drop it off, then,' he said. 'I'm coming up West this afternoon. Taking the twins to see Father Christmas.'

When Gregory had rung off, Strike said,

'You notice the Talbots are still convinced, forty years on—'

The phone rang in the outer office again.

'—that Margot was killed by Creed? I think I know what the symbol on this can of film is going to be, because—'

Pat knocked on the door of the inner office.

'Fuck's sake,' muttered Strike, whose throat was starting to burn. '*What?*'

'Charming,' said Pat, coldly. 'There's a Mister Shanker on the line for you. It diverted from your mobile. He says you wanted to—'

'Yeah, I do,' said Strike. 'Transfer it back to my mobile – please,' he added, and turning to Robin, he said, 'sorry, can you give me a moment?'

Robin left the room, closing the door behind her, and Strike pulled out his mobile.

'Shanker, hi, thanks for getting back to me.'

He and Shanker, whose real name he'd have been hard pressed to remember, had known each other since they were teenagers. Their lives had been moving in diametrically different directions even then, Strike heading for university, army and detective work, Shanker pursuing a career of ever-deepening criminality. Nevertheless, a strange sense of kinship had continued to unite them and they were, occasionally, useful to each other, Strike paying Shanker in cash for information or services that he could get no other way.

'What's up, Bunsen?'

'I wanted to buy you a pint and show you a photo,' said Strike.

'Up your way later today, as it goes. Going to Hamleys. Got the wrong fackin' Monster High doll for Zahara.'

Everything except 'Hamleys' had been gibberish to Strike.

'OK, call me when you're ready for a drink.'

'Fair dos.'

The line went dead. Shanker didn't tend to bother with goodbyes.

Robin returned carrying two fresh mugs of tea and closed the door with her foot.

'Sorry about that,' said Strike, absent-mindedly wiping sweat off his top lip. 'What was I saying?'

'That you think you know what symbol's on Talbot's can of old film.'

'Oh, yeah,' said Strike. 'Symbol for Capricorn. I've been having a go at deciphering these notes,' he added, tapping the leather-bound notebook sitting beside him, and he took Robin through the reasons Bill Talbot had come to believe that Margot had been abducted by a man born under the sign of the goat.

'Talbot was ruling out suspects on the basis that they weren't Capricorns?' asked Robin in disbelief.

'Yeah,' said Strike, frowning, his throat burning worse than ever. He took a sip of tea. 'Except that

435

Roy Phipps is a Capricorn, and Talbot ruled him out, too.'

'Why?'

'I'm still trying to deciper it all, but he seems to have been using a weird symbol for Phipps that I haven't been able to identify on any astrological site so far.

'But the notes explain why he kept interviewing Janice. Her star sign's Cancer. Cancer is Capricorn's "opposing" sign and Cancerians are psychic and intuitive, according to Talbot's notes. Talbot concluded that, as a Cancerian, Janice was his natural ally against Baphomet, and that she might have supernatural insights into Baphomet's identity, hence the dream diary.

'Even more significant in his mind was that Saturn, Capricorn's ruler—'

Robin hid a smile behind her mug of tea. Strike's expression, as he outlined these astrological phenomena, would have been appropriate to a man asked to eat weeks'-old seafood.

'—was in Cancer on the day of Margot's disappearance. From this, Talbot deduced that Janice knew or had had contact with Baphomet. Hence the request for a list of her sexual partners.'

'Wow,' said Robin quietly.

'I'm just giving you a hint of the nuttery, but there's plenty more. I'll email you the important points when I've finished deciphering it. But what's interesting is that there are hints of an actual detective trying to fight through his illness.

'He had the same idea that occurred to me: that Margot might've been lured somewhere on the pretext of someone needing medical assistance, although he dresses it all up in mumbo-jumbo – there was a stellium in the sixth house, the House of Health, which he decided meant danger associated with illness.'

'What's a stellium?'

'Group of more than three planets. The police did check out patients she'd seen a lot of in the run-up to the disappearance. There was Douthwaite, obviously, and a demented old woman on Gopsall Street, who kept ringing the surgery for something to do, and a family who lived on Herbal Hill, whose kid had had a reaction to his polio vaccination.'

'Doctors,' said Robin, 'have contact with *so many* people.'

'Yeah,' said Strike, 'and I think that's part of what went wrong in this case. Talbot took in a huge amount of information and couldn't see what to discard. On the other hand, the possibility of her being lured into a house on a medical pretext, or attacked by an angry patient isn't crazy. Medics walk unaccompanied into all kinds of people's houses . . . and look at Douthwaite. Lawson really fancied him as Margot's abductor or killer, and Talbot was very interested in him, too. Even though Douthwaite was a Pisces, Talbot tries to make him a Capricorn. He says "Schmidt" thinks Douthwaite's really a Capricorn—'

'Who's Schmidt?'

'No idea,' said Strike, 'but he or she is all over the notes, correcting signs.'

'All the chances to get actual evidence lost,' said Robin quietly, 'while Talbot was checking every-one's horoscope.'

'Exactly. It'd be funny if it wasn't so serious. But his interest in Douthwaite still smacks of sound copper instinct. Douthwaite seems pretty bloody fishy to me, as well.'

'Ha ha,' said Robin.

Strike looked blank.

'Pisces,' she reminded him.

'Oh. Yeah,' said Strike, unsmiling. The throbbing behind his eyes was worse than ever, his throat complaining every time he swallowed, but he couldn't have flu. It was impossible. 'I read that bit you marked in Oakden's book,' he continued. 'The stuff about Douthwaite changing his name when he went to Clacton to sing at a holiday camp, but I can't find any trace of a Steve, Steven or Stevie Jacks after 1976, either. One name change might be understandable after a lot of police atten-tion. Two starts to look suspicious.'

'You think?' said Robin. 'We know he was the nervous type, judging from his medical records. Maybe he was spooked by Oakden turning up at Butlin's?'

'But Oakden's book was pulped. Nobody beyond a couple of Butlin's Redcoats ever knew Stevie Jacks had been questioned about Margot Bamborough.'

'Maybe he went abroad,' said Robin. 'Died abroad. I'm starting to think that's what happened to Paul Satchwell, as well. Did you see, Satchwell's ex-neighbour said he went off travelling?'

'Yeah,' said Strike. 'Any luck on Gloria Conti yet?'

'Nothing,' sighed Robin. 'But I have got a *couple* of things,' she went on, opening her notebook. 'They don't advance us much, but for what they're worth . . .

'I've now spoken to Charlie Ramage's widow in Spain. The hot-tub millionaire who thought he saw Margot in the Leamington Spa graveyard?'

Strike nodded, glad of a chance to rest his throat.

'I think Mrs Ramage has either had a stroke or likes a lunchtime drink. She sounded slurred, but she confirmed that Charlie thought he'd seen Margot in a graveyard, and that he discussed it afterwards with a policeman friend, whose name she couldn't remember. Then suddenly she said, "No, wait – Mary Flanagan. It was Mary Flanagan he thought he saw." I took her back over the story and she said, yes, that was all correct, except that it was Mary Flanagan, not Margot Bamborough, he thought he'd seen. I've looked up Mary Flanagan,' said Robin, 'and she's been missing since 1959. It's Britain's longest ever missing person case.'

'Which of them would you say seemed more confused?' asked Strike. 'Mrs Ramage, or Janice?'

'Mrs Ramage, definitely,' said Robin. 'Janice definitely wouldn't have confused the two women, would she? Whereas Mrs Ramage might have done. She had no personal interest: to her, they were just two missing people whose names began with "M".'

Strike sat frowning, thinking it over. Finally he said, his tonsils burning,

'If Ramage was a teller of tall tales generally, his policeman mate can't be blamed for not taking him seriously. This is at least confirmation that Ramage believed he'd once met a missing woman.'

He frowned so intensely that Robin said,

'Are you in pain?'

'No. I'm wondering whether it'd be worth trying to see Irene and Janice separately. I'd hoped never to have to talk to Irene Hickson again. At the very least, we should keep looking for a connection between Margot and Leamington Spa. Did you say you had another lead?'

'Not much of one. Amanda Laws – or Amanda White, as she was when she supposedly saw Margot at that window on Clerkenwell Road – answered my email. I'll forward her reply if you want to read it, but basically she's angling for money.'

'Is she, now?'

'She dresses it up a bit. Says she told the police and nobody believed her, told Oakden and he didn't give her a penny, and she's tired of not being taken seriously and if we want her story she'd like to be paid for it this time. She claims she's endured a lot of negative attention, being called a liar and a fantasist, and she's not prepared to go through all of that again unless she gets compensated.'

Strike made a second note.

'Tell her it isn't the agency's practice to pay witnesses for their cooperation,' said Strike. 'Appeal to her better nature. If that doesn't work, she can have a hundred quid.'

'I think she's hoping for thousands.'

'And I'm hoping for Christmas in the Bahamas,' said Strike, as rain dotted the window behind him. 'That all you've got?'

'Yes,' said Robin, closing her notebook.

'Well, I've drawn a blank on the Bennie-abusing patient who claimed to have killed Margot, Applethorpe. I think Irene must've got the name wrong. I've tried all the variants that've occurred to me, but nothing's coming up. I might *have* to call her back. I'll try Janice first, though.'

'You haven't told me what you thought of the Oakden book.'

'Bog-standard opportunist,' said Strike, 'who did well to squeeze ten chapters out of virtually nothing. But I'd like to track him down if we can.'

'I'm trying,' sighed Robin, 'but he's another one who seems to have vanished off the face of the planet. His mother seemed to be his primary source, didn't she? I don't think he persuaded anyone who *really* knew Margot to talk to him.'

'No,' said Strike. 'You'd highlighted nearly all the interesting bits.'

'Nearly?' said Robin sharply.

'All,' Strike corrected himself.

'You spotted something else?'

'No,' said Strike, but seeing that she was unconvinced, he added, 'I've just been wondering whether someone might've put a hit on her.'

'Her husband?' said Robin, startled.

'Maybe,' said Strike.

'Or are you thinking about the cleaner's husband? Jules Bayliss, and his alleged criminal connections?'

'Not really.'

'Then why—'

'I just keep coming back to the fact that if she was killed, it was done very efficiently. Which might suggest—'

'—a contract killer,' said Robin. 'You know, I read a biography of Lord Lucan recently. They think he hired someone to kill his wife—'

'—and the killer got the nanny by mistake,' said Strike, who was familiar with the theory. 'Yeah. Well, if that's what happened to Margot, we're looking at an assassin a damn sight more efficient than Lucan's. Not a trace of her left behind, not so much as a drop of blood.'

There was a momentary silence, while Strike glanced behind him to see the rain and wind still buffeting the Christmas lights outside, and Robin's thoughts flew to Roy Phipps, the man whom Oonagh had called bloodless, conveniently bedridden on the day of Margot's disappearance.

'Well, I need to get going,' said Strike, pushing himself up out of his chair.

'I should, too,' sighed Robin, collecting her things.

'You're coming back into the office later, though?' Strike asked.

He needed to give her the as-yet-unbought Christmas present before she left for Yorkshire.

'I wasn't planning to,' said Robin. 'Why?'

'Come back in,' Strike said, trying to think of a reason. He opened the door into the outer office. 'Pat?'

'Yes?' said Pat, without looking round. She was once more typing fast and accurately, her electronic cigarette waggling between her teeth.

'Robin and I both need to head out now, but a man called Gregory Talbot's about to drop off a can of 16mm film. D'you think you can track down a projector that'll play it? Ideally before five o'clock?'

Pat swung slowly around on her desk chair to look at Strike, her monkey-ish face set, her eyes narrowed.

'You want me to find a vintage film projector by five o'clock?'

'That's what I said.' Strike turned to Robin. 'Then we can have a quick look at whatever Talbot had hiding in the attic before you leave for Masham.'

'OK,' said Robin, 'I'll come back at four.'

CHAPTER 27

His name was Talus, made of yron mould,
Immoueable, resistlesse, without end.
Who in his hand an yron flale did hould,
With which he thresht out falshood, and did
*   truth vnfould.*

Edmund Spenser
The Faerie Queene

S ome two and a half hours later, Strike stood beneath the awning of Hamleys on Regent Street, shopping bags by his feet, telling himself firmly that he was fine in spite of ample empirical evidence that he was, in fact, shivering. Cold rain was spattering all around him onto the dirty pavements, where it was kicked out of puddles by the marching feet of hundreds of passing pedestrians. It splashed over kerbs in the wake of passing vehicles and dripped down the back of Strike's collar, though he stood, theoretically, beneath shelter.

While checking his phone yet again for some sign

444

that Shanker hadn't forgotten they were supposed to be meeting for a drink, he lit a cigarette, but his raw throat didn't appreciate the sudden ingestion of smoke. With a foul taste in his mouth, he ground out the cigarette after one drag. There was no message from Shanker, so Strike picked up his bulky shopping bags and set off again, his throat burning every time he swallowed.

He'd imagined optimistically that he might have finished all his shopping within two hours, but midday had come and gone and he still wasn't done. How did people decide what to buy, when the speakers were all shrieking Christmas tunes at you, and the shops were full of too much choice, and all of it looked like junk? Endless processions of women kept ranging across his path, choosing items with apparently effortless ease. Were they genetically programmed to seek and find the right gift? Was there nobody he could pay to do this for him?

His eyes felt heavy, his throat ached and his nose had started running. Unsure where he was going, or what he was looking for, he walked blindly onwards. He, who usually had an excellent sense of direction, kept turning the wrong way, becoming disorientated. Several times he knocked into carefully stacked piles of Christmas merchandise, or buffeted smaller people, who scowled and muttered and scurried away.

The bulky bags he was carrying contained three identical Nerf blasters for his nephews; large plastic guns which shot foam bullets, which Strike had decided to buy on the dual grounds that he would have loved one when he was eleven, and the assistant had assured him they were one of the must-have gifts of the year. He'd bought his Uncle Ted a sweater because he couldn't think of anything else, his brother-in-law a box of golf balls and a bottle of gin on the same principle, but he still had the trickiest gifts to buy – the ones for the women: Lucy, Joan and Robin.

His mobile rang.

'Fuck.'

He hobbled sideways out of the crowd and, standing beside a mannequin wearing a reindeer sweater, shook himself free from a few of his bags so that he could pull out his mobile.

'Strike.'

'Bunsen, I'm near Shakespeare's 'Ead on Great Marlborough Street. See you there in twenty?'

'Great,' said Strike, who was becoming hoarse. 'I'm just round the corner.'

Another wave of sweat passed over him, soaking scalp and chest. It was, some part of his brain acknowledged, just possible that he had caught Barclay's flu, and if that was the case, he mustn't give it to his severely immunosuppressed aunt. He picked up his shopping bags again and made his way back to the slippery pavement outside.

The black and white timbered frontage of Liberty rose up to his right as he headed along Great Marlborough Street. Buckets and boxes of flowers lay all around the main entrance, temptingly light and portable, and already wrapped; so easy to carry to the Shakespeare's Head and take on to the office afterwards. But, of course, flowers wouldn't do this time. Sweating worse than ever, Strike turned into the store, dumped his bags once more on the floor beside an array of silk scarves, and called Ilsa.

'Hey, Oggy,' said Ilsa.

'What can I get Robin for Christmas?' he said. It was becoming difficult to talk: his throat felt raw.

'Are you all right?'

'I'm fantastic. Give me an idea. I'm in Liberty.'

'Um . . .' said Ilsa. 'Let's th . . . ooh, I know what you can get her. She wants some new perfume. She didn't like the stuff she—'

'I don't need backstory,' said Strike ungraciously. 'That's great. Perfume. What does she wear?'

'I'm trying to tell you, Oggy,' said Ilsa. 'She wants a change. Choose her something new.'

'I can't smell,' said Strike, impatiently, 'I've got a cold.'

But this basic problem aside, he was afraid that a perfume he'd personally picked out was too intimate a gift, like that green dress of a few years back. He was looking for something like flowers, but not flowers, something that said 'I like you', but not 'this is what I'd like you to smell like'.

'Just go to an assistant and say "I want to buy a perfume for someone who wears Philosykos but wants a—"'

'She what?' said Strike. 'She wears what?'

447

'Philosykos. Or she did.'

'Spell it,' said Strike, his head thumping. Ilsa did so.

'So I just ask an assistant, and they'll give me something like it?'

'That's the idea,' said Ilsa patiently.

'Great,' said Strike. 'Appreciate it. Speak soon.'

The assistant thought you'd like it.

Yeah, he'd say that. *The assistant thought you'd like it* would effectively de-personalise the gift, turn it into something almost as mundane as flowers, but it would still show he'd taken some care, given it some thought. Picking up his carrier bags again, he limped towards an area he could see in the distance that looked as though it was lined with bottles.

The perfume department turned out to be small, about the size of Strike's office. He sidled into the crowded space, passing beneath a cupola painted with stars, to find himself surrounded by shelves laden with fragile cargos of glass bottles, some of which wore ruffs, or patterns like lace; others which looked like jewels, or the kind of phial suitable for a love potion. Apologising as he forced people aside with his Nerf guns, his gin and his golf balls, he met a slim, black-clad man who asked, 'Can I help you?' At this moment Strike's eye fell on a range of bottled scents which were identically packed with black labels and tops. They looked functional and discreet, with no overt suggestion of romance.

'I'd like one of those,' he croaked, pointing.

'Right,' said the assistant. 'Er—'

'It's for someone who used to wear Philosykos. Something like that.'

'OK,' said the assistant, leading Strike over to the display. 'Well, what about—'

'No,' said Strike, before the assistant could remove the top of the tester. The perfume was called Carnal Flower. 'She said she didn't like that one,' Strike added, with the conscious aim of appearing less strange. 'Are any of the others like Philo—'

'She might like Dans Tes Bras?' suggested the assistant, spraying a second bottle onto a smelling strip.

'Doesn't that mean—?'

'"In your arms",' said the assistant.

'No,' said Strike, without taking the smelling strip. 'Are any of the others like Phi—?'

'Musc Ravageur?'

'You know what, I'll leave it,' said Strike, sweat prickling anew beneath his shirt. 'Which exit is nearest the Shakespeare's Head?'

The unsmiling assistant pointed Strike towards the left. Muttering apologies, Strike edged back out past women who were studying bottles and spraying on testers, turned a corner and saw, with relief, the pub where he was meeting Shanker, which lay just beyond the glass doors of a room full of chocolates.

Chocolates, he thought, slowing down and

incidentally impeding a group of harried women. *Everyone likes chocolates.* Sweat was now coming over him in waves, and he seemed to feel simultaneously hot and cold. He approached a table piled high with chocolate boxes, looking for the most expensive one, one that would show appreciation and friendship. Trying to choose a flavour, he thought he recalled a conversation about salted caramel, so he took the largest box he could find and headed for the till.

Five minutes later, another bag hanging from his hands, Strike emerged at the end of Carnaby Street, where music-themed Christmas decorations hung between the buildings. In Strike's now fevered state, the invisible heads suggested by giant headphones and sunglasses seemed sinister rather than festive. Struggling with his bags, he backed into the Shakespeare's Head, where fairy lights twinkled and chatter and laughter filled the air.

'Bunsen,' said a voice, just inside the door.

Shanker had secured a table. Shaven-headed, gaunt, pale and heavily tattooed, Shanker had an upper lip that was fixed in a permanent Elvis-style sneer, due to the scar that ran up towards his cheekbone. He was absent-mindedly clicking the fingers of the hand not holding his pint, a tic he'd had since his teens. No matter where he was, Shanker managed to emanate an aura of danger, projecting the idea that he might, on the slightest provocation, resort to violence. Crowded as the pub was, nobody had chosen to share his table. Incongruously, or so it seemed to Strike, Shanker, too, had shopping bags at his feet.

'What's wrong wiv ya?' Shanker said, as Strike sank down opposite him and disposed of his own bags beneath the table. 'Ya look like shit.'

'Nothing,' said Strike, whose nose was now running profusely and whose pulse seemed to have become erratic. 'Cold or something.'

'Well, keep it the fuck away from me,' said Shanker. 'Last fing we fuckin' need at home. Zahara's only just got over the fuckin' flu. Wanna pint?'

'Er – no,' said Strike. The thought of beer was currently repellent. 'Couldn't get me some water, could you?'

'Fuck's sake,' muttered Shanker, as he got up.

When Shanker had returned with a glass of water and sat down again, Strike said, without preamble,

'I wanted to ask you about an evening, must've been round about '92, '93. You needed to get into town, you had a car, but you couldn't drive it yourself. You'd done something to your arm. It was strapped up.'

Shanker shrugged impatiently, as much as to say, who could be expected to remember something so trivial? Shanker's life had been an endless series of injuries received and inflicted, and of needing to get places to deliver cash, drugs, threats or beatings. Periods of imprisonment had done nothing but temporarily change the environment in which he conducted business. Half the boys with whom he had associated in his teens were dead, most killed by knives or overdoses. One cousin had died in a police car chase, and another had been shot through the back of the head, his killer never caught.

'You had to make a delivery,' Strike went on, trying to jog Shanker's memory. 'Jiffy bag full of something – drugs, cash, I don't know. You came round the squat looking for someone to drive you, urgently. I said I'd do it. We went to a strip club in Soho. It was called Teezers.'

'Teezers, yeah,' said Bunsen. 'Long gone, Teezers. Closed ten, fifteen year ago.'

'When we got there, there was a group of men standing on the pavement, heading inside. One of them was a bald black guy—'

'Your fucking memory,' said Shanker, amused. 'You could do a stage act. "Bunsen, the Amazing Memory Man"—'

'—and there was a big Latin-looking bloke with dyed black hair and sideburns. We pulled up, you wound down the window and he came over and put his hand on the door to talk to you. He had eyes like a basset hound and he was wearing a massive gold ring with a lion's—'

'Mucky Ricci,' said Shanker.

'You remember him?'

'Just said 'is name, Bunsen, d'in I?'

'Yeah. Sorry. What was his real name, d'you know?'

'Nico, Niccolo Ricci, but everyone called 'im

"Mucky". Old-school villain. Pimp.'E owned a few strip clubs, ran a couple of knocking shops. Real bit of old London, 'e was. Got his start as part of the Sabini gang, when 'e was a kid.'

'How're you spelling Ricci? R – I – C – C – I, right?'

'What's this about?'

Strike tugged the copy of *Whatever Happened to Margot Bamborough?* out of his coat pocket, turned to the photographs of the practice Christmas party and held it out to Shanker, who took it suspiciously. He squinted for a moment at the partial picture of the man with the lion ring, then passed the book back to Strike.

'Well?' said Strike.

'Yeah, looks like 'im. Where's that?'

'Clerkenwell. A doctors' Christmas party.'

Shanker looked mildly surprised.

'Well, Clerkenwell, that was the old Sabini stamping ground, warn't it? And I s'pose even gangsters need doctors sometimes.'

'It was a party,' said Strike. 'Not a surgery. Why would Mucky Ricci be at a doctors' party?'

'Dunno,' said Shanker. 'Anyone need killing?'

'Funny you should ask that,' said Strike. 'I'm investigating the disappearance of a woman who was there that night.'

Shanker looked sideways at him.

'Mucky Ricci's gaga,' he said quietly. 'Old man now, innit.'

'Still alive, though?'

'Yer.'E's in an 'ome.'

'How d'you know that?'

'Done a bit o' business wiv 'is eldest, Luca.'

'Boys in the same line of work as their old man?'

'Well, there ain't no Little Italy gang any more, is there? But they're villains, yeah,' said Shanker. Then he leaned across the table and said quietly, 'Listen to me, Bunsen. You do not wanna screw wiv Mucky Ricci's boys.'

It was the first time Shanker had ever given Strike such a warning.

'You go fuckin' wiv their old man, you try pinnin' anyfing on 'im, the Ricci boys'll skin ya. Understand? They don't fuckin' care. They'll torch your fuckin' office. They'll cut up your girl.'

'Tell me about Mucky. Anything you know.'

'Did you 'ear what I just said, Bunsen?'

'Just tell me about him, for fuck's sake.'

Shanker scowled.

''Ookers. Porn. Drugs, but girls was 'is main thing. Same era as George Cornell, Jimmy Humphries, all those boys. That gold ring 'e wore, 'e used to say Danny the Lion gave it 'im. Danny Leo, the mob boss in New York. Claimed they were related. Dunno if it's true.'

'Ever run across anyone called Conti?' Strike asked. 'Probably a bit younger than Ricci.'

'Nope. But Luca Ricci's a fuckin' psycho,' said Shanker. 'When did this bint disappear?'

'1974,' said Strike.

He expected Shanker to say 'Nineteen seventy

454

fucking four?', to pour scorn on the likelihood of finding any kind of solution after all this time, but his old friend merely frowned at him, his clicking fingers recalling the relentless progress of the deathwatch beetle, and it occurred to the detective that Shanker knew more about old crimes and the long shadows they cast than many policemen.

'Name of Margot Bamborough,' said Strike. 'She vanished on her way to the pub. Nothing ever found, no handbag, door keys, nothing. Never seen again.'

Shanker sipped his beer.

'Professional job,' he said.

'That occurred to me,' said Strike. 'Hence—'

'Fuck your fucking "hence",' said Shanker fiercely. 'If the bint was taken out by Mucky Ricci or any of his boys, she's past fuckin' savin', in't she? I know you like bein' the boy scout, mate, but the last guy who pissed off Luca Ricci, his wife opened the door few days later and got acid thrown in her face. Blind in one eye, now.

'You wanna drop this, Bunsen. If Mucky Ricci's the answer, you need to stop askin' the question.'

CHAPTER 28

Greatly thereat was Britomart dismayd,
Ne in that stownd wist, how her selfe to
beare . . .

Edmund Spenser
The Faerie Queene

Somehow, Pat had managed to track down a vintage film projector. It had been promised for delivery at four, but Strike and Robin were still waiting for it at a quarter to six, at which time Robin told Strike she really did need to leave. She hadn't yet packed for her trip home to Yorkshire, she wanted an early night before catching the train and, if she was honest, she was feeling insulted by Strike's gift of unwrapped salted caramel chocolates, which he'd pulled hastily out of a Liberty bag when he saw her, and which she now suspected was the whole lousy reason he had forced her to come back to the office in the first place. As this had necessitated a long trip back to Denmark Street on a packed Tube, it was hard not to feel resentful about the time and trouble she had taken to find and wrap the DVD of two old Tom Waits concerts he'd mentioned wanting to watch, a few weeks previously. Robin had never heard of the singer: it had taken her some trouble to identify the man Strike had been talking about, and the concerts he'd never seen as those on *No Visitors After Midnight*. And in return, she got chocolates she was sure had been grabbed at random.

She left Strike's present behind, untouched, in Max's kitchen, before boarding the crowded train to Harrogate next morning. As she travelled north in her mercifully pre-booked seat, Robin tried to tell herself that her feeling of emptiness was merely tiredness. Christmas at home would be a wonderful break. She'd be meeting her new niece for the first time; there'd be lie-ins and home-cooked food and hours in front of the telly.

A toddler was shouting at the back of the carriage, his mother trying just as loudly to entertain and subdue him. Robin pulled out her iPod and put on headphones. She'd downloaded Joni Mitchell's album, *Court and Spark*, which Oonagh had mentioned as Margot Bamborough's favourite. Robin hadn't yet had time to listen to it, or, indeed, to any other music, for weeks.

But *Court and Spark* didn't soothe or cheer her. She found it unsettling, unlike anything she had ever listened to before. Expecting melodies and hooks, Robin was disappointed: everything felt unfinished, left open, unresolved. A beautiful soprano voice tumbled and swooped over piano or guitar chords that never led to anything as mundane as a chorus that you could settle into, or tap your foot to. You couldn't hum along, you couldn't have joined in unless you, too, could sing like Mitchell, which Robin certainly couldn't. The words were strange, and evoked responses she didn't like: she wasn't sure she'd ever felt the things Mitchell sang about, and this made her feel defensive, confused and sad: *Love came to my door, with a sleeping roll and a madman's soul . . .*

A few seconds into track three, she turned off the iPod and reached instead for the magazine she had brought with her. At the back of the carriage, the toddler was now howling.

Robin's mood of mild despondency persisted until she got off the train, but when she saw her mother standing on the platform, ready to drive her back to Masham, she was overtaken by a wave of genuine warmth. She hugged Linda, and for almost ten minutes afterwards, while they wended their way, chatting, towards the car, passing a café out of which jangling Christmas music was emanating, even the dour grey Yorkshire skies and the car interior, which smelled of Rowntree the Labrador, felt comforting and cheery in their familiarity.

'I've got something to tell you,' Linda said, when she had closed the driver's door. Instead of turning the key in the ignition, Linda turned to Robin, looking almost fearful.

458

A sickening jolt of panic turned Robin's stomach upside down.

'What's happened?' she said.

'It's all right,' Linda said hastily, 'everyone's well. But I want you to know before we get back to Masham, in case you see them.'

'See who?'

'Matthew,' said Linda, 'has brought . . . he's brought that woman home with him. Sarah Shadlock. They're staying with Geoffrey for Christmas.'

'*Oh*,' said Robin. 'Christ, Mum, I thought someone had died.'

She hated the way Linda was looking at her. Though her insides had just grown cold, and the fragile happiness that had briefly kindled inside her had been snuffed out, she forced a smile and a tone of unconcern.

'It's fine. I knew. Her ex-fiancé called me. I should've guessed,' she said, wondering why she hadn't, 'they might be here for Christmas. Can we get home, please? I'm dying for a cup of tea.'

'You *knew*? Why didn't you tell us?'

But Linda herself supplied the answer to that, as they drove. It neither soothed nor comforted Robin to have Linda storming about how outraged she'd been, when a neighbour told her that Matthew had been strolling hand in hand with Sarah through the middle of town. She didn't feel comforted by strictures against her ex-husband's morals and manners, nor did she appreciate having each family member's reaction detailed to her

('Martin was all for *punching* him again'). Then Linda moved on to the divorce: what was going on? Why wasn't it all settled yet? Did Robin *honestly* think mediation would work? Didn't Matthew's behaviour, *flaunting* this woman in front of the whole of Masham, *show* how utterly lost to shame and reason he was? Why, oh why, hadn't Robin agreed to let Harveys of Harrogate deal with it all, was she *sure* this London woman was up to it, because Corinne Maxwell had told Linda that when *her* daughter divorced without children it was all *completely* straightforward . . .

But at least there was little Annabel Marie, was the conclusion of Linda's monologue, as they turned onto Robin's parents' street.

'*Wait* till you see her, Robin, just *wait* . . .'

The front door opened before the car came to a halt. Jenny and Stephen were standing on the threshold, looking so excited that an onlooker might have suspected it was they who were about to see their baby daughter for the first time, not Robin. Realising what was expected of her, Robin hitched an eager smile onto her face, and within minutes found herself sitting on the sofa in her parents' living room, a warm little sleeping body in her arms, wrapped up in wool, surprisingly solid and heavy, and smelling of Johnson's baby powder.

'She's gorgeous, Stephen,' Robin said, while Rowntree's tail thumped against the coffee table. He was nosing at her, thrusting his head repeatedly under Robin's hand, confused as to why he wasn't receiving the fuss and love he was used to. 'She's gorgeous, Jenny,' Robin said, as her sister-in-law took photos of 'Auntie Robin' meeting Annabel for the first time. 'She's gorgeous, Mum,' Robin said to Linda, who had come back with a tea tray and a craving to hear what Robin thought of their twenty-inch-long marvel.

'Evens things out, doesn't it, having another girl?' said Linda delightedly. Her anger at Matthew was over now: her granddaughter was everything.

The sitting room was more cramped than usual, not only with Christmas tree and cards, but with baby equipment. A changing mat, a Moses basket, a pile of mysterious muslin cloths, a bag of nappies and an odd contraption that Jenny explained was a breast pump. Robin rhapsodised, smiled, laughed, ate biscuits, heard the story of the birth, admired some more, held her niece until she woke, then, after Jenny had taken back possession of the baby and, with a touch of new self-importance, settled herself down to breastfeed, said that she would nip upstairs and unpack.

Robin carried her bag upstairs, her absence unnoticed and unregretted by those below, who were lost in adoration of the baby. Robin closed the door of her old room behind her, but instead of unpacking, lay down on her old bed. Facial muscles aching from all her forced smiling, she closed her eyes, and allowed herself the luxury of exhausted misery.

CHAPTER 29

Thus warred he long time against his will,
Till that through weakness he was forced at last
To yield himself unto the mighty ill,
Which, as a victor proud, 'gan ransack fast
His inward parts and all his entrails waste . . .

Edmund Spenser
The Faerie Queene

With three days to go before Christmas, Strike was forced to abandon the pretence that he didn't have flu. Concluding that the only sensible course was to hole up in his attic flat while the virus passed through his system, he took himself to a packed Sainsbury's where, feverish, sweating, breathing through his mouth and desperate to get away from the crowds and the canned carols, he grabbed enough food for a few days, and bore it back to his two rooms above the office.

Joan took the news that he wouldn't be joining the festivities in Cornwall predictably hard. She went so far as to suggest that it would be fine for him to come, as long as they sat at opposite ends of the dinner table, but to Strike's relief, Ted overruled her. Strike didn't know whether he was being paranoid, but he suspected Lucy didn't believe he was genuinely ill. If she did, her tone suggested that he might have caught flu deliberately. He thought he heard a trace of accusation when she informed him that Joan was now entirely bald.

By five o'clock in the afternoon of Christmas Eve, Strike had developed a cough that made his lungs rattle and his ribs ache. Drowsing on his bed in a T-shirt and boxer shorts, his prosthetic leg propped against a wall, he was woken abruptly by a loud noise. Footsteps seemed to be moving down the stairs, away from his attic door. A paroxysm of coughing seized him before he could call out to the person he thought had woken him. Struggling back into a sitting position to clear his lungs, he didn't hear the second approach of footsteps until somebody knocked on his door. He greatly resented the effort it took to shout, 'What?'

'D'you need anything?' came Pat's deep, gravelly voice.

'No,' Strike shouted. The syllable emerged as a croak.

'Have you got food?'

'Yes.'

'Painkillers?'

'Yes.'

'Well, I'm leaving some things outside the door for you.' He heard her setting objects down. 'There are a couple of presents. Eat the soup while it's still hot. See you on the twenty-eighth.'

Her footsteps were clanging down the metal stairs before he could respond.

He wasn't sure whether he'd imagined the mention of hot soup, but the possibility was enough to make him drag his crutches towards himself and make his way laboriously to the door. The chill of the stairwell added gooseflesh to his fever sweats. Pat had somehow managed to carry the old video projector upstairs for him, and he suspected that it was the sound of her setting this down that had woken him. Beside it lay the can of film from Gregory Talbot's attic, a small pile of wrapped Christmas gifts, a handful of cards and two polystyrene tubs of hot chicken soup that he knew she must have walked to Chinatown to fetch. He felt quite pathetically grateful.

Leaving the heavy projector and the can of film where they were, he pulled and prodded the Christmas gifts and card across the floor into the flat with one of his crutches, then slowly bent down to pick up the tubs of soup.

Before eating, he took his mobile from the bedside table and texted Pat:

Thanks very much. Hope you have a good Christmas.

He then wrapped the duvet around himself and ate the soup straight out of the tubs, tasting nothing. He'd hoped the hot liquid would soothe his raw throat, but the cough persisted, and once or twice he thought he was going to choke everything back up again. His intestines also seemed unsure whether they welcomed food. Having finished the two tubs, he settled back down beneath the duvet, sweating while he looked at the black sky outside, guts churning, and wondering why he wasn't yet on the mend.

After a night of intermittent dozing interrupted by prolonged coughing fits, Strike woke on Christmas morning to find his fever unabated, and sweaty sheets tangled about him. His normally noisy flat was unnaturally quiet. Tottenham Court Road was suddenly, weirdly devoid of traffic. He supposed most of the taxi drivers were at home with their families.

Strike was not a self-pitying man, but lying alone in bed, coughing and sweating, his ribs sore and his fridge now virtually empty, he was unable to prevent his thoughts roaming back over Christmases past, especially those spent at Ted and Joan's in St Mawes, where everything proceeded as it did on the television and in story books, with turkey and crackers and stockings.

Of course, today was far from the first Christmas he'd spent away from family and friends. There'd been a couple such in the army, when he'd eaten foil trays of tasteless turkey in field canteens,

465

among camouflage-wearing colleagues wearing Santa hats. The structure he'd enjoyed in the military had then consoled him in the absence of other pleasures, but there was no camaraderie to sustain him today, only the dismal fact that he was alone, ill and one-legged, stuck up in a draughty attic, forced to endure the consequences of his own firm repudiation of any relationship that might offer support in moments of illness or sadness.

The memory of Pat's kindness became, this Christmas morning, still more touching in retrospect. Turning his head, he saw the few gifts that she'd brought upstairs still lying on the floor just inside the door.

He got up from his bed, still coughing, reached for his crutches and swung himself towards the bathroom. His urine was dark, his unshaven face in the mirror ashen. Though dismayed by his own debility and exhaustion, habits ingrained in him by the military prevented Strike from returning to bed. He knew that lying unwashed with his leg off would merely increase his hovering feeling of depression. He therefore showered, moving more carefully than usual to guard against the risk of falls, dried himself off, put on a clean T-shirt, boxers and dressing gown and, still racked with coughs, prepared himself a tasteless breakfast of porridge made with water, because he preferred to conserve his last pint of milk for his tea. As he'd expected to be well on the mend by now, his stocks of food had dwindled to some limp vegetables, a couple of bits of uncooked chicken two days out of date and a small chunk of hard Cheddar.

After breakfast Strike took painkillers, put on his prosthesis and then, determined to use what small amount of physical strength he could muster before the illness dragged him under again, stripped and remade his bed with clean sheets, removed his Christmas presents from the floor to his kitchen table, and carried the projector and roll of film inside from the landing where he had left them. The can, as he'd expected, bore the mark of Capricorn upon it, drawn in faded but clearly legible marker pen.

His mobile buzzed as he propped the can against the wall beneath his kitchen window. He picked it up, expecting a text from Lucy asking when he was going to call and wish everyone in St Mawes a Merry Christmas.

Merry Christmas, Bluey. Are you happy? Are you with someone you love?

It had been a fortnight since Charlotte had last texted him, almost as though she'd telepathically heard his resolution to contact her husband if her messages became any more self-destructive.

It would be so easy to answer; so easy to tell her he was alone, ill, unsupported. He thought of the naked photo she'd sent on his birthday, which he'd forced himself to delete. But he'd come such a long way, to a place of lonely security against

467

emotional storms. However much he'd loved her, however much she could still disturb his serenity with a few typed words, he forced himself, standing beside his small Formica table, to recall the only occasion on which he'd taken her back to St Mawes for Christmas. He remembered the row heard all through the tiny house, remembered her storming out past the family assembled around the turkey, remembered Ted and Joan's faces, because they'd so looked forward to the visit, having not seen Strike for over a year, because he was at that time stationed in Germany with the Special Investigation Branch of the Royal Military Police.

He set his mobile to mute. Self-respect and self-discipline had always been his bulwarks against lethargy and misery. What was Christmas Day, after all? If you disregarded the fact that other people were enjoying feasts and fun, merely a winter's day like any other. If he was currently bodily weak, why shouldn't he use his mental faculties, at least, to continue work on the Bamborough case?

Thus reasoning, Strike made himself a fresh cup of strong tea, added a very small amount of milk, opened his laptop and, pausing regularly for coughing fits, re-read the document he'd been working on before he'd fallen ill: a summary of the contents of Bill Talbot's symbol-laden, leather-bound notebook, which Strike had now spent three weeks deciphering. His intention was to send the document to Robin for her thoughts.

Talbot's Occult Notes

1. Overview
2. Symbol key
3. Possible leads
4. Probably irrelevant
5. Action points

Overview

Talbot's breakdown manifested itself in a belief that he could solve the Bamborough case by occult means. In addition to astrology, he consulted Aleister Crowley's Thoth tarot, which has an astrological dimension. He immersed himself in several occult writers, including Crowley, Éliphas Lévi and astrologer Evangeline Adams, and attempted magic rituals.

Talbot was a regular churchgoer before his mental health broke down. While ill, he thought he was hunting a literal embodiment of evil/the devil. Aleister Crowley, who seems to have influenced Talbot more than anyone else, called himself 'Baphomet' and also connected Baphomet both with the devil and the sign of Capricorn. This is probably where Talbot got the idea that Margot's killer was a Capricorn.

Most of what's in the notebook is worthless, but I think Talbot left three

Strike now deleted the number 'three' and substituted 'four'. As ever, when immersed in work, he felt a craving for a cigarette. As though in rebellion against the very idea, his lungs immediately treated him to a violent fit of coughing that necessitated the grabbing of kitchen roll to catch what they were trying to expel. Suitably chastened and shivering slightly, Strike drew his dressing gown more tightly around him, took a sip of tea he couldn't taste and continued to work.

Most of what's in the notebook is worthless, but I think Talbot left four possibly genuine leads out of the official police record, only recording them in 'the true book', ie, his leather notebook.

Symbol key

There are no names in the notebook, only zodiacal signs. I'm not listing unidentified eye witnesses – we've got no chance of tracing them on their star signs and nothing else – but by cross-referencing corroborative details, these are my best guesses at the identity of people Talbot thought were important to the investigation.

♈	Aries	Paul Satchwell (ex-boyfriend)
♉	Taurus	Wilma Bayliss (office cleaner)
♊	Gemini	Oonagh Kennedy
♊2	Gemini 2	Amanda Laws (saw M at window)

470

♋	Cancer	Janice Beattie (nurse)
♋2	Cancer 2	Cynthia Phipps (Anna's nanny/stepmother)
♌	Leo	Dinesh Gupta (GP)
♌2	Leo 2	Willy Lomax (saw M entering church)
♌3	Leo 3	? (from Talbot's notes, ♌3 seems to have been seen coming out of the practice by a member of the public. Hints that ♌3 is known to police and that ♌3 was there at night)

Strike now deleted the last paragraph and substituted a name and a new note.

♌3	Leo 3	Nico 'Mucky' Ricci (gangster who attended practice Christmas party. Nobody seems to have recognised him except an unnamed passer-by)
♍	Virgo	Dorothy Oakden (practice secretary)
♎	Libra	Joseph Brenner (GP)
♎2	Libra 2	Ruby Elliot (saw 2 struggling women)
♏	Scorpio	? (dead person)*
♏2	Scorpio 2	Mrs Fleury (was leading elderly mother across Clerkenwell Green on evening of Margot's disappearance)
♐	Sagittarius	Gloria Conti (receptionist)
♐2	Sagittarius 2	Jules Bayliss (husband of cleaner)
♒	Aquarius	Margot Bamborough (victim)
♑	Capricorn	The Essex Butcher/Baphomet
♓	Pisces	Steven Douthwaite (patient)
⚵	no idea	Roy Phipps (husband) **
⚶	no idea	Irene Bull/Hickson (receptionist)**

* I suggest an identity for Scorpio below, but could be someone we haven't yet heard of.

** No idea what either of these symbols mean. Can't find them on any astrological website. Talbot seems to

Schmidt

The name 'Schmidt' is all over the note-book. 'Schmidt corrects to (different star sign)', 'Schmidt changes everything', 'Schmidt disagrees'. Schmidt mostly wants to change people's star signs, which you'd think would be one certainty, given that birth dates don't change. I've checked with Gregory Talbot, and he can't remember his father ever knowing anyone of the name. My best guess is that Schmidt might have been a figment of Talbot's increasingly psychotic imagination. Perhaps he couldn't help noticing people weren't matching the star signs' supposed qualities and Schmidt was his rational side trying to reassert itself.

Possible leads

Joseph Brenner

In spite of Talbot's early determination to clear Brenner of suspicion on the basis of

---

have invented them. If he'd stuck to birth signs, Irene would have been one of the Geminis and Roy would have been Capricorn. Talbot writes that Phipps 'can't be true Capricorn' (because he's resourceful, sensitive, musical) then comes up with this new symbol for him, on the advice of Schmidt.

his star sign (Libra is 'the most trustworthy of the signs' according to Evangeline Adams), he later records in the notebook that an unidentified patient of the practice told Talbot that he/she saw Joseph Brenner inside a block of flats on Skinner Street on the evening Margot disappeared. This directly contradicts Brenner's own story (he went straight home), his sister's corroboration of that story, and possibly the story of the dog-walking neighbour who claims to have seen Brenner through the window at home at 11 in the evening. No time is given for Brenner's alleged sighting in Michael Cliffe House, which was a 3-minute drive from the St John's practice and consequently far nearer Margot's route than Brenner's own house, which was a 20-minute drive away. <u>None of this is in the police</u> notes and it doesn't seem to have been followed up.

Death of Scorpio

Talbot seems to suggest that somebody died, and that Margot may have found the death suspicious. Scorpio's death is connected to Pisces (Douthwaite) and Cancer (Janice), which makes the most likely candidate for Scorpio Joanna Hammond, the married woman Douthwaite had an affair with, who allegedly committed suicide.

The Hammond/Douthwaite/Janice explanation fits reasonably well: Margot could have voiced suspicions about Hammond's death to Douthwaite the last time she saw him, which gives us the reason he stormed out of her surgery. And as a friend/neighbour of Douthwaite's, Janice might have had her own suspicions about him.

The problem with this theory is that I've looked up Joanna Hammond's birth certificate online and she was born under Sagittarius. Either she isn't the dead person in question, or Talbot mistook her date of birth.

Blood at the Phipps house/Roy walking

When Lawson took over the case, Wilma the cleaner told him she'd seen Roy walking in the garden on the day Margot disappeared, when he was supposed to be bedbound. She also claimed she found blood on the spare bedroom carpet and cleaned it up.

Lawson thought this was the first time Wilma had mentioned either fact to the police and suspected she was trying to make trouble for Roy Phipps.

However, turns out Wilma <u>did</u> tell Talbot the story, but instead of recording it in the official police record, he put it in his astrological notebook.

Even though Wilma had already given him what you'd think is significant information, Talbot's notes indicate that he was sure she was concealing something else. He seems to have developed a fixation with Wilma having occult powers/secret knowledge. He speculates that Taurus might have 'magick' and even suggests the blood on the carpet might have been put there by Wilma herself, for some ritual purpose.

Tarot cards associated with Taurus, Wilma's sign, came up a lot when he was using them and he seems to have interpreted them to mean she knew more than she was letting on. He underlined the phrase 'black phantom' in regard to her, and associated her with 'Black Lilith', which is some astrological fixed point associated with taboos and secrets. In the absence of any other explanation, I suspect a good slug of old-fashioned racism.

Out on Charing Cross Road, a car passed, blaring from its radio 'Do They Know It's Christmas?' Frowning, Strike added another bullet point to 'possibly genuine new information', and began to type.

Nico 'Mucky' Ricci

According to Talbot, Leo 3 was seen leaving the practice one night by an unnamed passer-by, who told Talbot about it afterwards. Nico 'Mucky' Ricci was caught on camera in one of Dorothy Oakden's photos of the practice Christmas party in 1973. The picture's reproduced in her son's book. Ricci was a Leo (confirmed by d.o.b. in press report from 1968).

Ricci was a professional gangster, pornographer and pimp who in 1974 was living in Leather Lane, Clerkenwell, a short walk from the St John's practice, so should have been registered with one of the doctors there. He's now in his 90s and living in a nursing home, according to Shanker.

The fact that Ricci was at the party isn't in the official record. Talbot found the fact Ricci was at the practice significant enough to write down in the astrological notebook, but there's no sign he ever followed it up or told Lawson about it. Possible explanations: 1) as Ricci was Leo, not Capricorn, Talbot concluded he couldn't be Baphomet, 2) Talbot didn't trust the person who said he'd seen Ricci leaving the building, 3) Talbot knew, but didn't record in his book, that Ricci had an alibi for that night Margot disappeared, 4) Talbot knew Ricci had alibis for other Essex Butcher abductions.

Whichever applies, the presence of Ricci at that party needs looking into. He's a man who had the contacts to arrange a permanent disappearance. See action points below.

It cost Strike far more effort than it would usually have done to organise his thoughts on Mucky Ricci and set them down. Tired now, his throat raw and his intercostal muscles aching from coughing, he read through the rest of the document, which in his opinion contained little of real value other than the action points. After correcting a couple of typos, he attached the lot to an email and sent it to Robin.

Only after this had gone did it occur to him that some people might think emailing work colleagues on Christmas Day was unacceptable. However, he shrugged off any momentary qualms by telling himself that Robin was currently enjoying a family Christmas, and would be highly unlikely to check her email until tomorrow at the earliest.

He picked up his mobile and checked it. Charlotte hadn't texted again. Of course, she had twins, aristocratic in-laws and a husband to keep happy. He set the phone down again.

Little energy though he had, Strike found the absence of anything to do still more enervating. Without much curiosity, he examined a couple of the Christmas presents lying beside him, both of which were clearly from grateful clients, as they were addressed to both him and Robin. Shaking the larger one, he deduced that it contained chocolates.

He returned to his bedroom and watched a bit of television, but the relentless emphasis on Christmas depressed him and he switched off midway through a continuity announcer's wish that everyone was having a wonderful—

Strike returned to the kitchen and his gaze fell on the heavy projector and can of film lying just inside the door. After a moment's hesitation, he heaved the heavy machine onto his kitchen table, facing a blank stretch of kitchen wall and plugged it in. It seemed to be in working order. He then prised the lid off the tin to reveal a large roll of 16mm film, which he took out and fitted into the projector.

Doubtless because he wasn't thinking as clearly as usual, and also because of the need to stop regularly to cough up more sputum into kitchen roll, it took Strike nearly an hour to work out how to operate the old projector, by which time he realised that he had regained something of an appetite. It was now nearly two o'clock. Trying not to imagine what was going on in St Mawes, where a large turkey with all the trimmings was doubtless reaching the peak of bronzed perfection, but seeing this flicker of returned appetite as a sign of returning health, he took the pack of out-of-date chicken and the limp vegetables out of the fridge, chopped it all, boiled up some dried noodles and made a stir fry.

He could taste nothing, but this second ingestion of food made him feel slightly more human, and ripping the paper and cellophane off the box of chocolates, he ate several of them, too, before flicking the switch on the projector.

Onto the wall, pale in the sunlight, flickered the naked figure of a woman. Her head was covered in a hood. Her hands were bound behind her. A man's black-trousered leg entered the shot. He kicked her: she stumbled and fell to her knees. He continued to kick until she was prone on the ground of what looked like a warehouse.

She'd have screamed, of course, she couldn't have failed to scream, but there was no sound-track. A thin scar ran from beneath her left breast down to her ribs, as though this wasn't the first time knives had touched her. All the men involved had covered their faces with scarves or balaclavas. She alone was naked: the men merely pulled down their jeans.

She stopped moving long before they had finished with her. At one point, close to the end, when she was barely moving, when blood still dripped from her many stab wounds, the left hand of a man who seemed to have watched, but not participated, slid in front of the camera. It bore something large and gold.

Strike flicked off the projector. He was suddenly drenched in cold sweat. His stomach was cramping. He barely made it to the bathroom before he vomited, and there he remained, heaving until he was empty, until dusk fell beyond the attic windows.

CHAPTER 30

Ah dearest Dame, quoth then the Paynim bold,
Pardon the error of enraged wight,
Whome great griefe made forgett the raines to
  hold
Of reasons rule . . .

Edmund Spenser
The Faerie Queene

nnabel was wailing in Stephen's old bedroom, which was next door to Robin's own. Her niece had cried through a substantial portion of Christmas night and Robin had been awake along with her, listening to Joni Mitchell on her headphones to block out the noise.

Four days stuck in her parents' house in Masham had driven Robin back to Mitchell's sprawling, wandering tunes and the lyrics that had made her feel strangely lost. Margot Bamborough had found something there she had needed, and hadn't Margot Bamborough's life been far more complicated than her own? Ailing parents to support, a new daughter to love and to miss, a workplace full of cross currents and bullying, a husband who wouldn't talk to her, another man lurking in the background, promising that he'd changed. What were Robin's troubles, compared to those?

So Robin lay in the dark and listened as she hadn't on the train. Then, she had heard an alienating sophistication in the words the beautiful voice had sung. Robin hadn't had glamorous love affairs she could anatomise or lament: she'd had one proper boyfriend and one marriage, which had gone horribly wrong, and now she was home at her parents' house, a childless twenty-nine-year-old who was 'travelling in a different direction to the rest of us': in other words, backwards.

But in the darkness, really listening, she began to hear melodies among the suspended chords, and as she stopped comparing the music to anything she would usually have listened to, she realised that the images she had found alienating in their strangeness were confessions of inadequacy and displacement, of the difficulty of merging two lives, of waiting for the soulmate who never arrived, of craving both freedom and love.

It was with a literal start that she heard the words, at the beginning of track eight, '*I'm always running behind the times, just like this train . . .*'

And when, later in the song, Mitchell asked: 'what are you going to do now? You got no one to give your love to', tears started in Robin's eyes. Not a mile from where she lay, Matthew and Sarah

481

would be lying in bed in her ex-father-in-law's spare room, and here was Robin, alone again in a room that for her would forever have a hint of prison cell about it. This was where she had spent months after leaving university, pinioned within four walls by her own memories of a man in a gorilla mask, and the worst twenty minutes of her life.

Since arriving home, everyone in the house had been keen to accompany her into Masham, 'because you shouldn't have to hide'. The implication, no matter their kind intention, was that it would be a natural response for a woman whose ex-husband had found a new partner to hide. There was shame in being single.

But listening to *Court and Spark*, Robin thought that it was perfectly true that she was travelling in a different direction to anyone she knew. She was fighting her way back to the person she should have been before a man in a mask reached for her from the darkness beneath a stairwell. The reason nobody else understood was that they assumed that her true self was to be the wife Matthew Cunliffe had wanted: a woman who worked quietly in HR and stayed home safely after dark. They didn't realise that that woman had been the result of those twenty minutes, and that the authentic Robin might never have emerged if she hadn't been sent, by mistake, to a shabby office in Denmark Street.

With a strange sense of having spent her sleepless hours fruitfully, Robin turned off her iPod.

Four o'clock on Boxing Day morning and the house was silent at last. Robin took out her earbuds, rolled over and managed to fall asleep.

Two hours later, Annabel woke again, and this time, Robin got up and crept downstairs, barefooted, to the big wooden table beside the Aga, carrying her notebook, her laptop and her phone.

It was pleasant to have the kitchen to herself. The garden beyond the window, covered in a hard frost, was dark blue and silver in the winter predawn. Setting her laptop and phone on the table, she greeted Rowntree, who was too arthritic these days for early morning frolicking, but wagged his tail lazily from his basket beside the radiator. She made herself a cup of tea, then took a seat at the table and opened her laptop.

She hadn't yet read Strike's document summarising the horoscope notes, which had arrived while she was busy helping her mother cook Christmas lunch. Robin had been adding the Brussels sprouts to the steamer when she saw, out of the corner of her eye, the notification on her phone, which was charging on one of the few power points that wasn't taken up by some piece of baby equipment: bottle steriliser, baby alarm or breast pump. Seeing Strike's name, her heart had momentarily lifted, because she was sure that she was about to read thanks for the gift of the Tom Waits DVD, and the fact that he'd emailed on Christmas Day was an indicator of friendship such as she had perhaps never received from him.

However, when she opened the email she simply read:

FYI: summary of Talbot's horoscope notes and action points.

Robin knew her face must have fallen when she looked up and saw Linda watching her.

'Bad news?'

'No, just Strike.'

'On Christmas Day?' said Linda sharply.

And Robin had realised in that instant that Geoffrey, her ex-father-in-law, must have been spreading it around Masham that if Matthew had been unfaithful, it was only after being heinously betrayed himself. She read the truth in her mother's face, and in Jenny's sudden interest in Annabel, whom she was jiggling in her arms, and in the sharp look flung at her by Jonathan, her youngest brother, who was tipping bottled cranberry sauce into a dish.

'It's work,' Robin had said coldly. Each of her silent accusers had returned hastily to their tasks.

It was, therefore, with very mixed feelings towards the author that Robin now settled down to read Strike's document. Emailing her on Christmas Day had felt reproachful, as though she'd let him down by going back to Masham instead of remaining in London and single-handedly running the agency while he, Barclay and Morris were down with flu. Moreover, if he was going to email at all on Christmas Day, some kind of personal message might be seen as common politeness. Perhaps he'd simply treated her Christmas present with the same indifference she'd treated his.

Robin had just read to the bottom of 'Possible leads' and was digesting the idea that a professional gangster had been, on at least one occasion, in close proximity to Margot Bamborough, when the kitchen door opened, admitting baby Annabel's distant wails. Linda entered the room, wearing a dressing gown and slippers.

'What are you doing down here?' she asked, sounding disapproving, as she crossed to the kettle.

Robin tried not to show how irked she felt. She'd spent the last few days smiling until her face ached, helping as much as was physically possible, admiring baby Annabel until she doubted that a pore had been left unpraised; she'd joined in charades and poured drinks and watched films and unwrapped chocolates or cracked nuts for Jenny, who was constantly pinned to the sofa by the demands of breastfeeding. She'd shown an intelligent and sympathetic interest in Jonathan's university friends' exploits; she'd listened to her father's opinions on David Cameron's agricultural policy and she'd noticed, but shown no resentment about, the fact that not a single member of her family had asked what she was doing at work. Was she not allowed to sit quietly in the kitchen for half an hour, while Annabel rendered sleep impossible?

'Reading an email,' said Robin.

'They think,' said Linda (and Robin knew 'they' must be the new parents, whose thoughts and wishes were of all-consuming importance just now) 'it was the sprouts. She's been colicky all night. Jenny's exhausted.'

'Annabel didn't have sprouts,' said Robin.

'She gets it all through the breast milk,' explained Linda, with what felt to Robin like condescension for being excluded from the mysteries of motherhood.

Bearing two cups of tea for Stephen and Jenny, Linda left the room again. Relieved, Robin opened her notebook and jotted down a couple of thoughts that had occurred to her while reading 'Possible leads,' then returned to Strike's document to read his short list of 'Probably irrelevant' items gleaned from Talbot's notebook.

Paul Satchwell

After a few months, Talbot's mental state clearly deteriorated, judging by his notes, which become progressively more detached from reality.

Towards the end of the notebook he goes back to the other two horned signs of the zodiac, Aries and Taurus, presumably because he's still fixated on the devil. As stated above, Wilma comes in for a lot of unfounded suspicion, but he also goes to the trouble of calculating Satchwell's complete birth

486

horoscope, which means he must have got a birth time from him. Probably means nothing, but strange that he went back to Satchwell and spent this much time on his birth chart, which he didn't do for any other suspect. Talbot highlights aspects of the chart that supposedly indicate aggression, dishonesty and neuroses. Talbot also keeps noting that various parts of Satchwell's chart are 'same as AC' without explanation.

Roy Phipps and Irene Hickson

As mentioned above, the signs Talbot uses for Roy Phipps and Irene Hickson (who was then Irene Bull) haven't ever been used in astrology and seem to be inventions of Talbot's.

Roy's symbol looks like a headless stick-man. Exactly what it's supposed to represent I can't find out – presumably a constellation? Quotations about snakes recur around Roy's name.

Irene's invented sign looks like a big fish and—

The kitchen door opened again. Robin looked around. It was Linda again.

'You still here?' she said, still with a slight sense of disapproval.

'No,' said Robin, 'I'm upstairs.'

Linda's smile was reluctant. As she took more mugs from the cupboard, she asked,

'D'you want another tea?'

'No thanks,' said Robin, closing her laptop. She'd decided to finish reading Strike's document in her room. Maybe she was imagining it, but Linda seemed to be making more noise than usual.

'He's got you working over Christmas as well, then?' said Linda.

For the past four days, Robin had suspected that her mother wanted to talk to her about Strike. The looks she'd seen on her surprised family's faces yesterday had told her why. However, she felt under no obligation to make it easy for Linda to interrogate her.

'As well as what?' asked Robin.

'You know what I mean,' said Linda. 'Christmas. I'd have thought you were owed time off.'

'I get time off,' said Robin.

She took her empty mug over to the sink. Rowntree now struggled to his feet and Robin let him out of the back door, feeling the icy air on every bit of exposed skin. Over the garden hedge she could see the sun turning the horizon green as it made its way steadily up through the icy heavens.

'Is he seeing anyone?' Linda asked. 'Strike?'

'He sees lots of people,' said Robin, wilfully obtuse. 'It's part of the job.'

'You know what I mean,' said Linda.

'Why the interest?'

She expected her mother to back off, but was surprised.

'I think you know why,' she said, turning to face her daughter.

Robin was furious to find herself blushing. She was a twenty-nine-year-old woman. At that very moment, her mobile emitted a beep on the kitchen table. She was convinced that it would be Strike texting her, and so, apparently, was Linda, who, being nearer, picked up the phone to hand it to Robin, glancing at the sender's name as she did so.

It wasn't Strike. It was Saul Morris. He'd written:

Hope you're not having as shit a Christmas as I am.

Robin wouldn't normally have answered. Resentment at her family, and something else, something she didn't particularly want to admit to, made her text back, while Linda watched:

Depends how shit yours is. Mine's fairly shit.

She sent the message, then looked up at Linda.

'Who's Saul Morris?' her mother asked.

'Subcontractor at the agency. Ex-police,' said Robin.

'Oh,' said Linda.

Robin could tell that had given Linda fresh food for thought. If she was honest with herself, she'd meant to do exactly that. Picking her laptop off the table, she left the kitchen.

The bathroom was, of course, occupied. Robin returned to her room. By the time she lay back down on her bed, laptop open again, Morris had texted her again.

Tell me your troubles and I'll tell you mine. Problem shared and all that.

Slightly regretting that she'd answered him, Robin turned the mobile face down on her bed and continued reading Strike's document.

> Irene's invented sign looks like a big fish and Talbot's blunt about what he thinks it represents: 'the monster Cetus, Leviathan, the biblical whale, superficial charm, evil in depths. Headstrong, enjoys spotlight, a performer, a liar.' Talbot seems to have suspected Irene was a liar even before she was proven to have lied about her trip to the dentist, which Talbot never found out about, although there's no indication as to what he thinks she was lying about.

> **Margot as Babalon**
>
> This is only of relevance in as much as it shows just how ill Talbot was.
>
> On the night he was finally sectioned, he

attempted some kind of magic ritual. Judging by his notes, he was trying to conjure Baphomet, presumably because he thought Baphomet would take the form of Margot's killer.

According to Talbot, what manifested in the room wasn't Baphomet, but the spirit of Margot 'who blames me, who attacks me'. Talbot believed she'd become Babalon in death, Babalon being Baphomet's second-in-command/consort. The demon he 'saw' was carrying a cup of blood and a sword. There are repeated mentions of lions scribbled round the picture of the demon. Babalon rides a seven-headed lion on the card representing Lust in the Thoth tarot.

At some point after Talbot drew the demon, he went back and drew Latin crosses over some of the notes and on the demon itself, and wrote a biblical quotation warning against witchcraft across the picture. The appearance of the demon seems to have pushed him back towards religion, and that's where his notes end.

Robin heard the bathroom door open and close. Now desperate for a pee, she jumped up and headed out of her room.

Stephen was crossing the landing, holding his washbag, puffy-eyed and yawning.

'Sorry about last night, Rob,' he said. 'Jenny thinks it was the sprouts.'

'Yeah, Mum said,' Robin replied, edging around him. 'No problem. Hope she feels better.'

'We're going to take her out for a walk. I'll see if I can buy you some ear plugs.'

Once she'd showered, Robin returned to her room. Her phone beeped twice while she was dressing.

Brushing her hair in the mirror, her eyes fell on the new perfume she'd received as a Christmas present from her mother. Robin had told her she was looking for a new fragrance, because the old one reminded her too much of Matthew. She'd been touched that Linda remembered the conversation when she opened the gift.

The bottle was round; not an orb, but a flattish circle: Chanel Chance Eau Fraîche. The liquid was pale green. An unfortunate association of ideas now made Robin think of sprouts. Nevertheless, she sprayed some on her wrists and behind her ears, filling the air with the scent of sharp lemon and nondescript flowers. What, she wondered, had made her mother choose it? What was it about the perfume that made her think 'Robin'? To Robin's nostrils it smelled like a deodorant, generic, clean and totally without romance. She remembered her unsuccessful purchase of Fracas, and the desire to be sexy and sophisticated that had ended only in headaches. Musing about the disparity between the way people would like to be seen, and the way

492

others prefer to see them, Robin sat back down on her bed beside her laptop and flipped over her phone.

Morris had texted twice more.

Lonely and hungover this end. Not being with the kids at Christmas is shit.

When Robin hadn't answered this, he'd texted again.

Sorry, being a maudlin dickhead. Feel free to ignore.

Calling himself a dickhead was the most likeable thing she'd ever known Morris do. Feeling sorry for him, Robin replied,

It must be tough, I'm sorry.

She then returned to her laptop and the last bit of Strike's document, detailing actions to be taken, and with initials beside each to show which of them should undertake it.

Action points

Talk to Gregory Talbot again – CS

I want to know why, even after he got well, Bill Talbot never told colleagues about the leads in this notebook he'd withheld from colleagues during the investigation, ie, sighting of Brenner in Skinner Street the night Margot disappeared/blood on the Phippses' carpet/a death Margot might have been worried about/Mucky Ricci leaving the practice one night.

Speak to Dinesh Gupta again – CS

He might know who Brenner was visiting in Skinner Street that night. Could have been a patient. He might also be able to shed light on Mucky Ricci appearing at the party. Will also ask him about 'Scorpio' in case this refers to a patient whose death seemed suspicious to Margot.

Interview Roy Phipps – CS/RE

We've tiptoed around Phipps too long. Time to ring Anna and see whether she can persuade him to give us an interview.

Try and secure interview with one of Wilma Bayliss's children – CS/RE

Especially important if we can't get to Roy. Want to re-examine Wilma's story (Roy walking, blood on the carpet).

Find C. B. Oakden – CS/RE

Judging from his book, he's full of shit, but there's an outside possibility he knows things about Brenner we don't, given that his mother was the closest person to Brenner at the practice.

Find & interview Paul Satchwell – CS/RE

Find & interview Steven Douthwaite – CS/RE

Robin couldn't help but feel subtly criticised. Strike had now added his initials to action points that had previously been Robin's alone, such as finding Satchwell, and persuading Wilma Bayliss's children to give them interviews. She set the laptop down again, picked up her phone and headed back to the kitchen for breakfast.

An abrupt silence fell when she walked into the room. Linda, Stephen and Jenny all wore self-conscious looks of those who fear they might have been overheard. Robin put bread in the toaster, trying to tamp down her rising resentment. She seemed to sense mouthed speech and gesticulations behind her back.

'Robin, we just ran into Matthew,' said Stephen suddenly. 'When we were walking Annabel round the block.'

'Oh,' said Robin, turning to face them, trying to look mildly interested.

It was the first time Matthew had been spotted. Robin had avoided midnight mass out of conviction that he and Sarah would be there, but her mother had reported that none of the Cunliffes had attended. Now Linda, Stephen and Jenny were all looking at her, worried, pitying, waiting for her reaction and her questions.

Her phone beeped.

'Sorry,' she said, picking it up, delighted to have a reason to look away from them all.

Morris had texted:

Why's your Christmas so shit?

While the other three watched, she typed back:

My ex-father-in-law lives locally and my ex has brought his new girlfriend home. We're currently the local scandal.

She didn't like Morris, but at this moment he felt like a welcome ally, a lifeline from the life she had forged, with difficulty, away from Matthew and Masham. Robin was on the point of setting down the phone when it beeped again and, still with the other three watching her, she read:

That stinks.

It does, she texted back.

Then she looked up at her mother, Stephen and Jenny, forcing herself to smile.

'D'you want to tell me about it?' Robin asked Stephen. 'Or do I have to ask?'

'No,' he said hurriedly, 'it wasn't much – we were just pushing Annabel up to the Square and back, and we saw them coming towards us. Him and that—'

'Sarah,' supplied Robin. She could just imagine them hand in hand, enjoying the wintry morning, the picturesque town, sleepy in the frost and early sunshine.

'Yeah,' said Stephen. 'He looked like he wanted to double back when he saw us, but he didn't. Said, "Congratulations in order, I see."'

Robin could hear Matthew saying it.

'And that was it, really,' said Stephen.

'I'd've liked to have kicked him in the balls,' said Jenny suddenly. 'Smug bastard.'

But Linda's eyes were on Robin's phone.

'Who are you texting back and forth on Boxing Day?' she asked.

'I've just told you,' said Robin. 'Morris. He works for the agency.'

She knew exactly what impression she was giving Linda, but she had her pride. Perhaps there was no shame in being single, but the pity of her family, the thought of Matthew and Sarah walking through Masham, everyone's suspicion of her and Strike, and the fact that there was nothing whatsoever to tell about her and Strike, except that he thought he'd better start taking over some of her leads because she'd got no results: all made her want to clutch some kind of fig leaf to her threadbare dignity. Smarmy and overfamiliar as he might be, Morris was today, perhaps, more to be pitied than censured, and was offering himself up to save Robin's face.

She saw her mother and brother exchange looks and had the empty satisfaction of knowing that they were already haring after her false scent. Miserable, she opened the fridge and took out half a bottle of carefully re-corked champagne left over from Christmas Day.

'What are you doing?' asked Linda.

'Making myself a mimosa,' said Robin. 'Still Christmas, isn't it?'

One more night and she'd be back on the train to London. Almost as though she had heard Robin's antisocial thought, a cry of anguish issued through the baby monitor just behind her, making Robin jump, and what she was starting to think of as the baby circus relocated from the kitchen to the sitting room, Linda bringing a glass of water for Jenny to drink while breastfeeding and turning on the TV for her, while Stephen ran upstairs to fetch Annabel.

Drink, Robin decided, was the answer. If you splashed in enough orange juice, nobody had to know you were finishing off a bottle of champagne single-handedly, and those feelings of misery, anger and inadequacy that were writhing in the pit of your stomach could be satisfactorily numbed. Mimosas carried her through to lunchtime, when everyone had a glass of red, although Jenny drank 'just a mouthful' because of Annabel, and ignored Robin's suggestion that alcoholic breast milk might help her sleep. Morris was still texting, mostly stupid Christmas knock-knock jokes and updates on his day, and Robin was replying in the same mindless manner that she sometimes continued eating crisps, with a trace of self-loathing.

My mother's just arrived. Send sherry and excuses not to talk to her WI group about policework.

What's your mother's name? Robin texted back. She was definitely a little bit drunk.

Fanny, said Morris.

Robin was unsure whether to laugh or not, or, indeed, whether it was funny.

'Robs, d'you want to play Pictionary?' asked Jonathan.

'What?' she said.

She was sitting on an uncomfortable hard-backed chair in the corner of the sitting room. The baby circus occupied at least half the room. *The Wizard of Oz* was on the television but nobody was really watching.

'Pictionary,' repeated Jonathan, holding up the box. 'Oh, yeah, and Robs, could I come and stay with you for a weekend in February?'

I'm only kidding, texted Morris. **Frances.**

'What?' Robin said again, under the impression somebody had asked her something.

'Morris is obviously a very interesting man,' said Linda archly, and everyone looked around at Robin, who merely said,

'Pictionary, yes, fine.'

Got to play Pictionary, she texted Morris.

Draw a dick, came back the instant answer.

Robin set down her phone again. The drink was wearing off now, leaving in its wake a headache that throbbed behind her right temple. Luckily, Martin arrived at that moment with a tray full of coffees and a bottle of Baileys.

Jonathan won Pictionary. Baby Annabel screamed some more. A cold supper was laid out on the kitchen table, to which neighbours had been invited to admire Annabel. By eight o'clock in the evening, Robin had taken paracetamol and started to drink black coffee to clear her head. She needed to pack. She also needed, somehow, to shut down her day-long conversation with Morris, who, she could tell, was now very drunk indeed.

Mohter gone home, complaining not seeing grandchioldren enough. What shall we talk about now? What are you wearing?

She ignored the text. Up in her bedroom, she packed her case, because she was catching an early train. *Please, God, let Matthew and Sarah not be on it.* She resprayed herself with her mother's Christmas gift. Smelling it again, she decided that the only message it conveyed to bystanders was 'I have washed'. Perhaps her mother had bought her this boring floral antiseptic out of a subconscious desire to wipe her daughter clean of the suggestion of adultery. There was certainly nothing of the seductress about it, and it would forever remind her of this lousy Christmas. Nevertheless, Robin packed it carefully among her socks, having no wish to hurt her mother's feelings by leaving it behind.

By the time she returned downstairs, Morris had texted another five times.

I was joking.
Tell me u know I was joking.
Fukc have I offended u
Have I?
Answer me either way fuck's sake

Slightly riled, and embarrassed now by her stupid, adolescent pretence to her family that she, like Matthew, had found another partner, she paused in the hall to text back,

I'm not offended. Got to go. Need an early night.

She entered the sitting room, where her family were all sitting, sleepy and overfed, watching the

501

news. Robin moved a muslin cloth, half a pack of nappies and one of the Pictionary boards from the sofa, so she could sit down.

'Sorry, Robin,' said Jenny, yawning as she reached out for the baby things and put them by her feet.

Robin's phone beeped yet again. Linda looked over at her. Robin ignored both her mother and the phone, because she was looking down at the Pictionary board where Martin had tried to draw 'Icarus'. Nobody had guessed it. They'd thought Icarus was a bug hovering over a flower.

But something about the picture held Robin fixated. Again, her phone beeped. She looked at it.

Are you in bed?

Yes and so should you be, she texted back, her mind still on the Pictionary board. The flower that looked like a sun. The sun that looked like a flower.

Her phone beeped yet again. Exasperated, she looked at it.

Morris had sent her a picture of his erect dick. For a moment, and even while she felt appalled and repulsed, Robin continued to stare at it. Then, with a suddenness that made her father start awake in his chair, she got up and almost ran out of the room.

The kitchen wasn't far enough. Nowhere would be far enough. Shaking with rage and shock, she wrenched open the back door and strode out into the icy garden, with the water in the birdbath she'd unfrozen with boiling water already milky hard in

502

the moonlight. Without stopping to pause for thought, she called Morris's number.

'Hey—'

'How fucking dare you – *how fucking dare you send me that?*'

'Fuck,' he said thickly, 'I di'n – I thought – "wish you were here" or—'

'I said I was going to bloody bed!' Robin shouted. 'I did not ask to see your fucking dick!'

She could see the neighbours' heads bobbing behind their kitchen blinds. The Ellacotts were providing rich entertainment this Christmas, all right: first a new baby, then a shouting match about a penis.

'Oh shit,' gasped Morris. 'Oh fuck . . . no . . . listen, I di'n' mean—'

'Who the fuck does that?' shouted Robin. 'What's wrong with you?'

'No . . . shit . . . fuck . . . I'm s'rry . . . I thought . . . I'm so f'king sorry . . . Robin, don't . . . oh Jesus . . .'

'*I don't want to see your dick!*'

A storm of dry sobs answered her, then Robin thought she heard him lay down the phone on some hard surface. At a distance from the mouthpiece he emitted moans of anguish interspersed with weeping. Heavy objects seemed to be falling over. Then there was a clatter and he picked up his mobile again.

'Robin, I'm so fuckin' sorry . . . what've I done, what've I . . .? I thought . . . I should fucking kill myself . . . don't . . . don't tell Strike, Robin . . . I'm fuckin' begging you . . . if I lose this job . . . don't tell, Robin . . . I lose this, I lose fuckin' every- thing . . . I can't lose my little girls, Robin . . .'

He reminded her of Matthew, the day that she'd found out he was cheating. She could see her ex-husband as clearly as though he was there on the ice-crusted lawn, face in his hands as he gasped his apologies, then looking up at her in panic. *'Have you spoken to Tom? Does he know?'*

What was it about her that made men demand that she keep their dirty secrets?

'I won't tell Strike,' she said, shaking more with rage than with cold, 'because his aunt's dying and we need an extra man. But you'd better never send me anything other than an update on a case again.'

'Oh God, Robin . . . thank you . . . thank you . . . you are such a decent person . . .'

He'd stopped sobbing. His gushing offended her almost as much as the picture of his dick.

'I'm going.'

She stood in the dark, barely feeling the cold, her mobile hanging at her side. As the light in the neighbour's kitchen went off, her parents' back door opened. Rowntree came lolloping over the frozen lawn, delighted to find her outside.

'You all right, love?' Michael Ellacott asked his daughter.

'Fine,' said Robin, crouching to fuss Rowntree to hide her sudden rush of tears. 'It's all fine.'

PART IV

Great enemy . . . is wicked Time . . .

Edmund Spenser
The Faerie Queene

CHAPTER 31

Deare knight, as deare, as euer knight was deare,
That all these sorrowes suffer for my sake,
High heuen behold the tedious toyle, ye for me
take . . .

Edmund Spenser
The Faerie Queene

S trike's gastric upset added days to his illness, and he spent New Year's Eve in bed, reliant on takeaway pizzas but hardly able to touch them when they arrived. For the first time in his life he didn't fancy chocolate, because the truffles he'd consumed after his out-of-date chicken had been the first things to reappear during his prolonged vomiting. The only enjoyable thing he did was to watch the DVD of Tom Waits's *No Visitors After Midnight*, the taped concerts Robin had bought him for Christmas, which he finally unwrapped on New Year's Day. His text thanking her elicited a short 'you're welcome'.

By the time he felt fit enough to travel down to

Cornwall, clutching his belated Christmas gifts, Strike had lost over a stone, and this was the first thing an anxious Joan commented on when he finally appeared at her house in St Mawes, full of apologies for his absence at Christmas.

If he'd waited one more day to come down to Joan and Ted's, he'd have been unable to reach them, because no sooner had he arrived than a vicious weather front crashed over the south of Britain. Storms lashed the Cornish coast, train services were suspended, tons of sand washed off the beaches and flooding turned the roads of coastal towns into freezing canals. The Cornish peninsula was temporarily cut off from the rest of England, and while St Mawes had not fared as badly as Mevagissey and Fowey along the coast, sandbags had appeared at the entrances of buildings on the seafront. Waves smashed against the harbour wall, khaki and gunmetal grey. The tourists had melted out of sight like the seals: locals in sodden oilskins greeted each other with nods as they made their way in and out of local shops. All the gaudy prettiness of summertime St Mawes was wiped away and, like an actress when the stage-paint is removed, the town's true self was revealed, a place of hard stone and stiff backbone.

Though pelted with rain and pummelled by gales, Ted and Joan's house was, mercifully, set on high ground. Trapped there, Strike remembered Lucy telling him he was better suited to a crisis than to keeping a commitment going, and knew that there was truth in the accusation. He was well suited to emergencies, to holding his nerve, to quick thinking and fast reactions, but found the qualities demanded by Joan's slow decline harder to summon.

Strike missed the absence of an overriding objective, in pursuit of which he could shelve his sadness; missed the imperative to dismiss pain and distress in the service of something greater, which had sustained him in the military. None of his old coping strategies were admissible in Joan's kitchen, beside the flowered casserole dishes and her old oven gloves. Dark humour and stoicism would be considered unfeeling by the kindly neighbours who wanted him to share and show his pain. Craving diversionary action, Strike was instead expected to provide small talk and homely acts of consideration.

Joan was quietly delighted: hours and days alone with her nephew were compensation for the Christmas he'd missed. Resigned, Strike gave her what she wanted: as much companionship as possible, sitting with her and talking to her all day long. Chemotherapy had been discontinued, because Joan wasn't strong enough for it: she wore a headscarf over the wispy hair she had left, and her husband and nephew watched anxiously as she picked at food, and held themselves constantly ready to assist her when she moved between rooms. Either of them could have carried her with ease, now.

As the days went by, Strike noticed another change in his aunt that surprised him. Just as her storm-ravaged birthplace had revealed a different aspect in adversity, so an unfamiliar Joan was emerging, a Joan who asked open-ended questions that were not designed to elicit confirmation of her own biases, or thinly veiled requests for comforting lies.

'Why haven't you ever married, Cormoran?' she asked her nephew at midday on Saturday morning, when they sat together in the sitting room, Joan in the comfiest armchair, Strike on the sofa. The lamp beside her, which they'd turned on because of the overcast, rainy day, made her skin look as finely translucent as tissue paper.

Strike was so conditioned to tell Joan what she wanted to hear that he was at a loss for an answer. The honest response he'd given Dave Polworth seemed impossible here. She'd probably take it as her fault if he told her that he wasn't the marrying kind; she must have done something wrong, failed to teach him that love was essential to happiness.

'Dunno,' he said, falling back on cliché. 'Maybe I haven't met the right woman.'

'If you're waiting for perfection,' said the new Joan, 'it doesn't exist.'

'You don't wish I'd married Charlotte, do you?' he asked her. He knew perfectly well that both Joan and Lucy considered Charlotte little short of a she-devil.

'I most certainly don't,' said Joan, with a spark of her old fight, and they smiled at each other.

Ted popped his head around the door.

'That's Kerenza here, love,' he said. 'Her car's just pulled up.'

The Macmillan nurse, whom Strike had met on his first day there, was a blessing such as he could never have imagined. A slender, freckled woman his age, she brought into the house no aura of death, but of life continuing, simply with more comfort and support. Strike's own prolonged exposure to the medical profession had inured him to a certain brand of hearty, impersonal cheerfulness, but Kerenza seemed to see Ted and Joan as individuals, not as simple-minded children, and he heard her talking to Ted, the ex-lifeguard, about people trying to take selfies with their backs to the storm waves while she took off her raincoat in the kitchen.

'Exactly. Don't understand the sea, do they? Respect it, or stay well away, my dad would've said . . . Morning, Joan,' she said, coming into the room. 'Hello, Cormoran.'

'Morning, Kerenza,' said Strike, getting to his feet. 'I'll get out of the way.'

'And how're you feeling today, my love?' the nurse asked Joan.

'Not too bad,' said Joan. 'I'm just a bit . . .'

She paused, to let her nephew pass out of earshot. As Strike closed the door on the two women, he heard more crunching footsteps on the gravel path outside. Ted, who was reading the local paper at the table, looked up.

'Who's that, now?'

A moment later, Dave Polworth appeared at the glass panel in the back door, a large rucksack on his back. He entered, rainswept and grinning.

'Morning, Diddy,' he said, and they exchanged the handshake and hug that had become the standard greeting in their later years. 'Morning, Ted.'

'What're you doing here?' asked Ted.

Polworth swung his rucksack off, undid it and lifted out a couple of polythene-wrapped, frozen dishes onto the table.

'Penny baked a couple of casseroles. I'm gonna get some provisions in, wanted to know what you needed.'

The flame of pure, practical kindness that burned in Dave Polworth had never been more clearly visible to Strike, except perhaps on his very first day at primary school, when the diminutive Polworth had taken Strike under his protection.

'You're a good lad,' said Ted, moved. 'Say thanks very much to Penny, won't you?'

'Yeah, she sent her love and all that,' said Polworth dismissively.

'Wanna keep me company while I have a smoke?' Strike asked him.

'Go on, then,' said Polworth.

'Use the shed,' suggested Ted.

So Strike and Polworth headed together across

the waterlogged garden, heads bowed against the strong wind and rain, and entered Ted's shed. Strike lit up with relief.

'You been on a diet?' asked Polworth, looking Strike up and down.

'Flu and food poisoning.'

'Oh, yeah, Lucy said you'd been ill.' Polworth jerked his head in the direction of Joan's window. 'How is she?'

'Not great,' said Strike.

'How long you down for?'

'Depends on the weather. Listen, seriously, I really appreciate everything you've been—'

'Shut up, you ponce.'

'Can I ask another favour?'

'Go on.'

'Persuade Ted to get a pint with you this lunch-time. He needs to get out of this house for a bit. He'll do it if he knows I'm with her, but otherwise he won't leave.'

'Consider it done,' said Polworth.

'You're—'

'—a prince among men, yeah, I know I am. Arsenal through to the knockout stages, then?'

'Yeah,' said Strike. 'Bayern Munich next, though.'

He'd missed watching his team qualify before Christmas, because he'd been tailing Shifty through the West End. The Champions League, which should have been a pleasure and a distraction, was failing to grip him as it usually did.

'Robin running things in London while you're down here?'

'Yeah,' said Strike.

She'd texted him earlier, asking for a brief chat about the Bamborough case. He'd replied that he'd call her when he had a moment. He, too, had news on the case, but Margot Bamborough had been missing for nearly forty years and, like Kerenza the nurse, Strike was currently prioritising the living.

When he'd finished his cigarette, they returned to the house to find Ted and Kerenza in conversation in the kitchen.

'She'd rather talk to you than to me today,' said Kerenza, smiling at Strike as she shrugged on her raincoat. 'I'll be back tomorrow morning, Ted.'

As she moved towards the back door, Polworth said,

'Ted, come and have a pint.'

'Oh, no, thanks, lad,' said Ted. 'I'll bide here just now.'

Kerenza stopped with her hand on the door knob.

'That's a very good idea. Get a bit of fresh air, Ted – fresh water, today, I should say,' she added, as the rain clattered on the roof. 'Bye-bye, now.'

She left. Ted required a little more persuasion, but finally agreed that he'd join Polworth for a sandwich at the Victory. Once they'd gone, Strike took the local paper off the table and carried it back into the sitting room.

He and Joan discussed the flooding, but the

pictures of waves battering Mevagissey meant far less to her than they would have a couple of months ago. Strike could tell that Joan's mind was on the personal, not the general.

'What does my horoscope say?' she asked, as he turned the page of the paper.

'I didn't know you believed in that stuff, Joan.'

'Don't know whether I do or not,' said Joan. 'I always look, though.'

'You're . . .' he said, trying to remember her birthday. He knew it was in the summer.

'Cancer,' she said, and then she gave a little laugh. 'In more ways than one.'

Strike didn't smile.

'"Good time for shaking up your routine,"' he informed her, scanning her horoscope so he could censor out anything depressing, '"so don't dismiss new ideas out of hand. Jupiter retrograde encourages spiritual growth."'

'Huh,' said Joan. After a short pause, she said, 'I don't think I'll be here for my next birthday, Corm.'

The words hit him like a punch in the diaphragm.

'Don't say that.'

'If I can't say it to you, who can I say it to?'

Her eyes, which had always been a pale forget-me-not blue, were faded now. She'd never spoken to him like this before, as an equal. Always, she'd sought to stand slightly above him, so that from her perspective the six-foot-three soldier might still be her little boy.

'I can't say it to Ted or Lucy, can I?' she said. 'You know what they're like.'

'Yeah,' he said, with difficulty.

'Afterwards . . . you'll look after Ted, won't you? Make sure you see him. He does love you so much.'

Fuck.

For so long, she'd demanded a kind of falseness from all around her, a rose-tinted view of everything, and now at last she offered simple honesty and plain-speaking and he wished more than anything that he could be simply nodding along to news of some neighbourhood scandal. Why hadn't he visited them more often?

'I will, of course,' he said.

'I want the funeral at St Mawes church,' she said quietly, 'where I was christened. But I don't want to be buried, because it'd have to be in the cemetery all the way up in Truro. Ted'll wear himself out, travelling up and down, taking me flowers. I know him.

'We always said we wanted to be together, afterwards, but we never made a plan and he won't talk to me about it now. So, I've thought about it, Corm, and I want to be cremated. You'll make sure this happens, won't you? Because Ted starts crying every time I try and talk about it and Lucy just won't listen.'

Strike nodded and tried to smile.

'I don't want the family at the cremation. I hate cremations, the curtains and the conveyor belt. You say goodbye to me at the church, then take Ted to the pub and let the undertakers deal with the crematorium bit, all right? Then, after, you can pick up my ashes, take me out on Ted's boat and scatter me in the sea. And when his turn comes, you can do the same for Ted, and we'll be together. You and Lucy won't want to be worrying about looking after graves all the way from London. All right?'

The plan had so much of the Joan he knew in it: it was full of practical kindness and forethought, but he hadn't expected the final touch of the ashes floating away on the tide, no tombstone, no neat dates, instead a melding with the element that had dominated her and Ted's lives, perched on their seaside town, in thrall to the ocean, except during that strange interlude where Ted, in revolt against his own father, had disappeared for several years into the military police.

'All right,' he said, with difficulty.

She sank back a little in her chair with an air of relief at having got this off her chest, and smiled at him.

'It's so lovely, having you here.'

Over the past few days he'd become used to her short reveries and her non-sequiturs, so it was less of a surprise than it might have been to hear her say, a minute later,

'I wish I'd met your Robin.'

Strike, whose mind's eye was still following Joan's ashes into the sunset, pulled himself together.

'I think you'd like her,' he said. 'I'm sure she'd like you.'

'Lucy says she's pretty.'

'Yeah, she is.'

'Poor girl,' murmured Joan. He wondered why. Of course, the knife attack had been reported in the press, when Robin had given evidence against the Shacklewell Ripper.

'Funny, you talking about horoscopes,' Strike said, trying to ease Joan off Robin, and funerals, and death. 'We're investigating an old disappearance just now. The bloke who was in charge of the case . . .'

He'd never before shared details of an investigation with Joan, and he wondered why not, now he saw her rapt attention.

'But I remember that doctor!' she said, more animated than he had seen her in days. 'Margot Bamborough, yes! She had a baby at home . . .'

'Well, that baby's our client,' said Strike. 'Her name's Anna. She and her partner have got a holiday home in Falmouth.'

'That poor family,' said Joan. 'Never knowing . . . and so the officer thought the answer was in the stars?'

'Yep,' said Strike. 'Convinced the killer was a Capricorn.'

'Ted's a Capricorn.'

'Thanks for the tip-off,' said Strike seriously, and she gave a little laugh. 'D'you want more tea?'

While the kettle boiled, Strike checked his texts. Barclay had sent an update on Two-Times' girl-friend, but the most recent message was from an unknown number, and he opened it first.

Hi Cormoran, it's your half-sister, Prudence Donleavy, here. Al gave me your number. I do hope you'll take this in the spirit it's meant. Let me firstly say that I absolutely understand and sympathise with your reasons for not wanting to join us for the Deadbeats anniversary/album party. You may or may not know that my own journey to a relationship with Dad has been in many ways a difficult one, but ultimately I feel that connecting with him – and, yes, forgiving him – has been an enriching experience. We all hope very much that you'll reconsider —

'What's the matter?' said Joan.

She'd followed him into the kitchen, shuffling, slightly stooped.

'What are you doing? I can fetch anything you want—'

'I was going to show you where I hide the chocolate biscuits. If Ted knows, he scoffs the lot, and the doctor's worried about his blood pressure. What were you reading? I know that look. You were angry.'

He didn't know whether her new appreciation for honesty would stretch as far as his father, but somehow, with the wind and rain whipping around them, an air of the confessional had descended upon the house. He told her about the text.

'Oh,' said Joan. She pointed at a Tupperware box on a top shelf. 'The biscuits are in there.'

They returned to the sitting room with the biscuits, which she'd insisted he put on a plate. Some things never changed.

'You've never met Prudence, have you?' asked Joan, when she was resettled in her chair.

'Haven't met Prudence, or the eldest, Maimie, or the youngest, Ed,' said Strike, trying to sound matter of fact.

Joan said nothing for a minute or so, then a great sigh inflated, then collapsed, her thin chest, and she said,

'I think you should go to your father's party, Corm.'

'Why?' said Strike. The monosyllable rang in his ears with an adolescent, self-righteous fury. To his slight surprise, she smiled at him.

'I know what went on,' she said. 'He behaved very badly, but he's still your father.'

'No, he isn't,' said Strike. 'Ted's my dad.'

He'd never said it out loud before. Tears filled Joan's eyes.

'He'd love to hear you say that,' she said softly. 'Funny, isn't it . . . years ago, years and years, I was just a girl, and I went to see a proper gypsy fortune teller. They used to camp up the road. I thought she'd tell me lots of nice things. You expect them to, don't you? You've paid your money. D'you know what she said?'

Strike shook his head.

'"You'll never have children." Just like that. Straight out.'

'Well, she got that wrong, didn't she?' said Strike.

Tears started again in Joan's bleached eyes. Why had he never said these things before, Strike asked himself. It would have been so easy to give her pleasure, and instead he'd held tightly to his divided loyalties, angry that he had to choose, to label, and in doing so, to betray. He reached for her hand and she squeezed it surprisingly tightly.

'You should go to that party, Corm. I think your father's at the heart of . . . of a lot of things. I wish,' she added, after a short pause, 'you had someone to look after you.'

'Doesn't work that way these days, Joan. Men are supposed to be able to look after themselves – in more ways than one,' he added, smiling.

'Pretending you don't need things . . . it's just silly,' she said quietly. 'What does *your* horoscope say?'

He picked up the paper again and cleared his throat.

'"Sagittarius: with your ruler retrograde, you may find you aren't your usual happy-go-lucky self . . ."'

CHAPTER 32

Where euer yet I be, my secrete aide Shall follow you.

Edmund Spenser
The Faerie Queene

It was three o'clock in the afternoon and Robin, who was sitting in her Land Rover close to the nondescript house in Stoke Newington that Strike had watched before Christmas, had seen nothing of interest since arriving in the street at nine o'clock that morning. As rain drizzled down her windscreen she half-wished she smoked, just for something to do.

She'd identified the blonde owner-occupier of the house online. Her name was Elinor Dean, and she was a divorcee who lived alone. Elinor was definitely home, because Robin had seen her pass in front of a window two hours previously, but the squally weather seemed to be keeping her inside. Nobody had visited the house all day, least of all Shifty's Boss. Perhaps they were relatives, after all, and his pre-Christmas visit was simply one of those things you did in the festive season: pay social debts, give presents, check in. The patting on the head might have been a private joke. It certainly didn't seem to suggest anything sexual, criminal or deviant, which was what they were looking for.

Robin's mobile rang.

'Hi.'

'Can you talk?' asked Strike.

He was walking down the steeply sloping street where Ted and Joan's house lay, leaning on the collapsible walking stick he'd brought with him, knowing that the roads would be wet and possibly slippery. Ted was back in the house; they'd just helped Joan upstairs for a nap, and Strike, who wanted to smoke and didn't much fancy the shed again, had decided to go for a short walk in the relentless rain.

'Yes,' said Robin. 'How's Joan?'

'Same,' said Strike. He didn't feel like talking about it. 'You said you wanted a Bamborough chat.'

'Yeah,' said Robin. 'I've got good news, no news and bad news.'

'Bad first,' said Strike.

The sea was still turbulent, spray exploding into the air above the wall of the dock. Turning right, he headed into the town.

'The Ministry of Justice isn't going to let you interview Creed. The letter arrived this morning.'

'Ah,' said Strike. The teeming rain ripped through

the blueish haze of his cigarette smoke, destroying it. 'Well, can't say I'm surprised. What's it say?'

'I've left it back at the office,' said Robin, 'but the gist is that his psychiatrists agree non-cooperation isn't going to change at this stage.'

'Right,' said Strike. 'Well, it was always a long shot.'

But Robin could hear his disappointment, and empathised. They were five months into the case, they had no new leads worth the name, and now that the possibility of interviewing Creed had vanished, she somehow felt that she and Strike were pointlessly searching rockpools, while yards away the great white slid away, untouchable, into dark water.

'And I went back to Amanda White, who's now Amanda Laws, who thought she saw Margot at the printers' window. She wanted money to talk, remember? I offered her expenses if she wants to come to the office – she's in London, it wouldn't be much – and she's thinking it over.'

'Big of her,' grunted Strike. 'What's the good news?' he asked.

'Anna's persuaded her stepmother to speak to us. Cynthia.'

'Really?'

'Yes, but alone. Roy still doesn't know anything about us,' said Robin. 'Cynthia's meeting us behind his back.'

'Well, Cynthia's something,' said Strike. 'A lot, actually,' he added, after a moment's reflection.

His feet were taking him automatically towards the pub, his wet trouser leg chilly on his remaining ankle.

'Where are we going to meet her?'

'It can't be at their house, because Roy doesn't know. She's suggesting Hampton Court, because she works part time as a guide there.'

'A guide, eh? Reminds me: any news of Postcard?'

'Barclay's at the gallery today,' said Robin. 'He's going to try and get pictures of her.'

'And what're Morris and Hutchins up to?' Strike asked, now walking carefully up the wide, slippery steps that led to the pub.

'Morris is on Two-Times' girl, who hasn't put a foot wrong – Two-Times really is out of luck this time – and Hutchins is on Twinkletoes. Speaking of which, you're scheduled to submit a final report on Twinkletoes next Friday. I'll see the client for you, shall I?'

'That'd be great, thanks,' said Strike, stepping inside the Victory with a sense of relief. The rain dripped off him as he removed his coat. 'I'm not sure when I'm going to be able to get back. You probably saw, the trains have been suspended.'

'Don't worry about the agency. We've got every-thing covered. Anyway, I haven't finished giving you the Bamborough – oh, hang on,' said Robin.

'D'you need to go?'

'No, it's fine,' said Robin.

She'd just seen Elinor Dean's front door open. The plump blonde emerged wearing a hooded coat which, conveniently, circumscribed her field of vision. Robin slid out of the Land Rover, closed the door and set off in pursuit, still speaking on her mobile.

'Our blonde friend's on the move,' she said quietly.

'Did you just say you've got more good news on Bamborough?' asked Strike.

He'd reached the bar, and by simply pointing, was able to secure himself a pint, which he paid for, then carried to the corner table at which he'd sat with Polworth in the summer.

'I have,' said Robin, turning the corner at the end of the road, the oblivious blonde walking ahead of her. 'Wish I could say I'd found Douthwaite or Satchwell, but the last person to see Margot alive is something, right?'

'You've found Gloria Conti?' said Strike sharply.

'Don't get too excited,' said Robin, still trudging along in the rain. Elinor seemed to be heading for the shops. Robin could see a Tesco in the distance. 'I haven't managed to speak to her yet, but I'm almost sure it's her. I found the family in the 1961 census: mother, father, one older son and a daughter, Gloria, middle name Mary. By the looks of things, Gloria's now in France, Nîmes, to be precise, and married to a Frenchman. She's dropped the "Gloria", and she's now going by Mary Jaubert. She's got a Facebook page, but it's private. I found her through a genealogical website. One of her English cousins is trying to put together a family tree. Right date of birth and everything.'

'Bloody good work,' said Strike. 'You know, I'm not sure she isn't even more interesting than Satchwell or Douthwaite. Last to see Margot alive. Close to her. The only living person to have seen Theo, as well.'

Strike's enthusiasm did much to allay Robin's suspicion that he'd added himself to her action points because he thought she wasn't up to the job.

'I've tried to "friend" her on Facebook,' Robin continued, 'but had no response yet. If she doesn't answer, I know the company her husband works for, and I thought I might email him to get a message to her. I thought it was more tactful to try the private route first, though.'

'I agree,' said Strike. He took a sip of Doom Bar. It was immensely consoling to be in the warm, dry pub, and to be talking to Robin.

'And there's one more thing,' said Robin. 'I think I might have found out which van was seen speeding away from Clerkenwell Green the evening Margot disappeared.'

'What? How?' said Strike, stunned.

'It occurred to me over Christmas that what people thought might've been a flower painted on the side could have been a sun,' she said. 'You know. The planet.'

'It's technically a st—'

'Sod off, I know it's a star.'

The hooded blonde, as Robin had suspected,

was heading into Tesco. Robin followed, enjoying the warm blast of heat as she entered the shop, though the floor underfoot was slippery and dirty.

'There was a wholefoods shop in Clerkenwell in 1974 whose logo was a sun. I found an ad for it in the British Library newspaper archive, I checked with Companies House and I've managed to talk to the director, who's still alive. *I know I couldn't talk to him if he weren't,*' she added, forestalling any more pedantry.

'Bloody hell, Robin,' said Strike, as the rain battered the window behind him. Good news and Doom Bar were certainly helping his mood. 'This is excellent work.'

'Thank you,' said Robin. 'And get this: he sacked the bloke he had making deliveries, he thinks in mid-1975, because the guy got done for speeding while driving the van. He remembered his name – Dave Underwood – but I haven't had time to—'

Elinor turned abruptly, midway up the aisle of tinned foods, and walked back towards her. Robin pretended to be absorbed in choosing a packet of rice. Letting her quarry pass, she finished her sentence.

'—haven't had time to look for him yet.'

'Well, you're putting me to shame,' admitted Strike, rubbing his tired eyes. Though he now had a spare bedroom to himself rather than the sofa, the old mattress was only a small step up in terms of comfort, its broken springs jabbing him in the back and squealing every time he turned over.

'The best I've done is to find Ruby Elliot's daughter.'

'Ruby-who-saw-the-two-women-struggling-by-the-phone-boxes?' Robin recited, watching her blonde target consulting a shopping list before disappearing down a new aisle.

'That's the one. Her daughter emailed to say she's happy to have a chat, but we haven't fixed up a time yet. And I called Janice,' said Strike, 'mainly because I couldn't face Irene, to see whether she can remember the so-called Applethorpe's real name, but she's in Dubai, visiting her son for six weeks. Her answer machine message literally says "Hi, I'm in Dubai, visiting Kevin for six weeks". Might drop her a line advising her it's not smart to advertise to random callers that you've left your house empty.'

'So did you call Irene?' Robin asked. Elinor, she saw, was now looking at baby food.

'Not yet,' said Strike. 'But I have—'

At that very moment, a bleeping on his phone told him that someone else was trying to reach him.

'Robin, that might be him. I'll call you back.'

Strike switched lines.

'Cormoran Strike.'

'Yes, hello,' said Gregory Talbot. 'It's me – Greg Talbot. You asked me to call.'

Gregory sounded worried. Strike couldn't blame him. He'd hoped to divest himself of a problem by handing the can of old film to Strike.

'Yeah, Gregory, thanks very much for calling me back. I had a couple more questions, hope that's OK.'

'Go on.'

'I've been through your father's notebook and I wanted to ask whether your father happened to know, or mention, a man called Niccolo Ricci? Nicknamed "Mucky"?'

'Mucky Ricci?' said Gregory. 'No, he didn't really *know* him. I remember Dad talking about him, though. Big in the Soho sex shop scene, if that's the one I'm thinking of?'

It sounded as though talking about the gangster gave Gregory a small frisson of pleasure. Strike had met this attitude before, and not just in members of the fascinated public. Even police and lawyers were not immune to the thrill of coming within the orbit of criminals who had money and power to rival their own. He'd known senior officers talk with something close to admiration of the organised crime they were attempting to prevent, and barristers whose delight at drinking with high-profile clients went far beyond the hope of an anecdote to tell at a dinner party. Strike suspected that to Gregory Talbot, Mucky Ricci was a name from a fondly remembered childhood, a romantic figure belonging to a lost era, when his father was a sane copper and a happy family man.

'Yeah, that's the bloke,' said Strike. 'Well, it looks as though Mucky Ricci was hanging around

530

Margot Bamborough's practice, and your father seems to have known about it.'

'Really?'

'Yes,' said Strike, 'and it seems odd that information never made it into the official records.'

'Well, Dad was ill,' said Gregory defensively. 'You've seen the notebook. He didn't know what he was up to, half the time.'

'I appreciate that,' said Strike, 'but once he'd recovered, what was his attitude to the evidence he'd collected while on the case?'

'What d'you mean?'

Gregory sounded suspicious now, as though he feared Strike was leading him somewhere he might not want to go.

'Well, did he think it was all worthless, or—?'

'He'd been ruling out suspects on the basis of their star signs,' said Gregory quietly. 'He thought he saw a demon in the spare room. What d'you *think* he thought? He was . . . he was ashamed. It wasn't his fault, but he never got over it. He wanted to go back and make it right, but they wouldn't let him, they forced him out. The Bamborough case tainted everything for him, all his memories of the force. His mates were all coppers and he wouldn't see them any more.'

'He felt resentful at the way he was treated, did he?'

'I wouldn't say – I mean, he was justified, I'd say, to feel they hadn't treated him right,' said Gregory.

'Did he ever look over his notes, afterwards, to

make sure he'd put everything in there in the official record?'

'I don't know,' said Gregory, a little testy now. 'I think his attitude was, they've got rid of me, they think I'm a big problem, so let Lawson deal with it.'

'How did your father get on with Lawson?'

'Look, what's all this about?' Before Strike could answer, Gregory said, 'Lawson made it quite clear to my father that his day was done. He didn't want him hanging around, didn't want him anywhere near the case. Lawson did his best to completely discredit my father, I don't mean just because of his illness. I mean, as a man, and as the officer he'd been before he got ill. He told everyone on the case they were to stay away from my father, even out of working hours. So if information didn't get passed on, it's down to Lawson as much as him. Dad might've tried and been rebuffed, for all I know.'

'I can certainly see it from your father's point of view,' said Strike. 'Very difficult situation.'

'Well, exactly,' said Gregory, slightly placated, as Strike had intended.

'To go back to Mucky Ricci,' Strike said, 'as far as you know, your father never had direct dealings with him?'

'No,' said Gregory, 'but Dad's best mate on the force did, name of Browning. He was Vice Squad. He raided one of Mucky's clubs, I know that. I remember Dad talking about it.'

'Where's Browning now? Can I talk to him?'

'He's dead,' said Gregory. 'What exactly—?'

'I'd like to know where that film you passed to me came from, Gregory.'

'I've no idea,' said Gregory. 'Dad just came home with it one day, Mum says.'

'Any idea when this was?' asked Strike, hoping not to have to find a polite way of asking whether Talbot had been quite sane at the time.

'It would've been while Dad was working on the Bamborough case. Why?'

Strike braced himself.

'I'm afraid we've had to turn the film over to the police.'

Hutchins had volunteered to take care of this, on the morning that Strike had headed down to Cornwall. As an ex-policeman who still had good contacts on the force, he knew where to take it and how to make sure it got seen by the right people. Strike had asked Hutchins not to talk to Robin about the film, or to tell her what he'd done with it. She was currently in ignorance of the contents.

'What?' said Gregory, horrified. 'Why?'

'It isn't porn,' said Strike, muttering now, in deference to the elderly couple who had just entered the Victory and stood, disorientated by the storm outside, dripping and blinking mere feet from his table. 'It's a snuff movie. Someone filmed a woman being gang-raped and stabbed.'

There was another silence on the end of the

533

phone. Strike watched the elderly couple shuffle to the bar, the woman taking off her plastic rain hat as she went.

'Actually killed?' said Gregory, his voice rising an octave. 'I mean . . . it's definitely real?'

'Yeah,' said Strike.

He wasn't about to give details. He'd seen people dying and dead: the kind of gore you saw on horror movies wasn't the same, and even without a soundtrack, he wouldn't quickly forget the hooded, naked woman twitching on the floor of the warehouse, while her killers watched her die.

'And I suppose you've told them where you got it?' said Gregory, more panicked than angry.

'I'm afraid I had to,' said Strike. 'I'm sorry, but some of the men involved could still be alive, could still be charged. I can't sit on something like that.'

'I wasn't concealing anything, I didn't even know it was—'

'I wasn't meaning to suggest you knew, or you meant to hide it,' said Strike.

'If they think – we *foster kids*, Strike—'

'I've told the police you handed it over to me willingly, without knowing what was on there. I'll stand up in court and testify that I believe you were in total ignorance of what was in your attic. Your family's had forty-odd years to destroy it and you didn't. Nobody's going to blame you,' said Strike, even though he knew perfectly well that the tabloids might not take that view.

'I was afraid something like this was going to

happen,' said Gregory, now sounding immensely stressed. 'I've been worried, ever since you came round for coffee. Dragging all this stuff up again . . .'

'You told me your father would want to see the case solved.'

There was another silence, and then Gregory said,

'He would. But not at the cost of my mother's peace of mind, or me and my wife having our foster kids taken off us.'

A number of rejoinders occurred to Strike, some of them unkind. It was far from the first time he'd encountered the tendency to believe the dead would have wanted whatever was most convenient to the living.

'I had a responsibility to hand that film over to the police once I'd seen what was on it. As I say, I'll make it clear to anyone who asks that you weren't trying to hide anything, that you handed it over willingly.'

There was little more to say. Gregory, clearly still unhappy, rang off, and Strike called Robin back.

She was still in Tesco, now buying a packet of nuts and raisins, chewing gum and some shampoo for herself while, two tills away, the object of her surveillance bought baby powder, baby food and dummies along with a range of groceries.

'Hi,' Robin said into her mobile, turning to look out of the shopfront window while the blonde walked past her.

'Hi,' said Strike. 'That was Gregory Talbot.'

'What did he—? Oh yes,' said Robin with sudden interest, turning to follow the blonde out of the store, 'what was on that can of film? I never asked. Did you get the projector working?'

'I did,' said Strike. 'I'll tell you about the film when I see you. Listen, there's something else I wanted to say. Leave Mucky Ricci to me, all right? I've got Shanker putting out a few feelers. I don't want you looking for him, or making enquiries.'

'Couldn't I—?'

'*Did you not hear me?*'

'All right, calm down!' said Robin, surprised. 'Surely Ricci must be ninety-odd by—?'

'He's got sons,' said Strike. 'Sons *Shanker's* scared of.'

'*Oh,*' said Robin, who fully appreciated the implication.

'Exactly. So we're agreed?'

'We are,' Robin assured him.

After Strike had hung up, Robin followed Elinor back out into the rain, and back to her terraced house. When the front door had closed again, Robin got back into her Land Rover and ate her packet of dried fruit and nuts, watching the front door.

It had occurred to her in Tesco that Elinor might be a childminder, given the nature of her purchases, but as the afternoon shaded into evening, no parents came to drop off their charges, and no baby's wail was heard on the silent street.

CHAPTER 33

For he the tyrant, which her hath in ward
By strong enchauntments and blacke Magicke
  leare,
Hath in a dungeon deepe her close embard . . .
There he tormenteth her most terribly,
And day and night afflicts with mortall
  paine . . .

Edmund Spenser
The Faerie Queene

Now that the blonde in Stoke Newington had also become a person of interest, the Shifty case became a two-to-three-person job. The agency was watching Elinor Dean's house in addition to tracking the movements of Shifty's Boss and Shifty himself, who continued to go about his business, enjoying the fat salary to which nobody felt he was entitled, but remaining tight-lipped about the hold he had over his boss. Meanwhile, Two-Times was continuing to pay for surveillance on his girlfriend more, it seemed, out

537

of desperation than hope, and Postcard had gone suspiciously quiet. Their only suspect, the owlish guide at the National Portrait Gallery, had vanished from her place of work.

'I hope to God it's flu, and she hasn't killed herself,' Robin said to Barclay on Friday afternoon, when their paths crossed at the office. Strike was still stuck in Cornwall and she'd just seen the Twinkletoes client out of the office. He'd paid his sizeable final bill grudgingly, having found out only that the West End dancer with whom his feckless daughter was besotted was a clean-living, monogamous and apparently heterosexual young man.

Barclay, who was submitting his week's receipts to Pat before heading out to take over surveillance of Shifty overnight, looked surprised.

'The fuck would she've killed herself?'

'I don't know,' said Robin. 'That last message she wrote sounded a bit panicky. Maybe she thought I'd come to confront her, holding the postcards she'd sent.'

'You need tae get some sleep,' Barclay advised her.

Robin moved towards the kettle.

'No fer me,' Barclay told her, 'I've gottae take over from Andy in thirty. We're back in Pimlico, watchin' Two-Times' bird never cop off wi' any fucker.'

Pat counted out tenners for Barclay, towards whom her attitude was tolerant rather than warm. Pat's favourite member of the agency, apart from Robin, remained Morris, whom Robin had met

538

only three times since New Year: twice when swapping over at the end of a surveillance shift and once when he'd come into the office to leave his week's report. He'd found it difficult to meet her eye and talked about nothing but work, a change she hoped would be permanent.

'Who's next on the client waiting list, Pat?' she asked, while making coffee.

'We havenae got the manpower for another case the noo,' said Barclay flatly, pocketing his cash. 'Not wi' Strike off.'

'He'll be back on Sunday, as long as the trains are running,' said Robin, putting Pat's coffee down beside her. They'd arranged to meet Cynthia Phipps the following Monday, at Hampton Court Palace.

'I need a weekend back home, end o' the month,' Barclay told Pat, who in Strike's absence was in charge of the rota. As she opened it up on her computer, Barclay added, 'Migh' as well make the most of it, while I dinnae need a passport.'

'What d'you mean?' asked the exhausted Robin, sitting down on the sofa in the outer office with her coffee. She was, technically, off duty at the moment, but couldn't muster the energy to go home.

'Scottish independence, Robin,' said Barclay, looking at her from beneath his heavy eyebrows. 'I ken you English've barely noticed, but the union's about tae break up.'

'It won't really, will it?' said Robin.

'Every fucker I know's gonna vote Yes in September. One o' me mates from school called me an Uncle Tam last time I wus home. Arsehole won't be doin' that again,' growled Barclay.

When Barclay had left, Pat asked Robin,

'How's his aunt?'

Robin knew Pat was referring to Strike, because she never referred to her boss by name if she could help it.

'Very ill,' said Robin. 'Not fit for more chemotherapy.'

Pat jammed her electronic cigarette between her teeth and kept typing. After a while, she said,

'He was on his own at Christmas, upstairs.'

'I know,' said Robin. 'He told me how good you were to him. Buying him soup. He was really grateful.'

Pat sniffed. Robin drank her coffee, hoping for just enough of an energy boost to get her off this sofa and onto the Tube. Then Pat said,

'I'd've thought *he'd*'ve had somewhere to go, other than the attic.'

'Well, he had flu really badly,' said Robin. 'He didn't want to give it to anyone else.'

But as she washed up her mug, put on her coat, bade Pat farewell and set off downstairs, Robin found herself musing on this brief exchange. She'd often pondered the, to her, inexplicable animosity that Pat seemed to feel towards Strike. It had been clear from her tone that Pat had imagined Strike somehow immune to loneliness or vulnerability, and Robin was puzzled as to why, because Strike had never made any secret of where he was living or the fact that he slept there alone.

Robin's mobile rang. Seeing an unknown number, and remembering that Tom Turvey had been on the other end of the line the last time she'd answered one, she paused outside Tottenham Court Road station to answer it, with slight trepidation.

'Is this Robin Ellacott?' said a Mancunian voice.

'It is,' said Robin.

'Hiya,' said the woman, a little nervously. 'You wanted to talk to Dave Underwood. I'm his daughter.'

'Oh, yes,' said Robin. 'Thank you so much for getting back to me.'

Dave Underwood was the man who'd been employed to drive a wholefoods shop van at the time that Margot Bamborough went missing. Robin, who'd found his address online and written him a letter three days previously, hadn't expected such a quick response. She'd become inured to people ignoring her messages about Margot Bamborough.

'It was a bit of a shock, getting your letter,' said the woman on the phone. 'The thing is, Dad can't talk to you himself. He had a tracheotomy three weeks ago.'

'Oh, I'm so sorry to hear that,' said Robin, one finger in the ear not pressed to the phone, to block out the rumbling traffic.

'Yeah,' said the woman. 'He's here with me now, though, and he wants me to say . . . look . . . he's not going to be in trouble, is he?'

'No, of course not,' said Robin. 'As I said in my

letter, it really is just about eliminating the van from enquiries.'

'All right then,' said Dave's daughter. 'Well, it *was* him. Amazing, you working it out, because they all swore it was a flower on the side of the van, didn't they? He was glad at the time, because he thought he'd get in trouble, but he's felt bad about it for years. He went the wrong way on a delivery and he was speeding through Clerkenwell Green to try and put himself right. He didn't want to say, because the boss had had a go at him that morning for not getting deliveries out on time. He saw in the paper they were thinking maybe he'd been Dennis Creed and he just . . . well, you know. Nobody likes getting mixed up with stuff like that, do they? And the longer he kept quiet, the worse he thought it would look, him not coming forward straight away.'

'I see,' said Robin. 'Yes, I can understand how he felt. Well, this is very helpful. And after he'd made his delivery, did he—?'

'Yeah, he went back to the shop and he got a right telling-off anyway, because they opened the van and saw he'd delivered the wrong order. He had to go back out again.'

So Margot Bamborough clearly hadn't been in the back of the wholefoods van.

'Well, thanks very much for getting back to me,' said Robin, 'and please thank your father for being honest. That's going to be a great help.'

'You're welcome,' said the woman, and then,

quickly, before Robin could hang up. 'Are you the girl the Shacklewell Ripper stabbed?'

For a moment, Robin considered denying it, but she'd signed the letter to Dave Underwood with her real name.

'Yes,' she said, but with less warmth than she'd put into her thank you for the information about the van. She didn't like being called 'the girl the Shacklewell Ripper stabbed'.

'Wow,' said the woman, 'I told Dad I thought it was you. Well, at least Creed can't get you, eh?'

She said it almost jauntily. Robin agreed, thanked her again for her cooperation, hung up the phone and proceeded down the stairs into the Tube.

At least Creed can't get you, eh?

The cheery sign-off stayed with Robin as she descended to the Tube. That flippancy belonged only to those who had never felt blind terror, or come up against brute strength and steel, who'd never heard pig-like breathing close to their ear, or seen defocused eyes through balaclava holes, or felt their own flesh split, yet barely registered pain, because death was so close you could smell its breath.

Robin glanced over her shoulder on the escalator, because the careless commuter behind her kept touching the backs of her upper thighs with his briefcase. Sometimes she found casual physical contact with men almost unbearable. Reaching the bottom of the escalator she moved off fast to remove herself from the commuter's vicinity. *At least Creed can't get you, eh?* As though being 'got' was nothing more than a game of tag.

Or was it being in the newspaper had somehow made Robin seem less human to the woman on the end of the phone? As Robin settled herself into a seat between two women on the Tube, her thoughts returned to Pat, and to the secretary's surprise that Strike had nowhere to go when he was ill, and nobody to look after him. Was that at the root of her antipathy? An assumption that newsworthiness meant invulnerability?

When Robin let herself into the flat forty minutes later, carrying a bag of groceries and looking forward to an early night, she found the place empty except for Wolfgang, who greeted her exuberantly, then whined in a way that indicated a full bladder. With a sigh, Robin found his lead and took him downstairs for a quick walk around the block. After that, too tired to cook a proper meal, she scrambled herself some eggs and ate them with toast while watching the news on TV.

She was running herself a bath when her mobile rang again. Her heart sank a little when she saw that it was her brother Jonathan, who was in his final year of university in Manchester. She thought she knew what he was calling about.

'Hi, Jon,' she said.

'Hey, Robs. You didn't answer my text.'

She knew perfectly well that she hadn't. He'd sent it that morning, while she'd been watching Two-Times' girlfriend having a blameless coffee, alone with a Stieg Larsson novel. Jon wanted to know whether he and a female friend could come and stay at her flat on the weekend of the fourteenth and fifteenth of February.

'Sorry,' said Robin, 'I know I didn't, it's been a busy day. I'm not sure, to be honest, Jon. I don't know what Max's plans—'

'He wouldn't mind us crashing in your room, would he? Courtney's never been to London. There's a comedy show we want to see on Saturday. At the Bloomsbury Theatre.'

'Is Courtney your girlfriend?' asked Robin, smiling now. Jonathan had always been quite cagey with the family about his love life.

'Is she my *girlfriend*,' repeated Jonathan mockingly, but Robin had an idea that he was quite pleased with the question really, and surmised that the answer was 'yes'.

'I'll check with Max, OK? And I'll ring you back tomorrow,' said Robin.

Once she'd disposed of Jonathan, she finished running the bath and headed into her bedroom to fetch pyjamas, dressing gown and something to read. *The Demon of Paradise Park* lay horizontally across the top of her neat shelf of novels. After hesitating for a moment, she picked it up and took it back to the bathroom with her, trying as she did so to imagine getting ready for bed with her brother and an unknown girl in the room, as well. Was she prudish, stuffy and old before her time? She'd never finished her university degree: 'crashing' on floors in the houses of strangers had never been part of her life, and in the wake of the rape that had occurred in her halls of residence, she'd never had any desire to sleep anywhere except in an environment over which she had total control.

Sliding into the hot bubble bath, Robin let out a great sigh of pleasure. It had been a long week, sitting in the car for hours or else trudging through the rainy streets after Shifty or Elinor Dean. Eyes closed, enjoying the heat and the synthetic jasmine of her cheap bubble bath, her thoughts drifted back to Dave Underwood's daughter.

At least Creed can't get you, eh? Setting aside the offensively jocular tone, it struck her as significant that a woman who'd known for years that Creed hadn't been driving the sun-emblazoned van was nevertheless certain that he'd abducted Margot.

Because, of course, Creed hadn't *always* used a van. He'd killed two women before he ever got the job at the dry cleaner's, and managed to persuade women to walk into his basement flat even after he'd acquired the vehicle.

Robin opened her eyes, reached for *The Demon of Paradise Park* and turned to the page where she had last left it. Holding the book clear of the hot, foamy water, she continued to read.

One night in September 1972, Dennis Creed's landlady spotted him bringing a woman back to the basement flat for the first time. She testified at Creed's trial that she heard the front gate 'squeak' at close to midnight, glanced down from her bedroom window at the steps into the basement and saw Creed and a woman who 'seemed a bit drunk but was walking OK', heading into the house.

When she asked Dennis who the woman was, he told her the implausible story that she was a regular client of the dry cleaner's. He claimed he'd met the drunk woman by chance in the street, and that she had begged him to let her come into his flat to phone a taxi.

In reality, the woman Violet had seen Dennis steering into the flat was the unemployed Gail Wrightman, who'd been stood up that evening by a boyfriend. Wrightman left the Grasshopper, a bar in Shoreditch, at half past ten in the evening, after consuming several strong cocktails. A woman matching Wrightman's description was seen getting into a white van at a short distance from the bar. Barring Cooper's glimpse of a brunette in a light-coloured coat entering Creed's flat that night, there were no further sightings of Gail Wrightman after she left the Grasshopper.

By now, Creed had perfected a façade of vulnerability that appealed particularly to older women like his landlady, and a convivial, sexually ambiguous persona that worked well with the drunk and lonely. Creed subsequently admitted to meeting Wrightman in the Grasshopper, adding Nembutal to her drink and lying in wait outside the bar where, confused and unsteady on her feet, she was grateful for his offer of a lift home.

Cooper accepted his explanation of the dry-cleaning client who'd wanted to call a taxi 'because I had no reason to doubt it'.

In reality, Gail Wrightman was now gagged and chained to a radiator in Creed's bedroom, where she would remain until Creed killed her by strangulation in January 1973. This was the longest period he kept a victim alive, and demonstrates the degree of confidence he had that his basement flat was now a place of safety, where he could rape and torture without fear of discovery.

However, shortly before Christmas that year, his landlady visited him on some trivial pretext, and she recalled in the witness box that 'he wanted to get rid of me, I could tell. I thought there was a nasty smell about the place, but we'd had problems with next door's drains before. He told me he couldn't chat because he was waiting for a phone call.

'I know it was Christmastime when I went down there, because I remember asking him why he hadn't put any cards up. I knew he didn't have many friends but I thought someone must have remembered him and I thought it was a shame. The radio was playing 'Long-Haired Lover from Liverpool', and it was loud, I remember that, but that wasn't anything unusual. Dennis liked music.'

Cooper's surprise visit to the basement almost certainly sealed Wrightman's death warrant. Creed later told a psychiatrist that he'd been toying with the idea of simply keeping Wrightman 'as a pet' for the foreseeable future, to spare himself the risks that further abductions would entail, but that he reconsidered and decided to 'put her out of her misery'.

Creed murdered Wrightman on the night of January 9th 1973, a date chosen to coincide with a three-day absence of Vi Cooper to visit a sick relative. Creed cut off Wrightman's head and hands in the bath before driving the rest of the corpse in his van to Epping Forest by night, wrapped in tarpaulin, and burying it in a shallow grave. Back at home, he boiled the flesh off Wrightman's head and hands and smashed up the bones, as he'd done to the corpses of both Vera Kenny and Nora Sturrock, adding the powdered bone to the inlaid ebony box he kept under his bed.

On her return to Liverpool Road, Violet

Cooper noted that the 'bad smell' had gone from the basement flat and concluded that the drains had been sorted out.

Landlady and lodger resumed their convivial evenings, drinking and singing along to records. It's likely that Creed experimented with drugging Vi at this time. She later testified that she often slept so soundly on nights that Dennis joined her for a nightcap that she found herself still groggy the next morning.

Wrightman's grave remained undisturbed for nearly four months, until discovered by a dog walker whose terrier dug and retrieved a thigh bone. Decomposition, the absence of head and hands or any clothing rendered identification almost impossible given the difficulties of tissue typing in such circumstances. Only after Creed's arrest, when Wrightman's underwear, pantyhose and an opal ring her family identified as having belonged to her were found under the floorboards of Creed's sitting room, were detectives able to add Wrightman's murder to the list of charges against him.

Gail's younger sister had never lost hope that Gail was still alive. 'I couldn't believe it until I saw the ring with my own eyes. Until that moment, I honestly thought there'd been a mistake. I kept telling Mum and Dad she'd come back. I couldn't believe there was wickedness like that in the world, and that my sister could have met it.

'He isn't human. He played with us, with the families, during the trial. Smiling and waving at us every morning. Looking at the parents or the brother or whoever, whenever their relative was mentioned. Then, afterwards, after he was convicted, he keeps telling a bit more, and a bit more, and we've had to live with that hanging over us for years, what Gail said, or how she begged him. I'd murder him with my own bare hands if I could, but I could never make him suffer the way he made Gail suffer. He isn't capable of human feeling, is he? It makes you—'

There was a loud bang from the hall and Robin jumped so severely that water slopped over the edge of the bath.

'Just me!' called Max, who sounded uncharacteristically cheerful, and she heard him greeting Wolfgang. 'Hello, you. Yes, hello, hello . . .'

'Hi,' called Robin. 'I took him out earlier!'

'Thanks very much,' said Max, 'Come join me, I'm celebrating!'

She heard Max climbing the stairs. Pulling out the plug, she continued to sit in the bath as the water ebbed away, crisp bubbles still clinging to her as she finished the chapter.

It makes you pray there's a hell.'

In 1976, Creed told prison psychiatrist Richard Merridan that he tried to 'lie low' following the discovery of Wrightman's remains. Creed admitted to Merriman that he felt a simultaneous desire for notoriety and a fear of capture.

'I liked reading about the Butcher in the papers. I buried her in Epping Forest like the others because I wanted people to know that the same person had done them all, but I knew I was risking everything, not varying the pattern. After that, after Vi had seen me with her, and come in the flat with her there, I thought I'd better just do whores for a bit, lie low.'

But the choice to 'do whores' would lead, just a few months later, to Creed's closest brush with capture yet.

The chapter ended here. Robin got out of the bath, mopped up the spilled water, dressed in pyjamas and dressing gown, then headed upstairs to the living area where Max sat watching television, looking positively beatific. Wolfgang seemed to have been infected by his owner's good mood: he greeted Robin as though she'd been away on a long journey and set to work licking the bath oil off her ankles until she asked him kindly to desist.

'I've got a job,' Max told Robin, muting the TV. Two champagne glasses and a bottle were sitting on the coffee table in front of him. 'Second lead, new drama, BBC One. Have a drink.'

'Max, that's fantastic!' said Robin, thrilled for him.

'Yeah,' he said, beaming. 'Listen. D'you think your Strike would come over for dinner? I'm playing a veteran. It'd be good to speak to someone who's actually ex-army.'

'I'm sure he would,' said Robin, hoping she was right. Strike and Max had never met. She accepted a glass of champagne, sat down and held up her glass in a toast. 'Congratulations!'

'Thanks,' he said, clinking his glass against hers. 'I'll cook, if Strike comes over. It'll be good, actually. I need to meet more people. I'm turning into one of those "he always kept himself to himself" blokes you see on the news.'

'And I'll be the dumb flatmate,' said Robin, her thoughts still with Vi Cooper, 'who thought you were lovely and never questioned why I kept coming across you hammering the floorboards back down.'

Max laughed.

'And they'll blame you more than me,' said Max, 'because they always do. The women who didn't realise . . . mind you, some of them . . . who was that guy in America who made his wife call him on an intercom before he'd let her into the garage?'

'Jerry Brudos,' said Robin. Brudos had been mentioned in *The Demon of Paradise Park*. Like Creed, Brudos had been wearing women's clothing when he abducted one of his victims.

'I need to get a bloody social life going again,'

said Max, more expansive than Robin had ever known him under the influence of alcohol and good news. 'I've been feeling like hell ever since Matthew left. Kept wondering whether I shouldn't just sell this place and move on.'

Robin thought her slight feeling of panic might have shown in her face, because Max said,

'Don't worry, I'm not going to. But it's half-killed me, keeping it going. I really only bought the place because of him. "Put it all into property, you can't lose with property," he said.'

He looked as though he was going to say something else, but if so, decided against it.

'Max, I wanted to ask you something,' said Robin, 'but it's totally fine if the answer's no. My younger brother and a girlfriend are looking for a place to stay in London for the weekend of the fourteenth and fifteenth of February. But if you don't—'

'Don't be silly,' said Max. 'They can sleep on this,' he said, patting the sofa. 'It folds out.'

'Oh,' said Robin, who hadn't known this. 'Well, great. Thanks, Max.'

The champagne and the hot bath had made Robin feel incredibly sleepy, but they talked on for a while about Max's new drama, until at last Robin apologised and said she really did need to go to bed.

As she pulled the duvet over herself, Robin decided against starting a new chapter on Creed. It was best not to have certain things in your head if you wanted to get to sleep. However, once she'd turned out her bedside lamp she found her mind refusing to shut down, so she reached for her iPod.

She never listened to music on headphones unless she knew Max was in the flat. Some life experiences made a person forever conscious of their ability to react, to have advance warning. Now, though, with the front door safely double-locked (Robin had checked, as she always did), and with her flatmate and a dog mere seconds away, she inserted her earbuds and pressed shuffle on the four albums of Joni Mitchell's she'd now bought, choosing music over another bottle of perfume she didn't like.

Sometimes, when listening to Mitchell, which Robin was doing frequently these days, she could imagine Margot Bamborough smiling at her through the music. Margot was forever frozen at twenty-nine, fighting not to be defeated by a life more complicated than she had ever imagined it would be, when she conceived the ambition of raising herself out of poverty by brains and hard work.

An unfamiliar song began to play. The words told the story of the end of a love affair. It was a simpler, more direct lyric than many of Mitchell's, with little metaphor or poetry about it. *Last chance lost/The hero cannot make the change/Last chance lost/ The shrew will not be tamed.*

Robin thought of Matthew, unable to adapt himself to a wife who wanted more from life than a steady progression up the property ladder, unable to give up the mistress who had always, in truth, been better suited to his ideals and ambitions than Robin. So did that make Robin the shrew, fighting for a career that everyone but she thought was a mistake?

Lying in the dark, listening to Mitchell's voice, which was deeper and huskier on her later albums, an idea that had been hovering on the periphery of Robin's thoughts for a couple of weeks forced its way into the forefront of her mind. It had been lurking ever since she'd read the letter from the Ministry of Justice, refusing Strike permission to see the serial killer.

Strike had accepted the Ministry of Justice's decision, and indeed, so had Robin, who had no desire to increase the suffering of the victims' families. And yet the man who might save Anna from a lifetime of continued pain and uncertainty was still alive. If Irene Hickson had been bursting to talk to Strike, how much more willing might Creed be, after decades of silence?

Last chance lost/the hero cannot make the change.

Robin sat up abruptly, pulled out her earphones, turned the lamp back on, sat up and reached for the notebook and pen she always kept beside her bed these days.

There was no need to tell Strike what she was up to. The possibility that her actions might back-fire on the agency must be taken. If she didn't try, she'd forever wonder whether there hadn't been a chance of reaching Creed, after all.

CHAPTER 34

. . . no Art, nor any Leach's Might . . .
Can remedy such hurts; such hurts are hellish
Pain.

Edmund Spenser
The Faerie Queene

The train service between Cornwall and London resumed at last. Strike packed his bags, but promised his aunt and uncle he'd be back soon. Joan clung to him in silence at parting. Incredibly, Strike would have preferred one of the emotional-blackmail-laden farewells that had previously antagonised him.

Riding the train back to London, Strike found his mood mirrored in the monochrome winter landscape of mud and shivering trees he was watching through the dirt-streaked window. Joan's slow decline was a different experience to the deaths with which Strike was familiar, which had almost all been of the unnatural kind. As a soldier and an investigator, he'd become inured to the need to assimilate, without warning, the sudden, brutal extinction of a human being, to accept the sudden vacuum where once a soul had flickered. Joan's slow capitulation to an enemy inside her own body was something new to him. A small part of Strike, of which he was ashamed, wanted everything to be over, and for the mourning to begin in earnest, and, as the train bore him east, he looked forward to the temporary sanctuary of his empty flat, where he was free to feel miserable without either the need to parade his sadness for the neighbours, or to sport a veneer of fake cheerfulness for his aunt.

He turned down two invitations for dinner on Saturday night, one from Lucy, one from Nick and Ilsa, preferring to deal with the agency's books and review case files submitted by Barclay, Hutchins and Morris. On Sunday he spoke again to Dr Gupta and to a couple of relatives of deceased witnesses in the Bamborough case, preparatory to a catch-up with Robin the following day.

But on Sunday evening, while standing beside the spaghetti boiling on his single hob, he received a second text from his unknown half-sister, Prudence.

Hi Cormoran, I don't know whether you received my first text. Hopefully this one will reach you. I just wanted to say (I think) I understand your reasons for not wanting to join us for Dad's group

photo, or for the party. There's a little more behind the party than a new album. I'd be happy to talk to you about that in person, but as a family we're keeping it confidential. I hope you won't mind me adding that, like you, I'm the result of one of Dad's briefer liaisons (!) and I've had to deal with my own share of hurt and anger over the years. I wonder whether you'd like to have a coffee to discuss this further? I'm in Putney. Please do get in touch. It would be great to meet. Warmest wishes, Pru

His spaghetti now boiling noisily, Strike lit a cigarette. Pressure seemed to be building behind his eyeballs. He knew he was smoking too much: his tongue ached, and ever since his Christmas flu, his morning cough had been worse than ever. Barclay had been extolling the virtues of vaping the last time they'd met. Perhaps it was time to try that, or at least to cut down on the cigarettes.

He read Prudence's text a second time. What confidential reason could be behind the party, other than his father's new album? Had Rokeby finally been given his knighthood, or was he making a fuss over the Deadbeats' fiftieth anniversary in an attempt to remind those who gave out honours that he hadn't yet had one? Strike tried to imagine Lucy's reaction, if he told her he was off to meet a host of new half-siblings,

559

when her small stock of relatives was about to be diminished by one. He tried to picture this Prudence, of whom he knew nothing at all, except that her mother had been a well-known actress.

Turning off the hob, he left the spaghetti floating in its water, and began to text a response, cigarette between his teeth.

Thanks for the texts. I've got no objection to meeting you, but now's not a good time. Appreciate that you're doing what you think is the right thing but I've never been much for faking feelings or maintaining polite fictions to suit public celebrations. I don't have a relationship with—

Strike paused for a full minute. He never referred to Jonny Rokeby as 'Dad' and he didn't want to say 'our father', because that seemed to bracket himself and Prudence together in a way that felt uncomfortable, as she was a total stranger.

And yet some part of him didn't feel she was a stranger. Some part of him felt a tug towards her. What was it? Simple curiosity? An echo of the longing he'd felt as a child, for a father who never turned up? Or was it something more primitive: the calling of blood to blood, an animal sense of connection that couldn't quite be eradicated, no matter how much you tried to sever the tie?

—Rokeby and I've got no interest in faking one for a few hours just because he's putting out a new album. I hold no ill will towards you and, as I say, I'd be happy to meet when my life is less—

Strike paused again. Standing in the steam billowing from his saucepan, his mind roved over the dying Joan, over the open cases on the agency's books, and, inexplicably, over Robin.

—complicated. Best wishes, Cormoran.

He ate his spaghetti with a jar of shop-bought sauce, and fell asleep that night to the sound of rain hammering on the roof slates, to dream that he and Rokeby were having a fist fight on the deck of a sailing ship, which pitched and rolled until both of them fell into the sea.

Rain was still falling at ten to eleven the following morning, when Strike emerged from Earl's Court Tube station to wait for Robin, who was going to pick him up before driving to meet Cynthia Phipps at Hampton Court Palace. Standing beneath the brick overhang outside the station exit, yet another cigarette in his mouth, Strike read two recently arrived emails off his phone: an update from Barclay on Two-Times, and one from Morris on Shifty. He'd nearly finished them when the mobile rang. It was Al, and rather than let the call go to voicemail, Strike decided to put an end to this badgering once and for all.

'Hey, bruv,' said Al. 'How're you?'

'Been better,' said Strike.

He deliberately didn't reciprocate the polite enquiry.

'Look,' said Al, 'um . . . Pru's just rung me. She told me what you sent her. Thing is, we've got a photographer booked for next Saturday, but if you're not going to be in the picture – the whole point is that it's from all of us. First time ever.'

'Al, I'm not interested,' said Strike, tired of being polite.

There was a brief silence. Then Al said,

'You know, Dad keeps trying to reach out—'

'Is that right?' said Strike, anger suddenly piercing the fog of fatigue, of his worry about Joan, and the mass of probable irrelevancies he'd found out on the Bamborough case, which he was trying to hold in his head, so he could impart them to Robin. 'When would this be? When he set his lawyers on me, chasing me for money that was legally mine in the first—?'

'If you're talking about Peter Gillespie, Dad didn't know how heavy he was getting with you, I swear he didn't. Pete's retired now—'

'I'm not interested in celebrating his new fucking album,' said Strike. 'Go ahead and have fun without me.'

'Look,' said Al, 'I can't explain right now – if you can meet me for a drink, I'll tell you – there's a reason we want to do this for him now, the photo and the party—'

'The answer's no, Al.'

'You're just going to keep sticking two fingers up at him for ever, are you?'

'Who's sticking two fingers up? I haven't said a word about him publicly, unlike him, who can't give a fucking interview without mentioning me these days—'

'He's trying to put things right, and you can't give an inch!'

'He's trying to tidy up a messy bit of his public image,' said Strike harshly. 'Tell him to pay his fucking taxes if he wants his knighthood. I'm not his pet fucking black sheep.'

He hung up, angrier than he'd expected, his heart thumping uncomfortably hard beneath his coat. Flicking his cigarette butt into the road, his thoughts travelled inescapably back to Joan, with her headscarf hiding her baldness, and Ted weeping into his tea. Why, he thought, furiously, couldn't it have been Rokeby who lay dying, and his aunt who was well and happy, confident she'd reach her next birthday, striding through St Mawes, chatting to lifelong friends, planning dinners for Ted, nagging Strike over the phone about coming to visit?

When Robin turned the corner in the Land Rover a few minutes later, she was taken aback by Strike's appearance. Even though he'd told her by phone about the flu and the out-of-date chicken, he looked noticeably thinner in the face, and so enraged she automatically checked her watch, wondering whether she was late.

'Everything all right?' she asked, when he opened the passenger seat door.

'Fine,' he said shortly, climbing into the passenger seat and slamming the door.

'Happy New Year.'

'Haven't we already said that?'

'No, actually,' said Robin, somewhat aggravated by his surliness. 'But please don't feel pressured into saying it back. I'd hate you to feel railroaded—'

'Happy New Year, Robin,' muttered Strike.

She pulled out into the road, her windscreen wipers working hard to keep the windscreen clear, with a definite sense of déjà vu. He'd been grumpy when she'd picked him up on his birthday, too, and in spite of everything he was going through, she too was tired, she too had personal worries, and would have appreciated just a little effort.

'What's up?' she asked.

'Nothing.'

They drove for a few minutes in silence, until Robin said,

'Did you see Barclay's email?'

'About Two-Times and his girlfriend? Yeah, just read it,' said Strike. 'Ditched, and she'll never realise it was because she was too faithful.'

'He's such a freak,' said Robin, 'but as long as he pays his bill . . .'

'My thoughts exactly,' said Strike, making a

conscious effort to throw off his bad temper. After all, none of it – Joan, Pru, Al, Rokeby – was Robin's fault. She'd been holding the agency together while he dealt with matters in Cornwall. She was owed better.

'We've got room for another waiting list client now,' he said, trying for a more enthusiastic tone. 'I'll call that commodities broker who thinks her husband's shagging the nanny, shall I?'

'Well,' said Robin, 'the Shifty job's taking a lot of manpower at the moment. We're covering him, his boss and the woman in Stoke Newington. The boss went back to Elinor Dean yesterday evening, you know. Same thing all over again, including the pat on the head.'

'Really?' said Strike, frowning.

'Yeah. The clients are getting quite impatient for proper evidence, though. Plus, we haven't got any resolution on Postcard yet and Bamborough's taking up quite a bit of time.'

Robin didn't want to say explicitly that with Strike moving constantly between London and Cornwall, she and the subcontractors were covering the agency's existing cases by forfeiting their days off.

'So you think we should concentrate on Shifty and Postcard, do you?'

'I think we should accept that Shifty's currently a three-person-job and not be in a hurry to take anything else on just now.'

'All right, fair enough,' grunted Strike. 'Any

news on the guide at the National Portrait Gallery? Barclay told me you were worried she might've topped herself.'

'What did he tell you that for?' Robin said. She regretted blurting out her anxiety now: it felt soft, unprofessional.

'He didn't mean anything by it. Has she reappeared?'

'No,' said Robin.

'Any more postcards to the weatherman?'

'No.'

'Maybe you've scared her off.'

Strike pulled his notebook out of his pocket and opened it, while the rain continued to drum against the windscreen.

'I've got a few bits and pieces on Bamborough, before we meet Cynthia Phipps. That was great work of yours, eliminating the wholefoods van, by the way.'

'Thanks,' said Robin.

'But there's a whole new van on the scene,' said Strike.

'What?' said Robin sharply.

'I spoke to the daughter of Ruby Elliot yesterday. You remember Ruby—'

'The woman who saw the two women struggling from her car.'

'That's the one. I also spoke to a nephew of Mrs Fleury, who was crossing Clerkenwell Green, trying to get her senile mother home out of the rain.'

Strike cleared his throat, and said, reading from his notes:

'According to Mark Fleury, his aunt was quite upset by the description in the papers of her "struggling" and even "grappling" with her mother, because it suggested she'd been rough with the old dear. She said she was chivvying her mother along, not forcing her, but admitted that otherwise the description fitted them to a tee: right place, right time, rain hat, raincoat, etc.

'But Talbot leapt on the "we weren't grappling" discrepancy and tried to pressure Mrs Fleury into retracting her story and admitting that she and the old lady couldn't have been the people Ruby Elliot saw. Mrs Fleury wasn't having that, though. The description of them was too good: she was sure they were the right people.

'So Talbot went back to Ruby and tried to force her to change *her* story. You'll remember that there was another phone box at the opening of Albemarle Way. Talbot tried to persuade Ruby that she'd seen two people struggling in front of *that* phone box instead.

'Which is where things get mildly interesting,' said Strike, turning a page in his notebook. 'According to Ruby's daughter, Ruby was an absent-minded woman, a nervous driver and a poor map reader, with virtually no sense of direction. On the other hand, her daughter claims she had a very retentive memory for small visual details. She might not remember what street she'd met an acquaintance on, but she could describe down to the colour of a shoelace what they'd been wearing. She'd been a window dresser in her youth.

'Given her general vagueness, Talbot should have found it easy to persuade her she'd mistaken the phone box, but the harder he pushed, the firmer she stood, and the reason she stood firm, and said the two women couldn't have been in front of the Albemarle phone box, was because she'd seen *something else* happen beside that particular phone box, something she'd forgotten all about until Talbot mentioned the wedge-shaped building. Don't forget, she didn't know Clerkenwell at all.

'According to her daughter, Ruby kept driving around in a big circle that night, continually missing Hayward's Place, where her daughter's new house was. When he said, "Are you sure you didn't see these two struggling women beside the *other* phone box, near the wedge-shaped building on the corner of Albemarle Way?" Ruby suddenly remembered that she'd had to brake at that point in the road, because a transit van ahead of her had stopped beside the wedge-shaped building without warning. It was picking up a dark, stocky young woman who was standing in the pouring rain, beside the phone box. The woman—'

'Wait a moment,' said Robin, momentarily taking her eyes off the rainy road to glance at Strike. '"Dark and stocky?" It wasn't *Theo*?'

'Ruby thought it was, once she compared her memory of the girl in the rain with the artist's impressions of Margot's last patient. Dark-skinned, solid build, thick black hair – plastered to her face because it was so wet – and wearing a pair of—'

Strike sounded the unfamiliar name out, reading from his notebook.

'—*Kuchi* earrings.'

'What are Kuchi earrings?'

'Romany-style, according to Ruby's daughter, which might account for Gloria calling Theo "gypsyish". Ruby knew clothes and jewellery. It was the kind of detail she noticed.

'The transit van braked without warning to pick up the-girl-who-could-have-been-Theo, temporarily holding up traffic. Cars behind Ruby were tooting their horns. The dark girl got into the front passenger seat, the transit van moved off in the direction of St John Street and Ruby lost sight of it.'

'And she didn't tell Talbot?'

'Her daughter says that by the time she remembered the second incident, she was exhausted by the whole business, sick to death of being ranted at by Talbot and told she must have been mistaken in thinking the two struggling women hadn't been Margot and Creed in drag, and regretting she'd ever come forward in the first place.

'After Lawson took over the case, she was afraid of what the police and the press would say to her if she suddenly came up with a story of seeing someone who resembled Theo. Rightly or wrongly, she thought it might look as though, having had her first sighting proven to be worthless, she wanted another shot at being important to the inquiry.'

'But her daughter felt OK about telling you all this?'

'Well, Ruby's dead, isn't she? It can't hurt her now. Her daughter made it clear she doesn't think any of this is going to amount to anything, so she might as well tell me the lot. And when all's said and done,' said Strike, turning a page in his notebook, 'we don't know the girl *was* Theo . . . although personally, I think she was. Theo wasn't registered with the practice, so probably wasn't familiar with the area. That corner would make an easily identifiable place to meet the transit van after she'd seen a doctor. Plenty of space for it to pull over.'

'True,' said Robin slowly, 'but if that girl really *was* Theo, this lets her out of any involvement with Margot's disappearance, doesn't it? She clearly left the surgery alone, got a lift and drove—'

'Who was driving the van?'

'I don't know. Anyone. Parent, friend, sibling . . .'

'Why didn't Theo come forward after all the police appeals?'

'Maybe she was scared. Maybe she had a medical problem she didn't want anyone to know about. Plenty of people would rather not get mixed up with the police.'

'Yeah, you're not wrong,' admitted Strike. 'Well, I still think it's worth knowing that one of the last people to see Margot alive might've left the area in a vehicle big enough to hide a woman in.

'And speaking of the last person to see Margot alive,' Strike added, 'any response from Gloria Conti?'

'No,' said Robin. 'If nothing's happened by the end of next week, I'll try and contact her through her husband.'

Strike turned a page in his notebook.

'After I spoke to Ruby's daughter and the Fleury bloke, I called Dr Gupta back. Dunno whether you remember, but in my summary of the horoscope notes I mentioned "Scorpio", whose death, according to Talbot, worried Margot.'

'Yes,' said Robin. 'You speculated Scorpio might be Steve Douthwaite's married friend, who killed herself.'

'Well remembered,' said Strike. 'Well, Gupta can't remember any patient dying in unexplained circumstances, or in a way that troubled Margot, although he emphasised that all this is forty years ago and he can't swear there wasn't such a patient.

'Then I asked him whether he knew who Joseph Brenner might have been visiting in a block of flats on Skinner Street on the evening Margot disappeared. Gupta says they had a number of patients in Skinner Street, but he can't think of any reason why Brenner would have lied about going on a house call there.

'Lastly, and not particularly helpfully, Gupta remembers that a couple of men came to pick

Gloria up at the end of the practice Christmas party. He remembers one of the men being a lot older, and says he assumed that was Gloria's father. The name "Mucky Ricci" meant nothing to him.'

Midway across Chiswick Bridge, the sun sliced suddenly through a chink in the rain clouds, dazzling their eyes. The dirty Thames beneath the bridge and the shallow puddles flashed laser bright, but, seconds later, the clouds closed again and they were driving again through rain, in the dull grey January light, along a straight dual carriageway bordered by shrubs slick with rain and naked trees.

'What about that film?' said Robin, glancing sideways at Strike. 'The film that came out of Gregory Talbot's attic? You said you'd tell me in person.'

'Ah,' said Strike. 'Yeah.'

He hesitated, looking past the windscreen wipers at the long straight road ahead, glimmering beneath a diagonal curtain of rain.

'It showed a hooded woman being gang-raped and killed.'

Robin experienced a slight prickling over her neck and scalp.

'And people get off on that,' she muttered, in disgust.

He knew from her tone that she hadn't understood, that she thought he was describing a pornographic fiction.

'No,' he said, 'it wasn't porn. Someone filmed . . . the real thing.'

Robin looked around in shock, before turning quickly back to face the road. Her knuckles whitened on the steering wheel. Repulsive images were suddenly forcing their way into her mind. What had Strike seen, that made him look so closed up, so blank? Had the hooded woman's body resembled Margot's, the body Oonagh Kennedy had said was 'all legs'?

'You all right?' asked Strike.

'Fine,' she almost snapped. 'What – what did you see, how—?'

But Strike chose to answer a question she hadn't asked.

'The woman had a long scar over the ribcage. There was never any mention of Margot having a scarred ribcage in press reports or police notes. I don't think it was her.'

Robin said nothing but continued to look tense.

'There were four men, ah, involved,' Strike continued, 'all Caucasian, and all with their faces hidden. There was also a fifth man looking on. His arm came briefly into shot. It could've been Mucky Ricci. There was an out-of-focus big gold ring.'

He was trying to reduce the account to a series of dry facts. His leg muscles had tensed up quite as much as Robin's hands, and he was primed to grab the wheel. She'd had a panic attack once before while they were driving.

'What are the police saying?' Robin asked. 'Do they know where it came from?'

573

'Hutchins asked around. An ex-Vice Squad guy thinks it's part of a batch they seized in a raid made on a club in Soho in '75. The club was owned by Ricci. They took a load of hardcore pornography out of the basement.

'One of Talbot's best mates was also Vice Squad. The best guess is that Talbot nicked or copied it, after his mate showed it to him.'

'Why would he do that?' said Robin, a little desperately.

'I don't think we're going to get a better answer than "because he was mentally ill",' said Strike. 'But the starting point must have been his interest in Ricci. He'd found out Ricci was registered with the St John's practice and attended the Christmas party. In the notes, he called Ricci—'

'—Leo three,' said Robin. 'Yes, I know.'

Strike's leg muscles relaxed very slightly. This degree of focus and recall on Robin's part didn't suggest somebody about to have a panic attack.

'Did you learn my email off by heart?' he asked her.

It was Robin's turn to remember Christmas, and the brief solace it had been, to bury herself in work at her parents' kitchen table.

'I pay attention when I'm reading, that's all.'

'Well, I still don't understand why Talbot didn't chase up this Ricci lead, although judging by the horoscope notes, there was a sharp deterioration in his mental state over the six months he was in charge of the case. I'm guessing he stole

574

that can of film not long before he got kicked off the force, hence no mention of it in the police notes.'

'And then hid it so nobody else could investigate the woman's death,' said Robin. Her sympathy for Bill Talbot had just been, if not extinguished, severely dented. 'Why the hell didn't he take the film back to the police when he was back in his right mind?'

'I'd guess because he wanted his job back and, failing that, wanted to make sure he got his pension. Setting aside basic integrity, I can't see that he had a great incentive to admit he'd tampered with evidence on another case. Everyone was already pissed off at him: victims' families, press, the force, all blaming him for having fucked up the investigation. And then Lawson, a bloke he doesn't like, takes over and tells him to stay the fuck out of it. He probably told himself the dead woman was only a prostitute or—'

'Jesus,' said Robin angrily.

'*I'm* not saying "only a prostitute",' Strike said quickly. 'I'm guessing at the mindset of a seventies policeman who'd already been publicly shamed for buggering up a high-profile case.'

Robin said nothing, but remained stony-faced for the rest of the journey, while Strike, the muscles of his one-and-a-half legs so tense they ached, tried not to make it too obvious that he was keeping a covert eye on the hands gripping the steering wheel.

CHAPTER 35

. . . fayre Aurora, rysing hastily,
Doth by her blushing tell, that she did lye
All night in old Tithonus frosen bed,
Whereof she seemes ashamed inwardly.

Edmund Spenser
The Faerie Queene

'Ever been here before?' Strike asked Robin, as she parked in the Hampton Court car park. She'd been silent since he'd told her about the film, and he was trying to break the tension.

'No.'

They got out of the Land Rover and set off across the car park in the chilly rain.

'Where exactly are we meeting Cynthia?'

'The Privy Kitchen Café,' said Robin. 'I expect they'll give us a map at the ticket office.'

She knew that the film hidden in Gregory Talbot's attic wasn't Strike's fault. He hadn't put it there, hadn't hidden it for forty years, couldn't have known, when he inserted it in the projector, that he was about to watch a woman's last, terrified, excruciating moments. She wouldn't have wanted him to withhold the truth about what he'd seen. Nevertheless, his dry and unemotional description had grated on Robin. Reasonably or not, she'd wanted some sign that he had been repulsed, or disgusted, or horrified.

But perhaps this was unrealistic. He'd been a military policeman long before Robin had known him, where he'd learned a detachment she sometimes envied. Beneath her determinedly calm exterior, Robin felt shaken and sick, and wanted to know that when Strike had watched the recording of the woman's dying moments, he'd recognised her as a person as real as he was.

Only a prostitute.

Their footsteps rang out on the wet tarmac as the great red-brick palace rose up before them, and Robin, who wanted to drive dreadful images out of her mind, tried to remember everything she knew about Henry VIII, that cruel and corpulent Tudor king who'd beheaded two of his six wives, but somehow found herself thinking about Matthew, instead.

When Robin had been brutally raped by a man in a gorilla mask who'd been lurking beneath the stairs of her hall of residence, Matthew had been kind, patient and understanding. Robin's lawyer might be mystified by the source of Matthew's vindictiveness over what should have been a straightforward divorce, but Robin had come to believe that the end of the marriage had been a profound shock to Matthew, because he thought he was owed infinite credit for having helped her through the worst period of her life. Matthew, Robin felt sure, thought she was forever in his debt.

Tears prickled in Robin's eyes. Angling her umbrella so that Strike couldn't see her face, she blinked hard until her eyes were clear again.

They walked across a cobbled courtyard in silence until Robin came to a sudden halt. Strike, who never enjoyed navigating uneven surfaces with his prosthesis, wasn't sorry to pause, but he was slightly worried that he was about to be on the receiving end of an outburst.

'Look at that,' Robin said, pointing down at a shining cobblestone.

Strike looked closer and saw, to his surprise, a small cross of St John engraved upon a small square brick.

'Coincidence,' he said.

They walked on, Robin looking around, forcing herself to take in her surroundings. They passed into a second courtyard, where a school party in hooded raincoats was being addressed by a guide in a medieval jester's costume.

'Oh wow,' said Robin quietly, looking over her shoulder and then walking backwards for a few paces, the better to see the object set high in the wall above the archway. 'Look at *that*!'

Strike did as he was bidden and saw an enormous, ornate, sixteenth-century astronomical clock of blue and gold. The signs of the zodiac were marked on the perimeter, both with the glyphs with which Strike had become unwillingly familiar, and with pictures representing each sign. Robin smiled at Strike's expression of mingled surprise and annoyance.

'What?' he said, catching her look of amusement.

'You,' she said, turning to walk on. 'Furious at the zodiac.'

'If you'd spent three weeks wading through all Talbot's bollocks, you wouldn't be keen on the zodiac, either,' said Strike.

He stood back to allow Robin to enter the palace first. Following the map Strike had been given, they headed along a flagged, covered walkway towards the Privy Kitchen Café.

'Well, I think there's a kind of poetry to astrology,' said Robin, who was consciously trying to keep her mind off Talbot's old can of film, and her ex-husband. 'I'm not saying it works, but there's a kind of – of symmetry to it, an order . . .'

Through a door to the right, a small Tudor garden came into view. Brightly coloured heraldic beasts stood sentinel over square beds full of sixteenth-century herbs. The sudden appearance of the spotted leopard, the white hart and the red dragon seemed to Robin to cheer her on, asserting the potency and allure of symbol and myth.

'It makes a kind of – not literal sense,' Robin

said, as the whimsically strange creatures passed out of sight, 'but it's survived for a reason.'

'Yeah,' said Strike. 'People will believe any old shit.'

Slightly to his relief, Robin smiled. They entered the white-walled café, which had small leaded windows and dark oak furniture,

'Find us a discreet table, I'll get the drinks in. What d'you want, coffee?'

Choosing a deserted side room, Robin sat down at a table beneath one of the leaded windows and glanced through the potted history of the palace they'd received with their tickets. She learned that the Knights of St John had once owned the land on which the palace stood, which explained the cross on the cobblestone, and that Cardinal Wolsey had given Henry VIII the palace in a futile bid to stave off his own decline in influence. However, when she read that the ghost of nineteen-year-old Catherine Howard was supposed to run, screaming, along the Haunted Gallery, eternally begging her fifty-year-old-husband, the King, not to have her beheaded, Robin closed the pamphlet without reading the rest. Strike arrived with the coffees to find her with her arms folded, staring into space.

'Everything all right?'

'Yes,' she said. 'Just thinking about star signs.'

'Still?' said Strike, with a slight eye roll.

'Jung says it was man's first attempt at psychology, did you know that?'

'I didn't,' said Strike, sitting down opposite her. Robin, as he knew, had been studying psychology at university before she dropped out. 'But there's no excuse to keep using it now we've got actual psychology, is there?'

'Folklore and superstition haven't gone away. They'll never go away. People need them,' she said, taking a sip of coffee. 'I think a purely scientific world would be a cold place. Jung also talked about the collective unconscious, you know. The archetypes lurking in all of us.'

But Strike, whose mother had ensured that he'd spent a large portion of his childhood in a fug of incense, dirt and mysticism, said shortly,

'Yeah, well. I'm Team Rational.'

'People like feeling connected to something bigger,' said Robin, looking up at the rainy sky outside. 'I think it makes you feel less lonely. Astrology connects you to the universe, doesn't it? And to ancient myths and ideas—'

'—and incidentally feeds your ego,' said Strike. 'Makes you feel less insignificant. "Look how special the universe is telling me I am." I don't buy the idea that I've got anything more in common with other people born on November the twenty-third than I think being born in Cornwall makes me a person better than someone born in Manchester.'

'I never said—'

'You might not, but my oldest mate does,' said Strike. 'Dave Polworth.'

'The one who gets ratty when Cornish flags aren't on strawberries?'

'That's him. Committed Cornish nationalist. He gets defensive about it if you challenge him – "I'm not saying we're better than anyone else" – but he thinks you shouldn't be able to buy property down there unless you can prove Cornish ethnicity. Don't remind him he was born in Birmingham if you value your teeth.'

Robin smiled.

'Same kind of thing, though, isn't it?' said Strike. '"I'm special and different because I was born on this bit of rock." "I'm special and different because I was born on June the twelfth—"'

'Where you're born *does* influence who you are, though,' said Robin. 'Cultural norms and language have an effect. And there have been studies showing people born at different times of the year are more prone to certain health conditions.'

'So Roy Phipps bleeds a lot because he was born—? Hello there!' said Strike, breaking off suddenly, his eyes on the door.

Robin turned and saw, to her momentary astonishment, a slender woman wearing a long green Tudor gown and headdress.

'I'm *so sorry*!' said the woman, gesturing at her costume and laughing nervously as she advanced on their table. 'I thought I'd have time to change! I've been doing a school group – we finished late—'

Strike stood up and held out a hand to shake hers.

'Cormoran Strike,' he said. Eyes on her reproduction pearl necklace with its suspended initial 'B', he said, 'Anne Boleyn, I presume?'

Cynthia's laughter contained a couple of inadvertent snorts, which increased her odd resemblance, middle-aged though she was, to a gawky schoolgirl. Her movements were unsuited to the sweeping velvet gown, being rather exaggerated and ungainly.

'Hahaha, yes, that's me! Only my second time as Anne. You think you've thought of *all* the questions the kids might ask you, then one of them says "How did it feel to get your head cut off?", hahahaha!'

Cynthia wasn't at all what Robin had expected. She now realised that her imagination had sketched in a young blonde, the stereotypical idea of a Scandinavian au pair . . . or was that because Sarah Shadlock had almost white hair?

'Coffee?' Strike asked Cynthia.

'Oh – coffee, yes please, wonderful, thank you,' said Cynthia, over-enthusiastically. When Strike had left, Cynthia made a small pantomime of dithering over which seat to take until Robin, smiling, pulled out the seat beside her and offered her own hand, too.

'Oh, yes, hello!' said Cynthia, sitting down and shaking hands. She had a thin, sallow face, currently wearing an anxious smile. The irises of her large eyes were heavily mottled, an indeterminate colour between blue, green and grey, and her teeth were rather crooked.

'So you lead the tour in character?' asked Robin.

'Yes, exactly, as poor Anne, hahaha,' said Cynthia, with another nervous, snorting laugh. '"I couldn't give the King a son! They said I was a witch!" Those are the sort of things children like to hear; I have to work quite hard to get the politics in, hahaha. Poor Anne.' Her thin hands fidgeted.

'Oh, I'm still – I can take this off, at least, hahaha!'

Cynthia set to work unpinning her headdress. Even though she could tell that Cynthia was very nervous, and that her constant laughter was more of a tic than genuine amusement, Robin was again reminded of Sarah Shadlock, who tended to laugh a lot, and loudly, especially in the vicinity of Matthew. Wittingly or not, Cynthia's laughter imposed a sort of obligation: smile back or seem hostile. Robin remembered a documentary on monkeys she had watched one night when she was too tired to get up and go to bed: chimps, too, laughed back at each other to signal social cohesion.

When Strike returned to the table with Cynthia's coffee, he found her newly bare-headed. Her dark hair was fifty per cent grey, and smoothed back into a short, thin ponytail.

'It's very good of you to meet us, Mrs Phipps,' he said, sitting back down.

'Oh, no, not at all, not at all,' said Cynthia, waving her thin hands and laughing some more. 'Anything I can do to help Anna with – but Roy hasn't been well, so I don't want to worry him just now.'

'I'm sorry to hear—'

'Yes, thank you, no, it's prostate cancer,' said Cynthia, no longer laughing. 'Radiation therapy. Not feeling too chipper. Anna and Kim came over this morning to sit with him, or I wouldn't have been able – I don't like leaving him at the moment, but the girls are there, so I thought I'd be fine to . . .'

The end of the sentence was lost as she took a sip of coffee. Her hand trembled slightly as she replaced the cup onto the saucer.

'Your stepdaughter's probably told—' Strike began, but Cynthia immediately interrupted him.

'*Daughter.* I don't ever call Anna my stepdaughter. Sorry, but I feel *just* the same about her as I do about Jeremy and Ellie. No difference at all.'

Robin wondered whether that was true. She was uncomfortably aware that part of her was standing aside, watching Cynthia with judgemental eyes. *She isn't Sarah*, Robin reminded herself.

'Well, I'm sure Anna's told you why she hired us, and so on.'

'Oh, yes,' said Cynthia. 'No, I must admit, I've been expecting something like this for a while. I hope it isn't going to make things worse for her.'

'Er – well, we hope that, too, obviously,' said Strike, and Cynthia laughed and said, 'Oh, no, of course, yes.'

Strike took out his notebook, in which a few photocopied sheets were folded, and a pen.

'Could we begin with the statement you gave the police?'

'You've got it?' said Cynthia, looking startled. 'The original?'

'A photocopy,' he said, unfolding it.

'How . . . funny. Seeing it again, after all this time. I was eighteen. Eighteen! It seems a century ago, hahaha!'

The signature at the bottom of the uppermost page, Robin saw, was rounded and rather childish. Strike handed the photocopied pages to Cynthia, who took them looking almost frightened.

'I'm afraid I'm awfully dyslexic,' she said. 'I was forty-two before I was diagnosed. My parents thought I was bone idle, hahaha . . . um, so . . .'

'Would you rather I read it to you?' Strike suggested. Cynthia handed it back to him at once.

'Oh, thank you – this is how I learn all my guiding notes, by listening to audio discs, hahaha . . .'

Strike flattened out the photocopied papers on the table.

'Please interrupt if you want to add or change anything,' he told Cynthia, who nodded and said that she would.

'"Name, Cynthia Jane Phipps . . . date of birth, July the twentieth 1957 . . . address, "The Annexe, Broom House, Church Road" . . . that would be Margot's—?'

'I had self-contained rooms over the double garage,' said Cynthia. Robin thought she laid slight emphasis on 'self-contained'.

'"I am employed as nanny to Dr Phipps and Dr

Bamborough's infant daughter, and I live in their house—"'

'Self-contained studio,' said Cynthia. 'It had its own entrance.'

'"My hours . . ." Don't think we need any of that,' muttered Strike. 'Here we go. "On the morning of the eleventh of October I began work at 7 a.m. I saw Dr Bamborough before she left for work. She seemed entirely as usual. She reminded me that she would be late home because she was meeting her friend Miss Oonagh Kennedy for drinks near her place of work. As Dr Phipps was bedbound due to his recent accident—"'

'Anna told you about Roy's von Willebrand Disease?' said Cynthia anxiously.

'Er – I don't think *she* told us, but it's mentioned in the police report.'

'Oh, didn't she say?' said Cynthia, who seemed unhappy to hear it. 'Well, he's a Type Three. That's serious, as bad as haemophilia. His knee swelled up and he was in a lot of pain, could hardly *move*,' said Cynthia.

'Yes,' said Strike, 'it's all in the police—'

'No, because he'd had an accident on the seventh,' said Cynthia, who seemed determined to say this. 'It was a wet day, pouring with rain, you can check that. He was walking around a corner of the hospital, heading for the car park, and an out-patient rode right into him on a pushbike. Roy got tangled up in the front wheel, slipped, hit his knee and had a major bleed. These days he has

587

prophylactic injections so it doesn't happen the way it used to, but back then, if he injured himself, it could lay him up for weeks.'

'Right,' said Strike, and judging it to be the most tactful thing to do, he made careful note of all these details, which he'd already read in Roy's own statements and police interviews.

'No, Anna knows her dad was ill that day. She's always known,' Cynthia added.

Strike continued reading the statement aloud. It was a retelling of facts Strike and Robin already knew. Cynthia had been in charge of baby Anna at home. Roy's mother had come over during the day. Wilma Bayliss had cleaned for three hours and left. Cynthia had taken occasional cups of tea to the invalid and his mother. At 6 p.m., Evelyn Phipps had gone home to her bungalow to play bridge with friends, leaving a tray of food for her son.

'"At 8 p.m. in the evening I was watching television in the sitting room downstairs when I heard the phone ring in the hall. I would usually only ever answer the phone if both Dr Phipps and Dr Bamborough were out. As Dr Phipps was in, and could answer the phone from the extension beside his bed, I didn't answer.

'"About five minutes later, I heard the gong that Mrs Evelyn Phipps had placed beside Dr Phipps's bed, in case of emergency. I went upstairs. Dr Phipps was still in bed. He told me that it had been Miss Kennedy on the phone. Dr Bamborough hadn't turned up at the pub. Dr Phipps said he thought she must have been delayed at work or forgotten. He asked me to tell Dr Bamborough to go up to their bedroom as soon as she came in.

"'I went back downstairs. About an hour later, I heard the gong again and went upstairs and found Dr Phipps now quite worried about his wife. He asked me whether she'd come in yet. I said that she hadn't. He asked me to stay in the room while he phoned Miss Kennedy at home. Miss Kennedy still hadn't seen or heard from Dr Bamborough. Dr Phipps hung up and asked me what Dr Bamborough had been carrying when she left the house that morning. I told him just a handbag and her doctor's bag. He asked me whether Dr Bamborough had said anything about visiting her parents. I said she hadn't. He asked me to stay while he called Dr Bamborough's mother.

"'Mrs Bamborough hadn't heard from her daughter or seen her. Dr Phipps was now quite worried and asked me to go downstairs and look in the drawer in the base of the clock on the mantelpiece in the sitting room and see whether there was anything in there. I went and looked. There was nothing there. I went back upstairs and told Dr Phipps that the clock drawer was empty. Dr Phipps explained that this was a place he and his wife sometimes left each other private notes. I hadn't known about this previously.

"'He asked me to stay with him while he called

his mother, because he might have something else for me to do. He spoke to his mother and asked her advice. It was a brief conversation. When he hung up, Dr Phipps asked me whether I thought he ought to call the police. I said I thought he should. He said he was going to. He told me to go downstairs and let the police in when they arrived and show them up to his bedroom. The police arrived about half an hour later and I showed them up to Dr Phipps's bedroom.

"'I didn't find Dr Bamborough to be unusual in her manner when she left the house that morning. Relations between Dr Phipps and Dr Bamborough seemed completely happy. I'm very surprised at her disappearance, which is out of character. She is very attached to her daughter and I cannot imagine her ever leaving the baby, or going away without telling her husband or me where she was going.

"'Signed and dated Cynthia Phipps, 12 October 1974.'"

'Yes, no, that's . . . I haven't got anything to add to that,' said Cynthia. 'Odd to hear it back!' she said, with another little snorting laugh, but Robin thought her eyes were frightened.

'This is obviously, ah, sensitive, but if we could go back to your statement that relations between Roy and Margot—'

'Yes, sorry, no, I'm not going to talk about their marriage,' said Cynthia. Her sallow cheeks became stained with a purplish blush. 'Everyone rows, everyone has ups and downs, but it's not up to me to talk about their marriage.'

'We understand that your husband couldn't have—' began Robin.

'*Margot's* husband,' said Cynthia. 'No, you see, they're two completely different people. Inside my head.'

Convenient, said a voice inside Robin's.

'We're simply exploring the possibility that she went away,' said Strike, 'maybe to think or—'

'No, Margot wouldn't have just walked out without saying anything. That wouldn't have been like her.'

'Anna told us her grandmother—' said Robin.

'Evelyn had early onset Alzheimer's and you couldn't take what she said seriously,' said Cynthia, her tone higher and more brittle. 'I've always told Anna that, I've *always* told her that Margot would never have left her. I've *always* told her that,' she repeated.

Except, continued the voice inside Robin's head, *when you were pretending to be her real mother, and hiding Margot's existence from her.*

'Moving on,' said Strike, 'you received a phone call on Anna's second birthday, from a woman purporting to be Margot?'

'Um, yes, no, that's right,' said Cynthia. She took another shaky sip of coffee. 'I was icing the birthday cake in the kitchen when the phone rang, so not in any danger of forgetting what day it was, hahaha. When I picked up, the woman said, "Is that you, Cynthia?" I said "Yes", and she said "It's Margot here. Wish little Annie a happy birthday from her mummy. And make sure you look after her." And the line went dead.

'I just stood there,' she mimed holding an invisible implement in her hand, and tried to laugh again, but no sound came out, 'holding the spatula. I didn't know what to do. Anna was playing in the sitting room. I was . . . I decided I'd better ring Roy at work. He told me to call the police, so I did.'

'Did you think it was Margot?' asked Strike.

'No. It wasn't – well, it *sounded* like her, but I don't think it *was* her.'

'You think somebody was imitating it?'

'Putting it on, yes. The accent. Cockney, but . . . no, I didn't get that feeling you get when you just *know* who it is . . .'

'You're sure it was a woman?' said Strike. 'It couldn't have been a man imitating a woman?'

'I don't think so,' said Cynthia.

'Did Margot ever call Anna "little Annie"?' asked Robin.

'She called her all kinds of pet names,' said Cynthia, looking glum. 'Annie Fandango, Annabella, Angel Face . . . somebody could have guessed, or maybe they'd just got the name wrong . . . But the timing was . . . they'd just found bits of Creed's last victim. The one he threw off Beachy Head—'

'Andrea Hooton,' said Robin. Cynthia looked

slightly startled that she had the name on the tip of her tongue.

'Yes, the hairdresser.'

'No,' said Robin. 'That was Susan Meyer. Andrea was the PhD student.'

'Oh, yes,' said Cynthia. 'Of course . . . I'm so bad with names . . . Well, Roy had just been through the whole identification business with, um, you know, the bits of the body that washed up, so we'd had our hopes – not our hopes!' said Cynthia, looking terrified at the word that had escaped her, 'I don't mean that! No, we were obviously relieved it wasn't Margot, but you think, you know, maybe you're going to get an answer . . .'

Strike thought of his own guilty wish that Joan's slow and protracted dying would be over soon. A corpse, however unwelcome, meant anguish could find both expression and sublimation among flowers, speeches and ritual, consolation drawn from God, alcohol and fellow mourners; an apotheosis reached, a first step taken towards grasping the awful fact that life was extinct, and life must go on.

'We'd already been through it once when they found the other body, the one in Alexandra Lake,' said Cynthia.

'Susan Meyer,' muttered Robin.

'Roy was shown pictures, both times . . . And then this phone call, coming right after he'd had to . . . for the second time . . . it was . . .'

Cynthia was suddenly crying, not like Oonagh

Kennedy, with her head up and tears sparkling on her cheeks, but hunched over the table, hiding her face, her shaking hands supporting her forehead.

'I'm so sorry,' she sobbed. 'I knew this would be awful . . . we never talk about her any – any more . . . I'm sorry . . .'

She sobbed for a few more seconds, then forced herself to look up again, her large eyes now pink and wet.

'Roy wanted to believe it had been Margot on the phone. He kept saying "Are you sure, are you *sure*, it didn't sound like her?" He was on tenterhooks while the police traced the call . . .

'You're being very polite,' she said, and her laugh this time was slightly hysterical, 'but I know what you want to know, and what Anna wants to know, too, even though I've *told* her and *told* her . . . There was *nothing* going on between me and Roy before Margot disappeared, and not for *four years* afterwards . . . Did she tell you that Roy and I are related?'

She said it as though forcing herself to say it, although a third cousin was not, after all, a very close relationship. But Robin, thinking of Roy's bleeding disorder, wondered whether the Phippses, like the Romanovs, mightn't be well advised not to marry their cousins.

'Yes, she did,' said Strike.

'I was sick of the sound of his name before I went to work for them, actually. It was all, "Just look at Cousin Roy, with all his health problems, getting into Imperial College and studying medicine. If you'd only *work harder*, Cynthia . . ." I used to hate the very idea of him, hahaha!'

Robin recalled the picture of young Roy in the press: the sensitive face, the floppy hair, the poet's eyes. Many women found injury and illness romantic in a handsome man. Hadn't Matthew, in his worst effusions of jealousy against Strike, invoked his amputated leg, the warrior's wound against which he, whole-bodied and fit, felt unable to compete?

'You might not believe this, but as far as I was concerned at seventeen, the best thing about Roy was Margot! No, I thought she was *marvellous*, so – so fashionable and, you know, lots of opinions and things . . .

'She asked me over for dinner, after she heard I ploughed all my exams. Well, I hero-worshipped her, so I was thrilled. I poured my heart out, told her I couldn't face resits, I just wanted to get out in the real world and earn my own money. And she said, "Look, you're wonderful with children, how about coming and looking after my baby when I go back to work? I'll get Roy to do up the rooms over the garage for you."

'My parents were *livid*,' said Cynthia, with another brave but unsuccessful stab at a laugh. 'They were furious with her, *and* Roy, although actually, he didn't want me there in the first place, because he wanted Margot to stay at home and look after Anna herself. Mummy and Daddy said she was just after cheap labour. These days I do see it more from their point of view. I'm not sure *I'd* have been delighted if a woman had persuaded one of my girls to leave school and move in with them, and look after their baby. But no, I loved Margot. I was excited.'

Cynthia fell silent for a moment, a faraway look in her doleful eyes, and Robin wondered whether she was thinking about the huge and unalterable consequences of accepting the job as nanny, which instead of being a springboard to her own independent life had placed her in a house she would never leave, led to her raising Margot's child as her own, sleeping with Margot's husband, forever stuck in the shadow of the doctor she claimed to have loved. What was it like to live with an absence that huge?

'My parents wanted me to go away after Margot disappeared. They didn't like me being alone at the house with Roy, because people were starting to gossip. There were even hints in the press, but I swear to you on the lives of my children,' said Cynthia, with a kind of dull finality, 'there was *nothing* between Roy and me, ever, before Margot disappeared, and not for a long time afterwards, either. I stayed for Anna, because I couldn't bear to leave her . . . she'd become my daughter!'

She hadn't, said the implacable voice in Robin's head. *And you should have told her so.*

'Roy didn't date anyone for a long time after Margot disappeared. Then there was a colleague at work for a while,' Cynthia's thin face flushed again, 'but it only lasted a few months. Anna didn't like her.

'I had a kind of on-off boyfriend, but he packed me in. He said it was like dating a married woman with a child, because I put Anna and Roy first, always.

'And then I suppose . . .' said Cynthia shakily, one hand balled in a fist, the other clutching it, '. . . over time . . . I realised I'd fallen in love with Roy. I never dreamed he'd want to be with me, though. Margot was so clever, such a – such a big personality, and he was so much older than me, so much more intelligent and sophisticated . . .

'One evening, after I'd put Anna to bed, I was about to go back to my rooms and he asked me what had happened with Will, my boyfriend, and I said it was over, and he asked what had happened, and we got talking, and he said . . . he said, "You're a very special person and you deserve far better than him." And then . . . then, we had a drink . . .

'That was *four years* after she'd disappeared,' Cynthia repeated. 'I was eighteen when she vanished and I was twenty-two when Roy and I . . . admitted we had feelings for each other. We kept it secret, obviously. It was another three years before Roy could get a death certificate for Margot.'

'That must have been very hard,' said Strike.

Cynthia looked at him for a moment, unsmiling. She seemed to have aged since arriving at the table.

'I've had nightmares about Margot coming back and throwing me out of the house for nearly forty years,' she said, and she tried to laugh. 'I've never told Roy. I don't want to know whether he dreams about her, too. We don't talk about her. It's the only way to cope. We'd said everything we had to say to the police, to each other, to the rest of the family. We'd raked it all over, hours and hours of talking. "It's time to close the door", that's how Roy put it. He said, "We've left the door open long enough. She's not coming back."

'There were a couple of spiteful things said in the press, you know, when we got married. "Husband of vanished doctor marries young nanny." It's always going to sound sordid, isn't it? Roy said not to mind them. My parents were appalled by the whole thing. It was only when I had Jeremy that they came around.

'We never *meant* to mislead Anna. We were waiting . . . I don't know . . . trying to find the right moment, to explain . . . but how are you supposed to do it? She used to call me "Mummy",' whispered Cynthia, 'she was h- happy, she was a completely happy little girl, but then those children at school told her about Margot and it ruined *every*—'

From somewhere close by came a loud synthesiser version of 'Greensleeves'. All three of them looked startled until Cynthia, laughing her snorting laugh, said, 'It's my phone!' She pulled the mobile from a deep pocket in her dress and answered it.

'Roy?' she said.

Robin could hear Roy talking angrily from where she sat. Cynthia looked suddenly alarmed. She tried to get up, but stepped on the hem of her dress and tripped forwards. Trying to disentangle herself, she said,

'No, I'm – oh, she hasn't. Oh, God – Roy, I didn't want to tell you because – no – yes, I'm still with them!'

Finally managing to free herself from both dress and table, Cynthia staggered away and out of the room. The headdress she'd been wearing slid limply off her seat. Robin stooped to pick it up, put it back on the seat of Cynthia's chair and looked up to see Strike watching her.

'What?' asked Robin.

He was about to answer when Cynthia reappeared. She looked stricken.

'Roy knows – Anna's told him. He wants you to come back to Broom House.'

CHAPTER 36

He oft finds med'cine who his grief imparts;
But double griefs afflict concealing hearts,
As raging flames who striveth to suppress.

Edmund Spenser
The Faerie Queene

ynthia hurried away to change out of her Anne Boleyn costume and reappeared ten minutes later in a pair of poorly fitting jeans, a grey sweater and trainers. She appeared extremely anxious as they walked together back through the palace, setting a fast pace that Strike found challenging on cobblestones still slippery with the rain which had temporarily ceased, but the heavy grey clouds, gilt-edged though they were, promised an imminent return. Glancing upwards as they passed back through the gatehouse of the inner court, Robin's eye was caught by the gleaming gold accents on the astronomical clock, and noticed that the sun was in Margot's sign of Aquarius.

'I'll see you there,' said Cynthia breathlessly, as they approached the car park, and without waiting for an answer she half-ran towards a blue Mazda3 in the distance.

'This is going to be interesting,' said Robin.

'Certainly is,' said Strike.

'Grab the map,' said Robin, once both were back in the car. The old Land Rover didn't have a functioning radio, let alone satnav. 'You'll have to navigate.'

'What d'you think of her?' asked Strike, while he looked up Church Road in Ham.

'She seems all right.'

Robin became aware that Strike was looking at her, as he had in the café, a slightly quizzical expression on his face.

'What?' she said again.

'I had the impression you weren't keen.'

'No,' said Robin, with a trace of defensiveness, 'she's fine.'

She reversed out of the parking space, remembering Cynthia's snorting laughter and her habit of jumbling affirmatives and negatives together.

'Well—'

'Thought so,' said Strike, smugly.

'Given what might've happened to Margot, I wouldn't have kicked off the conversation with cheery decapitation jokes.'

'She's lived with it for forty years,' said Strike. 'People who live with something that massive stop being able to see it. It's the backdrop of their lives. It's only glaringly obvious to everyone else.'

It started to rain again as they left the car park: a fine veil laying itself swiftly over the windscreen.

'OK, I'm prejudiced,' Robin admitted, switching on the wipers. 'Feeling a bit sensitive about second wives right now.'

She drove on for a few moments before becoming aware that Strike was looking at her again.

'What?' she asked, for a third time.

'Why're you sensitive about second wives?'

'Because – oh, I didn't tell you, did I? I told Morris.' She'd tried not to think, since, about her drunken Boxing Day spent texting, of the small amount of comfort she had derived from it, or the immense load of discomfort. 'Matthew and Sarah Shadlock are together officially now. She left her fiancé for him.'

'Shit,' said Strike, still watching her profile. 'No, you didn't tell me.'

But he mentally docketed the fact that she'd told Morris, which didn't fit with the idea that he'd formed of Robin and Morris's relationship. From what Barclay had told him about Morris's challenges to Robin's authority, and from Robin's generally lukewarm comments on his new hire, he'd assumed that Morris's undoubted sexual interest in Robin had fizzled out for lack of a return. And yet she'd told Morris this painful bit of personal information, and not told him.

As they drove in silence towards Church Road,

he wondered what had been going on in London while he had been in Cornwall. Morris was a good-looking man and he, like Robin, was divorcing. Strike wondered why he hadn't previously considered the implications of this obvious piece of symmetry. Comparing notes on lawyers, on difficult exes, on the mechanics of splitting two lives: they'd have plenty to talk about, plenty of opportunities for mutual sympathy.

'Straight up here,' he said, and they drove in silence across the Royal Paddocks, between high, straight red walls.

'Nice street,' commented Robin, twenty minutes after they'd left Hampton Court Palace, as she turned the Land Rover into a road that might have been deep in countryside. To their left was dense woodland, to the right, several large, detached houses that stood back from the road behind high hedges.

'It's that one,' said Strike, pointing at a particularly sprawling house with many pointed, half-timbered gables. The double gates stood open, as did the front door. They turned into the drive and parked behind the blue Mazda3.

As soon as Robin switched off the engine, they heard shouting coming from inside the house: a male voice, intemperate and high pitched. Anna Phipps's wife, Kim, tall, blonde and wearing jeans and a shirt as before, came striding out of the house towards them, her expression tense.

'Big scenes,' she said, as Strike and Robin got out of the car into the mist of rain.

'Would you like us to wait—?' Robin began.

'No,' Kim said, 'he's determined to see you. Come in.'

They walked across the gravel and entered Broom House. Somewhere inside, male and female voices continued to shout.

Every house has its own deep ingrained smell, and this one was redolent of sandalwood and a not entirely unpleasant fustiness. Kim led them through a long, large-windowed hall that seemed frozen in the mid-twentieth century. There were brass light fittings, watercolours and an old rug on polished floorboards. With a sudden frisson, Robin thought that Margot Bamborough had once walked this very floor, her metallic rose perfume mingling with the scents of polish and old carpet.

As they approached the door of the drawing room, the argument taking place inside became suddenly comprehensible.

'—and if I'm to be talked about,' a man was shouting, 'I should have right of reply – my family deciding to investigate me behind my back, charming, *charming*, it really is—'

'Nobody's investigating *you*, for God's sake!' they heard Anna say. 'Bill Talbot was incompetent—'

'Oh, was he really? Were you there? Did you know him?'

'I didn't *have* to be there, Dad—'

Kim opened the door. Strike and Robin followed Kim inside.

It was like coming upon a tableau. The three people standing inside froze at their entrance. Cynthia's thin fingers were pressed to her mouth. Anna stood facing her father across a small antique table.

The romantic-looking poet of 1974 was no more. Roy Phipps's remaining hair was short, grey and clung only around his ears and the back of his head. In his knitted sweater vest, with his high, domed, shining pate and his wild eyes, slightly sunken in a blotchy face, he'd now be better suited to the role of mad scientist.

So furious did Roy Phipps look, that Robin quite expected him to start shouting at the newcomers, too. However, the haematologist's demeanour changed when his eyes met Strike's. Whether this was a tribute to the detective's bulk, or to the aura of gravity and calm he managed to project in highly charged situations, Robin couldn't tell, but she thought she saw Roy decide against yelling. After a brief hesitation, the doctor accepted Strike's proffered hand, and as the two men shook, Robin wondered how aware men were of the power dynamics that played out between them, while women stood watching.

'Dr Phipps,' said Strike.

Roy appeared to have found the gear change between intemperate rage and polite greeting a difficult one, and his immediate response was slightly incoherent.

'So you're – you're the detective, are you?' he said. Bluish-red blotches lingered in his pale cheeks.

'Cormoran Strike – and this is my partner, Robin Ellacott.'

Robin stepped forwards.

'How d'you do?' Roy said stiffly, shaking her hand, too. His was hot and dry.

'Shall I make coffee?' said Cynthia, in a half-whisper.

'Yes – no, why not,' said Roy, his ill-temper clearly jockeying with the nervousness that seemed to increase while Strike stood, large and unmoving, watching him. 'Sit, sit,' he said, pointing Strike to a sofa, at right angles to another.

Cynthia hurried out of the room to make coffee, and Strike and Robin sat where they'd been instructed.

'Going to help Cyn,' muttered Anna and she hurried out of the room, and Kim, after a moment's hesitation, followed her, leaving Strike and Robin alone with Roy. The doctor settled himself into a high-backed velvet armchair and glared around him. He didn't look well. The flush of temper receded, leaving him looking wan. His socks had bunched up around his skinny ankles.

There ensued one of the most uncomfortable silences Robin had ever endured. Mainly to avoid looking at Roy, she allowed her eyes to roam around the large room, which was as old fashioned as the hall. A grand piano stood in the corner. More

606

large windows looked out onto an enormous garden, where a long rectangular fish pond lay just beyond a paved area, at the far end of which lay a covered, temple-like stone structure where people could either sit and watch the koi carp, now barely visible beneath the rain-flecked surface of the water, or look out over the sweeping lawn, with its mature trees and well-tended flower-beds.

An abundance of leather-bound books and bronzes of antique subjects filled bookcases and cabinets. A tambour frame stood between the sofas, on which a very beautiful piece of embroidery was being worked in silks. The design was Japanese influenced, of two koi swimming in opposite directions. Robin was debating whether to pass polite comment on it, and to ask whether Cynthia was responsible, when Strike spoke.

'Who was the classicist?'

'What?' said Roy. 'Oh. My father.'

His crazy-looking eyes roamed over the various small bronzes and marbles dotted around the room. 'Took a first in Classics at Cambridge.'

'Ah,' said Strike, and the glacial silence resumed.

A squall of wind threw more rain at the window. Robin was relieved to hear the tinkling of teaspoons and the footsteps of the three returning women.

Cynthia, who re-entered the room first, set a tea tray down on the antique table standing between the sofas. It rocked a little with the weight. Anna added a large cake on a stand.

Anna and Kim sat down side by side on the free sofa, and when Cynthia had drawn up spindly side tables to hold everyone's tea, and cut slices of cake for those who wanted some, she sat herself down beside her stepdaughter-in-law, looking scared.

'Well,' said Roy at last, addressing Strike. 'I'd be interested to hear what you think your chances are of finding out what the Metropolitan Police has been unable to discover in four decades.'

Robin was sure Roy had been planning this aggressive opening during the long and painful silence.

'Fairly small,' said Strike matter-of-factly, once he'd swallowed a large piece of the cake Cynthia had given him, 'though we've got a new alleged sighting of your first wife I wanted to discuss with you.'

Roy looked taken aback.

'*Alleged* sighting,' Strike emphasised, setting down his plate and reaching inside his jacket for his notebook. 'But obviously . . . Excellent cake, Mrs Phipps,' he told Cynthia.

'Oh, thank you,' she said in a small voice. 'Coffee and walnut was Anna's favourite when she was little – wasn't it, love?' she said, but Anna's only response was a tense smile.

'We heard about it from one of your wife's ex-colleagues, Janice Beattie.'

Roy shook his head and shrugged impatiently, to convey non-recognition of the names.

'She was the practice nurse at the St John's surgery,' said Strike.

'Oh,' said Roy. 'Yes. I think she came here once, for a barbecue. She seemed quite a decent woman . . . Disaster, that afternoon. Bloody disaster. Those children were atrocious – d'you remember?' he shot at Cynthia.

'Yes,' said Cynthia quickly, 'no, there was one boy who was really—'

'Spiked the punch,' barked Roy. 'Vodka. Someone was sick.'

'Gloria,' said Cynthia.

'I don't remember all their names,' said Roy, with an impatient wave of the hand. 'Sick all over the downstairs bathroom. Disgusting.'

'This boy would've been Carl Oakden?' asked Strike.

'That's him,' said Roy. 'We found the vodka bottle empty, later, hidden in a shed. He'd sneaked into the house and taken it out of the drinks cabinet.'

'Yes,' said Cynthia, 'and then he smashed—'

'Crystal bowl of my mother's and half a dozen glasses. Hit a cricket ball right across the barbecue area. The nurse cleaned it all up for me, because – decent of her. She knew I couldn't – broken glass,' said Roy, with an impatient gesture.

'On the bright side,' said Cynthia, with the ghost of a laugh, 'he'd smashed the punch, so nobody else got sick.'

'That bowl was art deco,' said Roy, unsmiling. 'Bloody disaster, the whole thing. I said to Margot,' and he paused for a second after saying the name, and Robin wondered when he'd last spoken it, '"I don't know what you think this is going to achieve." Because *he* didn't come, the one she was trying to conciliate – the doctor she didn't get on with, what was his—?'

'Joseph Brenner,' said Robin.

'Brenner, exactly. *He'd* refused the invitation, so what was the point? But no, we still had to give up our Saturday to entertain this motley collection of people, and our reward was to have our drink stolen and our possessions smashed.'

Roy's fists lay on the arms of his chair. He uncoiled the long fingers for a moment in a movement like a hermit crab unflexing its legs, then curled them tightly in upon themselves again.

'That same boy, Oakden, wrote a book about Margot later,' he said. 'Used a photograph from that damn barbecue to add credibility to the notion that he and his mother knew all about our private lives. So, yes,' said Roy coldly, '*not* one of Margot's better ideas.'

'Well, she was trying to make the practice work better together, wasn't she?' said Anna. 'You've never really needed to manage different personalities at work—'

'Oh, you know all about my work, too, do you, Anna?'

'Well, it wasn't the same as being a GP, was it?' said Anna. 'You were lecturing, doing research, you didn't have to manage cleaners and receptionists and a whole bunch of non-medics.'

'They *were* quite badly behaved, Anna,' said

Cynthia, hurrying loyally to support Roy. 'No, they really were. I never told – I didn't want to cause trouble – but one of the women sneaked upstairs into your mum and dad's bedroom.'

'What?' barked Roy.

'Yes,' said Cynthia, nervously. 'No, I went upstairs to change Anna's nappy and I heard movement in there. I walked in and she was looking at Margot's clothes in the wardrobe.'

'Who was this?' asked Strike.

'The blonde one. The receptionist who wasn't Gloria.'

'Irene,' said Strike. 'Did she know you'd seen her?'

'Oh yes. I walked in, holding Anna.'

'What did she say when she saw you?' asked Robin.

'Well, she was a bit embarrassed,' said Cynthia. 'You would be, wouldn't you? She laughed and said "just being nosy" and walked back out past me.'

'Good God,' said Roy Phipps, shaking his head. 'Who *hired* these people?'

'Was she really just looking?' Robin asked Cynthia. 'Or d'you think she'd gone in there to—'

'Oh, I don't think she'd *taken* anything,' said Cynthia. 'And you never – Margot never missed anything, did she?' she asked Roy.

'No, but you should still have told me this at the time,' said Roy crossly.

'I didn't want to cause trouble. You were already . . . well, it was a stressful day, wasn't it?'

'About this alleged sighting,' said Strike, and he told the family the third-hand tale of Charlie Ramage, who claimed to have seen Margot wandering among graves in a churchyard in Leamington Spa.

'. . . and Robin's now spoken to Ramage's widow, who confirmed the basic story, though she couldn't swear to it that it was Margot he thought he'd seen, and not another missing woman. The sighting doesn't seem to have been passed to the police, so I wanted to ask whether Margot had any connection with Leamington Spa that you know of?'

'None,' said Roy, and Cynthia shook her head. Strike made a note.

'Thank you. While we're on the subject of sightings,' said Strike, 'I wonder whether we could run through the rest of the list?'

Robin thought she knew what Strike was up to. However uncomfortable the idea that Margot was still alive might be for the people in this room, Strike wanted to start the interview from a standpoint that didn't presume murder.

'The woman at the service station in Birmingham, the mother in Brighton, the dog walker down in Eastbourne,' Roy rattled off, before Strike could speak. 'Why would she have been out and about, driving cars and walking dogs? If she'd disappeared voluntarily, she clearly didn't want to be found. The same goes for wandering around graveyards.'

'True,' said Strike. 'But there was one sighting—'

'Warwick,' said Roy. 'Yes.'

A look passed between husband and wife. Strike waited. Roy set down his cup and saucer on the table in front of him and looked up at his daughter.

'You're quite sure you want to do this, Anna, are you?' he asked, looking at his silent daughter. 'Quite, *quite* sure?'

'What d'you mean?' she snapped back. 'What d'you think I hired detectives for? Fun?'

'All right, then,' said Roy, 'all right. That sighting caught . . . caught my attention, because my wife's ex-boyfriend, a man called Paul Satchwell, hailed originally from Warwick. This was a man she'd . . . reconnected with, before she disappeared.'

'Oh for God's sake,' said Anna, with a tight little laugh, 'did you *honestly* think I don't know about Paul Satchwell? Of course I do!' Kim reached out and put a hand on her wife's leg, whether in comfort or warning, it was hard to tell. 'Have you never heard of the internet, Dad, or press archives? I've seen Satchwell's ridiculous photograph, with all his chest hair and his medallions, and I know my mother went for a drink with him three weeks before she vanished! But it was only one drink—'

'Oh, was it?' said Roy nastily. 'Thanks for your reassurance, Anna. Thanks for your expert knowledge. How marvellous to be all-knowing—'

'Roy,' whispered Cynthia.

'What are you saying, that it was more than a

drink?' said Anna, looking shaken. 'No, it wasn't, that's a horrible thing to say! Oonagh says—'

'Oh, right, yes, I see!' said Roy loudly, his sunken cheeks turning purple as his hands gripped the arms of his chair, '*Oonagh* says, does she? Everything is explained!'

'What's explained?' demanded Anna.

'This!' he shouted, pointing a trembling, rope-veined, swollen-knuckled hand at Strike and Robin. 'Oonagh Kennedy's behind it all, is she? I should have *known* I hadn't heard the last of her!'

'For God's sake, Roy,' said Kim loudly, 'that's a preposterous—'

'*Oonagh Kennedy wanted me arrested!*'

'Dad, that's simply not true!' said Anna, forcibly removing Kim's restraining hand from her leg. 'You've got a morbid fixation about Oonagh—'

'Badgering me to complain about Talbot—'

'Well, why the bloody hell *didn't* you?' said Anna loudly. 'The man was in the middle of a fully fledged breakdown!'

'Roy!' whimpered Cynthia again, as Roy leaned forwards to face his daughter across the too-small circular table, with its precariously balanced cake. Gesticulating wildly, his face purple, he shouted,

'Police swarming all over the house going through your mother's things – sniffer dogs out in the garden – they were looking for any reason to arrest me, and I should lodge a formal complaint against the man in charge? *How would that have looked?*'

'He was incompetent!'

'Were you there, Miss Omniscient? Did you know him?'

'Why did they replace him? Why does everything written about the case say he was incompetent? The truth is,' said Anna, stabbing the air between her and her father with a forefinger, 'you and Cyn loved Bill Talbot because he thought you were innocent from the off and—'

'*Thought* I was innocent?' bellowed Roy. 'Well, thank you, it's good to know that nothing's changed since you were thirteen years old—'

'Roy!' said Cynthia and Kim together.

'—and accused me of building the koi pond over the place I'd buried her!'

Anna burst into tears and fled the room, almost tripping over Strike's legs as she went. Suspecting there was about to be a mass exodus, he retracted his feet.

'When,' Kim said coldly to her father-in-law, 'is Anna going to be forgiven for things she said when she was a confused child, going through a dreadful time?'

'And *my* dreadful time is nothing, of course? Nothing!' shouted Roy, and as Strike expected, he, too, left the room at the fastest pace he could manage, which was a speedy hobble.

'Christ's sake,' muttered Kim, striding after Roy and Anna and almost colliding at the door with Cynthia, who'd jumped up to follow Roy.

The door swung shut. The rain pattered on the pond outside. Strike blew out his cheeks, exchanged

615

looks with Robin, then picked up his plate and continued eating his cake.

'Starving,' he said thickly, in response to Robin's look. 'No lunch. And it's good cake.'

Distantly they heard shouting, and the slamming of another door.

'D'you think the interview's over?' muttered Robin.

'No,' said Strike, still eating. 'They'll be back.'

'Remind me about the sighting in Warwick,' said Robin.

She'd merely skimmed the list of sightings that Strike had emailed her. There hadn't seemed anything very interesting there.

'A woman asked for change in a pub, and the landlady thought she was Margot. A mature student came forward two days later to identify herself, but the landlady wasn't convinced that was who she'd seen. The police were, though.'

Strike took another large mouthful of cake before saying,

'I don't think there's anything in it. Well . . .' he swallowed and shot a meaningful look at the sitting room door, 'there's a bit more *now*.'

Strike continued to eat cake, while Robin's eyes roamed the room and landed on an ormolu mantel clock of exceptional ugliness. With a glance at the door, she got up to examine it. A gilded classical goddess wearing a helmet sat on top of the ornate, heavy case.

'Pallas Athena,' said Strike, watching her, pointing his fork at the figure.

In the base of the clock was a drawer with a small brass handle. Remembering Cynthia's statement about Roy and Margot leaving notes for each other here, she pulled the drawer open. It was lined in red felt and empty.

'D'you think it's valuable?' she asked Strike, sliding the drawer shut.

'Dunno. Why?'

'Because why else would you keep it? It's horrible.'

There were two distinct kinds of taste on view in this room and they didn't harmonise, Robin thought, as she looked around, all the time listening out for the return of the family. The leather-bound copies of Ovid and Pliny, and the Victorian reproductions of classical statues, among them a pair of miniature Medici lions, a reproduction Vestal virgin and a Hermes poised on tiptoe on his heavy bronze base, presumably represented Roy's father's taste, whereas she suspected that his mother had chosen the insipid watercolour landscapes and botanical subjects, the dainty antique furniture and the chintz curtains.

Why had Roy never made a clean sweep and redecorated, Robin wondered. Reverence for his parents? Lack of imagination? Or had the sickly little boy, housebound no doubt for much of his childhood, developed an attachment to these objects that he couldn't put aside? He and Cynthia seemed to have made little impression on the room other than in adding a few family pictures to faded black and white photos featuring Roy's parents and Roy as a child. The only one to hold Robin's interest was a family group that looked as though it had been taken in the early nineties, when Roy had still had all his hair, and Cynthia's had been thick and wavy. Their two biological children, a boy and a girl, looked like Anna. Nobody would have guessed that she'd had a different mother.

Robin moved to the window. The surface of the long, formal koi pond outside, with its stone pavilion at the end, was now so densely rain-pocked that the vivid red, white and black shapes moving beneath the surface were barely discernible as fish. There was one particularly big creature, pearl white and black, that looked as though it might be over two feet long. The miniature pavilion would normally be reflected in the pond's smooth surface, but today it merely added an extra layer of diffuse grey to the far end of the pond. It had a strangely familiar design on the floor.

'Cormoran,' Robin said, at the exact moment Strike said,

'Look at this.'

Both turned. Strike, who'd finished his cake, was now standing beside one of Roy's father's statuettes, which Robin had overlooked. It was a foot-high bronze of a naked man with a cloth around his shoulders, holding a snake. Momentarily puzzled, Robin realised after a second or two why Strike was pointing at it.

'Oh . . . the snaky invented sign Talbot gave Roy?'

'Precisely. This is Asclepius,' said Strike. 'Greek god of medicine. What've you found?'

'Look on the floor of the gazebo thing. Inlaid in the stone.'

He joined her at the window.

'Ah,' he said. 'You can see the beginnings of that in one of the photographs of Margot's barbecue. It was under construction.'

A cross of St John lay on the floor of the gazebo, inlaid in darker granite. 'Interesting choice of design,' said Strike.

'You know,' said Robin, turning to look at the room, 'people who're manic often think they're receiving supernatural messages. Things the sane would call coincidences.'

'I was thinking exactly that,' said Strike, turning to look at the figure of Pallas Athena, on top of the ugly mantel clock. 'To a man in Talbot's state of mental confusion, I'm guessing this room would've seemed crammed with astrological—'

Roy's voice sounded in the hall outside.

'—then don't blame me—'

The door opened and the family filed back inside.

'—if she hears things she doesn't like!' Roy finished, addressing Cynthia, who was immediately behind him, and looked scared. Roy's face was an unhealthy purple again, though the skin around his eyes remained a jaundiced yellow.

He seemed startled to see Strike and Robin standing at the window.

'Admiring your garden,' said Strike, as he and Robin returned to their sofa.

Roy grunted and took his seat again. He was breathing heavily.

'Apologies,' he said, after a moment or two. 'You aren't seeing the family at its best.'

'Very stressful for everyone,' said Strike, as Anna and Kim re-entered the room and resumed their seats on the sofa, where they sat holding hands. Cynthia perched herself beside them, watching Roy anxiously.

'I want to say something,' Roy told Strike. 'I want to make it perfectly clear—'

'Oh for God's sake, I've had *one* phone call with her!' said Anna.

'I'd appreciate it, Anna,' said Roy, his chest labouring, 'if I could finish.'

Addressing Strike, he said,

'Oonagh Kennedy disliked me from the moment Margot and I first met. She was possessive towards Margot, and she also happened to have left the church, and she was one of those who had to make an enemy of everyone still in it. Moreover—'

'Dr Phipps,' interrupted Strike, who could foresee the afternoon degenerating into a long row about Oonagh Kennedy. 'I think you should know that when we interviewed Oonagh, she made it quite clear that the person she thought we should be concentrating our energies on is Paul Satchwell.'

For a second or two, Roy appeared unable to fully grasp what had just been said to him.

'*See?*' said Anna furiously. 'You just implied that there was more between my mother and Satchwell than one drink. What did you mean? Or were you,' she said, and Robin heard the underlying hope, 'just angry and lashing out?'

'People who insist on opening cans of worms, Anna,' said Roy, 'shouldn't complain when they get covered in slime.'

'Well, go on then,' said Anna, 'spill your slime.'

'Anna,' whispered Cynthia, and was ignored.

'All right,' said Roy. 'All right, then.' He turned back to Strike and Robin. 'Early in our relationship, I saw a note of Satchwell's Margot had kept. "Dear Brunhilda" it said – it was his pet name for her. The Valkyrie, you know. Margot was tall. Fair.'

Roy paused and swallowed.

'Some three weeks before she disappeared, she came home and told me she'd run into Satchwell in the street and that they'd gone for an . . . *innocent* drink.'

He cleared his throat. Cynthia poured him more tea.

'After she – after she'd disappeared, I had to go and collect her things from the St John's practice. Among them I found a small—'

He held his fingers some three inches apart.

'—wooden figure, a stylised Viking which she'd been keeping on her desk. Written in ink on this figure's base was "Brunhilda", with a small heart.'

Roy took a sip of coffee.

'I'd never seen it before. Of course, it's *possible*

that Satchwell was carrying it around with him for years, on the off chance that he'd one day bump into Margot in the street. However, I concluded that they'd seen each other again and that he'd given her this – this token – on a subsequent occasion. All I know is, I'd never seen it before I collected her things from her surgery.'

Robin could tell that Anna wanted to suggest an alternative explanation, but it was very difficult to find a flaw in Roy's reasoning.

'Did you tell the police what you suspected?' Strike asked.

'Yes,' said Phipps, 'and I believe Satchwell claimed that there'd been no second meeting, that he'd given the figurine to Margot years before, when they were first involved. They couldn't prove it either way, of course. But *I'd* never seen it before.'

Robin wondered which would be more hurtful: finding out that a spouse had hidden a love token from a former partner, and taken to displaying it many years later, or that they'd been given it recently.

'Tell me,' Strike was saying, 'did Margot ever tell you anything about a "pillow dream"?'

'A what?' said Roy.

'Something Satchwell had told her, concerning a pillow?'

'I don't know what you're talking about,' said Roy, suspiciously.

'Did Inspector Talbot ever happen to mention

that he believed Satchwell lied about his where-abouts on the eleventh of October?'

'No,' said Roy, now looking very surprised. 'I understood the police were entirely satisfied with his alibi.'

'We've found out,' Strike said, addressing Anna, 'that Talbot kept his own separate case notes – separate from the official police record, I mean. After appearing to rule out Aries, he went back to him and started digging for more information on him.'

'"Aries"?' repeated Anna, confused.

'Sorry,' said Strike, irritated by his own lapse into astrological speak. 'Talbot's breakdown mani-fested itself as a belief he could solve the case by occult means. He started using tarot cards and looking at horoscopes. He referred to everyone connected with the case by their star signs. Satchwell was born under the sign of Aries, so that's what he's called in Talbot's private notes.'

There was a brief silence, and then Kim said, 'Jesus wept.'

'Astrology?' said Roy, apparently confounded.

'You *see*, Dad?' said Anna, thumping her knee with her fist. 'If Lawson had taken over earlier—'

'Lawson was a fool,' said Roy, who nevertheless looked shaken. 'An idiot! He was more interested in proving that Talbot had been inept than in finding out what happened to Margot. He insisted on going back over *everything*. He wanted to personally interview the doctors who'd treated me for the bleed on my knee, even though they'd given signed statements. He went back to my bank to check my accounts, in case I'd paid someone to kill your mother. He put pressure . . .'

He stopped and coughed, thumping his chest. Cynthia began to rise off the sofa, but Roy indicated with an angry gesture that she should stay put.

'. . . put pressure on Cynthia, trying to get her to admit she'd lied about me being in bed all that day, but he never found out a shred of new information about what had happened to your mother. He was a jobsworth, a bullying, unimaginative jobsworth whose priority wasn't finding *her*, it was proving that Talbot messed up. Bill Talbot may have been . . . he clearly *was*,' Roy added, with a furious glance at Strike, 'unwell, but the simple fact remains: nobody's ever found a better explanation than Creed, have they?'

And with the mention of Creed, the faces of the three women on the sofa fell. His very name seemed to conjure a kind of black hole in the room, into which living women had disappeared, never to be seen again; a manifestation of almost supernatural evil. There was a finality in the very mention of him: the monster, now locked away for life, untouchable, unreachable, like the women locked up and tortured in his basement. And Robin's thoughts darted guiltily to the email she had now written, and sent, without telling Strike what she'd done, because she was afraid he might not approve.

'Do any of you know,' Roy asked abruptly, 'who Kara Wolfson and Louise Tucker were?'

'Yes,' said Robin, before Strike could answer. 'Louise was a teenage runaway and Kara was a nightclub hostess. Creed was suspected of killing both of them, but there was no proof.'

'Exactly,' said Roy, throwing her the kind of look he might once have given a medical student who had made a correct diagnosis. 'Well, in 1978 I met up with Kara's brother and Louise's father.'

'I never knew you did that!' said Anna, looking shocked.

'Of course not. You were five years old,' snapped Roy. He turned back to Strike and Robin. 'Louise's father had made his own study of Creed's life. He'd gone to every place Creed had ever lived or worked and interviewed as many people who'd admit to knowing him. He was petitioning Merlyn-Rees, the then Home Secretary, to let him go and dig in as many of these places as possible.

'The man was half-insane,' said Roy. 'I saw then what living with something like this could do to you. The obsession had taken over his entire life. He wanted buildings dismantled, walls taken down, foundations exposed. Fields where Creed might once have walked, dug up. Streams dragged, which some schoolboy friend said Creed might have once gone fishing in. Tucker was shaking as he talked, trying to get me and Wolfson, who was a lorry driver, to join him in a TV campaign. We were to chain ourselves to the railings outside Downing Street, get ourselves on the news . . . Tucker's marriage had split up. He seemed on bad terms with his living children. Creed had become his whole life.'

'And you didn't want to help?' asked Anna.

'If,' said Roy quietly, 'he'd had actual evidence – any solid clue that linked Margot and Creed—'

'I've read you thought one of the necklaces in the basement might've been—'

'If you will get your information from sensationalist books, Anna—'

'Because you've always made it so *easy* for me to talk to you about my mother,' said Anna. 'Haven't you?'

'Anna,' whispered Cynthia again.

'The locket they found in Creed's basement wasn't Margot's, and I should know, because I gave it to her,' said Roy. His lips trembled, and he pressed them together.

'Just a couple more questions, if you wouldn't mind,' said Strike, before Anna could say anything else. He was determined to avert further conflict if he could. 'Could we talk for a moment about Wilma, the cleaner who worked at the practice and did housework for you here, as well?'

'It was all Margot's idea, hiring her, but she wasn't very good,' said Roy. 'The woman was having some personal difficulties and Margot thought the solution was more money. After Margot disappeared, she walked out. Never turned up again. No loss. I heard afterwards she'd been sacked from the practice. Pilfering, I heard.'

'Wilma told police—'

'That there was blood on the carpet upstairs, the day Margot went missing,' interrupted Roy. From Anna and Kim's startled expressions, Robin deduced that this was entirely new information to them.

'Yes,' said Strike.

'It was menstrual,' said Roy coldly. 'Margot's period had started overnight. There were sanitary wrappers in the bathroom, my mother told me. Wilma sponged the carpet clean. This was in the spare room, at the opposite end of the house to the marital bedroom. Margot and I were sleeping apart at that time, because of,' there was a slight hesitation, 'my injury.'

'Wilma also said that she thought she'd seen you—'

'Walking across the garden,' said Roy. 'It was a lie. If she saw anyone, it would have been one of the stonemasons. We were finishing the gazebo at that time,' he said, pointing towards the stone folly at the end of the fishpond.

Strike made a note and turned over a page in his notebook.

'Can either of you remember Margot talking about a man called Niccolo Ricci? He was a patient at the St John's practice.'

Both Roy and Cynthia shook their heads.

'What about a patient called Steven Douthwaite?'

'No,' said Roy. 'But we heard about him afterwards, from the press.'

'Someone at the barbecue mentioned that
Margot had been sent chocolates by a patient,'
said Cynthia. 'That was him, wasn't it?'

'We think so. She never talked about Douthwaite,
then? Never mentioned him showing an inappropriate interest in her, or told you he was gay?'

'No,' said Roy again. 'There's such a thing as
patient confidentiality, you know.'

'This might seem an odd question,' said Strike,
'but did Margot have any scars? Specifically, on
her ribcage?'

'No,' said Roy, unsettled. 'Why are you asking that?'

'To exclude one possibility,' said Strike, and
before they could ask for further details, he said,

'Did Margot ever tell you she'd received threatening notes?'

'Yes,' said Roy. 'Well, not notes in the plural. She
told me she'd got *one*.'

'She did?' said Strike, looking up.

'Yes. It accused her of encouraging young women
into promiscuity and sin.'

'Did it threaten her?'

'I don't know,' said Roy. 'I never saw it.'

'She didn't bring it home?'

'No,' said Roy shortly. He hesitated, then said,
'We had a row about it.'

'Really?'

'Yes. There can be serious consequences,' said
Roy, turning redder, '*societal* consequences, when

you start enabling things that don't take place in nature—'

'Are you worried she told some girl it was OK to be gay?' asked Anna, and yet again Cynthia whispered, '*Anna!*'

'I'm talking,' said Roy, his face congested, 'about giving reckless advice that might lead to marital breakdown. I'm talking about facilitating promiscuity, behind the backs of parents. Some very angry man had sent her that note, and she never seemed to have considered – considered—'

Roy's face worked. For a moment, it looked as though he was going to shout, but then, most unexpectedly, he burst into noisy tears.

His wife, daughter and daughter-in-law sat, stunned, in a row on the sofa; nobody, even Cynthia, went to him. Roy was suddenly crying in great heaving gulps, tears streaming down over his sunken cheeks, trying and failing to master himself, and finally speaking through the sobs.

'She – never seemed – to remember – that I couldn't – protect her – couldn't – do anything – if somebody tried – to hurt – because I'm a useless – bleeder . . . *useless . . . bloody . . . bleeder . . .*'

'Oh *Dad*,' whispered Anna, horrified, and she slid off the sofa and walked to her father on her knees. She tried to place her hands on his leg, but he batted her consoling hands away, shaking his head, still crying.

'No – no – I don't deserve it – you don't know everything – you don't know—'

'What don't I know?' she said, looking scared. 'Dad, I know more than you think. I know about the abortion—'

'There was never – never – *never* an abortion!' said Roy, gulping and sobbing. 'That was the one – one thing Oonagh Kennedy and I – we both knew – she'd *never – never* – not after you! She told me – Margot told me – after she had you – changed her views completely. *Completely!*'

'Then what don't I know?' whispered Anna.

'I was – I was c- cruel to her!' wailed Roy. 'I was! I made things difficult! Showed no interest in her work. I drove her away! She was going to l- leave me . . . I know what happened. I know. I've always known. The day before – before she went – she left a message – in the clock – silly – thing we used to – and the note said – *Please t- talk to me . . .'*

Roy's sobs overtook him. As Cynthia got up and went to kneel on Roy's other side, Anna reached for her father's hand, and this time, he let her hold it. Clinging to his daughter, he said,

'I was waiting – for an apology. For going to drink – with Satchwell. And because she hadn't – written an apology – I didn't t- talk to her. And the next day—'

'I know what happened. She liked to walk. If she was upset – long walks. She forgot about Oonagh – went for a walk – trying to decide what to do – leave me – because I'd made her – so – so

630

sad. She wasn't – paying attention – and Creed – and Creed – must have . . .'

Still holding his hand, Anna slid her other arm around her father's shaking shoulders and drew her to him. He cried inconsolably, clinging to her. Strike and Robin both pretended an interest in the flowered rug.

'Roy,' said Kim gently, at last. 'Nobody in this room hasn't said or done things they don't bitterly regret. Not one of us.'

Strike, who'd got far more out of Roy Phipps than he'd expected, thought it was time to draw the interview to a close. Phipps was in such a state of distress that it felt inhumane to press him further. When Roy's sobs had subsided a little, Strike said formally,

'I want to thank you very much for talking to us, and for the tea. We'll get out of your hair.'

He and Robin got to their feet. Roy remained entangled with his wife and daughter. Kim stood up to show them out.

'*Well*,' Kim said quietly, as they approached the front door, 'I have to tell you, that was . . . well, close to a miracle. He's never talked about Margot like that, *ever*. Even if you don't find out anything else . . . thank you. That was . . . healing.'

The rain had ceased and the sun had come out. A double rainbow lay over the woods opposite the house. Strike and Robin stepped outside, into clean fresh air.

'Could I ask you one last thing?' said Strike, turning back to Kim who stood in the doorway.

'Yes, of course.'

'It's about that summer house thing in the garden, beside the koi pond. I wondered why it's got a cross of St John on the floor,' said Strike.

'*Oh*,' said Kim. 'Margot chose the design. Yes, Cynthia told me, ages ago. Margot had just got the job at St John's – and funnily enough, this area's got a connection to the Knights Hospitaller, too—'

'Yes,' said Robin. 'I read about that, at Hampton Court.'

'So, she thought it would be a nice allusion to the two things . . . You know, now you mention it, I'm surprised nobody ever changed it. Every other trace of Margot's gone from the house.'

'Expensive, though,' said Strike, 'to remove slabs of granite.'

'Yes,' said Kim, her smile fading a little. 'I suppose it would be.'

CHAPTER 37

Spring-headed Hydres, and sea-shouldring
  Whales,
Great whirlpooles, which all fishes make to flee,
Bright Scolopendraes, arm'd with siluer scales
Mighty Monoceros, with immeasured tayles . . .
The dreadfull Fish, that hath deseru'd the name
Of Death . . .

Edmund Spenser
The Faerie Queene

Rain fell almost ceaselessly into February. On the fifth, the most savage storm yet hit the south. Thousands of homes lost power, part of the sea wall supporting the London-South West railway line collapsed, swathes of farmland disappeared under flood water, roads became rivers and the nightly news featured fields turned to seas of grey water and houses waist-deep in mud. The Prime Minister promised financial assistance, the emergency services scrambled to help the stranded, and high on her hill above the flooded St Mawes, Joan was deprived of a promised visit from Strike and Lucy, because they were unable to reach her either by road or train.

Strike sublimated the guilt he felt for not heading to Cornwall before the weather rendered the journey impossible by working long hours and skimping on sleep. Masochistically, he chose to work back-to-back shifts, so that Barclay and Hutchins could take some of the leave due to them because of his previous trips to see Joan. In consequence, it was Strike, not Hutchins, who was sitting in his BMW in the everlasting rain outside Elinor Dean's house in Stoke Newington on Wednesday evening the following week, and Strike who saw a man in a tracksuit knock on her door and be admitted.

Strike waited all night for the man to reappear. Finally, at six in the morning, he emerged onto the still dark street with his hand clamped over his lower face. Strike, who was watching him through night vision glasses, caught a glimpse of Elinor Dean in a cosy quilted dressing gown, waving him off. The tracksuited man hurried back to his Citroën with his right hand still concealing his mouth and set off in a southerly direction.

Strike tailed the Citroën until they reached Risinghill Street in Pentonville, where Strike's target parked and entered a modern, red-brick block of flats, both hands now in his pockets and nothing unusual about his mouth as far as the detective could see. Strike waited until the man was safely inside, took a note of which window showed a light five minutes later, then drove away, parking shortly afterwards in White Lion Street.

Early as it was, people were already heading off to work, umbrellas angled against the continuing downpour. Strike wound down the car window, because even he, inveterate smoker though he was, wasn't enjoying the smell of his car after a night's surveillance. Then, though his tongue ached from too much smoking, he lit up again and phoned Saul Morris.

'All right, boss?'

Strike, who didn't particularly like Morris calling him 'boss', but couldn't think of any way to ask him to stop without sounding like a dickhead, said,

'I want you to switch targets. Forget Shifty today; I've just followed a new guy who spent the night at Elinor Dean's.' He gave Morris the address. 'He's second floor, flat on the far left as you're looking at the building. Fortyish, greying hair, bit of a paunch. See what you can find out about him – chat up the neighbours, find out where he works and have a dig around online, see if you can find out what his interests are. I've got a hunch he and SB are visiting that woman for the same reason.'

'See, this is why you're the head honcho. You take over for one night and crack the case.'

Strike wished Morris would stop brown-nosing him, too. When he'd hung up, he sat smoking for a while, while the wind nipped at his exposed flesh, and rain hit his face in what felt like icy needle pricks. Then, after checking the time to make sure his early-rising uncle would be awake, he phoned Ted.

'All right, boy?' said his uncle, over the crackling phone line.

'Fine. How are you?'

'Oh, I'm fine,' said Ted. 'Just having some break-fast. Joanie's still asleep.'

'How is she?'

'No change. Bearing up.'

'What about food, have you got enough?'

'We're fine for food, don't you worry about that,' said Ted. 'Little Dave Polworth come over yesterday with enough to feed us for a week.'

'How the hell did he get to you?' asked Strike, who knew that a large chunk of the land between his aunt and uncle and Polworth's house was under several feet of water.

'Rowed part of the way,' said Ted, sounding amused. 'He made it sound like one of his Ironman competitions. All covered in oilskins he was when he got here. Big backpack full of shopping. He's all right, that Polworth.'

'Yeah, he is,' said Strike, momentarily closing his eyes. It oughtn't to be Polworth looking after his aunt and uncle. It should be him. He ought to have left earlier, knowing the weather was looking bad, but for months now he'd been juggling guilt about his aunt and uncle with the guilt he felt about the load he was putting on his subcontractors, and Robin especially. 'Ted, I'll be there as soon as they put the trains back on.'

'Aye, I know you will, lad,' said Ted. 'Don't worry about us. I won't take you to her, because she needs her rest, but I'll tell her you called. She'll be chuffed.'

Tired, hungry and wondering where he might get some breakfast, Strike typed out a text to Dave Polworth, his cigarette jammed between his teeth, using the nickname he'd had for Polworth ever since the latter had got himself bitten by a shark at the age of eighteen.

Ted's just told me what you did yesterday. I'll never be able to repay all this, Chum. Thank you.

He flicked his cigarette end out of the car, wound up the window and had just turned on the engine when his mobile buzzed. Expecting to see a response from Polworth, doubtless asking him when he'd turned into such a poof or a big girl (Polworth's language being always as far from politically correct as you could get), he looked down at the screen, already smiling in anticipation, and read:

Dad wants to call you. When would be a good time?

Strike read the text twice before understanding that it was from Al. At first, he felt only blank surprise. Then anger and profound resentment rose like vomit.

'Fuck off,' he told his phone loudly.

He turned out of the side street and drove away, jaw clenched, wondering why he should be hounded by Rokeby now, of all times in his life, when he was so worried about relatives who'd cared about him when there'd been no kudos to be gained from the association. The time for amends had passed; the damage was irreparable; blood wasn't thicker than fucking water. Consumed by thoughts of frail Joan, with whom he shared no shred of DNA, marooned in her house on the hill amid floods, anger and guilt writhed inside him.

A matter of minutes later, he realised he was driving through Clerkenwell. Spotting an open café on St John Street he parked, then headed through the rain into warmth and light, where he ordered himself an egg and tomato sandwich. Choosing a table by the window, he sat down facing the street, eye to eye with his own unshaven and stony-faced reflection in the rain-studded window.

Hangovers apart, Strike rarely got headaches, but something resembling one was starting to build on the left side of his skull. He ate his sandwich, telling himself firmly that food was making him feel better. Then, after ordering a second mug of tea, he pulled out his mobile again and typed out a response to Al, with the dual objective of shutting down Rokeby once and for all, and of concealing from both his half-brother and his father how much their persistence was disturbing his peace.

I'm not interested. It's too late. I don't want to fall out with you, but take this 'no' as final.

He sent the text and then cast around immediately for something else to occupy his tired mind. The shops opposite were ablaze with red and pink: February the fourteenth was almost here. It now occurred to him that he hadn't heard from Charlotte since he'd ignored her text at Christmas. Would she send him a message on Valentine's Day? Her desire for contact seemed to be triggered by special occasions and anniversaries.

Automatically, without considering what he was doing, but with the same desire for comfort that had pushed him into this café, Strike pulled his phone out of his pocket again and called Robin, but the number was engaged. Shoving the mobile back in his pocket, stressed, anxious and craving action, he told himself he should make use of being in Clerkenwell, now he was here.

This café was only a short walk from the old St John's surgery. How many of these passers-by, he wondered, had lived in the area forty years previously? The hunched old woman in her raincoat with her tartan shopping trolley? The grey-whiskered man trying to flag down a cab? Perhaps the ageing Sikh man in his turban, texting as he walked? Had any of them consulted Margot Bamborough? Could any of them remember a dirty, bearded man called something like Applethorpe, who'd roamed these very streets, insisting to strangers that he'd killed the doctor?

Strike's absent gaze fell on a man walking with a strange, rolling gait on the opposite side of the road. His fine, mousy hair was rain-soaked and plastered to his head. He had neither coat nor umbrella, but wore a sweatshirt with a picture of Sonic the Hedgehog on the front. The lack of coat, the slightly lumbering walk, the wide, childlike stare, the slightly gaping mouth, the stoic acceptance of becoming slowly drenched to the skin: all suggested some kind of cognitive impairment. The man passed out of Strike's line of vision as the detective's mobile rang.

'Hi. Did you just call me?' said Robin, and Strike felt a certain release of tension, and decided the tea was definitely soothing his head.

'I did, yeah. Just for an update.'

He told her the story of the tracksuited man who'd visited Elinor Dean overnight.

'And he was covering up his mouth when he left? That's weird.'

'I know. There's definitely something odd going on in that house. I've asked Morris to dig a bit on the new bloke.'

'Pentonville's right beside Clerkenwell,' said Robin.

'Which is where I am right now. Café on St John Street. I th – think,' a yawn overtook Strike, 'sorry – I think, seeing as I'm in the area, I might have another dig around on the late Applethorpe. Try and find someone who remembers the family, or knows what might've happened to them.'

'How're you going to do that?'

'Walk the area,' said Strike, and he became conscious of his aching knee even as he said it, 'have an ask around in any businesses that look long-established. I kn – know,' he yawned again, 'it's a long shot, but we haven't got anyone else claiming to have killed Margot.'

'Aren't you knackered?'

'Been worse. Where are you right now?'

'Office,' said Robin, 'and I've got a bit of Bamborough news, if you've got time.'

'Go on,' said Strike, happy to postpone the moment when he had to go back out into the rain.

'Well, firstly, I've had an email from Gloria Conti's husband. You know, the receptionist who was the last to see Margot? It's short. "*Dear Mr Ellacott—*"'

'Mister?'

'"Robin" often confuses people. "*I write for my wife, who is been very afflicted by your communications. She has not proofs or information that concern Margot Bamborough and it is not convenient that you contact her at my offices. Our family is private and desires to remain like that. I would like your assurances that you will not contact my wife another time. Yours sincerely, Hugo Jaubert.*"'

'Interesting,' agreed Strike, scratching his unshaven chin. 'Why isn't Gloria emailing back herself? Too afflicted?'

'I wonder why she's so affli – upset, I mean? Maybe,' Robin said, answering her own question, 'because I contacted her through her husband's office? But I tried through Facebook and she wouldn't answer.'

'You know, I think it might be worth getting Anna to contact Gloria. Margot's daughter might tug at her heartstrings better than we can. Why don't you draft another request and send it over to Anna, see whether she'd be comfortable letting you put her name to it?'

'Good thinking,' said Robin, and he heard her scribbling a note. 'Anyway, in better news, when you called me just now, I was talking to Wilma Bayliss's second-oldest daughter, Maya. She's the deputy headmistress. I think I'm close to persuading her to talk to us. She's worried about her older sister's reaction, but I'm hopeful.'

'Great,' said Strike, 'I'd like to hear more about Wilma.'

'And there's one other thing,' said Robin. 'Only, you might think this is a bit of a long shot.'

'I've just told you I'm about to go door to door asking about a dead nutter who definitely wasn't called Applethorpe,' said Strike, and Robin laughed.

'OK, well, I was back online last night, having another look for Steve Douthwaite, and I found this old "Memories of Butlin's" website, where ex-Redcoats chat to each other and reminisce and organise reunions and stuff – you know the kind of thing. Anyway, I couldn't find any mention of Douthwaite, or Jacks, as he was calling himself in Clacton-on-Sea, but I did find – I know it's probably totally irrelevant,' she said, 'and I don't know whether you remember, but a girl called Julie Wilkes was quoted in *Whatever Happened to Margot Bamborough?* She said she was shocked that Stevie Jacks hadn't told his friends that he'd been caught up in a missing woman case.'

'Yeah, I remember,' said Strike.

'Well . . . that girl drowned,' said Robin. 'Drowned at the holiday camp at the end of the 1985 holiday season. Her body was found one morning in the camp swimming pool. A group of them were discussing her death on the message boards on the website. They think she got drunk, slipped, hit her head and slid into the pool.

'Maybe it's horrible luck,' said Robin, 'but women do have a habit of dying in Douthwaite's vicinity, don't they? His married girlfriend kills herself, his doctor goes missing, and then there's this co-worker who drowns . . . Everywhere he goes, unnatural death follows . . . it's just odd.'

'Yeah, it is,' said Strike, frowning out at the rain. He was about to wonder aloud where Douthwaite had hidden himself, when Robin said in a slight rush,

'Listen, there's something else I wanted to ask you, but it's absolutely fine if the answer's no. My flatmate Max – you know he's an actor? Well, he's just been cast in a TV thing as an ex-soldier and he doesn't know anyone else to ask. He wondered whether you'd come over to dinner so he can ask you some questions.'

'Oh,' said Strike, surprised but not displeased. '. . . yeah, OK. When?'

'I know it's short notice, but would tomorrow suit you? He really needs it soon.'

'Yeah, that should be all right,' said Strike. He was holding himself ready to travel down to St Mawes as soon as it became practicable, but the sea wall looked unlikely to be repaired by the following day.

When Robin had hung up, Strike ordered a third mug of tea. He was procrastinating, and he knew why. If he was genuinely going to have a poke around Clerkenwell for anyone who remembered the dead man who claimed to have killed Margot Bamborough, it would help if he knew the man's real name, and as Janice Beattie was still in Dubai, his only recourse was Irene Hickson.

The rain was as heavy as ever. Minute to minute, he postponed the call to Irene, watching traffic moving through the rippling sheets of rain, pedestrians navigating the puddle-pocked street, and thinking about the long-ago death of a young Redcoat, who'd slipped, knocked her head and drowned in a swimming pool.

Water everywhere, Bill Talbot had written in his astrological notebook. It had taken Strike some effort to decipher that particular passage. He'd concluded that Talbot was referring to a cluster of water signs apparently connected with the death of the unknown Scorpio. Why, Strike asked himself now, sipping his tea, was Scorpio a water sign? Scorpions lived on land, in heat; could they even swim? He remembered the large fish sign Talbot had used in the notebook for Irene, which at one point he'd described as 'Cetus'. Picking up his mobile, Strike Googled the word.

The constellation Cetus, he read, known also as the whale, was named for a sea monster slain by Perseus when saving Andromeda from the sea god Poseidon. It resided in a region of the sky known as 'The Sea', due to the presence there of many other water-associated constellations, including Pisces, Aquarius the water bearer, and Capricorn, the fish-tailed goat.

Water everywhere.

The astrological notes were starting to tangle themselves around his thought processes, like an old net snagged in a propeller. A pernicious mixture of sense and nonsense, they mirrored, in Strike's opinion, the appeal of astrology itself, with its flattering, comforting promise that your petty concerns were of interest to the wide universe, and that the stars or the spirit world would guide you where your own hard work and reason couldn't.

Enough, he told himself sternly. Pressing Irene's

number on his mobile, he waited, listening to her phone ringing and visualising it beside the bowl of pot-pourri, in the over-decorated hall, with the pink flowered wallpaper and the thick pink carpet. At exactly the point where he'd decided, with a mixture of relief and regret, that she wasn't in, she answered.

'Double four five nine,' she trilled, making it into a kind of jingle. Joan, too, always answered her landline by telling the caller the number they'd just dialled.

'Is that Mrs Hickson?'

'Speaking.'

'It's Cormoran Strike here, the—'

'Oh, hello!' she yelped, sounding startled.

'I wondered whether you might be able to help me,' said Strike, taking out his notebook and opening it. 'When we last met, you mentioned a patient of the St John's practice who you thought might've been called Apton or Applethorpe—'

'Oh, yes?'

'—who claimed to have—'

'—killed Margot, yes,' she interrupted him. 'He stopped Dorothy in broad daylight—'

'Yes—'

'—but she thought it was a load of rubbish. I said to her, "What if he really did, Dorothy—?"'

'I haven't been able to find anyone of that name who lived in the area in 1974,' said Strike loudly, 'so I wondered whether you might've misremembered his na—'

'Possibly, yes, I might have done,' said Irene. 'Well, it's been a long time, hasn't it? Have you tried directory enquiries? Not directory enquiries,' she corrected herself immediately. 'Online records and things.'

'It's difficult to do a search with the wrong name,' said Strike, just managing to keep his tone free of exasperation or sarcasm. 'I'm right by Clerkenwell Road at the moment. I think you said he lived there?'

'Well, he was always hanging around there, so I assumed so.'

'He was registered with your practice, wasn't he? D'you remember his first—?'

'Um, let me think . . . It was something like . . . Gilbert, or – no, I can't remember, I'm afraid. Applethorpe? Appleton? Apton? *Everyone* knew him locally by sight because he looked so peculiar: long beard, filthy, blah blah blah. And sometimes he had his kid with him,' said Irene, warming up, 'really *funny*-looking kid—'

'Yes, you said—'

'—with *massive* ears. *He* might still be alive, the son, but he's probably – *you* know . . .'

Strike waited, but apparently he was supposed to infer the end of the sentence by Irene's silence.

'Probably—?' he prompted.

'Oh, *you* know. In a place.'

'In—?'

'A home or something!' she said, a little impatiently, as though Strike were being obtuse. 'He

647

was never going to be *right*, was he? – with a druggie father and a retarded mother, I don't care what Jan says. Jan hasn't got the same – well, it's not her fault – her family was – different standards. And she likes to look – in front of strangers – well, we all do – but after all, you're after the truth, aren't you?'

Strike noted the fine needle of malice directed at her friend, glinting among the disconnected phrases.

'Have you found Duckworth?' Irene asked, jumping subject.

'Douthwaite?'

'Oh, what am I like, I keep doing that, hahaha.' However little pleased she'd been to hear from him, he was at least someone to talk to. 'I'd *love* to know what happened to him, I really would, *he* was a fishy character if ever there was one. Jan played it down with you, but she was a bit dis-appointed when he turned out to be gay, you know. She had a soft spot for him. Well, she was very lonely when I first knew her. We used to try and set her up, Eddie and I—'

'Yes, you said—'

'—but men didn't want to take on a kid and Jan was a bit *you* know, when a woman's been alone, I don't mean *desperate*, but clingy – Larry didn't mind, but Larry wasn't exactly—'

'I had one other thing I wanted to ask—'

'—only *he* wouldn't marry her, either. He'd been through a bad divorce—'

'It's about Leamington Spa—'

'You'll have checked Bognor Regis?'

'Excuse me?' said Strike.

'For Douthwaite? Because he went to Bognor Regis, didn't he? To a holiday camp?'

'Clacton-on-Sea,' said Strike. 'Unless he went to Bognor Regis as well?'

'As well as what?'

Jesus fucking Christ.

'What makes you think Douthwaite was ever in Bognor Regis?' Strike asked, slowly and clearly, rubbing his forehead.

'I thought – wasn't he there, at some point?'

'Not as far as I'm aware, but we know he worked in Clacton-on-Sea in the mid-eighties.'

'Oh, it must've been that – yes, someone must've told me that, they're all – old-fashioned seaside – *you* know.'

Strike seemed to remember he'd asked both Irene and Janice whether they had any idea where Douthwaite had gone after he left Clerkenwell, and that both had said they didn't know.

'How did you know he went to work in Clacton-on-Sea?' he asked.

'Jan told me,' said Irene, after a tiny pause. 'Yes, Jan would've told me. *She* was his neighbour, you know, *she* was the one who knew him. Yes, I think she tried to find out where he'd gone after he left Percival Road, because she was worried about him.'

'But this was eleven years later,' said Strike.

649

'What was?'

'He didn't go to Clacton-on-Sea until eleven years after he left Percival Road,' said Strike. 'When I asked you both if you knew where he'd gone—'

'Well, you meant *now*, didn't you?' said Irene, 'where he is *now*? I've no idea. Have you looked into that Leamington Spa business, by the way?' Then she laughed, and said, 'All these seaside places! No, wait – it isn't seaside, is it, not Leamington Spa? But you know what I mean – *water* – I do *love* water, it's – Greenwich, Eddie knew I'd love this house when he spotted it for sale – *was* there anything in that Leamington Spa thing, or was Jan making it up?'

'Mrs Beattie wasn't making it up,' said Strike. 'Mr Ramage definitely saw a missing—'

'Oh, I didn't mean Jan would make it up, no, I don't mean that,' said Irene, instantly contradicting herself. 'I just mean, you know, odd place for Margot to turn up, Leamington – have you found any connection,' she asked airily, 'or—?'

'Not yet,' said Strike. '*You* haven't remembered anything about Margot and Leamington Spa, have you?'

'Me? Goodness, no, how should I know why she'd go there?'

'Well, sometimes people do remember things after we've talked to—'

'Have you spoken to Jan since?'

'No,' said Strike. 'D'you know when she's back from Dubai?'

650

'No,' said Irene. 'All right for some, isn't it? I wouldn't mind some sunshine, the winter we're – but it's wasted on Jan, she doesn't sunbathe, and I wouldn't fancy the flight all that way in Economy, which is how she has to – I wonder how she's getting on, six weeks with her daughter-in-law! Doesn't matter how well you get on, that's a long—'

'Well, I'd better let you get on, Mrs Hickson.'

'Oh, all right,' she said. 'Yes, well. Best of luck with everything.'

'Thank you,' he said, and hung up.

The rain pattered on the window. With a sigh, Strike retired to the café bathroom for a long overdue pee.

He was just paying his bill when he spotted the man in the Sonic the Hedgehog sweatshirt walking past the window, now on the same side of the street as the café. He was heading back the way he'd come, two bulging bags of Tesco shopping hanging from his hands, moving with that same odd, rocking, side-to-side gait, his soaking hair flat to his skull, his mouth slightly open. Strike's eyes followed him as he passed, watching the rain drip off the bottom of his shopping bags and from the lobes of his particularly large ears.

CHAPTER 38

So long in secret cabin there he held
Her captive to his sensual desire;
Till that with timely fruit her belly swell'd,
And bore a boy unto that salvage sire . . .

Edmund Spenser
The Faerie Queene

Asking himself whether he could possibly have got as lucky as he hoped, Strike threw a tip on the table and hurried outside into the driving rain, pulling on his coat as he went.

If the mentally impaired adult in the sopping Sonic sweatshirt was indeed the big-eared child once marched around these streets by his eccentric parent, he'd have been living in this corner of Clerkenwell for forty years. Well, people did that, of course, Strike reflected, particularly if they had support there and if their whole world was a few familiar streets. The man was still within sight, heading stolidly towards Clerkenwell Road in the pelting rain, neither speeding up, nor making any attempt to prevent himself becoming progressively more sodden. Strike turned up his coat collar and followed.

A short distance down St John Street, Strike's target turned right past a small ironmonger's on the corner, and headed into Albemarle Way, the short street with an old red telephone box at the other end, and tall, unbroken buildings on either side. Strike's interest quickened.

Just past the ironmonger's, the man set down both of his shopping bags on the wet pavement and took out a door key. Strike kept walking, because there was nowhere to hide, but made a note of the door number as he passed. Was it possible that the late Applethorpe had lived in this very flat? Hadn't Strike thought that Albemarle Way presented a promising place to lie in wait for a victim? Not, perhaps, as good as Passing Alley, nor as convenient as the flats along Jerusalem Passage, but better by far than busy Clerkenwell Green, where Talbot had been convinced that Margot had struggled with a disguised Dennis Creed.

Strike heard the front door close behind the large-eared man and doubled back. The dark blue door needed painting. A small push-button bell was beside it, beneath which was stuck the printed name 'Athorn'. Could this be the name Irene had misremembered as Applethorpe, Appleton or Apton? Then Strike noticed that the man had left the key in the lock.

With a feeling that he might have been far too dismissive of the mysterious ways of the universe, Strike pulled out the key and pressed the doorbell, which rang loudly inside. For a moment or two, nothing happened, then the door opened again and there stood the man in the wet Sonic sweatshirt.

'You left this in the lock,' said Strike, holding out the key.

The man addressed the third button of Strike's overcoat rather than look him in eye.

'I did that before and Clare said not to again,' he mumbled, holding out his hand for the key, which Strike gave him. The man began to close the door.

'My name's Cormoran Strike. I wonder whether I could come in and talk to you about your father?' Strike said, not quite putting his foot in the door, but preparing to do so should it be required.

The other's big-eared face stood out, pale, against the dark hall.

'My-Dad-Gwilherm's dead.'

'Yes,' said Strike, 'I know.'

'He carried me on his shoulders.'

'Did he?'

'Yeah. Mum told me.'

'D'you live alone?'

'I live with Mum.'

'Is her name Clare?'

'No. Deborah.'

654

'I'm a detective,' said Strike, pulling a card out of his pocket. 'My name's Cormoran Strike and I'd really like to talk to your mum, if that's OK.'

The man didn't take the card, but looked at it out of the corner of his eye. Strike suspected that he couldn't read.

'Would that be all right?' Strike asked, as the cold rain continued to fall.

'Yer, OK. You can come in,' said the other, still addressing Strike's coat button, and he opened the door fully to admit the detective. Without waiting to see whether Strike was following, he headed up the dark staircase inside.

Strike felt some qualms about capitalising on the vulnerabilities of a man like Athorn, but the prospect of looking around what he now strongly suspected was the flat in which the self-proclaimed killer of Margot Bamborough had been living in 1974 was irresistible. After wiping his feet carefully on the doormat, Strike closed the door behind him, spotting as he did so a couple of letters lying on the floor, which the son of the house had simply walked over; one of them carried a wet footprint. Strike picked up the letters, then climbed the bare wooden stairs, over which hung a naked, non-functioning light bulb.

As he climbed, Strike indulged himself with the fantasy of a flat which nobody other than the inhabitants had entered for forty years, with locked cupboards and rooms, or even – it had been known to happen – a skeleton lying in open view. For a split-second, as he stepped out onto the landing, his hopes surged: the oven in the tiny kitchen straight ahead looked as though it dated from the seventies, as did the brown wall tiles, but unfortunately, from a detective point of view, the flat looked neat and smelled fresh and clean. There were even recent Hoover marks on the old carpet, which was patterned in orange and brown swirls. The Tesco bags sat waiting to be unpacked on lino that was scuffed, but that had been recently washed.

To Strike's right stood an open door onto a small sitting room. The man he'd followed was standing there, facing a much older woman, who was sitting crocheting in an armchair beside the window. She looked, as well she might, shocked to see a large stranger standing in her hall.

'He wants to talk to you,' announced the man.

'Only if you're comfortable with that, Mrs Athorn,' Strike called from the landing. He wished Robin was with him. She was particularly good at putting nervous women at their ease. He remembered that Janice had said that this woman was agoraphobic. 'My name's Cormoran Strike and I wanted to ask a few questions about your husband. But if you're not happy, of course, I'll leave immediately.'

'I'm cold,' said the man loudly.

'Change your clothes,' his mother advised him. 'You've got wet. Why don't you wear your coat?'

'Too tight,' he said, 'you silly woman.'

He turned and walked out of the room past

Strike, who stood back to let him pass. Gwilherm's son disappeared into a room opposite, on the door of which the name 'Samhain' appeared in painted wooden letters.

Samhain's mother didn't appear to enjoy eye contact any more than her son did. At last, addressing Strike's knees, she said,

'All right. Come in, then.'

'Thanks very much.'

Two budgerigars, one blue, one green, chirruped in a cage in the corner of the sitting room. Samhain's mother had been crocheting a patchwork blanket. A number of completed woollen squares were piled on the wide windowsill beside her and a basket of wools sat at her feet. A huge jigsaw mat was spread out on a large ottoman in front of the sofa. It bore a two-thirds completed puzzle of unicorns. As far as tidiness went, the sitting room compared very favourably with Gregory Talbot's.

'You've got some letters,' Strike said, and he held up the damp envelopes to show her.

'You open them,' she said.

'I don't think—'

'You open them,' she repeated.

She had the same big ears as Samhain and the same slight underbite. These imperfections notwithstanding, there was a prettiness in her soft face and in her dark eyes. Her long, neatly plaited hair was white. She had to be at least sixty, but her smooth skin was that of a much younger woman. There was a strangely otherworldly air about her as she sat, plying her crochet hook beside the rainy window, shut away from the world. Strike wondered whether she could read. He felt safe to open the envelopes that were clearly junk mail, and did so.

'You've been sent a seed catalogue,' he said, showing her, 'and a letter from a furniture shop.'

'I don't want them,' said the woman beside the window, still talking to Strike's legs. 'You can sit down,' she added.

He sidled carefully between the sofa and the ottoman which, like Strike himself, was far too big for this small room. Having successfully avoided nudging the enormous jigsaw, he took a seat at a respectful distance from the crocheting woman.

'This one,' said Strike, referring to the last letter, 'is for Clare Spencer. Do you know her?'

The letter didn't have a stamp. Judging by the address on the back, the letter was from the ironmonger downstairs.

'Clare's our social worker,' she said. 'You can open it.'

'I don't think I should do that,' said Strike. 'I'll leave it for Clare. You're Deborah, is that right?'

'Yes,' she murmured.

Samhain reappeared in the door. He was now barefoot but wearing dry jeans and a fresh sweatshirt with Spider-Man on the front.

'I'm going to put things in the fridge,' he announced, and disappeared again.

'Samhain does the shopping now,' Deborah said, with a glance at Strike's shoes. Though timid, she didn't seem averse to talking to him.

'Deborah, I'm here to ask you about Gwilherm,' Strike said.

'He's not here.'

'No, I—'

'He died.'

'Yes,' said Strike. 'I'm sorry. I'm really here because of a doctor who used to work—'

'Dr Brenner,' she said at once.

'You remember Dr Brenner?' said Strike, surprised.

'I didn't like him,' she said.

'Well, I wanted to ask you about a *different* doc—'

Samhain reappeared at the sitting room door and said loudly to his mother,

'D'you want a hot chocolate, or not?'

'Yes,' she said.

'Do *you* want a hot chocolate, or not?' Samhain demanded of Strike.

'Yes please,' Strike said, on the principle that all friendly gestures should be accepted in such situations.

Samhain lumbered out of sight. Pausing in her crocheting, Deborah pointed at something straight ahead of her and said,

'That's Gwilherm, there.'

Strike looked around. An Egyptian ankh, the symbol of eternal life, had been drawn on the wall behind the old TV. The walls were pale yellow everywhere except behind the ankh, where a patch of dirty green survived. In front of the ankh, on top of the flat-topped television set, was a black object which Strike at first glance took for a vase. Then he spotted the stylised dove on it, realised that it was an urn and understood, finally, what he was being told.

'Ah,' said Strike. 'Those are Gwilherm's ashes, are they?'

'I told Tudor to get the one with the bird, because I like birds.'

One of the budgerigars fluttered suddenly across the cage in a blur of bright green and yellow.

'Who painted that?' asked Strike, pointing at the ankh.

'Gwilherm,' said Deborah, continuing to dextrously ply her crochet hook.

Samhain re-entered the room, holding a tin tray.

'Not on my jigsaw,' his mother warned him, but there was no other free surface.

'Should I—?' offered Strike, gesturing towards the puzzle, but there was no space anywhere on the floor to accommodate it.

'You close it,' Deborah told him, with a hint of reproach, and Strike saw that the jigsaw mat had wings, which could be fastened to protect the puzzle. He did so, and Samhain laid the tray on top. Deborah stuck her crochet hook carefully in the ball of wool and accepted a mug of instant hot chocolate and a Penguin biscuit from her son. Samhain kept the Batman mug for himself. Strike sipped his drink and said, 'Very nice,' not entirely dishonestly.

'I make good hot chocolate, don't I, Deborah?' said Samhain, unwrapping a biscuit.

'Yes,' said Deborah, blowing on the surface of the hot liquid.

'I know this was a long time ago,' Strike began again, 'but there was another doctor, who worked with Dr Brenner—'

'Old Joe Brenner was a dirty old man,' said Samhain Athorn, with a cackle.

Strike looked at him in surprise. Samhain directed his smirk at the closed jigsaw.

'Why was he a dirty old man?' asked the detective.

'My Uncle Tudor told me,' said Samhain. '*Dirty old man*. Hahahaha. Is this mine?' he asked, picking up the envelope addressed to Clare Spencer.

'No,' said his mother. 'That's Clare's.'

'Why is it?'

'I think,' said Strike, 'it's from your downstairs neighbour.'

'He's a bastard,' said Samhain, putting the letter back down. 'He made us throw everything away, didn't he, Deborah?'

'I like it better now,' said Deborah mildly. 'It's good now.'

Strike allowed a moment or two to pass, in case Samhain had more to add, then asked,

'Why did Uncle Tudor say Joseph Brenner was a dirty old man?'

'Tudor knew everything about everyone,' said Deborah placidly.

'Who was Tudor?' Strike asked her.

'Gwilherm's brother,' said Deborah. 'He always knew about people round here.'

'Does he still visit you?' asked Strike, suspecting the answer.

'Passed-away-to-the-other side,' said Deborah, as though it was one long word. 'He used to buy our shopping. He took Sammy to play football and to the swimming.'

'I do all the shopping now,' piped up Samhain. 'Sometimes I don't want to do the shopping but if I don't, I get hungry, and Deborah says, "It's your fault there's nothing to eat." So then I go shopping.'

'Good move,' said Strike.

The three of them drank their hot chocolate.

'Dirty old man, Joe Brenner,' repeated Samhain, more loudly. 'Uncle Tudor used to tell me some stories. Old Betty and the one who wouldn't pay, hahahaha. Dirty old Joe Brenner.'

'I didn't like him,' said Deborah quietly. 'He wanted me to take my pants off.'

'Really?' said Strike.

While this had surely been a question of a medical examination, he felt uncomfortable.

'Yes, to look at me,' said Deborah. 'I didn't want it. Gwilherm wanted it, but I don't like men I don't know looking at me.'

'No, well, I can understand that,' said Strike. 'You were ill, were you?'

'Gwilherm said I had to,' was her only response.

If he'd still been in the Special Investigation Branch, there would have been a female officer

662

with him for this interview. Strike wondered what her IQ was.

'Did you ever meet Dr Bamborough?' he asked. 'She was,' he hesitated, 'a lady doctor.'

'I've never seen a lady doctor,' said Deborah, with what sounded like regret.

'D'you know whether Gwilherm ever met Dr Bamborough?'

'She died,' said Deborah.

'Yes,' said Strike, surprised. 'People think she died, but no one knows for s—'

One of the budgerigars made the little bell hanging from the top of its cage tinkle. Both Deborah and Samhain looked around, smiling.

'Which one was it?' Deborah asked Samhain.

'Bluey,' he said. 'Bluey's cleverer'n Billy Bob.'

Strike waited for them to lose interest in the budgerigars, which took a couple of minutes. When both Athorns' attention had returned to their hot chocolates, he said,

'Dr Bamborough disappeared and I'm trying to find out what happened to her. I've been told that Gwilherm talked about Dr Bamborough, after she went missing.'

Deborah didn't respond. It was hard to know whether she was listening, or deliberately ignoring him.

'I heard,' said Strike – there was no point not saying it; this was the whole reason he was here, after all – 'that Gwilherm told people he killed her.'

Deborah glanced at Strike's left ear, then back at her hot chocolate.

'You're like Tudor,' she said. 'You know what's what. He probably did,' she added placidly.

'You mean,' said Strike carefully, 'he told people about it?'

She didn't answer.

'. . . or you think he killed the doctor?'

'Was My-Dad-Gwilherm doing magic on her?' Samhain enquired of his mother. 'My-Dad-Gwilherm didn't kill that lady. My uncle Tudor told me what really happened.'

'What did your uncle tell you?' asked Strike, turning from mother to son, but Samhain had just crammed his mouth full of chocolate biscuit, so Deborah continued the story.

'He woke me up one time when I was asleep,' said Deborah, 'and it was dark. He said, "I killed a lady by mistake." I said, "You've had a bad dream." He said, "No, no, I've killed her, but I didn't mean it."'

'Woke you up to tell you, did he?'

'Woke me up, all upset.'

'But you think it was just a bad dream?'

'Yes,' said Deborah, but then, after a moment or two, she said, 'but maybe he did kill her, because he could do magic.'

'I see,' said Strike untruthfully, turning back to Samhain.

'What did your Uncle Tudor say happened to the lady doctor?'

'I can't tell you that,' said Samhain, suddenly grinning. 'Uncle Tudor said not to tell. Never.' But he grinned with a Puckish delight at having a secret. 'My-Dad-Gwilherm did that,' he went on, pointing at the ankh on the wall.

'Yes,' said Strike, 'your mum told me.'

'I don't like it,' said Deborah placidly, looking at the ankh. 'I'd like it if the walls were all the same.'

'I like it,' said Samhain, 'because it's different from the other walls . . . you silly woman,' he added abstractedly.

'Did Uncle Tudor—' began Strike, but Samhain, who'd finished his biscuit, now got to his feet and left the room, pausing in the doorway to say loudly,

'Clare says it's nice I still got things of Gwilherm's!'

He disappeared into his bedroom and closed the door firmly behind him. With the feeling he'd just seen a gold sovereign bounce down a grate, Strike turned back to Deborah.

'Do *you* know what Tudor said happened to the doctor?'

She shook her head, uninterested. Strike looked hopefully back towards Samhain's bedroom door. It remained closed.

'Can you remember *how* Gwilherm thought he'd killed the doctor?' he asked Deborah.

'He said his magic killed her, then took her away.'

'Took her away, did it?'

Samhain's bedroom door suddenly opened

again and he trudged back into the room, holding a coverless book in his hand.

'Deborah, is this My-Dad-Gwilherm's magic book, is it?'

'That's it,' said Deborah.

She'd finished her hot chocolate, now. Setting down the empty mug, she picked up her crochet again.

Samhain held the book wordlessly out to Strike. Though the cover had come off, the title page was intact: *The Magus* by Francis Barrett. Strike had the impression that being shown this book was a mark of esteem, and he therefore flicked through it with an expression of deep interest, his main objective to keep Samhain happy and close at hand for further questioning.

A few pages inside was a brown smear. Strike halted the cascade of pages to examine it more closely. It was, he suspected, dried blood, and had been wiped across a few lines of writing.

> This I will say more, to wit, that those who walk in their sleep, do, by no other guide than the spirit of the blood, that is, of the outward man, walk up and down, perform business, climb walls and manage things that are otherwise impossible to those that are awake.

'You can do magic, with that book,' said Samhain. 'But it's my book, because it was My-Dad-

Gwilherm's, so it's mine now,' and he held out his hand before Strike could examine it any further, suddenly jealous of his possession. When Strike handed it back, Samhain clutched the book to his chest with one hand and bent to take a third chocolate biscuit.

'No more, Sammy,' said Deborah.

'I went in the rain and got them,' said Samhain loudly. 'I can have what I want. Silly woman. *Stupid* woman.'

He kicked the ottoman, but it hurt his bare foot, and this increased his sudden, childish anger. Pink-faced and truculent, he looked around the room: Strike suspected he was looking for something to disarrange, or perhaps break. His choice landed on the budgies.

'I'll open the cage,' he threatened his mother, pointing at it. He let *The Magus* fall onto the sofa as he clambered onto the seat, looming over Strike.

'No, don't,' said Deborah, immediately distressed. 'Don't do that, Sammy!'

'And I'll open the window,' said Samhain, now trying to walk his way along the sofa seats, but blocked by Strike. 'Hahaha. You stupid woman.'

'No – Samhain, don't!' said Deborah, frightened.

'You don't want to open the cage,' said Strike, standing up and moving in front of it. 'You wouldn't want your budgies to fly away. They won't come back.'

'I know they won't,' said Samhain. 'The last ones didn't.'

His anger seemed to subside as fast as it had come, in the face of rational opposition. Still standing on the sofa, he said grumpily, 'I went out in the rain. I got them.'

'Have you got Clare's phone number?' Strike asked Deborah.

'In the kitchen,' she said, without asking why he wanted it.

'Can you show me where that is?' Strike asked Samhain, although he knew perfectly well. The whole flat was as big as Irene Hickson's sitting room. Samhain frowned at Strike's midriff for a few moments, then said,

'All right, then.'

He walked the length of the sofa, jumped off the end with a crash that made the bookcase shake, and then lunged for the biscuits.

'Hahaha,' he taunted his mother, both hands full of Penguins. 'I got them. Silly woman. *Stupid* woman.'

He walked out of the room.

As Strike inched back out of the space between ottoman and sofa, he stooped to pick up *The Magus*, which Samhain had dropped, and slid it under his coat. Crocheting peacefully by the window, Deborah Athorn noticed nothing.

A short list of names and numbers was attached to the kitchen wall with a drawing pin. Strike was pleased to see that several people seemed interested in Deborah and Samhain's welfare.

'Who're these people?' he asked, but Samhain

shrugged and Strike was confirmed in his suspicion that Samhain couldn't read, no matter how proud he was of *The Magus*. He took a photo of the list with his phone, then turned to Samhain.

'It would really help me if you could remember what your Uncle Tudor said happened to the lady doctor.'

'Hahaha,' said Samhain, who was unwrapping another Penguin. 'I'm not telling.'

'Your Uncle Tudor must have really trusted you, to tell you.'

Samhain chewed in silence for a while, then swallowed and said, with a proud little upwards jerk of the chin, 'Yer.'

'It's good to have people you can trust with important information.'

Samhain seemed pleased with this statement. He ate his biscuit and, for the first time, glanced at Strike's face. The detective had the impression that Samhain was enjoying another man's presence in the flat.

'I did that,' he said suddenly and, walking to the sink, he picked up a small clay pot, which was holding a washing-up brush and a sponge. 'I go to class on Tuesdays and we make stuff. Ranjit teaches us.'

'That's excellent,' said Strike, taking it from him and examining it. 'Where were you, when your uncle told you what happened to Dr Bamborough?'

'At the football,' said Samhain. 'And I made this,' he told Strike, prising a wooden photo frame off the fridge, where it had been attached with a magnet. The framed picture was a recent one of Deborah and Samhain, both of whom had a budgerigar perched on their finger.

'That's very good,' said Strike, admiring it.

'Yer,' said Samhain, taking it back from him and slapping it on the fridge. 'Ranjit said it was the best one. We were at the football and I heard Uncle Tudor telling his friend.'

'Ah,' said Strike.

'And then he said to me, "Don't you tell no one."'

'Right,' said Strike. 'But if you tell me, I can maybe help the doctor's family. They're really sad. They miss her.'

Samhain cast another fleeting look at Strike's face.

'She can't come back now. People can't be alive again when they're dead.'

'No,' said Strike. 'But it's nice when their families know what happened and where they went.'

'My-Dad-Gwilherm died under the bridge.'

'Yes.'

'My Uncle Tudor died in the hospital.'

'You see?' said Strike. 'It's good you know, isn't it?'

'Yer,' said Samhain. 'I know what happened.'

'Exactly.'

'Uncle Tudor told me it was Nico and his boys done it.'

It came out almost indifferently.

'You can tell her family,' said Samhain, 'but nobody else.'

'Right,' said Strike, whose mind was working very fast. 'Did Tudor know how Nico and the boys did it?'

'No. He just knew they did.'

Samhain picked up another biscuit. He appeared to have no more to say.

'Er – can I use your bathroom?'

'The bog?' said Samhain, with his mouth full of chocolate.

'Yes. The bog,' said Strike.

Like the rest of the flat, the bathroom was old but perfectly clean. It was papered in green, with a pattern of pink flamingos on it, which doubtless dated from the seventies and now, forty years later, was fashionably kitsch. Strike opened the bathroom cabinet, found a pack of razor blades, extracted one and cut the blood-stained page of *The Magus* out with one smooth stroke, then folded it and slipped it in his pocket.

Out on the landing, he handed Samhain the book back.

'You left it on the floor.'

'Oh,' said Samhain. 'Ta.'

'You won't do anything to the budgies if I leave, will you?'

Samhain looked up at the ceiling, grinning slightly.

'*Will* you?' asked Strike.

'No,' sighed Samhain at last.

Strike returned to the doorway of the sitting room.

'I'll be off now, Mrs Athorn,' he said. 'Thanks very much for talking to me.'

'Goodbye,' said Deborah, without looking at him.

Strike headed downstairs, and let himself back onto the street. Once outside, he stood for a moment in the rain, thinking hard. So unusually still was he, that a passing woman turned to stare back at him.

Reaching a decision, Strike turned left, and entered the ironmonger's which lay directly below the Athorns' flat.

A sullen, grizzled and aproned man behind the counter looked up at Strike's entrance. One of his eyes was larger than the other, which gave him an oddly malevolent appearance.

'Morning,' said Strike briskly. 'I've just come from the Athorns, upstairs. I gather you want to talk to Clare Spencer?'

'Who're you?' asked the ironmonger, with a mixture of surprise and aggression.

'Friend of the family,' said Strike. 'Can I ask why you're putting letters to their social worker through their front door?'

'Because they don't pick up their phones at the bloody social work department,' snarled the ironmonger. 'And there's no point talking to *them*, is there?' he added, pointing his finger at the ceiling.

'Is there a problem I can help with?'

'I doubt it,' said the ironmonger shortly. 'You're probably feeling pretty bloody pleased with the situation, are you, if you're a friend of the family?

Nobody has to put their hand in their pocket except me, eh? Quick bit of a cover-up and let someone else foot the bill, eh?'

'What cover-up would this be?' asked Strike.

The ironmonger was only too willing to explain. The flat upstairs, he told Strike, had long been a health risk, crammed with the hoarded belongings of many years and a magnet for vermin, and in a just world, it ought not to be *he* who was bearing the costs of living beneath a pair of actual morons—

'You're talking about friends of mine,' said Strike.

'*You* do it, then,' snarled the ironmonger. '*You* pay a bleeding fortune to keep the rats down. My ceiling's sagging under the weight of their filth—'

'I've just been upstairs and it's perfectly—'

'Because they mucked it out last month, when I said I was going to bloody court!' snarled the ironmonger. 'Cousins come down from Leeds when I threaten legal action – nobody give a shit until then – and I come back Monday morning and they've cleaned it all up. Sneaky bastards!'

'Didn't you want the flat cleaned?'

'I want compensation for the money I've had to spend! Structural damage, bills to Rentokil – that pair shouldn't be living together without supervision, they're not fit, they should be in a home! If I have to take it to court, I will!'

'Bit of friendly advice,' said Strike, smiling. 'If you behave in any way that could be considered threatening towards the Athorns, their friends will make sure it's *you* who ends up in court. Have a nice day,' he added, heading for the door.

The fact that the Athorns' flat had recently been mucked out by helpful relatives tended to suggest that Margot Bamborough's remains weren't hidden on the premises. On the other hand, Strike had gained a bloodstain and a rumour, which was considerably more than he'd had an hour ago. While still disinclined to credit supernatural intervention, he had to admit that deciding to eat breakfast on St John Street that morning had been, at the very least, a most fortuitous choice.